Louise Brown has lived in Nepal and travelled extensively in India, sparking her enduring love of South Asia. She was a Senior Lecturer in Sociology and Asian Studies at the University of Birmingham, where she worked for nearly twenty years. In research for her critically acclaimed non-fiction books she's witnessed revolutions and even stayed in a Lahore brothel with a family of traditional courtesans. She has written two novels, *Eden Gardens* and *The Himalayan Summer*.

Louise has three grown-up children and lives in Birmingham.

By Louise Brown

Eden Gardens
The Himalayan Summer

THE
Himalayan
SUMMER
LOUISE BROWN

REVIEW

First published in Great Britain in 2017 by Headline Review
An imprint of HEADLINE PUBLISHING GROUP

First published in paperback in 2017 by Headline Review
An imprint of HEADLINE PUBLISHING GROUP

1

Cataloguing in Publication Data is available from the British Library

ISBN 978 1 4722 2613 6

Typeset in Bembo MT Pro 11.25/15 pt by
Palimpsest Book Production Limited, Falkirk, Stirlingshire

Printed and bound in Great Britain by
Clays Ltd, St Ives plc

MIX
Paper from
responsible sources
FSC® C104740

Headline's policy is to use papers that are natural, renewable and recyclable
products and made from wood grown in sustainable forests. The logging
and manufacturing processes are expected to conform to the environmental
regulations of the country of origin.

HEADLINE PUBLISHING GROUP
An Hachette UK Company
Carmelite House
50 Victoria Embankment
London EC4Y 0DZ

www.headline.co.uk
www.hachette.co.uk

For my mother, Julie Hawley Brown. With love.

Prologue
California,18 April 1906

WHEN THE EARTH shook, the great houses on San Francisco's hills stood firm. Windows cracked, plates smashed and ornaments were broken. Nearer the water, on acres of badly reclaimed land, the poor in their shoddy homes sank into liquefying sands, and the residents of Chinatown were entombed in their collapsing tenements. When the tremors stopped, the silence was eerie and unnerving. Then the screams began, and the fires started to spread.

Across the bay in Oakland, the damage was minimal, except for a grand old house set high in the tree-lined hills. The first jolt woke the children and sent the little boy running from his room. He jumped into his big sister's bed, clutching his teddy, and buried his face in the pillow. A second later, the room shook. It was thrust up and spun round. The quake twisted the tall chimneys skywards and weakened the ageing mortar. They snaked back and forth and then the tallest leaned forward, suspended at an impossible angle for several moments, before toppling, at first in slow motion, and then in a torrent of bricks that smashed through the roof and into an attic room where two maids had slept only half an hour before. The floor timbers broke under the weight, and the chimney crashed into the room below, driving the girl's bed down into the dining room, where it landed on the walnut table, snapping its legs instantly.

The roar of the quake died and the dawn sky was visible through a gaping hole cut through the heart of the house. Under a pile of bricks, rafters and floorboards, Ellie couldn't see a single chink of daylight. She reached out her hand. She felt the soft fur of her brother's teddy, and then his arm. He didn't move and she couldn't pull him closer because she was pinioned by a web of splintered wood. Dust and soot from the chimney coated the inside of her mouth. She could smell wood smoke, and she would have shouted for help if the weight of the bricks hadn't stopped her filling her lungs with air.

She whispered, 'Bobby.'

He didn't respond and his breathing was shallow. Stretching her arm until it hurt, she wrapped her fingers around his wrist. 'Bobby,' she said again.

He moaned but didn't move, and she began to cry. Dust, soot and tears clogged her eyes and made them sting. As she tried lifting her other hand to wipe them, the debris creaked, shifted, and settled more heavily on her.

Ellie listened to her brother's breath grow fainter.

'Bobby, don't go to sleep on me, you hear,' she said, trying to generate enough saliva to loosen the dry coating from her mouth. 'Pa is going to buy you a bicycle for your birthday. Mom told me.'

Bobby didn't stir, and gradually his breathing grew so shallow she thought it might have stopped. 'Stay with me, Bobby,' she pleaded. As his skin cooled slowly under her hand, she talked to him, and to God, her voice rasping, begging her brother to live. When the rescuers lifted them off the bed, she realised that no one had been listening. Bobby lay limp in a man's arms, perfect and untouched except for the dust on his pyjamas and the soot that turned his golden hair black.

1

Darjeeling District, June 1933

SOON AFTER BREAKFAST, a wall of water crashed through the forest and dropped a veil over the tea gardens. The deluge thundered on the red tin roof of the bungalow and beat the chrysanthemums to the ground. By mid-morning the first rain of the monsoon had slowed to a steady drizzle and clouds cloaked the mountains. The bright saris of the pluckers were soaked to their waists as the women worked among the flat, tightly packed tea bushes spreading like a soft green blanket over the steep mountainsides, down to the river and up over the next ridge.

Ellie sat in a cane chair and watched water drip from bright green tree ferns on to earth that smelled of fertility and decay. She looked up to see Shushila, the new ayah, walk on to the veranda, a thread from the thin blue fabric of her sari catching on the silver chain around her ankle.

'Where were you last night?' Ellie asked. 'It's almost ten o'clock now, and it's the first time I've seen you.'

The girl looked blank, pretending she didn't understand, even though she spoke perfect English. She held her head high and thrust her chin forward, just short of insolent. Instead of replying, she spun very slowly on the smooth, buffed skin of her heel and sauntered along the veranda, humming and looking out over the misty hills, then drifted into the bungalow without giving Ellie a glance. God knows why Francis hired her, Ellie thought. She's useless; she doesn't even like children.

A bearer brought Ellie tea on a tray. It was the estate's second flush, and although a big fuss was made about it being the finest in Darjeeling, Ellie knew it was an insipid drink. She rarely took tea, even in England, preferring coffee, the way they made it at home. She toyed with a slice of lemon, holding it with tiny silver tongs before dropping it into the tea with a splash. It sank slowly through the amber liquid to the bottom of the porcelain cup.

When the untouched tea had grown cold, she returned to the bedroom. The toys were arranged neatly and the sheets had been changed by a servant she'd neither seen nor heard. She spotted her reflection in the dressing table mirror, and paused. Hazy light from the open door to the veranda fell across her face. The soft glow should have been flattering, but the angle was all wrong. Ellie winced at the middle-aged woman whose cheeks were slowly hollowing out. She imagined them sliding down her face; soon they'd be gathering in little puffy bags around her jaw.

Nanny Barker's brown brogues made a loud clomping noise as she strode along the veranda. She stopped and dropped on to a cane planter's chair, looking grey, her energy sapped by the short walk from her room at the far end of the bungalow.

'Are you feeling good today?' Ellie asked.

'Much better, thank you,' Nanny said, and then looked around. 'Where are the children?' she asked.

'The house servants have taken them for a walk,' Ellie said.

Nanny Barker bridled. 'I hope they're not feeding them foreign food.' On any other day she would have marched off to find the twins, but, exhausted by the last purges of 'hill diarrhoea', she remained in the chair, and for a moment there was an uncomfortable silence because she knew she really shouldn't be sitting there.

Ellie glanced at Nanny's salt-and-pepper hair that was escaping from its tight bun and winding itself into wild, frizzy curls around her ears and over her forehead. In one of his especially mean moments, her husband, Francis, had said that Nanny Barker had the perfect face for a nanny. He meant that she was so ugly no one was likely to marry her, and so she could be relied on to stay in service. She'd been plain even when she was young and had spent her days wiping his snotty nose and organising the nursery for him and his brothers. But for some reason, Francis liked her. Ellie thought he might even have loved her, which seemed inexplicable, because she'd never warmed to the woman herself. She always had the feeling that she fell short in Nanny's opinion: she was too old to be a mother; she didn't have a suitable aristocratic pedigree; and she certainly wasn't good enough for Francis. Ellie frequently felt Nanny's watery hazel eyes on her. They were cold as a dead fish, and her mouth was all too often tight with disapproval.

Today, though, sitting crumpled on the cane chair, Nanny hadn't the energy to be judgemental. She didn't even have the strength to stir from the chair when a car horn blared repeatedly in the drive. Several servants shouted at once, and Ellie ran with them to deal with the crisis at the front of the bungalow.

The hunters had returned from the shoot, and Francis was grimacing as he walked slowly, supported by Davies, his gunman, and Black, the owner of the tea garden. Rain had plastered Black's shirt to his thin torso, and his old-fashioned moustache drooped on a face that was too big for his body. Davies was swearing, uttering such a torrent of vile expletives that Ellie winced. She'd once thought the gunman's voice was charming, but now she associated it with Davies's behaviour, which he'd learned in the worst parts of London's East End and honed during fifteen years in the Indian Army and five in the Burmese police.

'What's happened?' she gasped.

Francis pushed aside Black and Davies and hobbled on to the veranda, his boots squeaking. He shivered and shed foliage over the floor.

'He has a nasty injury,' Black said.

'It was the niggers' fault,' Davies said, nodding his head towards a group of Indians standing on the lawn.

Ellie couldn't see her husband's injury. She scanned him for bloodstains, knowing that even a small wound could be deadly. A tiger's claws were hollow and filled with the decaying flesh of its last kill so that a simple scratch could lead to infection and a painful death.

'*Jungli suir* is a *saitan* pig, sahib,' one of the Indians said. He was older than the others, and seemed to be their leader.

'We know. You keep telling us,' Davies snapped. 'He's a big fucking devil pig who eats your crops and pisses on the ones he doesn't eat.'

Ellie shuddered, thinking Francis had been slashed by a boar's razor-sharp tushes.

Black ordered a bearer to bring them burra pegs: Francis would need a large whisky to help him tolerate the pain.

'The pig was holed up in elephant grass,' Black said. 'I could smell him, and there's nothing worse than the stink of an old boar. The beaters made a complete mess driving him out. They did it too fast. Half the jungle was sent down the funnel towards us. We were stampeded by deer, a peacock, a whole family of porcupines, and a dozen wild chickens. Then the big fellow came charging at us from nowhere. He was the biggest, blackest boar I've ever seen. His tushes were a foot long.'

'Longer,' Francis said, shaking. He leaned against the wall and Ellie watched his hands tremble.

'Did you kill him?' she asked.

'Your husband got him in the shoulder but it wasn't enough to bring him down. Worst thing you can do, really,' Black said gravely. 'An injured boar is a dangerous creature.'

'He was four foot away from us. I thought my fucking innards would end up on the jungle floor,' Davies exclaimed.

'What did you do?' Ellie said.

Black cleared his throat, and looked at his feet.

None of the men wanted to say that Francis and Black had dropped their rifles and climbed a tree, and that Davies, out of ammunition, had scaled another. The Indian beaters had seen the sahibs sitting among the branches looking down as the angry boar snorted and paced about below them, and they had turned on their heels and fled, because if burra sahibs with rifles could be outwitted by the *saitan* pig, then what chance did they have armed only with staves and drums?

This story wouldn't have surprised Ellie, if anyone had had the courage to tell her. She'd married a professed crack shot, a hunter who trailed big game and who'd vowed to bag an eight-hundred-pound tiger. But although Francis had new guns from Manton's on Calcutta's Chowringhee and an entire wardrobe of hunting clothes made by Hall and Anderson, shikari specialists on Park Street, he rarely returned from a hunt with much to show for his days in the wilderness. His best bag had been a wild chicken and a stubby pig.

'Will the sahibs kill the *jungli suir* tomorrow?' the villager leader asked.

Black waved them away. 'I'll deal with the beast myself,' he said. 'Lord Northwood needs to recover from his injuries.'

Francis staggered through the bungalow and into the bedroom. He began to unbutton his shirt.

'Let me help you,' Ellie said, taking the shirt. 'Is Black calling a doctor?'

Francis let his shorts drop to the floor, and at once Ellie saw the extent of his wounds. She stifled a laugh. He hadn't been mauled by a tiger or slashed by a boar's tushes. Two dozen thorns had embedded themselves in his backside when he'd slipped in the mud and fallen into a bush on the long trudge back from the inglorious pig hunt.

Francis lay face down on the bed while Ellie dug the thorns out of his buttocks with tweezers and applied iodine to the punctured skin with cotton wool. He was completely silent and perfectly still, his muscles tense, his teeth gritted. When it was over and the wounds were covered in lint dressings, he rolled over and winced. He watched Ellie tidying away the first-aid kit.

'Get me another drink, will you?' he said.

'I'll tell the bearer.'

'I need one now, Ellie. This minute.'

'Don't shout; I'm getting a headache.'

'What's wrong? Bloody mountain sickness?'

'I didn't sleep last night. There was no electricity because the generator stopped working, then I ran out of oil for the lamp and couldn't find any candles.'

'For God's sake, I'm married to an invalid,' Francis sighed. 'You drag around like it's the end of the fucking world.' He looked away from her and stared blankly at the ceiling fan. 'It's all in your head.' He turned to look at her and tapped his forefinger on his temple.

Ellie backed away from him.

'Where are you going?' he asked.

'I'm going to write to Momo.'

'Get me that Scotch.'

She picked up her battered leather writing case and threw open the louvred doors. As she walked along the veranda, heavy with wisteria, she heard him laughing.

Francis was a drunk; Ellie had known it when she married him, but at that point he was a charming, playful drunk given to endearing, if very formal, displays of affection. A year after the wedding, he'd abandoned the charm, the humour was a memory, and he'd become an unadorned, angry drunk.

They'd met in the south of France while she was on vacation with her friend Margaret 'Momo' Jackson, who was recovering from her second divorce. Ellie and Momo were unlikely friends: Ellie was tall and serious, and wore sensible clothes; while

Momo was beautiful and petite, and always in trouble. The only things they had in common were that they were rich and their parents had been killed when they were children. Ellie's parents had died in the great San Francisco earthquake, and Momo's were hit by a 'death driver' in one of the city's first automobile accidents.

Both girls had attended the Hamlin School, where they sought each other's company because they were the odd ones out: they never invited friends to their homes; they didn't have family to talk about; and they were both looked after by a long line of people who were paid to do the job and who didn't bother to pretend they enjoyed it.

Almost thirty years on, Ellie had known Momo well enough to predict that their European tour was going to be accompanied by scandal. They'd made a similar pilgrimage to the Old World in 1926, following Momo's first divorce, and Ellie wasn't very keen on repeating the experience.

'But we girls need a vacation,' Momo stated.

Except that we're no longer girls, Ellie thought. They were, in fact, fast approaching forty, and Ellie wondered where their youth had gone. Momo had spent hers, and some of her fortune, on unruly men and wild times. Ellie tried to think how she'd spent her own youth, and found she couldn't remember. She certainly hadn't lived it in a giddy whirl. It had simply passed her by, because she made an effort to shy away from life and big emotions, as if by enjoying herself too much and loving too deeply, she would risk everything being snatched away. Ellie protected herself by asking for little, and expecting less.

Momo's good intentions on the post-divorce holiday lasted

exactly a fortnight. In Rome, she met an Italian count at a lavish party.

'Do you think the count would look like an orange-picker without his military uniform?' she asked Ellie as they lay on their beds in the hotel room. She adjusted her eye mask, bothered by the soft light from the standard lamp Ellie insisted on leaving on all night. 'He's very dark.'

'And very handsome,' Ellie added as she admired Momo's short, wavy copper-coloured hair on the snow-white pillows.

'He says he's a close friend of Mussolini,' Momo said. 'And he's married.' She lifted the corner of the mask to gauge Ellie's reaction.

Momo clearly didn't care if he looked like a Mexican fruit picker, or if he was married, because the next night Ellie returned alone to their hotel.

The affair lasted until they left Rome. Momo spent the next few days pining for her lost love, but then they arrived in Nice and met a group of young Englishmen, all three of them titled, and all embarrassingly poor. They were wintering on the Riviera and staying in barely respectable lodgings well away from the seafront because it was cheaper than the big hotels on the Promenade des Anglais, and certainly cheaper than trying to keep up appearances at home. Momo and Ellie invited the men for drinks and luncheon at their hotel, the Negresco, because Momo needed something to take her mind off the count, and the English crowd lifted her spirits.

'They're very young,' Ellie said as she looked over their room's wrought-iron balcony to where England's penurious nobles were making their way very slowly down the Promenade.

Momo snorted. 'Listen, Ellie. Take a rest now, because tonight we're going dancing.'

'We are?'

'Sure we are. I saw the way you clicked with that sweet English lord.'

That night, Ellie danced demurely with the blue-eyed Lord Northwood, who held her at arm's length and kissed her hand when they parted.

The next day they sat together on a seat overlooking the Bay of Angels and marvelled at the azure water. During the following days they visited Monte Carlo and he drove her at high speed along the Grande Corniche in a burnished red Mercedes Benz roadster, borrowed from a wealthier friend.

'You could be British royalty if you married Lord Northwood,' Momo sighed.

'Francis is eight years younger than me,' Ellie said.

'What is wrong with you? He's handsome – if you like English lords. And his accent is adorable.'

Ellie hesitated, feeling she was on the brink of a precipice, and wondering whether she should abandon a lifetime of caution.

Four weeks later, Ellie and Francis were married in a quiet ceremony in London. The following morning, as they stood on the deck of a liner and embarked on their honeymoon in South Africa, Francis stared down at Momo, who was waving ecstatically from the dockside. Then he turned to look at Ellie, his blue eyes suddenly icy.

'Your friend is a fucking trollop,' he said. 'Don't see her again.'

A knot tightened in Ellie's stomach, and she gazed at Momo's overjoyed face. She'd been swept along on a tide of wine and champagne. She'd listened to her friend's reckless views of the world, and she hadn't obeyed her own usually solid judgement. I know nothing about this man, she thought, and looked at Francis properly for the first time. I must be a total fool. Who else but an idiot would take advice on men from the mouth of Momo Jackson?

Leather-skinned tea planters in khaki shorts gathered at the bar, drinking pink gins beneath a portrait of Clive of India. At the far end of the club, a group of young Scottish assistant managers kept their straight backs turned to the English. Ellie sat at a side table and watched Francis and Black walk to the bar. The men greeted Black and nodded at Francis, unaware who he was. She knew they would fawn when they were introduced.

'Got your Mr Stripes yet?' a heavyset, freckled man called to Black. He was covered in a thick mat of red hair and rested a boot on a copper rail running around the base of the bar. Ellie was fascinated by the luxuriant fuzz that ran up his calves and over his kneecaps. It sprouted from his open collar and coated his bare arms below his short-sleeved shirt. From a distance it looked like a golden aura.

The men brought their drinks to the table and sat with Ellie.

'Mr Stripes has eluded me so far, Johnson,' Black said stiffly and slightly apologetically, because everyone knew you couldn't be called a genuine shikari until you'd bagged your first tiger.

Another group of men settled down to play cards at a table near the entrance to the bar. They were probably up from Calcutta and had come to fish in the Teesta. The sportsmen with Ellie knew their sort and gave them dismissive glances:

the newcomers were pansies and poodle fakers who were happy to waste time playing cards and who were far too much at ease talking with women. They didn't have the grit and dedication of true shikaris.

'You made a good choice coming here,' Johnson said to Francis. 'We've some of the finest hunting in India. Only Kashmir has better game.'

The hairy planter was right: the local jungle was a sportsman's paradise, although Francis pointed out that it was not a patch on Kenya, which was still populated with plenty of animals and where hunting laws were easy to flout. Francis knew this because he'd lived in Kenya, in Happy Valley, for three years, enjoying the life of an aristocrat on the cheap. That was in the days before Ellie's money allowed him to behave like nobility at home and not just in the colonies.

'Kashmir's not what it was,' Black said, with a shake of his oversized head. 'The ibex are finished.'

'True,' Johnson said thoughtfully. 'Nepal is the new frontier. Old King George bagged thirty-nine tigers in the plains.'

'By himself?' Ellie asked, paying closer attention now someone had mentioned Nepal.

'With help from the Nepalese maharaja, the Viceroy, a troop of hunting elephants and five hundred coolies,' Johnson said.

'Gentlemen,' Black announced, twirling his moustache, 'you are looking at the first Englishman to hunt in the Nepal Terai since old King George himself.'

'You?' Johnson exclaimed, aghast.

'Lord Northwood,' Black said, pointing to Francis.

Johnson smiled, mollified now he knew the honour was being given to a titled man. 'By God, how did you manage that?' he said as his wife came to sit beside her substantial and colourful husband. She looked very small and insipid in her flowery dress. She stared in awe at Francis, who was growing in stature.

Ellie had heard Francis's story a dozen times during the previous month, and the tale changed slightly each time he told it. She knew some of it was true because she'd been there to witness it.

Three months ago, at the start of the hot season, they had been in Calcutta, where Francis was busy ordering guns and having hunting clothes made. Then he went to the Sundarbans to bag a Royal Bengal tiger or two, and left Ellie and the twins in a suite in the Great Eastern Hotel, with only Nanny Barker for company. It was like a prison. Outside, everything baked. The Maidan, Calcutta's great green park, turned a crisp brown, and the city was covered in a choking layer of dust. Nanny Barker became ever more officious and Ellie was increasingly nervy. She was so miserable that she was pleased when Francis returned from the hunt, tigerless as usual. A few days later, he appeared with an ayah, a Bengali girl, whom he insisted they needed because Nanny Barker was getting old, and her puffy ankles were a sure sign she wasn't coping with the heat. The new girl looked at Ellie without smiling.

Francis seemed happy for a week and then became irritable. 'I need to be back on the hunt,' he explained to Ellie. 'You won't understand, but there's nothing quite like it. It's man against beast; you pit your wits against the King of the Jungle.'

What a load of garbage, Ellie thought, totting up the carnage Francis had wreaked during his career as a sportsman: the small animals he'd maimed and slaughtered; the creatures who had

17

crawled into the jungle to die after being wounded by her husband's wide shots.

Francis spent every evening in the hotel bar or in one of Calcutta's many clubs. He was invited by members who were eager to be seen with a peer of the realm, and he recounted his exploits in the Sundarbans, Kenya and South Africa to a rapt audience. Every night, he returned to the Great Eastern raging drunk, and usually in a vicious temper.

'They're the most bloody awful plebs,' he said to Ellie, launching himself on to the bed after a long evening at the Tollygunge Club. 'They've got the natives running after them like they're royalty.' He lay on his back, lit a cigarette, put one arm behind his head and blew smoke very slowly through his nostrils.

The next night he planned to go to a bar on Park Street, where, he told Ellie, he was less likely to meet offensive middle-class products of minor public schools and Oxbridge.

When he returned, he was twitchy with excitement. 'The place was full of adventurers, explorers, hunters,' he explained, though he couldn't pinpoint exactly which bar he was referring to. He wasn't specific when he told the tale to others, either. The club, he said, was packed and he was just about to order a drink when a foreigner – an enormous Dane – elbowed him and then pushed a tiny Indian man out of the way. The Indian fell, sprawling on the floor, and when Francis remonstrated, the man threatened in his thick, guttural accent to kick his head in. Francis rose to the challenge, stood his ground, ducked a few punches and then cleanly and surgically, with a single well-placed blow, knocked the brute out.

The Indian picked himself up off the floor, dusted himself

down and, to Francis's surprise, revealed he wasn't Indian after all. He was, in fact, Nepali, the favourite nephew of Nepal's maharaja and a great shikari himself. So, over a bottle of Scotch, the peer of the British realm and the nephew of the Maharaja became fast friends, and Francis was persuaded to visit Nepal and teach the Maharaja's nephew all about the excellence of British sporting traditions. He was going to explain the practicalities of hunting with hounds, and the possibility of developing grouse shooting in the mountain kingdom. In return, the Maharaja's nephew promised to take him to a camp in the Nepal Terai, where they would ride in bejewelled howdahs on the backs of giant tuskers and shoot more tigers than the old British king.

The version of the story that Francis told the planters in Darjeeling was embellished by details of the Dane's enormous size and belligerence, the impressiveness of Francis's own chivalry, and the fervent gratitude of the Maharaja's nephew. The essence remained the same, however, including the outcome: in January they were going to travel to Kathmandu as guests of Maharaja Juddha Shumsher Rana, Prime Minister of Nepal, and his ill-treated nephew.

The planters were quiet, and envious.

'You'll have a very varied bag. I daresay you'll have a shot at elephants and wild buffalo, even rhino,' Johnson said.

Mrs Johnson looked at Ellie. 'My dear, will you be staying here or in Calcutta while your husband goes on his shoot?'

'I'm going too,' Ellie said.

'No,' Mrs Johnson said, her voice rising to a hoot. 'It's frightfully dangerous. There's not a single European woman in the whole country.' She reconsidered for a moment. 'Well, no more than a handful.' She thought again, and looked to her husband for support. 'I can't imagine there'll be a single American either,' she added in a rush.

'They don't call it a closed kingdom for nothing,' a red-skinned planter added. He'd been severely sunburned over so many decades that his face looked like a skinned tomato.

When Francis had first announced the trip, he'd insisted Ellie should return to England. 'It will be better for the children,' he said.

Ellie shuddered at the thought of Francis's vast, shabby house in the bleak countryside of eastern England. Draughts blew through enormous, sparsely furnished rooms, and a chill wind whistled down the long, dark corridors, along which the lino curled up at the edges and had thinned over decades to form holes where the servants' footfall was heaviest.

'I'm coming with you,' she told him.

'You are?' he said, both incredulous and disappointed. 'You've never stayed in a forty-pound tent in the thick of the jungle, surrounded by hyenas and tigers. You'll be bitten by mosquitoes and caked in mud. And don't imagine we're going to drive to Kathmandu. We can't take a plane either. You'll have to climb over the damned mountains to get there.'

Ellie was unwavering: she wasn't going to leave Francis to travel the subcontinent, spending her money. She'd probably never see him again. Even more importantly, she wanted to visit Nepal because it was in the heart of the Himalayas and near to Tibet, one of the last unmapped places on the planet.

In the Planters' Club, everyone was waiting for her to speak. 'We're all going,' she told them.

'All?' Johnson's washed-out wife said, appalled.

'Yes. I'm going and so are the children, with Nanny, and the ayah if she's still with us.'

'Surely you're not going to take the children?' Johnson's eyes boggled. Ellie nodded and fixed her gaze on a large fish, stuffed and mounted in a display case on the far wall. The sportsmen turned their attention to the vexed question of the best gun to take down an elephant.

Ellie wished she hadn't come to the club. She didn't want to listen to the bragging, the shikar tales and endless dissections of memorable hunts. The men laughed, the women brayed, and the wife of the furred ginger planter sat opposite her and spoke in a clipped, nasal voice while giving her savage little looks.

Ellie stood up. 'I'm going to get some fresh air. I won't be long.'

On the veranda, she didn't notice that the clouds had lifted from the mountains. The wind blew snow from the peaks of Kanchenjunga, forming a white plume, like smoke, lifting up and westward into a blue sky. To the south, a mass of white-topped, grey-bottomed clouds gathered, ready to bring more rain.

It was good to be away from the planters, and from Francis. She leaned against a pillar and closed her eyes.

'Had enough of the view?' a man asked.

Her heart sank; one of them had followed her out of the bar.

'You should come out of season. It's much better, much quieter,' he added.

She didn't reply. Opening her eyes a fraction, she glanced at him, not caring if she seemed rude. To her surprise, the man wasn't one of the sportsmen. He was several inches taller than her, and slim, with dark auburn hair and a golden tan.

'I saw you with the nobs in there,' he said.

She looked directly at him. He grinned as if testing her reaction.

'One of those nobs is my husband.'

'I'm sorry,' he said.

She wanted to reply, 'So am I,' but laughed instead.

'Are you running away from them?' he asked.

'I can't stand listening to any more boasting and shikar stories, and pink gin makes me sick.'

'Come to the bazaar with me and have some tea.'

'I don't like tea either.'

'I bet you haven't had it the Indian way.'

'I have, in Calcutta, and besides, I don't even know you.'

'I'm Hugh Douglas. You know me now.' He was smiling, and what she wanted was to say, 'Yes, I'll have some tea in the bazaar,' but then the voice of caution in her head told her to be quiet, and next thing she knew, someone was gripping her arm.

'There you are,' Mrs Johnson said. 'I've left the men getting a teeny bit tight and thought it would be marvellous to have a walk down the Mall. Who knows when we'll get the chance to do it again now the dirty weather is here.' She steered Ellie around the man. 'Must skedaddle,' she told him.

Ellie looked back and saw he was watching her.

'I wish I'd known he'd cornered you,' Mrs Johnson hissed as she manoeuvred Ellie off the veranda. 'I would have rescued you sooner. He's a thoroughly bad hat. I can't imagine why he was in the Planters' Club; he hardly ever comes to town, and when he does, he spends his time down in the bazaar. He lives over in Kalimpong and has gone native. People say he's happier with lice-infested Nepali hill men and Tibetans than he is with his own kind.'

She stopped. 'He didn't bother you, did he?' she said, breathing gin over Ellie. 'I can ask my husband to speak to the club secretary and we can have him barred.'

Ellie shook her head. 'He was okay. He was an unusual guy.'

'Unusual is certainly the word.' Mrs Johnson sniffed delicately. 'He's almost a recluse. He never married and has a native girl living with him. He absolutely flaunts her. It's a disgrace. The Douglas family used to have such a good name, but if you ask me, they stayed in India too long.'

They walked slowly down towards the Mall, which was one of the only bits of flat land in Darjeeling. The town clung to a hillside, and many of its steep streets turned into rivers in the monsoon. The rain channelled into gullies, and created torrents that threatened to sweep the chalets, bungalows, hotels and government buildings downhill.

'It reminds me so much of home,' Mrs Johnson sighed.

Baffled, Ellie considered the scene. A long line of heavily laden porters trudged between mock-Tudor buildings; a mule train stood outside the English parish church; and a holidaying Indian family weaved between a group of colourfully dressed Tibetan traders.

'Now where are your children?' Mrs Johnson said. 'Your husband said they're taking a constitutional with their nanny.'

Ellie pointed to Nanny Barker, who was striding towards them pushing a majestic pram. The Tibetans scattered as she cut through the crowds. The twins, dressed in white, sat in splendour. Lizzie held her doll, Jean, and Tom hugged his woolly lamb. Mrs Johnson greeted them, marvelling at their golden hair and their chubby, rosy cheeks.

'The mountain air does wonders for British children,' she gushed. Tom's bottom lip began to quiver as the woman fixed her gaze on him.

'You certainly can't take them to Nepal,' Mrs Johnson stated. 'They're only babies.'

'My great-grandparents crossed the whole of America with three children in a wagon train, so I reckon we can make it to Kathmandu.'

'But you have no idea of the danger,' Mrs Johnson continued, astonished by Ellie's lack of common sense. Nanny Barker scrunched her mouth into a little puckered hole, a sure sign, Ellie thought, that she agreed with the sharp woman in the flowery dress.

'Anyway,' Mrs Johnson said briskly, seeing she was getting nowhere, 'it must be such a comfort to have a British nanny. I've lost track of the children who've been ruined by native ayahs. Did you know they keep opium under their fingernails and give it to the babies to keep them quiet?'

'We have an ayah too,' Ellie said. 'She helps Nanny Barker.'

Shushila, who had been looking in a shop window, sauntered slowly towards them. Mrs Johnson flinched at the sight of her. Perhaps she was surprised by Shushila's languid walk, or the roll of her hips under the thin fabric of her sari. There was power in that walk, and in the tilt of Shushila's head.

Mrs Johnson turned her back to the ayah. 'Look, take my advice,' she said to Ellie. 'You're new to India, and I've been here for twenty years. I'm an old hand, so believe me when I say you need to get rid of that girl. Bengalis from the plains are sly and work-shy. You need a hill girl; they're filthy but loyal, and they always have a smile on their face.'

Mrs Johnson beamed too fulsomely at the children, the smile grotesque. Tom grizzled, while Lizzie blinked and then smiled back prettily. 'Such a little poppet,' Mrs Johnson said.

Clouds were building again over the mountains.

'Be glad you're going back to Calcutta,' Mrs Johnson said. 'Darjeeling will be the wettest place in India for the next few months.'

Ellie looked below the icy peaks to the lower slopes of the Himalayan foothills. 'Where's Kalimpong?' she asked.

'Over there,' Mrs Johnson said, pointing a small, bony finger to buildings scattered over a distant ridge. 'There's no point going; it looks close from here but would take you three or four hours by road. Anyway, Darjeeling is much more interesting. Kalimpong is a backwater, and it's full of foreigners.'

Nanny Barker jiggled Tom's woolly lamb in front of him. He quietened and buried his face in its fur. Lizzie twisted Jean's head round and giggled.

A group of Indians gathered around the perambulator, admiring the golden children in their little chariot. Nanny shooed them away, then turned to face Ellie, the colour drained from her face.

'I'm going to the public conveniences,' she said urgently, and headed up the Mall at a trot. Hill diarrhoea could linger for weeks and erupt at the most inconvenient moments.

For the first time, Shushila was placed in charge of the perambulator, which was usually guarded jealously by Nanny Barker. She jabbed at the brake with her sandalled foot and began walking, Ellie and Mrs Johnson following closely. She stopped when they came to Commercial Row, and turned her attention to a jewellery shop. She had lost interest in the pram because she didn't have to fight over it with Nanny Barker.

Ellie thought it was a good time to get rid of Mrs Johnson; she was weary of her grating voice and didn't know how much longer she could be polite. Mrs Johnson was so full of advice and opinions, you couldn't have a simple conversation with her. She was too certain of her own views, and too limited in her knowledge of the world. She seemed to think being a memsahib in a tea garden taught you everything there was to know.

A green Baby Austin with a dented radiator, its wheels and running boards caked in mud, drew alongside them and a man waved through the driver's window. He seemed too big to fit inside the little car. It was Hugh Douglas, the man from the Planters' Club. Ellie was surprised, because it seemed odd for him to be driving such a small, battered car when British people in India were supposed to be rich.

As he turned down Old Post Office Road, Ellie thought she saw someone in the passenger seat, but before she could take a second look to see if it was the native girl Mrs Johnson had described, a shout made her swivel round. The perambulator was trundling down a steep lane to the lower bazaar, gathering speed. It bounced over a bump, landing, stately and cushioned by its suspension, like a liner pitching and yawing in heavy seas. Lizzie's eyes widened and her mouth opened in a perfect circle of surprise. Tom screamed and flung himself flat in the pram.

'Stop!' Ellie shrieked, and ran after the twins. She could see disaster unfolding; she saw the pram accelerating into the bazaar, busy with taxis and tikka garries, and the way it would career and crash, the children's heads cracking open on the road.

She reached out, her fingertips just touching the lacquered wood handle, but before she could get a grip, she stumbled, and the handle drew away from her.

Two youths sprinted past and grabbed the pram. They skidded to a halt, and the twins were thrown forward with the sudden deceleration. The youths were porters, dressed in ragged clothes, and they had nothing on their feet. They pushed the pram back to the junction with Commercial Street and Ellie thanked them so many times they seemed embarrassed.

'What a dreadful incident that could have been,' Mrs Johnson said in a hushed voice. Her face had some colour for the first time. 'It just goes to show that your ayah is a liability. The stupid girl left the pram at the top of a hill and didn't apply the brake.'

I didn't see the risk either, Ellie thought, even though I spend most of my life worrying about disasters. She kissed the children, her tears wetting their cheeks. Lizzie lifted her arms, asking to be picked up and comforted, and Tom clung tightly to his toy lamb. Unclipping Lizzie's harness, Ellie held her daughter and stroked Tom's soft hair.

'It's okay,' she said, over and over, as if to remind herself that India really was a safe place to be.

Nanny Barker gasped in horror at the long queue outside the public conveniences and then sprinted, doubled over, towards the Everest Hotel. She didn't see Davies watching her as he ate a sandwich on the Mall, the contents spilling from his mouth. If she had spotted him, it wouldn't have surprised her. She knew Davies was common and had no manners. He thought nothing of eating in the street and talking with his mouth full. Today, though, she wouldn't have cared much about the gunman's loutish behaviour; the only thing on her mind was making it to the bathroom.

The lobby of the hotel was packed and her heart sank as her bowels convulsed. The ladies' powder room was filled with tourists and she had to push through a party of holidaymakers who were checking in at reception. Please, please, she thought, let me make it upstairs. She had to go all the way to the communal bathroom next to her small single room on the third floor, which was advertised as suitable for higher-ranking domestic servants. She barrelled through a group of travellers on the red-carpeted stairs.

'For God's sake, woman. Are you mad?' an elderly florid gentleman exclaimed as he was thrust back against the wall.

Nanny Barker put her head down and ploughed forward. She was nearly there; nearly at the bathroom door. She flung it open and groaned with relief.

Sitting on the rather old and badly stained toilet, she put her elbows on her knees and her head in her hands. Whatever disorder was afflicting her bowels was not going away. The virulence of the condition was on the wane, but it struck now and again, and always at the most embarrassing times, as if the foul gremlins living in her belly knew when they could inflict most damage. It's the curse of this place, she thought, and then reminded herself it was just one of many torments, like the insect bites that made her skin blister and ooze; and the heat and humidity that gave her prickly heat rash no amount of talcum powder would ease.

Darjeeling, she admitted, was better than Calcutta, the miserable, insanitary city on the plains. The whole district looked nice, like a postcard of the Lake District, only on a much bigger scale. The mountains were higher and topped with snow all year, but the effect was the same. It made Nanny feel almost at home as she walked around the town, drinking in the atmosphere until the gremlins stirred and wrung her intestines like a piece of twisted cloth.

She stood up straight for the first time since the cramps had crippled her on the Mall, and in the mirror she saw a fat woman on the cusp of old age.

How did I end up like this? she thought. She should have been pushing the grand Silver Cross perambulator around Kensington Gardens, basking in the respect of lesser nannies whose children were not aristocrats, and who didn't have a crest on the side of their prams. She should have a proper nursery, with nursery maids she could train to do her bidding, unlike Shushila, who was the most sloppy, nonchalant girl she'd ever met. If she had her way, the ayah would be sent packing, but Lord Northwood – her own dear Francis – had a soft spot for her. He was too kind for his own good and it was so like him to take pity on one of the natives and give her a chance to better herself. It was a shame, though, that she, Nanny Barker, paid the price for the ayah's incompetence, and it was galling to put up with her insolence. It would never be tolerated at home. Lady Northwood was slack about discipline. She was too friendly with the staff, always wanting them to call her Ellie.

Nanny Barker examined the red spots on her cheeks in the mirror. Mother had those too, she thought. Her mother, though, had had pretty features, whereas Nanny Barker had her father's face. She knew that was why she'd never married – that, and the fact that her fiancé, Bertie, who was a groom and the only man ever to show an interest in her, had died when he was kicked by a mare in the stables. His skull was caved in and his body trampled to a bloody mess among the straw.

If he'd lived, she wouldn't be in heathen India; she'd have her own little cottage, and children to look after her in her old age. Instead, she'd followed the only family she had halfway across the world, and now she wondered whether it would be the death of her. She was too old to be traipsing round the Empire. Going to Nepal, which people said was like the book *The Land that Time Forgot*, would be worse than Calcutta, because at least there she'd been able to see white people, whereas everyone said there were only natives in Nepal. They probably meant it was full of savages, because how could anyone expect to be civilised if they lived in the Land that Time Forgot? Nanny Barker had read novels about lost worlds full of beast men and monsters, and she knew what Nepal had in store for them. She would have refused to go if she had any alternative, but she was a practical woman and she needed to be with Francis. He would take care of her; he'd pay her back for all the years she'd loved him and cared for him.

Someone knocked loudly on the bathroom door and she looked at herself one last time in the mirror. I pray he will, she thought.

In the lobby, Ellie and the children had returned from their walk and Nanny Barker was pleased to see they'd shaken off Mrs Johnson. She didn't like the way the woman talked; she had an almost perfect accent but she wasn't really class. She was probably a shopkeeper's daughter and was just putting on airs and graces. Nanny Barker had seen plenty like her in India; she had a fine nose for social climbers, and the place was riddled with them. Although they could get away with lording it over the natives, Nanny Barker wasn't so easily duped. She'd lived among nobility; admittedly only because she had cleaned up after them, but she knew a real aristocrat when she met one.

Nanny knew Ellie wasn't class either, but that, she reasoned, was probably because she was foreign, and they didn't have old families in America. It was a new country, full of cowboys and movie stars, though in truth, Ellie looked nothing like a glamorous film star. She wasn't the wife Nanny Barker thought Francis deserved; she was too old, too tall and thin, and while she wasn't plain, most people described her as 'striking' or 'handsome', which was damning in itself. Only her hair was truly beautiful. It was a shade or two darker than the children's. Perhaps her hands were good too, Nanny thought grudgingly. Her fingers were long, like a pianist's, although they were a little too manly for Nanny's taste.

The twins toddled around the lobby, creating a commotion among the guests. Ellie gazed about her, oblivious to the disapproving looks.

Nanny scooped Tom up. He babbled in her face and Lizzie tugged at her long dress and then swung on it, lifting her feet off the ground. Nanny's brown brogues stood firm on the polished floor while Ellie walked towards the stairs.

'Come with me to my rooms,' Ellie said. 'I've had a terrible shock.' Her hands were trembling, and Nanny could see a sheen of sweat on her high forehead.

In her suite, Ellie took the stopper out of a glass bottle of Veronal pills. She didn't want to take them. She'd promised herself she wouldn't, not any more. She hesitated, then tipped back her head and swallowed.

She heard the children playing with Nanny Barker in the other room, and stopped to listen, spellbound by their laughter. I love them too much, she thought. They were perfect, and they were hers; the little family she couldn't bear to lose.

She looked up and out of the wide panoramic windows towards Kanchenjunga. The setting sun tinged the snow orange and pink against a darkening indigo sky. She breathed deeply; there was something solid and reassuring about the mountains. Her heartbeat slowed and her breathing steadied. There was no need to worry, she told herself. The Himalayas were ancient and unchanging, the mountains unshakeable under her feet.

2

The Himalayan Foothills, January 1934

RAXAUL STATION WAS tiny, and surprisingly empty. Three
men stood, surrounded by boxes and bags, at the far end
of the platform and nodded a greeting to the foreigners, politely
ignoring the sniping between Nanny Barker and Davies. The
men wore white jodhpurs that were tight around their calves
and yet so wrinkled they looked as if they had been made for
someone a foot taller. Over their white shirts they wore thick,
colourful belts and dark jackets cut in the European style. They
each carried a large black umbrella, proof against sun and rain.

A small train stopped in a cloud of steam, and two dozen
passengers climbed aboard carrying lumpy bundles, trunks and
boxes. The men in the white jodhpurs sat at the far end of the
first carriage, well away from the warring foreigners.

Davies swore at the porters stacking the luggage haphazardly
on the overhead racks and between the hard benches. 'For
fuck's sake, mind the guns,' he barked in the voice of a furious
sergeant.

Nanny Barker blanched at the language, and hurried the
children to sit by the window. Ellie sat opposite Nanny, and

Shushila took a seat behind them, ignoring everyone while picking dirt from under her nails with a sharp, thin stick. She can't have hidden any opium there, Ellie thought. Lizzie climbed on to Ellie's lap, chattering and asking questions but without pausing for her mother to answer. Tom sat quietly and held his lamb to the window so it could watch a couple run up the platform and dive into the train moments before the station-master blew his whistle.

Francis and Davies, who had set up camp well away from the women and children, turned to look at the commotion. A middle-aged European man, with a three-day-old beard and dark auburn hair, was helping a young native woman arrange her luggage as the train pulled out of the station. The two Englishmen spoke quietly, and Davies guffawed, leering at the girl. She was especially pretty, in that very particular way Davies appreciated. Like many women in northern India and Burma, she had high cheekbones and almond eyes. She also had a childlike quality that Davies had found easy to purchase in the brothels of Calcutta and Rangoon. She was about twenty, and could pass for fourteen.

Ellie swivelled in her seat to take a better look at the couple. The man saw her and grinned. It was Douglas, the strange man from the terrace of the Planters' Club. Ellie thought there was something different about him. Perhaps it was the stubble, which he really should have tended to, or maybe he was a little slimmer. She couldn't decide. He glanced to where Francis and Davies were taking nips from a hip flask, and then settled back to study a map.

Ellie assumed the girl must be the one Mrs Johnson was incensed about: the one she said Douglas flaunted so shamelessly.

And looking at them, Ellie had to admit the woman had a point. Hugh Douglas and the girl made an odd couple, not only because he was white and she was Indian, but because she was so young it was distasteful. The things men could do, Ellie mused. She heard Francis talking to Davies in his familiar voice of authority, and she looked at her husband, spread out over the seats. I've married a buffoon, she thought, but at least he's not a womaniser. She was grateful for this small mercy.

The girl pointed to the map and then to something out of the window, though Ellie couldn't think what it could be as there was nothing unusual to see. It was the typical Indian scene: a few factories and warehouses that appeared derelict; a cluster of scruffy houses; a man driving a bullock cart; and boys playing in the dust in the shabby outskirts of a town before it petered out into a countryside of flat fields.

Shushila lolled sleepily across the length of a bench, her head rocking with the movement of the train. Lizzie lay in Ellie's arms, her eyelashes and lids flickering as her eyes moved under the thin, pale skin. Tom curled up, his lamb's pink felt nose pressed against his own, and Ellie melted at the sight. He was smaller than his sister and had learned to walk and talk several months later than her. Lizzie outstripped him in everything except the love Ellie felt for the gentle, quiet boy with hair the colour of gold – soft and bright, like Bobby's. She reached over and patted his chubby legs as if to reassure herself he was really there.

On the bench opposite, Nanny Barker fanned herself wearily with her hat. The poor woman couldn't tolerate the heat, even though it was the cool season and felt no worse than a hot summer day in England. Sweat patches darkened her blue cotton dress and white apron, and despite her best efforts with carbolic soap and splashes of 4711 eau de cologne, and a dhobi's constant washing, the cotton of her uniform was impregnated with the faint but unmistakable smell of stale sweat. A musky miasma accompanied her wherever she went.

Ellie was surprised to see Nanny had given up wearing stockings. She'd stuck her legs out across the carriage in a very unladylike way, presumably to increase ventilation, and her bare ankles and the bottoms of her calves were covered in a dozen red bites, the recent ones raw and oozing and the older ones crusted over and capped with solidified fluid that looked like small nuggets of amber. The pale, puffy flesh must have been a feast for the mosquitoes, and Ellie reminded herself to tell Nanny to use more citronella as a defence against bites, though in truth she thought it would also help the fuggy atmosphere.

Not long afterwards, they stopped at Birgunj, just over the border in Nepal. The town looked exactly like the one on the Indian side of the border. Nanny grabbed Tom's arm as he tried to climb down from the bench.

'We're not there yet,' she said.

A dozen or more people clambered into the carriage. There were a couple of farmers, some men who looked like traders, and a family with excited young children, a little older than Lizzie and Tom. They were driven like a flock of goslings along the carriage by their grandmother. The woman adjusted the long shawl wrapped round her shoulders and settled down on a bench to feed the children from parcels made out of leaves.

Although the train was slow, the wind from the open windows blew through Ellie's hair and made the curls spring free from Nanny's bun. Ellie was hoping for an interesting view, but all she could see were low trees, dense scrub and the occasional tall palm tree. She had hoped for more from the Terai, expecting something to match its reputation, but the twenty-mile tract of impenetrable jungle, home to dangerous animals and even more frightening strains of malaria, looked surprisingly ordinary after her journey to the tea estate on the picturesque Darjeeling Himalayan Railway.

Ellie was untangling her hair when the train jolted and the driver pulled the whistle cord. The wheels screeched and the passengers were thrown forward. The grandmother, who was standing, searching in a bundle for more food, was catapulted along the carriage. Ellie and Lizzie bumped down on to the floor, and Nanny Barker and Tom were pressed into the back of the bench. The train came to a halt as the driver put the engine into reverse. Ellie stood up, rubbing the bottom of her spine, and stuck her head out of the window. Nothing was visible ahead because the engine was expelling giant clouds of steam. Then the driver and stoker appeared out of a white mist.

'*Hathi!*' the driver shouted.

'What did he say?' Ellie asked.

'Elephant,' Douglas replied, jumping from the carriage.

Suddenly animated, Francis and Davies flung open the gun box, took out their rifles and followed Douglas. The three men in crinkly white jodhpurs joined them, while the merchants leaned out of the windows and shouted to the passengers from the other carriages, some of whom were making their way forward to find out what was happening. Ellie leaped down too.

The train had stopped in the middle of nowhere. They were

surrounded by thick grass, three or four feet high, which was dotted with termite mounds. To the left, a forest of tall sal trees spread north and south as far as she could see, and to the right, a single enormous palm tree stood among dense scrub.

The girl who'd boarded the train with Douglas leaned out of the window and spoke to Ellie. 'You'd best stay inside,' she said. 'Elephants can be dangerous.'

Lizzie stood on the bench and looked out of the window at her mother. Tom stayed low and held his lamb aloft, the toy's glass eyes just visible from where Ellie stood. Ellie followed the men and stopped behind them.

Seventy yards ahead, a colossal elephant, far bigger than the steam engine, stood astride the tracks.

The driver spoke to the men in the jodhpurs in a language Ellie assumed must be Nepali. Douglas added something, and there was general agreement. The Nepali men nodded their heads from side to side in a way Ellie still found peculiar.

Francis stepped forward, lifted his rifle and aimed at the elephant.

'No,' Douglas said. 'You'll turn her savage.' Placing his fingers under the barrel of the gun, he lifted it to the sky.

'What the fuck do you think you're doing?' Francis said. 'What the hell do you know about killer elephants?'

Douglas smiled. 'This isn't a killer elephant. She's a grand-mother, and she's protecting her family from this iron beast. When she feels it's safe, she'll go to join them, over there in the forest.' He pointed left, and Ellie squinted, unable to see any elephants until a calf appeared from behind the cover of the sal trees.

'My guess is they're on their way west,' Douglas said calmly, 'probably to one of the royal hunting grounds, where they'll be slaughtered by the Maharaja and his family.'

Ellie wished he would stop speaking in that way. Francis had a short fuse and he'd be humiliated to have this stranger instruct him on his greatest passion. Thank goodness, she thought, that only she, Davies and the jodhpur men seemed to understand English.

'Now I suggest we all get back on the train,' Douglas said. 'Hopefully this old girl will soon be on her way.' He turned to the other passengers and must have said the same thing in Nepali or Hindi, because they began to disappear back into their carriages.

'It is a good thing you are so well armed, sir,' the oldest man in jodhpurs said to Francis. 'It could have saved us from an unpleasant fate if the cow had been ready to charge.'

His words restored some of Francis's pride, and Ellie gave the man a look of thanks. She walked back to the carriage with him.

'I'm Ellie,' she said, not using her title because it felt too formal. Then she changed her mind and added, 'Lady Northwood,' because she knew it eased her passage through any situation.

The man bowed slightly, pressed his palms together and lifted them to his forehead. 'Namaskar, Lady Northwood. I'm Dr Prasad.'

'Are you going to Kathmandu?'

'Indeed I am. It's my home, though I've worked in Calcutta for years. I'm hoping to start a new practice in Nepal. That's why I'm returning with my sons. They've both been educated in India.'

On board the train, Dr Prasad tended to the grandmother, who had sustained a bad cut on the bridge of her nose. Lizzie and Tom clambered over Ellie, treading on her bladder and reminding her that she needed the bathroom. Nanny Barker gave the twins some paper and wax crayons to keep them busy and then had to confiscate them because Tom had scribbled all over his white topi. The pith helmet was covered in orange crayon.

Shushila was curled up, asleep. Dr Prasad's sons read books but didn't seem to be able to concentrate very well; one of the young men kept glancing out of the window, and the other was jumpy, his eyes darting from his book to the rest of the travellers. Douglas's pretty mistress studied her map, while Douglas himself stayed with the driver until the old elephant swished her trunk at the train, trumpeted a few times and lumbered slowly into the forest.

The passengers had to wait another half-hour before the journey continued because the engine had to be stoked to generate a sufficient head of steam. In the meantime, everyone in the first carriage grew tense as Francis and Davies inspected their guns. Francis stroked his new Holland & Holland .375, and Davies oiled his pistols while chewing tobacco and spitting out of the window. After a while, Francis began taking pot shots at passing animals and birds. Shushila woke with a start. The merchants edged to the far end of the carriage, and then got out without a fuss and moved further down the train. When the journey resumed, Francis's shots became wilder, and Davies joined in, his aim a little truer. Dr Prasad and his sons became agitated.

'Gentlemen,' Douglas called, walking towards the hunters. 'You're flouting the first law of shikar. You can't shoot an animal and leave it without knowing whether it's dead. Perhaps the wildlife you've shot is wounded. I think the noise of the engine will have driven game further into the forest, and your shots are unlikely to have harmed a single creature, but you can't rely on it. Besides, the noise is unsettling the ladies.'

Dr Prasad and his sons waggled their heads in agreement.

Francis withdrew his rifle from the open window, and although Ellie couldn't be sure, he seemed to point it at Douglas. Dr Prasad and his sons clearly thought the same because she saw their bodies stiffen and their jaws slacken.

'What's your name?' Francis asked.

'Hugh Douglas.'

'No title? No rank?'

'I was a lieutenant in the 8th Gurkhas.'

Francis smirked; he was dealing with a retired junior officer. 'Indian Army,' he said to Davies as he sat down and handed the gunman his rifle. Davies chuckled.

Hugh Douglas made to return to his seat and then stopped, pausing to look back at Francis. 'There's no place here for big shots,' he said. 'The war finished them. No one has the stomach for slaughter any more.'

Francis pretended not to hear.

The train rattled on. Ellie tied a scarf around her hair to stop the wind whipping it into knots. She began to feel calmer as the tension in the carriage slowly defused. Then, from the corner of her eye, she saw Shushila watching her from the bench. Ellie turned to look directly at her, and froze; the look in the girl's eyes was malevolent and fierce. Shushila smiled, but her eyes did not.

'When do we get off this damned cattle wagon?' Francis called down the carriage to no one in particular. Everyone avoided his eye. He was pumped up by the shooting, and riled by Douglas. The fellow didn't know his place. To add to Francis's woes, the train was slow and uncomfortable. The benches were unforgiving, and there were no overhead fans. Such privations, he reminded himself, were only to be expected, and other hunters had suffered far more in pursuit of their sport. What was really testing him, though, was the continual delay. It was intolerable. Nine exasperating months had passed since he'd rescued the Maharaja's nephew, and the promise of stalking game in the great virgin plains of the Nepal Terai had seemed increasingly elusive, as if the opportunity would vanish, rather like the Maharaja's nephew, into the vastness of the Himalayas. The dawdling train, jolting along on its narrow tracks, or stationary in the face of the old cow elephant, had only heightened his irritation. To top it all, he was sick and tired of the unsuitable party accompanying him. There was no question that women were bad for shikar. It was infuriating that he was saddled with them, but unavoidable when his wife was financing the expedition.

Francis's lack of patience made him a shocking sportsman. It was why he didn't take time to internalise jungle lore or learn the rules of shikar. It was the kill rather than the craft he craved, as if you could have one without the other. Despite a run of bad luck and a failure to bag any decent game, he was convinced he was going to be one of the renowned shikaris of the age. He'd become a legend, crowned in a glory that would eclipse the memory of his two heroic brothers, killed in the trenches of northern France. It was hard to compete with dead men, Francis thought bitterly, especially when there was no war left to fight and your grieving mother refused to allow you to join the army.

He glanced at Nanny Barker and looked away quickly. What was happening to the woman? She was perspiring heavily. It seemed she couldn't regulate her temperature, as if the climate, or just being abroad, had disrupted every bodily function, puffing up her skin so she looked as if she was wrapped in lavender quilting. Perhaps she's too old for this, he thought, feeling guilty for a moment. But then he dismissed the thought: it wasn't his fault the children were here and needed a nanny. It was absurd to bring them to such a remote place; they should be at home, growing up in an English climate, learning English ways.

If he'd had any say in the matter, they wouldn't have come to India, never mind Nepal, but the galling fact was, he couldn't order Ellie round like she was a normal wife. Ellie insisted she was going to accompany him, and she was adamant she'd bring the twins too. She wanted to see India and she was obsessed by the mountains in the north. She was captivated by the romance of the names, and the strangeness of the places. It was as if she believed she'd discover something special there, some idyll she wouldn't find anywhere else in the world. I've married a fruitcake, Francis told himself, and cursed his misfortune.

Ellie wasn't right in the head. She took pills when she had one of her funny spells, and she was terrified of the dark, which was ridiculous. Her brother and parents had died almost thirty years ago, Bobby under a collapsed chimney and her parents lost somewhere in the fires raging across San Francisco. It couldn't feel that raw any longer, Francis had told her, but some people just couldn't pull themselves together. What Ellie needed was a stiff upper lip like his own. Unfortunately, as she had control of their money, he was at her mercy. His gaze lingered on the case containing the expensive guns and he felt a little warmer towards his wife. Yes, he thought, as wives went, she could have been a hell of a lot worse.

Ellie wasn't beautiful, but she had something about her, or at least that was what his friends said. Perhaps they meant her fortune, and it was true that she was outrageously wealthy, even by American standards. It was a pity, though, that the family's money was so recently acquired. It still carried a whiff of mine camps in the Sierra Nevada and the toxic sludge filling California's rivers. Whatever the attractions of Ellie's money, however, Francis couldn't shake off the thought that there was something mannish about her. And it wasn't just her style, the way she strode around in trousers or jodhpurs, trying, he assumed, to look like Amelia Earhart about to fly solo over the Atlantic. It wouldn't surprise him one bit if she were to appear at breakfast in a flying jacket and aviation helmet. No, he thought, it's not just her clothes that are odd; her face has a decidedly unfeminine strength. Francis looked at his wife in pity, and was surprised to feel a little tug at his heart, a feeling almost like fondness. The wind from the open window tousled her thick, silky hair, which had escaped from under her head-scarf, and he admitted it made a very striking picture. He looked at the ayah lying on the bench, her eyes half closed. His gaze lingered on her soft feet, decorated with henna, and his penis twitched.

The train came to a halt in Amlekhganj, a dusty little town that was, quite literally, at the end of the line. Most of the passengers vanished immediately. Dr Prasad and his sons gathered their large collection of luggage and boarded a decrepit bus that didn't look as if it was going anywhere. Three trucks, one rather inferior to the other two, were parked at the side of the station. Their uniformed drivers saluted the foreigners and a Nepali official in very elaborate formal dress greeted them with a bow, his hands pressed against his chest. He introduced himself as Major Thapa, secretary to the Maharaja's nephew.

'We have two parties travelling to Kathmandu today,' he said with a smile. 'Lord Northwood and his family will be in the first two automobiles.'

That meant Hugh and the native girl were allocated the shabbier truck.

'God knows why he's going to Kathmandu,' Francis said, raking Douglas with an imperious gaze. 'Let's hope the bugger's not here for the game.' He looked down at Ellie as he climbed into the truck. 'You travel with the children and the other women,' he said. 'Davies and I will go ahead with Major Thapa and the luggage.'

The first part of the road journey was not unlike the trip in the train – the land was flat; there were fields and farms and patches of forest – and then, abruptly, they began to climb. The road swung back and forth, twisting up the Himalayan foothills. The gradient grew steeper, the road narrower and more hazardous, so that at points it was chiselled into the mountains. Nanny Barker was rigid in her seat, her eyes shut tight, muttering a prayer and holding tightly to Tom. Ellie pulled Lizzie away from the window. Even Shushila, who usually took everything in her stride, looked terrified, her eyes fixed on the streams edged with mosses and lichens that trickled down the rock and over the road.

Shrines were dotted at odd intervals along the route. Sometimes they were no more than a stone strung with wilting garlands; at other times they were crude miniature temples, or little idols placed in a cleft in the earth.

The driver kept turning to the women and grinning, excited by the danger. Ellie was sure he was enjoying his passengers' discomfort.

'Shushila, please tell him to keep his eyes on the road, will you?' Ellie said.

'I do not speak Nepali,' Shushila replied. 'I am Bengali.'

Although Francis and Davies's truck was two hundred yards ahead, the many twists in the road meant they rarely saw it. They'd left the truck carrying Hugh Douglas far behind them, its engine belching out smoke and struggling to haul its passengers up the steadily increasing gradient.

The wooden slats of a bridge creaked under the weight of the truck when they crossed a deep gorge. Only one of the headlights worked as they chugged through a long, narrow tunnel, shiny with moisture, water dripping from its roof. Halfway through, Tom was violently sick into Ellie's lap, and she spent the rest of the drive gagging at the stink of vomit.

'I've never been so glad to finish a journey,' Nanny Barker said when they stopped. Climbing backwards out of the truck, she dangled a leg, searching for the ground, while her dress rode up to reveal the edges of her long drawers. She may have given up stockings, but she clung firmly to the safety of old-fashioned bloomers.

Major Thapa looked away, flustered, and fixed his eyes on a

distant peak. 'Memsahib,' he said, mistaking Nanny Barker for a burra mem, an important white lady, 'our journey has only just begun. This is Bhimphedi: it is the end of the road. From here we must walk.'

Shushila sighed and sank on to a rock, and Nanny Barker looked at the man in disbelief.

'You ladies, of course, do not need to walk.' He laughed, and pointed to three sedan chairs. 'We have dolis to take you to Kathmandu.'

Ellie watched the porters take the luggage, including the children's pram, to the ropeway that would carry it over the mountains to Kathmandu.

'We'll take the guns,' Davies barked. 'Can't risk those going astray.'

The men mounted sturdy ponies that seemed too small to carry them, and the women looked dubiously at the dolis, which were wooden boxes upholstered in badly frayed, sun-bleached purple velvet. Bamboo poles were threaded through hoops on either side, and four bearers stood by each chair, waiting to lift the travellers on to their shoulders.

'I'll walk,' Nanny Barker said firmly. Shushila hid a smile behind her hand. The wood of the doli was old and Nanny Barker was heavy from a diet of nursery food: cake, endless rounds of bread and butter, and sweet milky puddings.

The bearers grunted in unison and lifted the first doli. Ellie and Lizzie were jolted sideways as the men adjusted the poles on their shoulders and began walking. Shushila and Tom followed in the next, and Nanny Barker stomped behind in a slather of sweat, trailed by her empty doli and the bearers, who were in no rush to carry the plump English nanny. When the gradient increased, however, she admitted defeat and squeezed into the wooden chair. The men lifted her, staggered, and then moved forward, chanting to help them negotiate the most difficult, treacherous sections of the climb.

The road to Kathmandu was a path of broken stones, so steep and unrelenting in its ascent that Ellie was afraid to look back. She imagined slipping and falling, plunging down, unable to stop as the loose rocks and stones tumbled with her. The bearers paused occasionally to shift their loads, moving the bamboo poles on their skinny shoulders, but as a rule, they kept the momentum steady. As the incline increased and the ground beneath their feet became unstable, the men's chants grew louder.

'Narayan-ah, Narayan-ah,' they chorused.

The shadeless trail zigzagged, cutting back on itself, and then grew steeper as it turned another corner. Ellie adjusted Lizzie's bonnet and called to Shushila, telling her to put Tom's sola topi back on. The pith helmet was still too big for him and he hated wearing it because it kept slipping down and covering his eyes.

Four porters, wearing loose loincloths, leaned against a bank of rocks and watched the foreigners go by. Their enormous bundles of goods were fastened to their backs with a single broad strap that ran across their foreheads. An old man hobbled slowly downhill, supported by a long staff, and smiled at the twins.

Just before the trail turned again, Francis and Davies halted their ponies. A cloud of dust hung in the air and there was a noisy hum. Rounding the corner, the travellers stopped in surprise. Over a hundred men blocked the road. They were carrying a Rolls-Royce on a wooden frame. At the front of the column, about forty men pulled the car up on ropes, while perhaps sixty laboured behind it to stop the Rolls slipping downhill.

The porters stopped when their foreman shouted. They shuffled sideways and the car creaked. The trail was just wide enough at that point for the sahibs' party to pass. A few of the bearers stared at them, the men's faces strained and covered in perspiration. The Rolls, which was green under the layer of dust kicked up from the road, rested without its wheels on the timber frame. Ellie thought it would have looked wonderful on the roads of London or San Francisco, but it appeared monstrous when hauled up a mountain by half-starved men.

Ellie had often imagined crossing the Himalayas, but she'd never thought she'd be carried over them. She'd dreamed of walking and climbing on to the roof of the world. Her muscles would ache, her feet would blister, and the journey would be a trial, an ordeal to test her. She looked at the tense shoulders of the porters carrying the doli, at the way the bamboo poles pressed against their skin and bones, and she felt it was all wrong. It was not the way it was supposed to be. Francis thought she was accompanying him to Nepal because it was a fancy of hers, something decided on a whim in the lounge of the Great Eastern Hotel, but there were things Ellie kept secret from her husband, not because they were forbidden and dangerous things, but because she knew he would think her mad.

In the spring of 1926, Ellie and Momo were in Paris on the long vacation they took after Momo's first divorce. They had been up the Eiffel Tower, visited Notre-Dame and Sainte-

Chapelle, and Momo's mood was lifting. She'd regained her zest for life, especially when they met a philosopher, quite by chance, at the Louvre. He clearly had an eye for copper-haired American heiresses as well as dusty old books.

The dashing intellectual spoke in heavily accented English, which Momo said made her swoon, and then in French.

Momo opened her eyes wide and turned to Ellie. 'I can't understand a word he's saying,' she whispered.

'He wants to take us to a lecture,' Ellie explained.

'Oh,' Momo said, perplexed; she'd never been to a lecture in her life.

'It's being given by Alexandra David-Néel,' the philosopher explained, switching back to English.

'Is she an actress?' Momo asked.

He laughed, charmed, Ellie hoped, by her friend's exuberance. She worried though that he might think Momo a bit scatty. 'She's many things,' he said. 'She's an explorer, a spiritualist, a searcher for truth. She's been to places we only dream about.'

'The Arctic?' Momo said.

'More remote than that.'

'Darkest Africa?' Momo suggested.

'Tibet and the Himalayas.'

Momo frowned. Geography was not one of her strong points.

'Where the mountaineers saw the Abominable Snowman?' Ellie asked.

'If you believe in such things, then yes, that's the place. On the map it is just a blank space; one of the last great unexplored wildernesses on the planet. I promise you, mademoiselles, this talk will open your eyes.'

The philosopher was right, the evening opened Ellie's eyes.

It also did more than that: it changed her life, though sometimes, she would later think, not necessarily for the better.

There was a buzz in the Collège de France. More and more people were arriving, pushing into the back of the lecture hall and creating an uncomfortable crush. Alexandra David-Néel glided on to the stage and hush descended. She was a small, stout woman in late middle age, and she commanded the room, moving so that her flowing robes swirled around her. She was accompanied by a young man dressed in the robes of a lama, a Tibetan Buddhist priest, and who was introduced as her Tibetan adopted son, Yogden.

'My God, I was right,' Momo said, breathing heavily in Ellie's ear. 'She really is an actress: it's like going to the theatre. Look at the crazy costumes.'

Ellie ignored her friend, too captivated by the woman on stage to listen to Momo's commentary. The explorer was talking about the spell cast by the world's highest peaks, about the glory of Tibet's mountain fastness, its secret places, and the sacred knowledge cradled behind the fortress of the Himalayas. When they began the slide show, the images made Ellie breathe faster because she couldn't have been any more amazed if she had been shown a photograph of the Abominable Snowman himself.

Although the black and white slides were grainy, and a few were scratched, they drew Ellie in so she sat on the very edge of her seat. She saw snow-capped Himalayas, devil dancers, priests in robes, mountain eyries, monasteries like impregnable forts, nomads standing stiffly outside yak-hair tents.

She wondered later if she had mistranslated David-Néel's

words, giving them a meaning that was not intended. Much of the language was complex, and the explorer sprinkled her speech with Tibetan phrases. Ellie, though, wasn't sure it mattered. She understood that high in the Himalayas there was one last enchanted land where David-Néel had found the happiness and wisdom lost to the West. It all makes so much sense, she thought, such perfect sense.

The rapt audience sighed and gasped. David-Néel had walked for months through hostile terrain, braving snow blindness, frost bite, arrest and attack. It was a pilgrimage, she said, and it was only the true yearning of her heart that had finally got her to Lhasa, the Tibetan capital.

Her son began to recite poetry in his mother tongue and David-Néel translated from Tibetan into French. Ellie tried to make sense of the lama's words and looked at the philosopher for help.

'He means "coral-red mountains",' the philosopher said to her over the top of Momo's meticulously coiffured hair.

What would coral-red mountains look like? Ellie wondered.

Eight years later, jiggling in the doli towards Sisaghari, she wondered whether the lama might have meant something like the colour of Kanchenjunga as the last rays of the sun touched its snows and dusk fell over Darjeeling. No, she thought, those reds, oranges and pinks weren't the colour of coral. Maybe I'll see the coral mountains when I get to Kathmandu. Nepal wasn't Tibet, she reasoned, but it was damn close, and like Tibet, it was a forbidden land. In her heart, though, she felt the lama's visions lay further north, over the great barrier of the high Himalayas, where the coral-red mountains would rise from the deserts of the Tibetan plateau. And if she ever went there, she decided as she sat in her doli borne by emaciated men, she would do it like Alexandra David-Néel, on her own two feet, like a pilgrim, going in search of something she did not yet fully understand.

The small town of Sisaghari was built on one of the only bits of flat land in the foothills. Two officers from the fort that guarded the entrance to Nepal made an elaborate display of checking the travellers' papers, and then detailed half a dozen soldiers to escort them to the government guest house. Before they went inside, Ellie looked back over the trail they had just climbed. To the south, the plains of India spread as far as she could see. She turned in the opposite direction and watched Major Thapa talking to Francis and pointing up to a track that cut through the high forests and towards the Chandragiri Pass, the gateway to Kathmandu.

Ellie and Francis ate on the veranda of the guest house. It grew chilly very quickly and Ellie felt the tiny hairs on her arms lift. She pulled a shawl around her shoulders, thankful that the bearer was kindling a fire in her damp and unaired bedroom. Shushila had disappeared into the bazaar, suddenly remembering enough Hindustani to speak with the local people, who understood the language almost as well as their own Nepali tongue. As usual, Nanny Barker had settled the twins to sleep without Shushila's help. Both children were exhausted, and Ellie was sure Tom was out of sorts and suffering a touch of sunstroke because of the length of time he'd spent without his topi.

After dinner, Davies reappeared from the bazaar and he and Francis opened a bottle of Scotch. Ellie decided to turn in, knowing they were set for a long bout of drinking and telling tall shikar tales. She wished Francis goodnight, and as she opened the door to the guest house, she glimpsed several figures making their way up the road from India. Hugh Douglas, his mistress, their guide and half a dozen porters emerged out of the dusk. Ellie closed the door behind her, glad the guest house was full and that their fellow travellers would have to find other accommodation. Something about Hugh and his companion made her uneasy. She told herself that it was the age gap. If she was honest, though, it wasn't only the girl's youth that made her uncomfortable: for the first time she could remember, Ellie felt the prickle of envy.

The moon is brighter in the hills, Shushila decided as she walked out of her lodgings and along the path to the fort. She craned her head to look at the deep midnight-blue sky that arced over the hills. Although it was a revelation to see so many stars, Shushila wasn't sure that she liked being in the countryside. She certainly didn't like the lodgings she'd been given. In the government guest house, the bearers had dragged a cot into the hall outside the children's room and motioned her towards it. The bed was a horrible, knotty string cot, the kind a lowly servant would use. The fat old English nanny had a comfy bed, two pillows and a heap of blankets, but you always got good things if you were white.

The sahib had seen Shushila's livid expression and Major Thapa had quickly arranged a room for her in a private guest house. It wasn't ideal, but at least the sahib would be happy. He'd be able to visit her once Mem was asleep, and when he did, she was going to remind him that she wanted her own room in the heart of a palace.

Maybe their stay in Kathmandu would be better, she thought, wrapping her shawl around her shoulders. A cloud crossed the face of the moon, darkness claimed the town for a moment, and she shivered. It never got so cold in Calcutta. The Himalayas smelled different too. In the centre of Sisaghari the smells were similar to those in Calcutta. The hill town was rank with wood smoke, kerosene and shit, and the familiar odour of men's sweat wafted round the tea shop, but on the treacherous path that wound its way from Bhimphedi, her senses had been assailed by the smell of rich earth and forest.

'I'd get back inside,' a man said gruffly as he brushed past. 'Never know who's about, do you? You can't be too careful.'

She recoiled. It was that donkey, Davies, doing his funny walk, his muscled shoulders hunched up around his ears and his bulky arms unable to hang by his sides.

Shushila pretended not to understand, which was a useful tactic and one she'd perfected.

'See this lot of bleeding niggers,' he said, pointing to the open-fronted tea shop, where a handful of men were eating and drinking in the soft light of an oil lamp. 'They'd steal the clothes off my back if I stood still long enough.'

She ignored him.

'Did you hear what I said?' he barked. He came so close she could see that the whites of his eyes were like jelly. He blasted whisky-laden breath over her. She would have recoiled but she'd learned to harden herself to the stink of British men.

Shushila was an accomplished actress, and she looked blankly at him.

'Fucking stupid bitch,' he muttered, and stomped away.

The men smoking and drinking in the tea shop watched

her. Women weren't supposed to walk around alone, especially at night, but she wasn't going to be bound by what a lot of peasants and coolies thought. She glanced at them and thanked the pantheon of gods and goddesses that she lived in the city, not in some dirt-poor farm clinging to the side of a mountain.

Shushila hadn't always lived in the city; she'd grown up on a jute mill compound on the banks of the Hooghly, where her mother was an ayah to the manager's children. The manager's bungalow had wide, airy verandas and enormous rooms with shuttered windows and ceiling fans, and the bathrooms had hot running water and toilets that flushed.

All the supervisors in the mill were sahibs with red faces and white suits, and they lived in similar, but smaller, bungalows. Shushila watched them and their families go to the club house on the compound. They played tennis and took off their clothes and splashed about in a swimming pool, looking foolish. There was a diving board on which the men showed off, jumping into the pool and spraying everyone with water. The shameless women appeared in their underclothes, and everyone could see the bare flesh of their legs. A couple of older, fatter ladies refused to join in the silliness and sat on cane loungers looking overheated and bad-tempered.

When Shushila was five, she began helping her mother with the children. In the bathrooms, she stood on a chair, pulled a long chain and watched the little sahibs' and sahibas' shit vanish with a gurgle down a hole in the bottom of the pan. Soon, though, the miracle of bathroom fittings and sanitary progress became boring, and the smell of meat eater's faeces repulsive, and her mother had to nag Shushila to check the toilets.

'What will Mem say if she sees such a mess?' her mother asked.

'I'm not a sweeper, Ma,' Shushila cried, her face screwed tight with indignation.

'No, but we are poor. Who will pay for your food if we don't work?' Her mother touched the girl's head and smiled, but Shushila scowled and ran off.

Her mother knew nothing, she decided. Shushila had seen plenty of memsahibs who didn't work but who still had an endless amount of food: mutton chops, devilled kidneys, tinned peaches, kedgeree, shepherd's pie, plum duff pudding, more fried *bekti* than anyone could ever eat. They sat around all day playing cards and talking while they smoked and drank alcohol. On weekends they went to church, and sailed to Calcutta on the mill's own boat to go shopping and eat in restaurants. Sometimes their husbands drove them, and Shushila was sure none of this counted as work, even though she heard the mems complain about how tired they were, and how being 'out East' sapped your energy. If life was so hard on the compound, she wondered, why didn't they go back to wherever they came from? But the funny thing was, when they did go home every few years, they always returned saying how much they'd missed the place, and how hard it had been without their servants.

When she was fifteen, the manager and his family came back from a long leave, and his wife told Shushila that she'd grown an awful lot in the months they'd been away, and that it was good to see her running errands around the compound. The manager glanced up from his paper and was startled. He took a sip from his burra peg. He too had noticed how much she'd grown.

'Don't wrap your sari so tightly,' her mother said every morning, tugging at the fabric. 'And that blouse is too small for you now. Go and change it.'

Why should I? Shushila thought. When she dressed like that, and walked with a slight roll of her hips, she knew she wouldn't have to flush toilets again or pretend to like babies. It served the memsahibs right. Why should they, with their big, ungainly figures, live like queens while she was their servant? She wanted what they had, and by the age of fifteen, she knew how to get it.

Several jobs later, she realised she had to be circumspect. She'd been sacked by three memsahibs who had suddenly seen their simple, devoted ayah in a new light, and it was proving hard to get a new job because sensible mems didn't employ attractive ayahs if they wanted to keep their husbands to themselves. She had a number of excellent chits written by former sahibs, but the problem was she didn't really like children or memsahibs, and it showed very quickly. Her current mem, the wife of the burra sahib in one of the big managing agencies, was growing increasingly wary, almost certainly doubting the glowing recommendations from her previous employers.

Only important Britishers went to the Tollygunge Club. In the withering heat of May, some of the idiotic sahibs were still sitting outside eating lunch at tables on the fine, close-cropped lawn. From the shade of the trees, Shushila watched her own mem and sahib eating while she minded their youngest child. The little sahib sat on the rug, staring open-mouthed at her bracelets. He's such a gormless child, Shushila thought, irritated by his pudgy pink face and miserable whine.

His father was proving even more of a problem, because he

remained stubbornly immune to Shushila's charms. She observed him being served another drink and decided he must be ill, or maybe that he preferred boys. And then as he smiled at his plain wife, who was wearing an ill-fitting linen dress that made her look like a sinewy old chicken, a bizarre thought occurred to Shushila: he might actually love Mem. He might not want another woman – even Shushila. She was saved from this disturbing idea by the arrival of a new party of guests, at the centre of which was a man everyone else seemed to treat as a god. The burra sahibs fawned around him, respectful, smiling, offering seats and ordering drinks. He must be the biggest of the burra sahibs, Shushila reasoned. Perhaps he was the King of England. Realising he wasn't with a queen, Shushila left the halfwit child alone on the blanket. Then she walked slowly between the tables, her eyes meeting those of the confused bearers, the shocked mems and the surprised sahibs. Two hours later, she became an ayah to British nobility, and her new sahib didn't even ask to see her chits.

On the edge of Sisaghari, Shushila shivered in the crisp mountain air. I should go to my room, she decided, and turned to follow Davies back into the village. It was late and the sahib would be looking for her. Out of the corner of her eye, she saw a figure moving fast. Something white, like a billowing sail, disappeared into the darkness along the road from the fort. She shuddered. It must have been a ghost or an evil spirit luring unsuspecting travellers to its forest lair.

She slowed when she heard angry voices, and as she approached the lodge, a door burst open and Davies and Douglas fell into the street, one on top of the other. They stood up, and staggered. As she watched, Davies stepped on a large loose stone and twisted his ankle. He steadied himself and began to run towards the government guest house, Douglas close behind. The sahib appeared in the doorway and looked at the damage.

'Fucking idiots,' he said, slurring his words. 'It's going to be pistols at dawn.'

The chimney in Ellie's bedroom in the government guest house was rudimentary and the wood in the hearth was damp. It burned slowly and smoke leaked into the room through gaps in the brickwork. Ellie made her way to the next room, where Nanny Barker was stretched out on a bed made for a smaller person, the mound of blankets covering her quivering with each reverberating breath. The twins slept in cots, Tom more fitfully than his sister, as if he was still being jiggled by the movement of the doli.

She left the door ajar and returned to the murk of her own room. The pathetic fire barely warmed the air, and she climbed into bed and pulled the blankets up around her chin. They were impregnated with the smell of the smokehouse. A candle burned on the bedside table and she watched the flame flicker as she tried to sleep. A pack of jackals howled and began chattering to one another outside the barred and shuttered window. By the time the leopard came prowling around the garden and coughed under her window, she was dozing as restlessly as her son.

An hour later, she woke with a jolt. Something was caught in the back of her throat. She was sure she was going to choke, and the taste of smoke coated the inside of her mouth. The candle had burned to a waxy puddle and the room was almost pitch black. Terror flipped her stomach over and slammed her heart against her ribs. She could just make out the beams, the walls, and the stone of the chimney. Somewhere nearby, she heard a child moan. She sat up and turned her head, sure that the wall had moved. The chimney was leaning into the centre of the room. She drew up her legs and buried her face in her hands. The ceiling was bearing down, the big beams buckling under the pressure. The room was collapsing in on itself and pressing against her so tightly she couldn't breathe.

She scrabbled in the dark, trying to find another candle, but in her panic, she knocked over the box and sent the candles spinning under the bed. She fumbled in a rucksack, looking for her Veronal tablets, and couldn't find them. She stood up unsteadily, unbalanced by the rotating floor, and staggered into the children's room. Picking up the twins, one in each arm, she balanced them on her hips and carried them down the stairs and on to the veranda. They were no longer babies and were too heavy for her to carry far. Tom wriggled and arched his back, and as she stepped on to the road, she almost dropped him. She held on tighter and ran blindly, putting as much distance as possible between herself and the collapsing guest house.

The night was lit by a bright moon that shone through the pristine mountain air like weak winter sun. She slowed, no longer feeling the ground sway. She could see the edges of the forest, and the trail descending back down to Bhimphedi and the plains. The outskirts of the bazaar looked unchanged. It was the same small collection of buildings, decorated with flags. A lamp hung from a shop, and a dog tethered to a house woke and eyed her before falling back to sleep. Every house and shop was still standing. Half a dozen porters sitting in the tea shop stared at her in bemused silence. She leaned her head back and breathed in cold, clear air. It filled her lungs and her heart began to slow. She turned around and saw the guest house, solid and undamaged in the moonlight.

She put the children down and they sat in the road. After a few minutes she led them back towards the guest house, grateful that they didn't meet anyone on the way. What would people think if they saw her dressed in her nightgown, leading two toddlers in pyjamas through a hill bazaar in the middle of the night? What kind of mother did that sort of thing? She knew the answer: it was the worst kind – the mad kind.

They stepped on to the veranda of the guest house, and the chowkidar and a bearer appeared from nowhere and rushed about looking alarmed. It took Ellie a moment to realise that no one was paying any attention to her as she stood stricken in the doorway, the twins clinging to her legs.

'For fuck's sake,' Davies shouted, storming on to the veranda. He was drunk, and his face glowed red.

Hugh Douglas followed Davies and grabbed the collar of his safari shirt. Swinging him around, he shoved him against the wall. 'What do you think you were doing?' he spat, his face an inch from Davies's.

Davies bared his teeth. 'I understand. You want to keep her to yourself. I just thought she might like a bit of extra business. No harm meant.'

'She's not a whore, you fool. She's my daughter.'

He banged Davies's head so hard against the wall that the chowkidar howled, 'Stop, stop!'

Francis appeared from the bazaar a few moments later looking equally drunk and even more dishevelled. Hugh relaxed his grip on Davies and then released him. 'If you go anywhere near her again, I'll kill you,' he said. He barged past Francis, knocking his shoulder as he stepped off the veranda and returned to his lodgings.

'When will you learn, Davies?' Francis said, his words slurred. 'It's no good slinking off to the whorehouse whenever the fancy takes you. You need more discretion. Be more like a gentleman: take a mistress.' He belched, then, seeing his wife, pulled himself up straight and brushed back his hair.

'Sorry to disturb you, darling. Davies and I went for a little night hunting. I don't suppose you heard the leopards?'

Ellie didn't reply. She took the oil lamp offered to her by the chowkidar and led the children back to their room. She settled them to sleep, stroking their faces and smiling at them so they could see she was happy. Nanny Barker hadn't budged. She was sleeping soundly, unaware of the panic that had possessed Ellie, or of the fight on the veranda.

When Ellie returned to her room, Francis was already asleep, still fully dressed. She placed the lamp on the bedside table and lay until dawn watching the flame flicker in the safety of its glass case. It illuminated the room with a gentle glow that kept the walls straight, the ceiling high and the floor steady. If she looked at the flame long and hard enough, there would be no darkness and no disaster.

The descent from Sisaghari was easier than the previous day's climb. Ellie elected to walk; she couldn't bear to spend any more time on the inadequately padded seat of the sedan chair, and the base of her spine was still sore from the bump she'd had on the train. Francis and Davies rode on ahead, while the bearers carried the dolis. Lizzie sat with Nanny Barker, and Tom with Shushila, who had rigged up an umbrella over her doli to protect herself from the sun.

Ellie had barely noticed the country on the climb from Bhimphedi, but today she was more aware of the beauty of their surroundings. A few flowers still bloomed even though it was January, and she kept pausing to examine the plants edging the road. The rest of the party pulled further ahead, and she was relieved. She wanted to get away from Francis, who was acting as if he were organising an invasion of the country, and away from Nanny Barker, who didn't complain but who radiated fury and disapproval. She also wanted a break from the bearers, with their repetitive 'Narayan-ah' chorus. Their chanting was less intrusive from a distance and sounded almost melodic.

The hillsides were intricately terraced into narrow paddy fields that had been harvested a few weeks before. On some terraces, rice stubble stuck out of cracked soil. Others had been planted with wheat, and a few with vegetables. Where the long descent into the Chitlong Valley ended and the land flattened into broader fields, she heard bells tinkling behind her. A man ran past, his feet barely touching the ground as he seemed to skim along the road to Kathmandu.

'That's the postman,' Hugh Douglas said, drawing alongside her.

She jumped in surprise.

'Perhaps I should wear bells too,' he said.

'I didn't see you.'

'You were dawdling and it seems your companions have

forgotten you. Perhaps we should both wear bells. The unfortunate postman, though, is required to; he'll be flogged if his bells go silent. That's how the Maharaja keeps the mail moving so fast.'

Two or three hundred yards back up the track, Ellie spotted Hugh's daughter being carried into the valley in a doli. She was glad the girl wasn't his mistress; it gave her an odd sense of satisfaction, as if things were made right with the world. Hugh Douglas didn't strike her as a man who'd prey on young girls; he seemed solid and reliable. But then she caught sight of Francis and Davies up ahead, buying cigarettes from a roadside stall, and reminded herself that when it came to evaluating men, she was an idiot.

'Where's your pony?' she asked.

'Still at Sisaghari. She's lame and far too old to be carrying someone like me.'

They walked together without speaking, and Ellie was surprised to find it was a comfortable silence. They were both busy observing the beauty of the valley, its pretty houses, the mountainsides clad in pine, oak, alder and chestnut. There were many more people on the trail from Chitlong than she'd imagined. A group of heavily laden porters marched towards Kathmandu, leaning forward, the straps that held their loads pulled tight around their foreheads. A couple of old women carried giant bundles of firewood, and a man drove a herd of goats along the trail towards them and then veered off along a narrow path running between the fields, whacking the last, tardy goat on its flanks with a cane.

'Namaste. Good morning, Lady Northwood,' someone said from under a large black umbrella as he overtook them. The man lifted his sunshade and nodded to Hugh. 'Mr Douglas,' he said.

'Namaste, Dr Prasad,' Ellie answered and waved.

The doctor hurried on, followed by his sons, who hadn't opened their umbrellas but had hooked the handles over the back of their jacket collars. The men were trailed by a line of porters who carried their bags and boxes.

'Ellie,' she shouted after him. 'Call me Ellie.'

Dr Prasad turned and bobbed his umbrella up and down.

'So you know Dr Prasad,' Ellie said to Hugh.

He turned quickly. 'No.'

'He knew your name.'

'He must have heard it when we were on the train and I had that cheery conversation with your husband.'

Ellie jumped aside as a drowsy boy, who was clearly thinking about something other than tending his bullocks, drove the animals towards them. She and Hugh took refuge among some shrubs until they had passed.

'Are you going hunting too?' Ellie asked.

He laughed. 'Not for game. I'm going to examine monuments and inscriptions in the valley.'

'Oh,' Ellie said. She was disappointed; it sounded so dreary. She'd imagined him to be an explorer and mountaineer rather than an academic. He looked as if he should be more in rapture at the thought of scaling Everest than cataloguing old inscriptions.

'I've spent the last five years trying to get an invitation from the Nepali government,' he said. 'An Italian professor has visited for a few weeks, and a few journalists have made a study of Kathmandu, but my daughter, Maya, and I are planning something more ambitious, if they'll give us the time. We're writing a book about the ancient history of the valley.'

Ellie looked back at Maya, squinting to see her better. 'She seems very young to be working on such a serious subject,' she said.

'She's formidably clever.'

'Didn't her mother want to come on the trip too?' Ellie asked.

'She's dead. She died years ago.'

'I'm sorry,' Ellie said, annoyed with herself for being tactless.

'It was a tragedy,' Hugh said, and Ellie heard the sorrow in his voice.

She wanted to change the subject and said the first thing that came into her head.

'Do you work in a university or a museum?'

'No. I used to be a political officer.'

'That sounds, well . . .' She searched for something polite to say.

'You mean boring,' he laughed. 'Well, it isn't as dull as you imagine. At least not here. I was based in Sikkim for a while.'

'Were you fired?'

He blew air through his teeth so it sounded like a hiss, and then laughed again. 'I think I fired myself.'

She looked at him properly for the first time that day. The ends of his auburn hair were burnished gold by the sunlight, and his eyes were a warm brown. He was handsome, she thought, and he looked absolutely nothing like a scholar. He had the tanned, rugged face of a ranch hand, and the body of a hard-working man. She was certain he hadn't spent a lifetime in libraries. Hugh Douglas must be a liar.

Hugh wasn't a liar; he just didn't tell the entire truth, but he had no intention of lying to the American woman unless it was absolutely necessary. He was enjoying her company on the walk through the Chitlong Valley. They talked for a while and then slipped into an easy silence. She didn't fill the beautiful morning with empty chatter, and there was no brittleness or edge to her. He breathed deeply, feeling the ache in his legs from yesterday's climb and this morning's fast descent into the valley. He liked that ache; he hadn't felt it for a long time. It was a memory, deep within his body, of other journeys; not like this one over the Mahabharat hills to Kathmandu, but walks in the mountains around his home in Kalimpong, and expeditions over the high passes into Tibet. Ellie stopped to look at the strings of red chillies and corn hanging from the roof of a house, and when she began walking again, she smiled at him but remained quiet, caught entirely in the spell cast by the winter sunshine on the Himalayan valley. Hugh smiled back. He felt the warmth of the sun on his face, he smelled fields and forest, and heard the gentle flow of the river, and he judged it perfect.

The wives of Darjeeling District said Hugh's father should have sent the boy to England long before his chee-chee accent became hard to shift. The man was irresponsible, they said, and far too busy cataloguing the orchids of the Himalayas to pay the child proper attention. That was what happened to widowers in the hills: they went a bit doolally. Hugh should have gone home when he was seven, like other decent Anglo-Indian boys. It was horrifying to think that he'd turned eleven and was still in India picking up all kinds of bad habits from the servants.

Later, when they explained the scandalous story to new arrivals in town, they said that the Douglas boy was a real-life version of Kipling's Kim, a vagabond cut off from his own kind. Such characters were all very well in fiction, but in the flesh they disturbed the good order of society.

Hugh didn't want to go to England. He didn't like the sound of it; he liked the house in the hills near Kalimpong, where he could do as he liked and skip school as much as possible.

'Keep missing lessons and I'll be arranging a prep school for you in England sooner than I wanted,' his father said.

Hugh knew it was an empty threat, because Captain Douglas, formerly of the 5th Gurkhas, was happy to let his son do exactly as he had done in his own youth in the foothills of the Himalayas.

'To hell with what the prissy ladies at that bloody Gymkhana Club think,' his father roared when the Reverend Smyth came to express the community's concern for the dishevelled boy they saw running about the trails in Kalimpong, the deep red and gold in his hair the only thing distinguishing him from the natives.

Captain Douglas thought it was good to let his son speak the local languages, and learn to fish, hunt and climb mountains. He wanted Hugh to be a proper boy before he parcelled him up and sent him to school to be whittled into a functionary of the Empire.

Hugh had no memory of his mother. She'd died giving birth to him, and he was raised by an ayah, a gentle woman who gave him a mother's love. She also had a son of her own, Suresh, who was only a few weeks older than Hugh. So instead of learning Greek and Latin at school, Hugh learned Hindustani and Tibetan, and from Kamala and Suresh he learned Nepali, speaking it as if it was his mother tongue, which in a way it was. And although he knew nothing about algebra and trigonometry, he knew every trail around Kalimpong and how to distinguish a tiger cub's pug marks from a leopard's. Hugh and Suresh ate together, played together and hunted together. In winter they climbed to the snow line, and in summer they fished in the rivers, caught wild chickens that they cooked over camp fires, and were reprimanded repeatedly for poaching. They were burned by the sun, Suresh to a shade that was almost black, and Hugh to a golden brown.

When he was twelve, Hugh was hauled home again by the police. They said he was setting a bad example to the natives, who had to understand that hunting was a noble pursuit and the preserve of the British. Poaching, on the other hand, was an Indian vice, which had to be punished. Reluctantly, Captain Douglas was persuaded that the time had come to end Hugh's days of freedom. The ladies of Darjeeling District were relieved; it was a weight off their minds, though they agreed it would have been preferable to enrol Hugh in a better school, one people had heard of, rather than some small establishment in an uncharted part of Shropshire, which was almost as bad as being in Wales.

Hugh sailed home in the care of an Englishwoman, the wife of a district judge, who was taking her two much younger sons to a superior prep school. She was kind to Hugh, and pretended not to notice when he cried.

'You probably feel a teeny bit sad, but you'll make plenty of chums in no time,' she said when she left him at school. They were watched from the refectory windows by dozens of eyes, keen to get a look at the awkward boy with the peculiar accent.

'The sports will be first rate,' she said, 'and before you know it, you'll fall in love with the place. Believe me, dear, the time will fly and soon you won't even want to go back to India.' She adjusted the collar of his shirt and briefly touched his hair, as if she felt she had to play the part of his dead mother.

The time didn't fly and he never loved the place. It was cruel and alien. From the classroom window Hugh saw a winter plagued by grey, scudding rain. And he didn't make lots of chums either. His few friends were from the motley group of misfits rejected by the popular boys.

'Are you Welsh?' a small boy asked on his second day. The boy wore glasses and had bright red hair.

'No,' Hugh said miserably, rearranging his clothes in his dormitory cupboard.

'You sound Welsh.'

'Well, I'm not.'

'Pierce Harrington says you're a colonial.' Pierce Harrington was captain of the rugby team, and had narrow eyes and broad fists.

'Clear off, will you,' Hugh said.

The red-haired boy didn't go, instead hovering around Hugh, anxious to make a friend. 'There's another colonial in the form below us. He's from Canada,' he said.

'I lived in India.'

'Do you speak Indian?'

'There are lots of languages in India.'

'Speak some, go on.'

Hugh said a mix of things in Hindustani and Nepali. The other boys became interested and asked for some good curses and swear words. Hugh got into his stride, showing off in

Tibetan and switching back to Nepali, the words from home filling his mouth like comforting food, familiar and reassuring.

'Sounds like you grew up in the jungle,' Pierce Harrington said, sauntering into the dorm with a couple of henchmen to see what the excitement was about. He made some monkey sounds, swung his arms to and fro, and scratched his armpits. 'We'll call you Mowgli – the Jungle Boy.'

It was meant as mockery, but Hugh didn't see it that way. If only I *were* Mowgli, he thought that night, lying awake, unable to sleep. His heart and soul ached and there was a dragging in his stomach that felt like pain and loneliness all rolled into one. He had been wrenched from the place he belonged, and he wanted to be back in India, in the hills and jungles of Kalimpong, with Father, Suresh and Kamala. He'd return soon; he'd write to his father and plead to go home. He'd be back on the ship by Christmas. But Christmas came and went, and then another year, and still he kept on writing, always expecting to be sent tickets for the passage to Bombay. It was good he had so much hope, good that the Jungle Boy didn't know it would take him ten years to return to India, and that when he did, his world would be turned upside down.

'We are coming to the end of our journey,' Major Thapa said as the foreigners gathered together before beginning the climb to the Chandragiri Pass. The stragglers caught up with Francis and Davies, who were impatient to get on, kicking their confused ponies and then reining them back when they started to trot up the path.

The road cut through green forest. A group of girls and

young women with flowers in their hair skipped towards them. They were singing, and when they saw the white people, who in reality were bright pink, they stopped to discuss the strange visitors. They hooted at something amusing, held hands and continued their journey into the Chitlong Valley, the sound of their singing gradually fading and their laughter ringing through the trees.

The track turned to greasy red clay as they climbed higher. It was slippery, and the bearers slid back, waves of mud rippling over their feet. Ellie walked slowly, stopping to look at the wild apple trees while she caught her breath. She hadn't realised she was so unfit.

Mist drifted over the mountains so she didn't know how far they'd climbed, or that they were about to scale the saddle of the pass. The track turned, the foliage parted and they stopped in surprise. The Kathmandu Valley spread before them like a deep basin carved into the mountains. The fields were a mosaic of colours: brilliant greens; rich yellow where the mustard was flowering early; and black where crops had been recently harvested and the earth was left bare. Rivers meandered across the valley floor, and to the north, the Himalayas stretched as far as they could see, the backbone of the range formed by jagged snow-capped peaks that jutted into a cloudless sky.

There were many small towns and three cities in the valley. Buildings with red tiled roofs, and tiered pagoda temples with golden finials clustered tightly together, and the large palaces and public buildings of Kathmandu were startlingly white in the January sun.

'It was once a great lake,' Major Thapa said, with a wide

sweep of his arm. 'And then the saint Manjushri took his sword and cut a path through the hills. The water flowed out and left us this blessed land.'

Davies rolled his eyes.

'Indeed,' Francis said, nodding. 'Good for old Manju.'

'I must take a photograph of this,' Ellie said. She fumbled with her Leica, but just as she took the shot, a finger of mist swirled around the pass, obscuring the view. It drifted around the trees and then was gone. She tried again, and this time she thought she'd made a better job of it.

'Now I want one of the children,' she said.

Hugh lifted Tom out of Shushila's doli and sat him with Lizzie and Nanny Barker. The bearers muttered among themselves and raised the doli with a shout of, 'Narayan-ah.'

'Take off your topi, Tom,' Ellie said.

Tom sat grinning at his mother, and Hugh reached over to take the pith helmet from the boy.

'Smile,' Ellie said, pointing the camera at the twins.

Lizzie lifted both hands and laughed, and Tom grew suddenly serious. He sat up straight and held tightly to the side of the doli.

'That will be a great photograph,' Hugh said.

The mist returned suddenly and a cloud of minute droplets enveloped them. Hugh coughed, abruptly turning away and walking into the forest. He leaned against a tree trunk and coughed again.

He returned a few minutes later. 'Apologies: a legacy of childhood asthma,' he said.

'Let us depart quickly,' Major Thapa declared. 'We must begin our descent to Thankot before these coolies get in our way.'

An army of porters was carrying a grand piano up the path from the Chitlong Valley.

Ellie took Tom from Nanny Barker, kissed him and put him back in Shushila's lap. Then they hurried towards the giant steps that would take them down through the forest and into the valley. At the first step, she stopped and turned round. Hugh followed at a distance with Maya, his face grey and his lips tinged blue.

3

The Kathmandu Valley, January 1934

THE FOREIGNERS ARRIVED in Kathmandu travel-stained and tired. Francis's party trundled from Thankot, on the edge of the valley, to Kathmandu in two new Rolls-Royces, and Hugh and Maya followed in an older model that belched smoke. Ellie spent the journey screwing up her eyes to get a better view of the city ahead. The Bhim Sen Tower, the tallest building in Kathmandu, grew larger, and the tiered pagoda roofs of the temples made her think the city was going to be as beautiful as promised.

Hugh and Maya were taken to the government guest house near the Bagmati River, while Francis and Ellie went with the rest of their party to the great palace on the northern outskirts of Kathmandu that belonged to the Maharaja's nephew. As Ellie stood in the drive, she felt let down: it wasn't an ancient Himalayan palace constructed of red bricks and age-darkened carved wood. The building had little charm, and looked like a copy of a clunky European museum. It was covered in stucco and was so big it would take hours to walk through its hundreds of rooms.

Major Thapa made hurried arrangements, instructing bearers and porters, and promised that the luggage from the ropeway would soon be delivered. The twins staggered, exhausted after a long day. Lizzie held Jean by the foot, the doll's head banging on the steps up to the portico and the main doors of the palace. Unable to go any further, Tom dropped his lamb, sat down and lifted his arms. Ellie picked him up. He was heavy but still felt like a baby. He was soft and plump, and she hugged him, breathing in the warm, intoxicating scent he'd had since he was a newborn.

'You're going to like it here,' she said, surprised to hear the uncertainty in her own voice. She stopped in the ostentatious reception hall to look at a crystal fountain that gushed rose water. 'Look at this,' she said to the twins. 'See how it sparkles.'

Tom was already asleep, his head resting on her shoulder. She carried him on her hip as Major Thapa ushered them through grand rooms, the walls hung with gilt mirrors and oil paintings, the marble floors covered in Axminster and Wilton carpets. The ceilings of the apartments were decorated with ornate coving and plaster fleur-de-lis picked out in gold. They followed him along labyrinthine corridors to a far wing of the building. It was sufficiently distant from the palace's heart that the presence of the foreigners wouldn't pollute the building or the family of the Maharaja's nephew.

Francis had his own rooms, stuffed with opulent furniture. There were cabinets stacked with treasures from Europe, China and Japan. An enormous crystal chandelier hung from the high ceiling and two Greek marble nudes flanked the door. Ellie and the children, together with Nanny and Shushila, were accommodated separately in a secluded corner of the same wing.

77

Similar sumptuous furniture, rich fabrics and imported luxuries filled the women's quarters. Ellie flopped with Tom on to a Louis XVI tapestry couch. She was shocked and dazed by her surroundings. It wasn't what she'd imagined; they were staying in a Nepali copy of the Palace of Versailles.

It was one of the best times of year to visit Kathmandu. The mountains weren't as clear as they were in November, but the valley continued to be exquisitely beautiful in the depths of winter. In January, the sun was warm and soft. The mornings were suffused by a delicate haze, and in the late afternoons, the mellow yellow light faded to gold, and then to orange. The nights were cool, the sky star-studded, and a chill breeze spilled down from the Himalayas. Occasionally a crisp frost touched the grass, and at dawn, fog slid down the hills and settled over the fields and cities.

Next morning, when Ellie, Nanny Barker and the twins were driven into Kathmandu in a gold-painted Bentley, fog still lingered in the streets, shrouding the temples and lying like a densely woven blanket over the Tundikhel, the great field where the army paraded almost every day.

The twins had slept well for the first time in weeks, and they sat, sublimely angelic, in the pram that the porters had carried into the city on their shoulders. Tom didn't try to take off his topi, and he hadn't grizzled once. Instead, he beamed at a group of local people who gathered round, intrigued by the beautiful children in the odd contraption, which was the first of its kind ever seen on the city's streets. They pointed at Tom's toy lamb, at the crest on the side of the pram, and spoke rapidly before gazing again at the children.

Ellie had known the twins would be well-behaved. She'd been sure the atmosphere of the city would rub off on all of them. Nanny Barker was less enchanted by the magic. She stood gripping the handle of the pram so tightly her knuckles had turned white. She pushed the pram twenty feet up the road and then stopped. A wheel was caught in a rut. She manoeuvred it out, and a moment later, the wheel on the opposite side became stuck. They made slow progress until the group of youths accompanying them began to lift the pram over obstacles, potholes and collapsed drains.

'They're turning it into a doli,' Ellie said.

Nanny Barker sucked in air through pursed lips. She didn't want to relinquish the perambulator. Pushing it made her walk a little taller. It was a solid, knowable thing in a strange, unknowable place that was populated by people she could never understand because, when all was said and done, they acted oddly and looked different.

The morning was cold, but not freezing. The local people, though, were dressed as if they were in the Arctic, their scarves wrapped twice around their necks. The chill didn't seem to slow them down, however, and Ellie was surprised by the number of traders crowding the bazaars. A group of men in long red coats strode past them and glanced at the pram. They were tall, with long black braided hair, and their brown skin was weather-beaten into creases, their cheeks made rosy by webs of tiny broken veins. They had the eyes of the people to the north, Ellie thought. They looked like Chinese people; like Hugh's daughter.

Kathmandu was filled with temples and palaces. Carved archways led to courtyards and shrines. In the main square, the pagoda roofs of the temples and the old royal palace were exactly like the pictures Ellie had seen in the memoirs of intrepid travellers. It was their wood carvings she liked best; the way the windows of even modest houses were latticed and decorated with birds and flowers. Some of the carving on the smaller temples had been painted, the bright colours mellowing over the years.

They walked along lanes bathed in patches of bright sunlight at one moment, and sunk in deep shadows the next. Little idols stood in alcoves in the walls, or in shrines on street corners. They were smeared in vermillion and ghee, and festooned with marigold flowers.

'It's beautiful,' Ellie exclaimed.

'It's filthy,' Nanny Barker said, fixing her gaze on a pile of rotting food dumped at the edge of the street, and at the rat making a meal of it. A sadhu with matted waist-length hair walked past leaning on a stick. Nanny shuddered and closed her eyes; the holy man's skeletal body was covered with nothing but ash.

At the end of the lane, a group of women were bathing, still in their saris, in a tank of scummy green water. They stood on the ledge of the tank as fresh water piped down from the hills gushed out of half a dozen spouts. It washed their long black hair into glistening sheets that flowed and rippled down their backs.

One of the women glanced up in surprise, and then said something to the others, who all looked at Ellie. They began to talk fast, and then to hoot at the hilarious, shocking sight of her jodhpur-clad legs. She looked so shameful, and so funny, standing there with her legs apart, just like a man.

Ellie and Nanny Barker retreated up a busy road, accompanied by the young men who were now carrying the pram.

'I must get some pictures of that,' Ellie said, pointing through a narrow archway into a pretty courtyard surrounded by buildings with elaborately carved windows and wooden balconies. The youths lowered the pram to the ground. One of them said something to Ellie as she began to climb a staircase into the most ornate house, which was three storeys tall. She wouldn't have understood the boy even if she'd heard him.

The steps were worn by use, and she had to lower her head to avoid hitting it on a low beam. On the first-floor balcony, she leaned out over the panels carved with peacocks and apples, and began to adjust the lens, then the angle of the shot, as she pointed the camera first one way, then another.

A woman's piercing scream nearly made her lose her balance. A man shouted and lurched on to the balcony, waving his arms. He was joined by another, both of them gesticulating angrily. An old man jumped towards her waving a brush made of sticks. From the dark interior of the house a woman wailed.

Ellie rushed down the stairs, bashing her head on the low beam. She was followed by the old man and two women, all incandescent with rage. They stood in the courtyard shouting at her and poking her with the brush. The youths had abandoned the pram, and Nanny Barker pushed it over the uneven courtyard, making for the archway and their escape route back into the bazaar. Lizzie lay back, stricken by the angry voices, while Tom wriggled out of his harness and stood screaming in terror.

What have I done? Ellie thought, dumbfounded. Are they like the Africans, who think the camera will steal their souls?

She stumbled after Nanny Barker as dozens of Nepalis gathered in the courtyard. Women and children leaned out from every balcony and a large group of onlookers was waiting for them in the main road. Two policemen in blue uniforms and red hats skidded to a halt by the pram.

Someone took her arm, and she yanked it away.

'They won't harm you,' a man said. 'They are just very angry and insulted.'

She spun round. It was Dr Prasad, his hat slightly askew.

'What did you think you were doing, going into someone's home uninvited?' he asked.

'I just wanted a picture of the courtyard. I don't know why these people are treating me like I'm a criminal or a monster.'

'Would you be happy if they traipsed through your home? And to make matters worse, they think you're unclean.'

'But I'm American,' she said.

'These people don't know what that is. They are Newars; they practise a mixture of Hinduism and Buddhism, and to them you are an outcast because you aren't a Hindu. You are like the cow-eating British, and you've contaminated their home by going into it. Now they will have to sweep and scrub it. And after that, they will have to whitewash the inside and employ a priest to purify it.'

'How stupid.'

'Not to them.' He glanced at her legs. 'And may I suggest that you modify your dress. You're not in Calcutta now. British rules don't apply here.'

The tone of his words was harsh but his face quickly softened, and she was glad of his arm leading her through the archway.

'I'm setting up a practice here for the poor of the city,' he said, nodding to a ground-floor room in an old building. 'You'll be able to find me here if you ever need me. Everyone knows this place because it's one of the main commercial districts.' He pointed to a busy intersection a little way up the road. 'That's Asan Tole. Can you remember the name?'

She nodded.

He frowned and pushed his spectacles up his nose as he examined her face. 'You've had a nasty bump, though at least the skin isn't broken.'

A red lump the size of an egg was swelling on her forehead.

'You are staying at the British Legation?' he asked.

'No. We're guests of the Maharaja's nephew.'

'Which one? There are hundreds.'

'The favourite one. We're staying in his palace.'

Dr Prasad furrowed his brow and then nodded. He walked with her, pointing out things she might find interesting.

The twins grizzled in the pram, and Nanny Barker muttered silent curses as the wheels became jammed time after time in the rutted road. 'Are you okay, Nanny?' Ellie asked, noticing the two flaming patches high on Nanny Barker's cheeks.

Nanny glanced at her, her eyes boggling for a second, before she looked back at the children lolling listlessly in the pram, the tears dried on their faces.

The street met a broad road, and ahead of them was the Tundikhel. To their left stretched Rani Pokhari, a five tier clock tower reflected in the still water of the giant tank.

'Lizzie, Tom, look,' Ellie exclaimed. The twins sat upright. An elephant ambled slowly past with a bejewelled howdah on its back. A golden canopy sheltered its occupants from the sun.

Three young boys in the opulent clothes of royalty stared down at them, as did their simply dressed ayahs and a grey-haired woman in the stuffy clothes of an English governess.

'Good morning,' the woman said, lifting a gloved hand as the elephant swung by. The mahout, perched on the animal's neck, stabbed its ear with a short stick and the elephant increased its pace, the end of its tail swishing so close to Ellie she felt the hairs tickle her face.

'Are they princes and princesses?' she asked.

'They aren't the King's children,' Dr Prasad said. 'They are from the Rana family. They are relatives of the Maharaja.'

'The Maharaja isn't the King?'

Dr Prasad laughed, although he didn't sound amused. 'The Maharaja is the Prime Minster. His family keep members of the royal family, including King Tribhuvan, prisoners in their own palace. You won't see the royal children parading through the streets like this.'

Political intrigue wasn't what Ellie had expected in the enchantment of the Kathmandu Valley, and it took her aback.

'You don't like the Ranas, Dr Prasad?'

'You don't ask questions like that, Lady Northwood,' he said sharply.

Ellie's surprise showed on her face.

'I'm sorry. I see you know nothing about this country,' he said more gently. He continued almost in a whisper. 'The Ranas run Nepal for their own benefit. They are a giant parasitic family that grows by the day, and they leech off peasants who scrape a living from the land and who can barely feed and clothe themselves.'

Ellie felt uncomfortable. She didn't want her dreams of

Kathmandu so quickly dismissed by an angry man who, by his own admission, hadn't lived in the Himalayas for years.

'You sound like a revolutionary, Dr Prasad.'

He turned on her, his voice sharp and low. 'That's dangerous talk.'

'I'm not in any danger. I've been told a hundred times that Nepal is dangerous and that I shouldn't come here with the children, but as far as I can see, it's perfect. It's almost as if it's lost in time.'

Dr Prasad pushed his glasses up his nose and leaned close. 'It's not dangerous for you, but it is for me and my sons, so I'd appreciate it if you watched your tongue.'

Ellie was shocked by his bluntness; people in India had always been polite to the point of obsequious, and yet this doctor spoke to her as if he were a teacher reprimanding a disruptive pupil.

'We can find our way from here, thank you,' she said briskly.

He pressed his hands together in front of his chest and made a little bow. 'Namaste,' he said.

Ellie watched him disappear up a crowded lane. 'Let's get back to the palace,' she said to the twins. 'You must be hungry.'

She turned left. That wasn't the way back to the palace. She turned right. No, she thought, that's not the way either. Where had the driver parked the gold Bentley? It didn't make any sense to go straight ahead, because on the other side of the Tundikhel was Singha Durbar, the Maharaja's thousand-roomed palace. From a distance it looked like a giant cake slathered in brittle royal icing. She spun on her heel and looked down the congested street into the heart of the city. That was the way, she told herself. They were going to have to retrace their steps.

Kathmandu was small, more like a town than a city, and it couldn't be too hard to find your way around.

Nanny Barker sighed, exasperated by Ellie's stupid decision not to bring a guide. She pushed the pram forward, leaning on the handle. It hardly budged. Ellie examined the front wheels, which seemed to be offset, and the axle looked slightly twisted. She beckoned to some porters, who stared blankly at the foreigners, and pointed to the pram. Looking confused, they spoke among themselves, then took the coins from her outstretched palm. They lifted the twins into baskets and put them on the backs of two of the men, who followed Ellie towards Asan Tole. As Nanny Barker entered the shade of the lane, she looked round and groaned at the sad sight of the chrome sparkling on the majestic pram as it sat abandoned in the sun at the edge of the Tundikhel.

A quarter of a mile away, Davies strolled around the giant tank to the north of the parade ground and decided that he liked Calcutta a hell of a lot more than Kathmandu. India was a better country than Nepal. In fact, even shitty Burma had been a nicer place to stay. Actually, he thought, Burma had been best of all, because you had more freedom. There were fewer do-good officials wanting to do right by the natives. In Burma, most of the other white men were like him: they enjoyed being a sahib and they made the most of it. They didn't poke their noses into other fellers' business, and they stood together when they had to. No matter where you came from, even if home was the most stinking part of old Blighty, you always had the darkies under you, in one way or another. That was why he'd come out East. He wanted a leg-up in the world, and to have things he'd never get at home, like a bit of money, and a lot of respect. Fucking respect, he thought, sucking in air through narrowed lips.

The sun was hot on the back of his neck, which was permanently reddened by the sun and so coarse it was almost reptilian. He strode through a group of Nepali men standing in the road. They parted before him like a curtain because it was clear he was about to plough into them. He heard them gabble and he sighed, wondering whether he should go back to the palace and find Northwood, who'd been missing since the previous night. Perhaps he was off getting pissed with the Maharaja's nephew, Davies thought. Or maybe he was shacked up somewhere with the tart.

Davies didn't know why he'd got himself lumbered with a daft nob like Northwood. The very second they were back in Calcutta, he planned to ditch him. Life was too short to waste it sucking up to toffs. He'd left home to get away from all that bollocks. He was sick of trailing round after the great hunter, because despite the fortune Northwood had spent on guns and a whole bloody wardrobe of shikar clothes, the fucker couldn't hit a tusker at ten paces. He was the worst shikari Davies had ever known. The native Burmese police were better shots with their fifty-year-old rifles.

Northwood wasn't a real man's man: he couldn't hold his drink, and got plastered after a couple of pegs. He talked big but he was weak, you could see it in his eyes. He wasn't sure of himself. But sometimes you had to feel sorry for him. Davies didn't know how he put up with that American wife. She pretended to be shocked by the posh Britishers and their snobbery, and yet she was as obsessed by the little gradations of status as they were. You never saw her get her hands dirty: she never cleaned the kids' arses, and she didn't change their clothes. She left all that to the ugly old nanny, and instead cooed over them for a while before sending them away to be looked after by someone else while she wrote long letters to God knows who, or took pills that knocked her out cold. Her drawling accent got on his wick, and she was always going on about something dippy, most recently the magic and spirituality of this place. It was a laugh really, because it was a dump and you couldn't find a single bar. It was bone dry; there wasn't a drop of Scotch in the entire bloody valley.

Mind you, at times he pitied the silly American cow. It wasn't right that the uppity ayah thought she was better than her memsahib. It wasn't right either that Northwood flaunted the woman, even if his stupid wife seemed oblivious to it. Davies had no problem fucking the natives, but you couldn't let them think they were better than the memsahibs. Northwood should have been more discreet, and it was embarrassing to see him fawning over the tart. She had a pretty face when she wasn't looking sullen or mocking, although she certainly wasn't his type. She was overdone: her breasts were too large, her hips too round.

I'm surrounded by bleeding idiots, Davies said to himself as he sauntered down a lane. He'd been walking for a long time and he needed something to distract him, something to make the piss-awful journey worthwhile.

A middle-aged man stepped out from a dark passage and spoke to him.

'Speak English,' Davies said loudly.

The man beckoned him into the shadows, and though he

couldn't comprehend the words, Davies understood his gestures well enough.

He followed the man to a miserable lane of shacks. In the front room of a house, the pimp and the madam, a plump middle-aged woman with very few teeth, couldn't stop smiling at the new customer, hoping he'd bring the riches of the white man's world into the brothel. The madam pushed forward a girl in a tight red sari. She looked at the floor. The madam said something, and laughed as she cupped one of the girl's breasts.

Davies shook his head. He placed his hands flat on his chest and brushed them downwards.

The pimp and the madam looked at one another and smiled.

They can't be as stupid as they look, Davies thought. He'd never had a problem finding what he wanted in India or Burma.

A few moments later, the madam appeared from the back room with a youth dressed in women's clothes.

What a fucking freak, Davies thought. He shook his head and the woman's face fell.

Davies turned and looked at the child sitting in the doorway. The girl, who was no more than eight or nine, glanced up from scratching a picture in the dirt. Davies pointed at her, and as the room grew quiet, the madam clicked her tongue.

In the heart of Kathmandu, Ellie was disorientated and the city no longer felt magical. The twins were hungry, Tom needed the toilet, and Nanny Barker's anger simmered very close to the surface of her overheated face. Neither of the women spoke a word of Nepali, the great Durbar Square was too crowded, and its many-tiered temples and pagoda roofs seemed strange rather than exotic. People were staring at them as if they were in a show.

'We came that way,' Ellie said without any confidence. She tried to regain her poise. Francis always told her that the British ruled by prestige, by making the natives believe they should be in charge by some natural right. 'I'm sure we came from the north,' she added, pointing towards a lane flanked by houses that were top-heavy with wooden balconies.

Nanny Barker grunted dissent. 'We need to find that doctor again,' she stated flatly, and then sank on to a step leading to one of the smaller temples. She was exhausted by the walking and the foreignness of it all.

A flock of women surrounded her, talking loud and fast. She stood up, and they shooed her away.

Tom wriggled to get out of the basket, desperate for a wee. He did a little dance until Ellie held him by the hand and took him to an open drain running along a side street. He relieved himself, watched by an audience of ten. The child had only just been potty-trained and Ellie knew he couldn't wait any longer.

Lizzie darted between the legs of the onlookers, glad to be out of the scratchy basket.

A policeman spoke to them in Nepali, and Ellie looked despairing.

'Asan Tole,' she said. They would have to throw themselves on the mercy of the grouchy doctor.

The policeman grinned and they all followed him past Hanuman Dhoka, through the open square and down a paved road. As he talked, Ellie smiled and nodded, not understanding a word.

Ellie and Nanny were obliged to carry the twins because the porters had vanished into the crowds. Where the road turned, Nanny stopped. She slid Tom to the ground and then sat down again with a bump, her head in her hands.

A man ran out from his open-fronted shop and began wafting her with a wicker tray.

'Give me a moment,' she said.

'Is it hill diarrhoea again?' Ellie asked.

'My head's spinning but I'll be right in a tick.'

'I'll fetch Dr Prasad,' Ellie said, scooping up the children. Surely it wasn't far, she thought. That must be Asan Tole up ahead.

Two minutes later, she stopped to catch her breath. Putting the children down, she scanned the road. Yes, this is it, she thought, ignoring the policeman, who was still talking like they were old friends. He held out his arms as if offering to carry the twins himself. Ellie looked at him, at his earnest face and his brown eyes crinkling into a smile. She held the look for a long time, transfixed as the crinkles faded and his smile was erased.

When she looked around, the world was moving in slow motion, creating a kaleidoscope. The colours were bright; the mist had been burned off by the sun, and the air was clear. The sari of a woman standing next to her was the most vibrant red; the vivid blue cotton woven into her plait was electric against the black of her hair. The twins' clothes were startlingly white, and their hair was the colour of gold.

Suddenly the earth heaved upwards, slammed to the left and then dropped down again with a deafening crash. The twins rocked and fell sideways. Ellie and the policeman both reached out towards them, but the shaking of the road stopped them moving.

Blinded by panic, Ellie couldn't work out what was happening. A memory flashed through her mind and she remembered falling, hurtling through the floor, timber and bricks cascading around her.

Unable to stand, she crouched, looking down in terror, expecting a hole to open and swallow them.

A hundred miles south, the earth was cracking and realigning itself. For two minutes, northern India and eastern Nepal shook. The Kathmandu Valley seemed to spin as the Himalayas bit more deeply into central Asia. The ground undulated and a deep fissure opened up in the Tundikhel. Trees bent as if whipped by a great storm; the scummy green water was thrown out of the tank where the women were bathing; and the glassy surface of Rani Pokhari, where Ellie had admired the reflection of the clock tower only an hour before, was turned into a choppy sea.

As she looked up towards Asan Tole, the road moved as if a series of powerful waves were rolling up a beach. Earth burst up through the paving stones and the ground began to oscillate. Ellie watched the children as she felt the world narrowing, pulling them into a whirlpool. The quake roared from deep within the earth, while on its surface, the temples and shrines of Kathmandu began to crumble. Bricks thundered to the ground a few feet from the twins. Further up the road, the front of a house separated from the rest of the building, swung forward, suspended for a moment at forty-five degrees, and then slapped back into place. It remained intact for a few seconds and then disintegrated in a torrent of mud bricks, knocking the porters gathered below to the ground and covering them in a rubble tomb.

The collapsing temples echoed the rumble and growl of the quake. Tom held his lamb in one hand and reached out to Ellie with the other, his mouth open, trying to scream, but no sound came out. Behind the twins, Ellie saw the houses flanking the road slide sideways and then begin to twist over them. Small pieces of furniture and utensils were flung from the balconies. A little copper dish flew through the air and bounced off the policeman's head.

They're going to be buried alive, Ellie thought in terror. She got to her feet, but was thrown to the ground. She stood again and lurched towards the twins, grasping at thin air. They were too far apart. She couldn't reach both of them. Out of the corner of her eye she saw the policeman stumbling towards them too, his arms outstretched.

I can only save one, she thought, and in an instant, she grabbed Lizzie, then reeled back and hurled herself to the left as the houses listed and tumbled in a cloud of dust. All she could sense before darkness overtook her was the feel of a small body in her arms.

On the day of the earthquake, Shushila slept later than usual and woke on a soft, deep mattress. She opened her eyes, unsure for a moment where she was. The room was big, with high ceilings, and shafts of light streamed through the partially opened shutters of the tall windows. Two marble nudes stood either side of the door, and the walls were covered in gilt mirrors and oil paintings. I'm in a palace, she remembered.

She saw the indentation in the pillow where the sahib's head had rested. She was glad he'd gone; glad not to have to wake up next to him and feign desire, or even affection.

A servant brought her tea on a tray. The girl was from the hills, and had almond eyes and high cheekbones. Despite her youth, she was plain, her body already stout and her hair scraped back into a tight plait.

'Where is the sahib?' Shushila asked, speaking Hindi because most Nepali speakers could understand it.

The girl opened the shutters and pointed into the garden. Shushila wrapped herself in a shawl and walked languidly to the window.

Below, in the glorious gardens, amid a profusion of flowers, Francis strolled with the Maharaja's nephew, who was wearing a magnificent headdress. Even to Shushila, who loved rich display, it looked faintly ridiculous. The cap was studded with jewels. Diamonds, pearls, emeralds and rubies sparkled in the sun, and an elegant bird-of-paradise plume swept up from the crown and extended over the back of the man's head.

The Maharaja's nephew had worn the same cap when they'd arrived at the palace. Shushila had been surprised by the welcome ceremony in the evening. She'd spent her whole life watching the Britishers being worshipped like gods, and yet she saw with her own eyes the way the Brahmin priest moved to begin purification rituals as soon as the sahib left the grand reception room. The Maharaja's nephew had shaken hands with the eminent white visitor and was tainted by the touch of a *mleccha* – a cow-eating, alcohol-drinking outcast from across the black waters, the seas surrounding India. It might have been acceptable to shake hands in the British way in a Calcutta bar, but things were different here in Kathmandu. It was one of the last sacred Hindu places in the world unsullied by foreigners. Now, as the Maharaja's nephew walked in the garden, Shushila looked at him with a sharper interest, her gaze sliding over the man's short stature and slight stoop. In Calcutta he had been just another little brown princeling; in Kathmandu he was almost divine.

By early afternoon, Shushila thought she should go and look for Nanny Barker and the children. The bed looked comfy, though, and so she lay down instead. In the distance she heard a temple bell ring, and heard children playing, and was pleased they weren't her own little sahib and sahiba, who looked pretty and sweet but were tiresome and noisy, especially bossy little Lizzie.

Shushila called the plain servant girl, who hurried in and stood at the end of the bed, looking vacant.

'Massage me,' she ordered.

The girl clambered on to the bed and began kneading Shushila's legs.

'Harder,' Shushila said, closing her eyes and enjoying the pressure of the girl's hands on her skin.

She snapped her eyes open when the bed began to tremble. A wave passed through the room, making the floor undulate and the fancy ornaments jump. The marble nudes danced, pirouetted and fell to the floor. The largest gilt mirror buckled and cracked.

The servant girl jumped up and dragged Shushila from the bed. They stumbled across the room, finding it difficult to move forward as they were thrust this way and that, and the floor beneath them kept shifting. As they ran downstairs, the palace groaned. At the entrance to the reception hall, a suit of armour that must have belonged to a medieval European knight swayed across their path, and the girl yanked Shushila sideways as a crystal column split open and fell, narrowly missing her head.

The main doors to the palace were jammed because the masonry above the portico had collapsed and pinched the wooden doors shut.

'Come,' the girl shouted. Shushila was paralysed by fear, unable to move her legs, and so the girl shoved her and then stumbled towards a side door and out into the garden. At the opposite end of the palace a stream of young women fled from the building and clung to each other among the flower beds. The wing of the palace from which they'd escaped was tilting, its windows distorting. The front wall bulged, the stucco cracked, distending until fragments shattered in tiny pieces over the stricken girls.

The jolting stopped. Shushila thought the horror was over, but then another tremor swept her feet from under her and flung her on to the drive. When it stopped, she got up gingerly and leaned on one of the Maharaja's nephew's gold-painted limousines. The air was so thick with dust she could barely see the far end of the palace, but she heard the collapse when it came. A splintering and then a deep rumble echoed through the gardens. The far end of the mud-brick palace with its bright, brittle coating slid over the flower beds, and the walls became a pair of massive white stucco jaws that devoured the young women who had tried to flee. They made no sound as the teeth snapped shut around them.

The rumbling subsided and everything was quiet. There was no birdsong, no barking dogs. The Kathmandu Valley was shocked into silence. Shushila looked down at her ripped sari, at a cut on her foot and the blood forming a little pool on the drive. She watched the dust settling, tiny particles sinking slowly to earth. In the clearing air she could see the devastation, and the servant girl rocking her head from side to side, one of her eyeballs lying on her cheek and weeping blood.

Davies didn't experience the full force and terror of the earthquake; instead he felt it through a veil thrown by the valley's finest ganja. The madam had offered to send a boy to fetch some millet beer, brought down from a hill village, because she knew all foreigners were alcoholics, and although Davies was gagging for a drink, he refused. The girl was too pretty for him to want to dull his senses with a local brew. Instead, after half an hour on a bamboo mat in the back room – a half-hour he decided was well worth the money – he took the ganja from the boy who was dressed as a girl, and puffed away until his thoughts became mellow and fuzzy. Forgetting about lice and bed bugs, he laid his head on a rolled-up blanket. He turned to offer the girl a drag, and to tell her she was pretty, but she was gone.

A young woman stared at him from the door. It must be the girl's sister, he decided, they looked so similar, though the older one already had a bit of meanness about her mouth and a sallow tone to her skin. He tried focusing on her impassive face and the glitter that was visible in her black eyes even in the shade of the room. Unlike every other native woman he'd seen around the valley, this one didn't drop her gaze. It's a shame how quickly they're spoiled, he reflected as he drifted into a deep, dreamless sleep. He liked them before time had

had a chance to ruin them, when they were unmarked and still unfinished.

He woke as the tremors were subsiding. The roof of khas grass hadn't fallen in, and unlike the brick houses, the wood and bamboo walls of the shack had swayed rather than collapsed. He staggered out of the house into a dusty silence. The residents were huddled together in little groups. Pi-dogs slunk by, chickens dashed back and forth, and a cow with long strands of vegetation hanging from its mouth was struggling to lift its hind legs out of a three-foot fissure in the road. He stopped to button his flies and noticed the girl's blood on his trousers. Good job there's been an earthquake, he thought: it'll make it easy to explain that dirty stain.

Ellie woke in the dark. Pain stabbed at her temples and pulsated behind her eyes. I'm in the old house in Oakland, she thought for a moment, and then realised the bed was strangely saggy. It was nothing but ropes strung over a narrow frame, and Bobby wasn't there. She could hear breathing, but it wasn't that of a child. When she tried to sit up, her hair stuck to a cushion, and she gingerly reached round the back of her head and felt a mat of hair, thick with blood that was dried at the edges and still soft and liquid in the centre. I smell like freshly butchered meat, she thought.

'Lie down,' a man said firmly. 'You're concussed; a doctor will be here soon.'

'What happened?' she said, jerking upwards and ripping her hair from the cushion.

'You've had a bash on your head. Two, in fact. There's a smaller bump on your forehead.'

A confused memory made her gasp, 'The children.'

The man brought a lamp to the side of her bed, and in the flickering light she saw Hugh Douglas, dishevelled and worried.

'Lizzie is fast asleep in the next room,' he said. 'There's not a scratch on her and my daughter is keeping an eye on her.'

Ellie's stomach tightened into a knot. She remembered the twins standing looking at her as the wall behind them toppled; she saw a policeman with his arms outstretched, and the fear on Tom's face. She saw herself grabbing Lizzie.

'Where's Tom?' she cried.

'You and Lizzie were brought here, but so far there's no news about Tom.'

Ellie tried to get to her feet. She wobbled, her vision distorted so that the light from the lamp was multiplied and it seemed as if there were three or four men in the room.

'I've got to find him,' she said, shaking her head in an effort to clear it.

'You're not going anywhere. Half the city has been destroyed. It's the middle of the night and you won't be able to find him in the dark. In your present state, you'll only hinder the rescuers.'

She tipped backwards, and for a second she thought she was going to faint. Hugh grabbed her arm and held it tight.

'It's another aftershock,' he said. 'Big quakes are often followed by smaller tremors.'

'I know what earthquakes are like,' she half screamed, consumed by a rising hysteria.

The building creaked and sighed as it settled.

'I'm going to find him,' she said. 'He'll be buried. He'll be terrified. He'll die if I don't look for him right now.'

'We'll go at first light, I promise.' He led her back to the bed. 'For now, you have to rest. You'll be no use to anyone if you collapse. A doctor from Bir Hospital is on his way.'

Ellie sank back on to the bed.

'Where are we?' she asked

'Tri-Chandra College. It's right in the centre of the city, next to Rani Pokhari. Most of the foreigners have been brought here, though no one seems to be seriously injured. Even that cut on the back of your head is quite superficial. We need to take care, though: a knock on the head can be more serious than it first appears.'

Ellie looked around the room for a few seconds before the thumping pain forced her to close her eyes again.

'We're in the chowkidar's room,' Hugh said.

'Doesn't he need it?' she asked through teeth clenched so tightly she thought they might crack.

'No. He was killed when the clock tower collapsed.'

Ellie opened one eye, trying to see his expression in the gloom. 'Who brought us here?' she asked.

'Soldiers. One of the saving graces of this catastrophe was that the army was in the middle of a drill on the Tundikhel. Most of the soldiers were uninjured and they were deployed the moment the tremors ended.'

'Is my husband here?' Ellie said, remembering Francis.

'Not now, though you're not to worry. He's fine: I saw him just before sunset with your ayah and his gunman.'

Ellie began to shiver. Her teeth chattered and her body trembled.

'I'm going to puke,' she said.

Hugh snatched up an old pot and thrust it under her chin. She grabbed it, hung over the bed and retched. When she'd finished, she wiped her mouth on the back of her hand because there was nothing else she could use apart from some filthy blankets on the bed. Hugh took the pot and gave her his handkerchief, which she pressed to her face. It smelled freshly laundered and carried a trace of sandalwood.

'You're in shock,' Hugh said.

Ellie looked at him, her grief desperate. 'I left him,' she said slowly, as if she could hardly believe it herself. 'I took Lizzie, but I couldn't get to Tom.'

'You did what you could.'

'I could have saved him, but I didn't. I chose Lizzie. I let him die.'

'Nonsense,' Hugh said firmly. 'He's probably in the safe hands of some Nepali matron.'

But Ellie wasn't listening to him. She was imagining Tom, all alone, crushed among the debris, the life ebbing from him and his body growing cold.

She curled into a ball and closed her eyes, drifting in and out of a terrifying sleep, so that she didn't know if she was delirious, or even conscious at all. She woke now and again, wondering where she was, feeling things were bad, and then realising they were worse than she could ever have imagined. She slept again in the flickering light, knowing Hugh was sitting near her. In her dreams, Tom was talking to her, but not in his baby voice. He sounded older, like five-year-old Bobby, so that the two boys merged in her mind, and she didn't know which one had died or whether both of them had been taken from her. They looked the same, with their hair of spun gold.

In the depths of her delusion she half woke and saw that Hugh had moved from the chair by the side of the bed and was standing talking with another man. She saw their silhouettes, the way their shadows, monstrously huge and ill-defined, loomed over the far wall. Hugh had bent his head to speak to the much shorter man. They were whispering, but she caught the urgency in their tone, the way the shorter man shook his head and the candlelight shone for a moment on his glasses.

'Dr Prasad?' she called in a feeble voice, a sharp pain running through her head as she lifted herself on to her elbow. The smaller man stepped back into the darkness.

'There'll be a doctor here soon,' Hugh said.

'Where's Dr Prasad gone?'

'There's no doctor here yet. Go back to sleep,' Hugh said softly.

I must be dreaming, she thought.

An hour or two later, a young doctor came from Bir Hospital. He cleaned Ellie's wound, dressed it, and wrapped a bandage round her head. When he left, he insisted she must rest.

All she could think was that she'd had plenty of rest and that her headache was no longer excruciating. Her double vision was clearing and she was just about to tell Hugh they were wasting valuable time when she heard raised voices.

'Where is he?' Francis shouted, bursting through the door. 'Where is my son?'

Ellie stumbled back and sank on to the bed. She covered her face with her hands.

'I told you to stay in the bloody palace,' Francis said in fury. 'You put the children in danger.'

Ellie was unable to respond; her guilt was paralysing.

'How could she know there was going to be an earthquake?' Hugh said.

'Don't get involved in this,' Francis barked. 'You have no idea what you're dealing with. She's queer in the head. She thinks we're in the bloody Garden of Eden, and that bad things never happen here. I tell you, she's fucking mad. She can't be trusted with the children.'

'She's concussed and this isn't helping her,' Hugh said, angry because nothing good could come of Francis abusing his despairing wife. He glanced down at Ellie. She didn't look insane, or an unfit mother.

'They might not have been safe even if they'd stayed in the palace,' he said in a measured voice. 'In fact, the pukka buildings, the ones made of brick and mortar, have suffered the worst damage. No one was safe. Two of the King's daughters were killed.'

'But if she'd stayed where she was supposed to, at least we'd know where my son was. Instead, we have to search the whole of Kathmandu.'

'Not quite. The soldiers said they were near Asan Tole.'

'Where the hell is that?'

'The commercial district.'

'Are you coming?' Francis said to Hugh, as if he was laying down a challenge.

'Where?'

'To look for my son in Asan Tole.'

A heavy frost crept over the ruined city during the night. At dawn, Ellie left Tri-Chandra College and skirted around the rubble of the Gantaghar. The clock tower had toppled on to the road outside the college, crushing the chowkidar who was standing beneath it. On the opposite side of the great tank,

Durbar High School was razed to the ground. To the left, the Tundikhel had been turned into a makeshift town, crammed with the homeless and people too terrified to re-enter their houses. Further away, across the parade ground, the Bhim Sen Tower had lost five of its nine tiers.

Ellie held Lizzie tight as they walked around the edge of the tank. They stopped on Kanti Path, the road broken by fissures, and Hugh turned to help her. He was covered in a layer of dust from top to toe, his hair thick with a pinkish powder. He and Francis had spent the early hours digging fruitlessly through the rubble of Kathmandu. Ellie paused, utterly overwhelmed by the devastation. How would she be able to find one small boy among the ruins?

Two soldiers led a woman with wild bushy hair towards them through the mist. The woman's blank face, ripped dress and dusty white legs concentrated Ellie's attention, and it took her a few moments to realise she was looking at Nanny Barker. She was shot through with more guilt; she'd forgotten all about Nanny and hadn't even wondered whether she was alive or dead.

She ran to the older woman. 'Have you seen Tom?' she asked.

'Tom?' Nanny frowned and then smiled. 'Yes, Tom. He was on the train.'

'Not on the train. Did you see him during the earthquake?' Ellie wanted to pinch Nanny to wake her up.

Nanny stared, and dust settled into the furrows on her forehead. Hugh spoke to the soldiers in Nepali, and the men led her towards Tri-Chandra College.

Near Bir Hospital, which was scarred by a large crack zigzagging across its facade, they passed a group of well-dressed people. The women wore a lot of gold jewellery and brightly coloured saris, and looked as if they were going to a wedding. Hugh stopped and spoke to them. Their grave expressions didn't suggest they were preparing to celebrate.

'They think the world is about to end,' he said. 'So they've decided to wear their best.'

Ellie understood how they felt: it wouldn't have surprised her either if the world was ending.

'Did you go this way?' Francis asked her.

Ellie turned a full circle, scanning the devastation. There's Rani Pokhari, she thought, and there's the Tundikhel. And that way is the centre of the old city, and perhaps that's the road we took back to Asan Tole. The problem, she decided, was it all looked so different because half the buildings had collapsed.

'We'll go this way,' Hugh said. 'It seems the most obvious route.' He stopped and turned to Ellie. 'Give me Lizzie,' he said.

Ellie resisted for a few seconds but then handed her daughter to Hugh. She was heavy and it was hard to hold her as they scrambled over piles of bricks and weaved between the larger pieces of debris, their path blocked by buildings that had slid across the road.

Everywhere she looked, Ellie saw grief. A man staggered past them carrying an infant wrapped in rags. The baby's arm hung out of the bundle, limp and lifeless. Half a dozen men were digging inside the shell of a collapsed house. Its floors had dropped neatly, one on to the next, so the three-storey structure was now only seven feet tall. Two women watched, an older woman consoling a younger one whose face was swollen with crying.

Francis walked on, and Hugh stopped to help the men lift a beam pinning down a section of floor. A girl lay beneath it, crushed by a wooden chest. The distraught younger woman wailed as the men lifted her daughter's smashed body slowly and with respect. Ellie hurried to catch Francis, and heard the heartbreaking sound of the mother's grief. It mirrored the scream in her head.

A twenty-foot-high pile of bricks, carved balconies, windows and lengths of timber rose ahead of them. Francis had already climbed it and was on the other side. 'For fuck's sake, keep up,' he shouted.

Ellie stumbled over the debris. The bricks shifted and her foot struck a dog's head that poked out of the wreckage. Its eyes were wide open and a swollen blue tongue protruded from its mouth.

Francis surveyed the destruction and shouted orders in English to bemused Nepalis who were tending to the wounded and searching for survivors.

'Is this where you were?' he asked Ellie. 'Do you recognise any of it?'

'Of course not,' Ellie said in exasperation. 'Yesterday the buildings were still standing.'

The day before, she'd thought Kathmandu was an idyll. Today it looked like a war zone; a scene of bloody annihilation and unfathomable grief.

She glanced up at the nearest building. It bulged over the street. A jagged scar ran from the tiled roof down through the balcony to a crack that split the lintel above the door on the ground floor.

'Wait,' she said, as Francis and Hugh began to move on. 'We were here. I remember this shop.'

Yesterday the shop had been crammed with baskets of pulses and different types of rice, but today it was empty, ransacked by looters.

'Yes, here,' she said, suddenly frantic.

The men began to shift aside a section of wall.

'He's under there, I know he is,' Ellie cried, and began tearing at the bricks.

'Stand back and take Lizzie with you,' Hugh said. 'The house over there is about to come down.'

The roof of the neighbouring building had fallen in and was resting on the first floor. Another tremor would send it crashing on to the road. Ellie understood and backed away, pulling Lizzie with her.

Someone tugged at her shirt. Transfixed by the search, she ignored the tug. A woman no more than four feet tall, her back bent with age, turned her head sideways so she could look up at Ellie. She spoke slowly, wrinkling her face. Her milky eyes were focused on Ellie and she was intent on what she was saying. Ellie couldn't understand a word, and decided the old woman was another person driven crazy by the catastrophe.

'Here?' Francis said, casting aside a section of wooden lattice-work.

Ellie jumped forward, shrugging off the old woman.

Francis and Hugh knocked away a few more bricks and then brushed the dirt from some blue material.

Ellie groaned. She saw a head, the hair black under a coating of brick dust. 'It's the cop,' she cried. She remembered the way he'd propelled himself forward against the lurch of the earth and tried to grab Tom. 'He was next to Tom,' she said.

She looked on, paralysed with fear, as the men rolled the policeman's body over. Tom wasn't beneath him.

'Keep looking,' she said. 'I know he's here.'

The old woman hadn't given up. She tugged again on Ellie's shirt.

Anxious and frustrated, Ellie shouted at her, 'get away from me.'

'She want to help you,' a passer-by said in heavily accented English. The man stopped and took a long drag on a cigarette. He was young and sharp-eyed, and had the look of the men from the north. He carried a heavy rucksack and seemed like a Gurkha soldier. He listened to the old woman, her gnarled and twisted fingers waving as if she were describing something momentous. She came close to Ellie, staring right in her face, and Ellie couldn't work out if she was fierce and angry or was just fixed on telling her story.

The young man turned to Ellie.

'She says she know who you look for. A child, yes? Last night she saw a man pull child from under here.'

The man spoke to the old woman, checking something.

'She say he was a boy with gold hair.'

'He was alive?' Ellie said.

He talked with the woman, who craned her neck sideways, her big hooped earrings swinging with the intensity of her nodding.

'Yes, he live,' the man said.

'Where is he now?'

It seemed to take an eternity before the man finished speaking to the woman and formulated his reply. 'She don't know. The man took him.'

'What man?'

'Bhotia man.'

'Bhotia?'

'Tibetan man. A trader. In a red coat.'

A shout from Hugh drew her attention away from the man and the old woman. Ellie's heart leaped. He was holding something covered in dust. She sprang towards him, guessing what it was.

'He's not here,' Hugh said, shaking his head.

Francis wiped the sweat from his face with his sleeve, and Ellie saw he was crying.

'There's only this,' Hugh said, holding out Tom's lamb, its fur caked in mud.

Ellie took it gingerly and pressed it to her chest.

'He isn't dead,' she stated, looking at Hugh and Francis. 'This lady saw a man pulling him from the rubble. Ask her,' she said, turning to the old woman. There was no one there. Ellie looked left and right, and into the darkness of the shop, thinking the old woman might be taking a rest. Only the shopkeeper and a group of puzzled ragged children stared back.

'She was here a moment ago,' Ellie said.

Hugh and Francis looked back at her as if they thought she'd lost her mind.

'He'll tell you,' she continued, and looked round for the man. He wasn't there either.

'They were here, both of them,' she exclaimed. 'There was an old woman in a blue sari and a man who spoke English. He had a soldier's rucksack.'

Hugh took her arm. She yanked it away from him.

'Listen to me. The old woman said a Tibetan man in a red

coat pulled Tom out of the wreckage last night. She saw it with her own eyes.'

They scanned the street. There were a few old women and lots of men, but not the ones Ellie described.

'We'll take you back to the college,' Hugh said. 'And then we'll carry on searching.'

'I can't go back; I've got to find Tom. We need to find the Tibetan man.'

'You are going to the palace,' Francis said. 'It's safer there.'

'You need to rest,' Hugh said gently, realising that harsh orders were only sharpening her resolve.

A slight tremor made them all sway backwards for a second, and the building above them creaked. A stool slid across the collapsed floor and toppled on to the road.

Hugh snatched up Lizzie. The child's eyes were wide with surprise. 'We'll take you back, for her sake,' he said to Ellie. 'And I promise we'll not stop searching for Tom.'

They began to weave their way through the obstacles, passing other families searching for relatives. Hugh lifted Lizzie on to his shoulders and grimaced, wishing he hadn't. Her knickers were wet.

They walked in single file, Ellie taking up the rear. Her head was pounding again. It's my fault, she repeated to herself. I brought him here when everyone said I shouldn't. I took him to Asan Tole, and when the quake came, I saved Lizzie. I left my baby to fight for his life under an avalanche of bricks. And now he's God knows where with a man he doesn't know. He'll be terrified, and it's all because of me. She wanted to stop and tear at her hair, to scream and scream so all of Kathmandu would hear, so that Tom, wherever he was, would hear and know she was sorry, and that she was going to find him.

Instead, she walked in silence, stroking the caked fur of Tom's lamb. She ran her fingers over the felt nose and wiped the dirt from its eyes. One shone bright, the brown glass still shiny. She touched the second one and it looked back at her, badly cracked and the lustre gone. A moment later, it crumbled to powder in her hand.

The stench of decomposition settled like early-morning fog over the valley. Unlike fog, however, it didn't lift, but grew denser and fouler throughout the day, permeating the scarves and cloths that survivors tied over their mouths and noses. The stink made Ellie gag. So many people had died that there wasn't enough wood left to cremate the bodies stacked on the ghats beside the holy Bagmati River, and the bereaved foraged for timber among homes levelled by the quake.

The winter days were short and looters scavenged during the long, dark nights. Thieves were whipped on the Tundikhel, and then the army began shooting them on sight. A curfew was declared at eight in the evening and remained in force until the early morning, when a cannon was fired across the ruins of the city.

Ellie waited for the dawn. She sat at an east-facing window of the palace, watching for a soft glow to spread over the hills, and for sunlight to flood the valley. When the cannon was fired, she joined a steady stream of people heading into the flattened heart of Kathmandu.

No one else was confident about finding Tom. After searching for two days, Francis seemed to give up. He went through the motions but Ellie could tell his heart wasn't in it. After four days he declared that his son was dead, and that was an end to it. He stayed in the palace, refusing to go out, and told Ellie the search was futile.

Hugh was more positive, and he often accompanied her around the city, but even then, she wondered if she saw doubt in his quizzical expression. Perhaps everyone reckons I'm crazy, she thought. They think I made up that old lady because I can't deal with the truth. She knew that grief could do strange things to your mind, and yet she was adamant the woman wasn't a figment of her imagination. She walked through the wreckage of the city, looking at every old woman to check if she was the one who'd seen a golden-haired boy pulled from the rubble. She scanned faces for the soldier who'd translated the woman's words, and she kept a watch for men in red coats. Each night, though, when she returned to the palace, to Francis's miserable 'I told you so' face, she was without a single piece of information that would lead her to her son.

On a cold morning five days after the earthquake, Ellie stood alone in the road where she'd last seen Tom. Most of the bricks had been moved and the undamaged ones were stacked in neat piles so that a clear path had been opened to Asan Tole. She squinted in the sunshine, sure she recognised the man who was standing by a group of rescuers shifting a tangle of heavy beams. He carried a medical bag and must have been waiting to treat possible survivors.

'Dr Prasad,' she called.

When the men had eased the timbers to the ground and the people beneath were found to be dead, he turned to look at her. His face was deeply lined and there were dark purple shadows under his eyes.

'I'm glad to see you are unscathed,' he said with a faint smile. He sank on to one of the beams, his legs seeming to give way. Then he looked up and focused properly on her. 'Actually, you look wretched,' he said.

She sat down next to him.

'Tell me about your children,' he said. 'Did you find the boy?'

'Lizzie is well. She doesn't have a single scratch. But Tom . . .' His name caught in her throat.

'He was killed?'

'No. An old woman saw him being pulled from under a collapsed building. He's alive, and a Tibetan man has him.'

Dr Prasad searched her eyes, and then scanned the rest of her.

'What about your injuries?'

'Only a little bump.' She pointed to the back of her head, glad she'd torn off the bandage a nurse kept wrapping tightly around her head. She didn't want to look like an invalid when she didn't feel like one. The swelling was almost gone, the cut was small, and her hair covered it. In a few days the scab would fall off and no one would ever know she'd been injured in any way. It's not my body that's sick, she thought.

'How did you know Tom was missing?' she asked.

Dr Prasad hesitated. 'Kathmandu has a flourishing rumour mill,' he said. He stretched out his legs as if they were stiff and giving him pain. His white Nepali trousers were filthy, and brick dust was rubbed into the fabric of his dark jacket.

'We are still finding people under the wreckage,' he said

gently. 'That's why I'm here. They thought they heard a woman cry. Yesterday they found a baby in Patan, the city across the river, but if I'm honest, I doubt anyone will still be alive. You have to prepare yourself, just in case. You know how cold the nights are. If anyone was still trapped, they would probably die from hypothermia.'

Ellie shook her head. 'You don't understand. He isn't trapped. Someone saved him.'

'I see,' Dr Prasad said carefully.

He's like Francis, Ellie thought. He thinks I'm certifiable and making it up.

A woman marched along the road and stood right in front of them. She talked fast in a loud, angry voice, swinging her arms in the air and pointing into the clear blue sky.

Dr Prasad spoke firmly but quietly and told the woman to go away. She stood with her hands on her hips.

'I think I know her,' Ellie said.

'You were the uninvited guest in her house a few days ago, and you haven't left a good impression,' Dr Prasad said. 'She no longer has a home and she thinks you have something to do with it.'

'And I suppose I'm responsible for the destruction of this whole city too?'

'That's what she's saying.'

'It's crazy.'

He spoke gently to the woman, and her fury was replaced by despair.

'What have I done?' Ellie asked.

'It's what your people have done. I'm afraid you're guilty by association.'

'How could we cause an earthquake?'

'Last year a British team flew over Everest for the first time. Their plane took off from Purnea in India, flew over the Himalayas, circled Everest and then flew back.'

'What the hell has that got to do with an earthquake? And, anyway, I'm American, not British.'

'You are white. The people here don't know the difference. All they know is that the flight was sacrilege. The mountains are holy, and the flight disturbed the peace of Shivaji, who is meditating in Mount Kailash. This woman thinks the earthquake was the god's response.'

'Idiotic,' Ellie said.

'It is to you. But you understand the world in a different way. How would you explain it?'

Ellie watched the woman walk slowly away. Her sari sagged and her head was bent. Ellie sighed. I don't have any explanation, she thought, and an idea, cold and unwelcome, entered her mind. What were the chances of being in two earthquakes in a single lifetime; of losing people you loved to a rupturing of the earth twice over? What was the common denominator in both those cataclysmic events? She pushed the thought away, as a little voice answered: you are.

She turned the question around. 'Why do you think this happened?'

Dr Prasad sighed. 'Fate,' he said.

'Just that? It was chance?'

'Chance is not fate,' he said. 'Chance is random. Fate is what is meant to be.'

'This was meant to happen?' Ellie said, incredulous.

'Fate is not always a good thing.'

'You're damn right. And I guess there's nothing we could have done to stop it?'

'No. Although if we'd built our homes in a different way, maybe they would have withstood the shock better and more people would have survived.'

'You really believe it was fate?'

'I have to. If I don't, I will not be able to accept it.'

'Your family think this too?

'My brother thinks it happened because of the sins of the world. He is a traditional man; he thinks God is a serpent, or a fish, and that the earth rests on his shoulders. For a long time now God has been unable to bear the burden of human sin he carries, and so he shifted the earth to his other shoulder. This is what my brother thinks happened on Saturday.'

'It's a screwy idea,' Ellie said.

'It is his faith. He believes what his faith tells him is true, even though logic suggests otherwise.'

Ellie thought it was silly to imagine the world sitting on a fish. I mean, she thought, fish don't even have shoulders.

Dr Prasad grinned, seeing the amusement in her eyes. 'Don't you believe in certain things, Lady Northwood, when common sense tells you they are wrong?'

Ellie stared at the gap in the buildings where the house had been, and at the spot in the road where it had tumbled on to her and the children and the earnest policeman. She looked back at Dr Prasad and laughed for the first time in days, and not at the idea of God as a fish, but at her own lack of humility.

'I have a kind of faith, too,' she said. 'And I'm going to keep true to it.'

He nodded. 'I wish you luck, Lady Northwood.'

'Do you know, it's the strangest thing, but when I was half delirious in Tri-Chandra College, I could have sworn you were there. I saw you talking to Hugh Douglas.'

Dr Prasad laughed. 'That's what comes from having a bump on your head.' Then, with an effort that seemed to cost him dear, he got to his feet. 'I must go,' he said. 'I should be at Bir Hospital. I'm a volunteer there and I have, quite literally, hundreds of patients.'

Ellie remained sitting and looked up at him. 'How are your sons, Dr Prasad?'

'They are working with the Earthquake Relief Organisation.'

'And your wife? She must be happy to have you back home even under these terrible circumstances.'

'Our house was in the south of the city. It collapsed in the quake, and sadly my wife was inside on Saturday afternoon, preparing food for a party to celebrate our return.'

Ellie opened her mouth to speak, but hesitated, unable to find the right words.

'It was fate, Lady Northwood,' he said.

All the foreigners who witnessed the aftermath of the quake said Davies was a good man. He'd learned some handy skills in the Indian Army and he wasn't afraid to get his hands dirty. In the days after the catastrophe, he worked ceaselessly for the Earthquake Relief Organisation, a motley group of Europeans and Nepalis who added their own efforts to those of the Nepalese Army. He was brave, everyone said so. He risked his life and went into dangerously fragile buildings to bring out survivors, even though aftershocks still jolted the valley. He was a leader of men and directed teams of rescuers, and when they misunderstood his instructions because he bellowed at them in English, he demonstrated what he meant, tearing at the debris with his own blistered fingers, lifting entire sections of wall and hauling broken timbers, until the natives cottoned on and did what they were supposed to do.

'He is a treasure,' a lady from the British Legation said on her visit to the relief operations.

Ellie watched Davies wipe the sweat from his brow with his forearm, and although she found it hard to disagree, something niggled at her. She'd never imagined him as a hero; he'd always seemed more of a bully than a saviour, but she couldn't deny that he was genuinely concerned about the poor and homeless. The people lauded him; the men were grateful and the women garlanded him with flowers and offered him small gifts. The children gazed at him in a kind of wonder, and he smiled back, touched by their trust, and by their need. Heroes like him were treated well. He appreciated that. They respected him, and if the poorest couldn't thank him adequately with gifts and reverence, they could always be persuaded to pay in kind.

Five days after the earthquake, water from the hills began to be piped back into Kathmandu. Electricity once again lit the most important streets in the city, because by some miracle, the new hydroelectric power plant in Sundarijal was undamaged. Davies strutted around as if he'd had a personal hand in all these triumphs of man over nature.

Although Francis and Ellie had returned to the damaged palace, which had swiftly been clad in a net of bamboo scaffolding, Davies said he preferred to take a room in private lodgings close to where he was needed. I'm freer that way, he decided. I don't want to be at Northwood's beck and call.

Perhaps, he thought, it's time for me to give up the whole arrangement with that daft cunt of a lord. There was no chance they'd be heading for the Terai with the Maharaja's nephew, particularly when the Maharaja himself was moving in the opposite direction. He'd been on a tiger shoot in the plains when the earthquake struck and was now returning to his ruined capital. No decent hunting was on the cards, and Davies couldn't carry on playing flunkey to Northwood. He didn't want to see him, his Yankee wife, the tart, the fat nanny or the squealing brat ever again. He didn't want to be some nob's lackey when here, among the people who needed him, he was king.

In the early afternoon of the fifth day, he stretched out on the bamboo mat in the back room of the madam's brothel, and took a long drag of ganja. It was first-rate stuff, the best he'd had. The girl, whose name he couldn't remember – Lanksi or Laxmi, something like that – sat facing away from him, her legs drawn up and her chin resting on her knees. She was good, too, he thought, though he reckoned she must be deaf and dumb because he'd never heard her say a word. Only the madam and the boy-girl ever said his name; they called him Davvy. The idiots even managed to get that wrong.

Excited voices came from the road, and then the other room. Davies wished they'd pipe down. He wanted to relax, but all he could hear were the whores jabbering away. Maybe they've spotted another customer, he thought, and bristled. It was bound to be a local, and that wasn't on. It made him feel dirty to think he might be with a girl who'd also been with a native. He didn't want anyone messing with Lansi, or whatever her name was. He didn't want her spoiled and riddled with the clap. Anyway, whoever they were, they could piss off, because he'd paid good money and he was going to take his time.

The madam laughed, and Davies thought how much he disliked her. She was a mean, calculating bitch. All the madams were the same: hard as fucking nails.

In fact, the madam and her workers weren't discussing another customer. They were alarmed and amused by the strange figure walking down the lane. At first they thought it was a *hijra* – half man, half woman – but then they decided it was just a tall white woman in men's clothes.

'Is it Davvy's wife?' the boy-girl asked.

'If it is, no wonder he comes here,' the madam said, and grinned at the odd woman, who was peeping into every shack.

The boy-girl edged inside the house and peered round the door as Ellie came close.

'Hello,' Ellie said, trying to look friendly. She wanted to put the women and girls at their ease.

Inside the shack, Davies held his breath and then cursed. It sounded like Northwood's bloody American wife. What the hell was she doing on the outskirts of town?

'I'm looking for a little boy,' Ellie said to the women. She was miming, first rocking a baby, then showing them how tall Tom was. Then she pointed to her own hair. Finally, she did an impression of a building falling down in the earthquake.

They laughed, and thought she was utterly mad.

Suddenly a small girl darted out of the dim interior of the shack. She was doubled over and her shoulder struck Ellie's leg. The girl stumbled and fell, and Ellie reached out and took her arm. The girl flinched and shied away, and Ellie saw terror in her heart-shaped face and a blank deadness in her eyes.

Ellie surveyed the shack, scanning the shadows of the first room. She stepped into the darkness, and it took a moment for the indistinct form in the back room to take shape.

Davies was looking up at her from a mat.

'Davies?' she said, astonished.

'Having a bit of a kip, your ladyship,' he said.

'Here?'

'It's as good a place as any.'

Ellie stared at him, perplexed. 'But it's filthy. And these people,' she said, waving her hand, not knowing what to say.

'They're the salt of the earth, your ladyship. They'll do anything for you. They let me rest here and have a bite to eat before I start work again.'

Ellie backed out of the hut. She didn't like it; the air was heavy and something felt wrong, though she couldn't tell what it was, except that she knew there was unhappiness in that place. It was woven into the very walls, impregnating the bamboo and the grass roof. She thought of the little girl's frightened eyes and her tiny pinched face, and she decided to hurry back across the city to check that Lizzie was safe in Nanny Barker's care.

Davies listened to the madam cackle and the others talk as Ellie walked quickly down the lane. Jabber. Jabber. Jabber.

He chucked aside the smouldering ganja. Lady fucking Northwood knows my game, he thought. The stupid cow's on to me.

Ellie had spent only a few minutes with Lizzie in the palace before Francis sent a bearer to find her. She was led to his room and stood, dusty and defiant, in a shaft of sunlight. She had forgotten they had an invitation to visit the British Legation.

'I don't want to have tea at the Legation,' she said, her voice rising to a shout.

Francis paced the room and stopped to look at himself in the cracked gilt mirror. He stood straighter and put his shoulders back.

'We have to observe the formalities if we want to stay in this country,' he said wearily.

'But I want to carry on searching. I'm not going to quit. Every moment matters.'

'It matters that all foreign visitors are required to visit the Legation if requested to do so. I don't like paying homage to middle-class clerks, but in this case we have to go. We could be requested to leave at any moment. The Maharaja could withdraw our permits, and then the shoot in the Terai would be cancelled.'

'You're kidding? You're going hunting when Tom's missing?'

'We have men searching the whole valley. If he's alive, they'll find him.'

Ellie stood between the two marble nudes, her hands on her hips. One of the statues had lost her head in the quake, the other her arms. Francis looked at Ellie and a shiver ran up his spine. She looked threatening, like an Amazon, and why was she wearing those filthy jodhpurs and battered leather boots? For God's sake, she looked like a farmhand. Francis wanted her to soften; he felt unsettled by determined women and preferred Ellie when she'd taken a few pills to smooth the edges off her obsessions.

'You think you're the only one grieving,' he said. 'But Tom was my son too.'

'That's the point, Francis: I'm not grieving, and you won't see me crying for Tom because I know he's not dead.'

'For fuck's sake, Ellie. Take some Veronal, or whatever you need to cope with this.'

'I haven't got any Veronal. I lost the bottle in Sisaghari, and you know I don't always take it. I didn't when I was pregnant, and I don't want any now. I don't want to calm down, or slow down, because time is against me.'

Francis leaned closer to the mirror, and then stepped sideways so the crack didn't run down the centre of his face. His eyes were still red from crying. It was appalling that poor Tom had died like that, he thought. He imagined him in his sailor suit, playing with his lamb, and then lying in his cot, sleeping like an angel. Yes, he'd been a fine boy. He took a deep breath as a lump came to his throat. Enough is enough, he told himself sharply, and stood straighter. Life had to go on. He wasn't going to end up like his mother, who grieved for years for the sons killed in France while acting as if they were more important than the one boy left alive.

He glanced at Ellie's reflection. She'd begun pacing the room. She's like a bloody caged lion, he said to himself. If she carries on this way, I'll have to send her to Ranchi.

He turned the idea over in his head, energised for the first time in days, and wondered why he hadn't thought of it before. Sending his wife for a spell in the European mental hospital would be embarrassing – he didn't want people to know he'd married a lunatic – but he could deal with the shame, and it wouldn't be as bad as being lumbered with a hysterical woman night and day. He'd be able to go hunting whenever he wanted, and that would help take his mind off the tragedy of his son.

The plan unfolded before him. Nanny Barker could take Lizzie back to England, where she could stay in his old nursery and they wouldn't have to worry about her catching tropical diseases. He could relax and there'd be no need to fret about being caught in flagrante with Shushila. What's more, he thought, I'll be able to spend a few pounds without her looking over my shoulder. All I have to do is persuade a couple of tame doctors that she's lost the power of reason. He watched her twitching with energy as she prepared to resume the search. It won't be hard to convince the psychiatrists, he decided; not if she keeps moving like that. They'll be fitting her into a straitjacket the moment she walks into the clinic.

Francis sighed. 'Look, I promise you,' he said, sounding patient, 'the reward we're offering for information is staggering, even by English standards. It would make your average Nepali a very rich man. My friend the Maharaja's nephew tells me the search is a top priority for the Prime Minister, and they won't leave a brick or stone unturned.'

Ellie's voice almost reached a scream. 'They don't need to search under bricks; they need to find the Tibetan man.'

'Calm down. You're not helping yourself, or Tom,' Francis said, his voice mellow and cajoling now he'd decided to play the long game and to turn the family tragedy to his advantage. 'And it will be best if we visit the Legation this afternoon. We can use the whole might of the British Empire to help us.' He handed her a comb. 'Why don't you clean yourself up a bit? Wear a dress, get the tangles out of your hair and put on some lipstick.'

Ellie dragged the comb ferociously through her hair and

thought that one day, quite soon, she would come to hate Francis.

'That's a good girl,' he said. 'You can look so pretty when you try.'

The British Legation was in Lainchaur, north-west of Kathmandu, not far from the Maharaja's nephew's palace. Unlike the palace, it was surprisingly humble, and Ellie was taken aback because it was not what she had expected. Everyone knew the British loved grand buildings, and the Legation was far from imposing. It looked like an oversized Swiss chalet covered in begonias. The bedrooms on the first floor had wide verandas, and there was an incongruous tower tacked on to the left-hand side of the house, from which a limp Union Flag hung on a flagpole that tilted to the right.

The garden was full of trees. There were crepe myrtles near the house and tall Scots pines in the untended parts of the grounds. Ellie stood on the lawn, her heels sinking into the grass, and wished she wasn't there. She scowled, and didn't care if people thought she was odd. I have a decent excuse, she thought: everyone thinks Tom's dead and that I'm a grieving mother. She didn't listen properly to what people were saying, and glared fiercely at Francis, who was talking to Colonel Smith, the Legation's surgeon. They were locked in conversation, Colonel Smith nodding his head, his brow furrowed. He glanced up at her, and she didn't return his hesitant smile.

The two men walked towards her. Colonel Smith pointed towards the residence, saying, 'A structural engineer is coming from Calcutta as soon as possible because the tower has suffered serious damage and we're not sure the building is salvageable.

Our own house is completely uninhabitable. It'll have to be demolished and rebuilt; until then, we're living in a tent on the lawn.'

Mrs Smith, who looked immaculate, and not as if she lived in a tent, hurried towards Ellie. 'I'm so sorry to hear about your son, Lady Northwood,' she said. She leaned forward, her white glove touching Ellie's hand, which was covered in scabs from where she had torn at the debris in Asan Tole. 'They tell me the government is doing everything it can. The Red Cross too, and of course the envoy's escort has been unstinting.'

She looked slightly alarmed at Ellie's wild eyes in her stony face and must have thought it a good idea to change the subject. 'Anyway, we need to keep our spirits up,' she went on. 'We're such a tight-knit community and there are so few of us that it's marvellous to see new people. Sir Clendon Daukes, the envoy, is away in India at the moment, so my husband is standing in for him, and I thought it would do us good to carry on as normal. We've been quite fortunate, I suppose: the tennis court is undamaged and the billiard room isn't too dangerous.'

Ellie couldn't bring herself to speak. She looked at the other people assembling on the lawn around a few tables and thought how typical it was of the British to hold an event like this in the middle of a crisis. They were being kind to her in that very structured British way. Their voices were all the same, their mannerisms uncannily similar. They were saying soothing things but she couldn't respond to their sympathy when they were clearly expressing condolences for Tom's death.

Mrs Smith steered Ellie to a chair and sat next to her while they listened to Colonel Smith telling Francis about the casualties

that kept arriving at the Legation clinic, and how he had minis-
tered to the injured on the streets after the earthquake.

Ellie's attention wandered to Hugh Douglas and his daughter,
who were sitting at a nearby table talking to Mr Kilbourne, an
electrical engineer who oversaw the Sundarijal hydroelectric
plant. He was telling Hugh the dramatic story of how his own
daughter had narrowly escaped being crushed during the quake
when the front wall of their house in Kathmandu had collapsed
not two feet from her.

Hugh had his back to Ellie so she couldn't see his face.
Although he'd accompanied her on her search several times in
the last few days, she'd been so intent on finding Tom, she
hadn't actually looked at him properly since they'd walked
together through the Chitlong Valley. His sun-burnished hair
touched the collar of his short-sleeved shirt, and his tanned
arms rested on the sides of the chair.

She gazed at Maya sitting next to him and was struck by
how exquisite she was. Her mother must have been a beauty,
she decided, which was clearly why Hugh had broken all the
rules of polite British society to be with her. Ellie searched the
girl's features and saw very little of Hugh. She turned away,
willing herself not to look at him again. He unsettled her, and
she didn't like it.

She focused instead on Davies, who troubled her in a different
way. Her unease over him came from a place and a feeling she
couldn't quite pinpoint. Two hours earlier she'd seen him lying
on the floor of a shack. And now he was in the heart of imperial
privilege, standing with his legs wide apart, his boots planted
firmly on the lawn, as if bracing himself to withstand another
earthquake. It must be unusual, Ellie thought, to have a guest like

him at the Legation, someone without even a junior commission in the army and with an accent and bearing that marked him as inferior. But Davies didn't seem to be intimidated by his surroundings or his betters. He seemed to relish being out of place.

The wife of the British forestry officer walked towards them across the lawn, holding a child's hand. The boy toddled, his step uncertain. Ellie gasped, suddenly overwhelmed with emotion. The boy was slightly younger than Tom, but he had the same expression of wonder, the same vulnerability.

'Sit with this ayah while I talk to the ladies,' his mother said, passing his fat little hand to Hugh's daughter.

Maya flinched. 'I'm not an ayah,' she said, aghast.

The forestry officer's wife coloured. 'I beg your pardon. Please forgive me,' she stammered, taken aback, Ellie assumed, by Maya's perfect English. Flustered, the woman joined Mrs Smith and Ellie, dragging along the child, who was grinning and holding out a pudgy arm towards Maya.

'It's an easy mistake to make,' Mrs Smith said quietly to the forestry officer's wife. 'Apparently the girl is a student of history and languages. She's in the valley to help catalogue and transcribe ancient inscriptions.'

'And who's that angry-looking chap with her?' the woman asked.

'An antiquarian of sorts. He's ex-Political Department and has wangled an invitation from the Durbar. Goodness knows how,' Mrs Smith said. They were joined by Francis and Colonel Smith, who caught the end of their conversation. Colonel Smith lowered his voice. 'Very odd fellow, I'm given to believe. From what I've heard, he's not quite pukka. He mixes with all sorts of questionable people.'

Lizzie came rushing through the ornamental bushes, Nanny Barker in pursuit and panting heavily, her shoes scuffing the lawn. Lizzie flung herself on to her mother's legs, and Ellie picked her up and sat her in her lap.

'Look at the monkeys, Mama,' Lizzie said, pointing into the trees. The monkeys chattered and bared their teeth, and Lizzie shrank back a little. She watched the plump son of the forestry officer rolling on the grass and getting his white shirt very dirty.

'Where's Tom?' she said, looking up at Ellie. 'Is he with the man?'

Ellie answered this question several times a day, because Lizzie couldn't get used to being without her brother.

'Yes, and we're going to find him soon.' She spoke with such certainty, the other women looked away from her as if her hope made them uncomfortable.

Lizzie jumped off Ellie's knee. 'Tom. Tom,' she shouted, gambolling back into the bushes. 'Where are you?'

Nanny Barker headed after her with a leaden step.

'I've got to go,' Ellie said, standing quickly. She heard Francis sigh.

'You need someone to accompany you, Lady Northwood,' Mrs Smith said.

'I'll be okay,' Ellie said. 'Francis, please will you take Nanny Barker and Lizzie back to the palace with you?'

She began to stride away, then stopped, cursing her stupid outfit. She couldn't walk properly in a dress and pretty court shoes.

Hugh caught her arm. 'I'll come with you,' he said.

Ellie didn't hear him, her attention fastened instead on the people murmuring behind her.

'Poor thing,' Mrs Smith said. 'It's been the most terrible trauma.'

'I can't imagine what it would be like to lose my darling boy,' the wife of the forestry officer said. 'It would make me quite mad.'

'She can't accept our son is dead,' Francis said. 'I'm afraid it's driving her insane with grief.'

'Pi-dogs,' Davies said loudly.

'Pi-dogs?' Mrs Smith's whisper was barely audible.

'Feral dogs eat the corpses. That's why there's no trace of the poor little nipper.'

'Ghastly,' the forestry officer's wife breathed, and a sob caught in her throat.

Ellie turned. Francis jerked slightly in his chair and bowed his head. Davies, though, looked her straight in the eye, and she was instantly chilled, sensing his glee and the play of a smile on his lips.

Maya was glad to leave the Legation. She hated the way the Britishers had come from the other side of the earth and yet they all talked about the same boring things in the same awful accents. And the very worst thing about the afternoon was that stupid woman who'd thought she was an ayah. Why, Maya fumed, did so many white people think she was a servant? She threw open the shutters of the house her father had rented in Lazimpat. The late-afternoon sun revealed a heavy patina of grime. The servants had cleaned the room in the morning, but the air was so loaded with dust that it built up again within hours, coating the floor, shelves and furniture in a pinkish-brown powder.

Heavy rain during the previous night had rinsed away the debris clinging to the trees along the lane to the house, but the valley remained choked by the smell of death. Maya watched an elderly woman weed rows of vegetables in the field opposite. Further away, a man ploughed with two young buffalo in the black soils that led down to Kathmandu. How strange, and yet comforting, she thought, that everyday farming tasks went on in the middle of a disaster.

She was relieved the servants hadn't touched the maps and papers strewn over the table. There was an order to them despite their apparent chaos. She pulled up a chair. I'll have to work quickly, she realised. The sun would soon set and she'd have to light a lamp, whose kerosene was fast running out. The house had lost its electricity in the quake, and although the power supply had been reinstated in some central parts of Kathmandu, on the outskirts of the city they had to make do with candles and oil lamps. Dusk would bring a chill as well as darkness to the house, and they'd have no fire to warm them because there was so little wood left.

Maya examined a map dotted with pins and small clay markers, like pawns on a chessboard. She consulted a list in an old book with a broken spine and soft, yellowed pages, and carefully, with a confident precision, moved a red-topped pin from one location to another. She stood back, and then sighed, suddenly deflated. The task before them was virtually impossible. Centuries of Nepal's history and ancient culture had been smashed or buried, and many of the things they had come to catalogue were lost or impossible to reach. They had a week left on their permit, and instead of working, her father was helping in the relief operation or spending time on a wild-goose chase, searching for a dead boy while trying to console his deluded mother.

The only good thing was that her father was so interested in helping the American woman, he had taken his eye off Maya for a moment. He'd even allowed her to walk back to the house from the Legation on her own, which was a miracle in itself. Usually he treated her so much like a child that it was unbearable. He was so keen to know where she was, and if she was safe, that he could have been her jailer. It was strangely good to get a break from him while he was off hunting for the missing boy.

The sun was sinking behind the western hills and the air chilled quickly. Maya pulled a shawl around her shoulders and asked a servant to bring her a drink. As dusk fell, she bent over a book and warmed her hands around a clay bowl of hot, sweet tea. The light was almost too poor to read and so she lit a candle. Placing it near the book, she noticed the tea move in its bowl, the surface of the liquid quivering. She held her breath as her chair seemed to tilt backwards and then right itself. Her paper clips danced on the table, a pen rolled on to the floor, and there was a crash as glass broke in her father's room. The house creaked and sighed before easing again into silence. It was the third aftershock that day, and she thought each one might level what was left of the valley's buildings.

She checked the damage in her father's room. Two small bottles of medication had slid off a chest and smashed. A sweeper came in and began to clear the mess, collecting shards of glass and mopping up the liquid while Maya rearranged the phials, syrups and bottles of pills on top of the chest.

'That was the worst aftershock yet,' her father called from the main room. He had returned looking tired and weary, and older than his forty-three years.

'Are you feeling all right, Father?' Maya asked.

'Just a damned cough,' he said, running his fingers through hair that was loaded with dust.

'You shouldn't be digging through rubble. Besides, it's pointless now, isn't it?'

'Perhaps.'

A bearer knocked at the door and entered. 'There is a boy here to see you, Sahib.'

'Send him in,' Hugh said.

The boy stood by the table, moving from foot to foot while he wrung his hat.

'What's the news?' Hugh asked.

'He's in Bhadgaon, Sahib,' the boy said, grinning and revealing his big new teeth, brilliant white against his brown skin.

Hugh was puzzled. 'Who's in Bhadgaon?'

'The boy with gold hair,' the messenger said proudly. He wiggled his grubby toes in excitement as he explained how Tom was with a family on the second floor of a house on a narrow lane just off the main square.

'You're sure?' Hugh asked.

'My uncle said so. And Sahib . . .' The boy paused. 'How do we get the reward?'

While the messenger boy ran at top speed to get home before the curfew began, in the great sagging palace north of Kathmandu, the Maharaja's nephew ordered a bearer to open a second bottle of wine.

'You have a fine cellar,' Francis declared. 'I thought Kathmandu was supposed to be dry.'

Half an hour later, the Maharaja's nephew was too drunk to

bother with caste rules, and he shared a bowl of spicy wild boar with Francis. They lay in his new, hastily improvised women's quarters on uncomfortable sofas dragged from a grand, rarely used reception room in a distant part of the palace. The room must have been damp because the upholstery smelled of mould and rotting horsehair.

'Let's be friends the way we were in Calcutta,' the Maharaja's nephew said. 'Call me Mohan again. To hell with formalities and rules. We are princes, Francis. We can do what we want. I am a prince of Nepal and you are a prince of England.'

Francis was about to clarify their titles, because he was a lord not a prince, and he didn't think Mohan had a drop of royal blood in his veins, but he thought better of it, realising his mind was too foggy to sustain a logical argument.

Mohan raised a bottle of 1923 red Burgundy, an excellent vintage he claimed, and emptied it from a great height into long-stemmed blue Venetian crystal glasses, at least half of it splashing on the marble floor. He'd forgotten he shouldn't drink; forgotten he shouldn't eat with the foreigner. His magnificent headdress lay abandoned on the floor, the end of the bird-of-paradise plume soaking in a pool of wine.

'Careful, Mohan old man,' Francis said, grabbing at the jewel-encrusted cap. He missed it, reached for it again, and snatched it from the floor. He plonked it on his own head. The white plume was wet and stained purple at the end. It dangled before his eyes, and he kept batting it away with his hand. 'You can't leave a fine hat like this on the floor,' he said.

'Pah,' Mohan exclaimed. 'What do I care? What's the point of having treasures when you have lost your greatest love?'

Sinking back, he stared up at the bulging ceiling, too intoxicated to realise it hung four feet lower than usual and that a wide crack snaked across it.

Francis wondered if Mohan was talking about his wife. It didn't seem possible. He'd had a brief, forbidden glimpse of her that morning as she went to the royal palace to visit an injured relative. She was related to the King in some way, but the blue blood didn't stop her looking grim and stolid. To Francis's mind, she didn't look like anyone's greatest love.

'Your wife?'

Mohan expelled a lot of air through his nostrils.

'Your mother?' Francis asked.

'Tipu, love of my life,' Mohan wailed.

'Tipu?'

'A Gurung girl. They're always the prettiest.'

Francis had just enough sense left to realise that Mohan was talking about a concubine. He'd not seen these girls; he hadn't had the opportunity because they'd all been safely secluded in a kind of purdah, and then most of them had been crushed to death when the far end of the palace had folded into the garden. But he'd heard about them and their beauty. They were peasant girls sent by their villages as tribute to the Ranas. He wondered what had been so special about this Tipu; most of the hill girls looked indistinguishable to him.

'She was exquisite, and so fair. You know what it's like when they're young, and they're plump but still firm,' Mohan went on. 'Now I have only two left,' he said, gesturing to a couple of girls chatting on a giant sofa in the corner of the room. They kept glancing fleetingly at the men, and then looking quickly away.

'I became too fond of her, that's the trouble,' he continued. He pondered for a while. 'My uncle has the right idea.'

'The Maharaja?'

'He doesn't become attached. Well, not for long, anyway. I should follow his example. Whenever someone takes his fancy, he gives the family a few rupees and takes her off home. And then when he's finished, he sends her back.'

'Does this mean he has lots of children?' Francis asked.

'Over a hundred and twenty at the last count.'

'Christ, the expense.'

'Oh, he pays for the upkeep of the sons but I'm not sure he gives anything for the daughters.'

Francis thought for a moment about the difficulty of having so many children. How on earth would you remember their names? His heart sank at the memory of Tom, and he knew that he would never, ever forget *his* name. He took another slug of wine, his sadness beginning to morph into anger. Tom would still be alive if his idiotic dreamer of a wife hadn't brought him to this outpost of civilisation, this crummy little country with its big mountains and tin-pot rulers. Mohan was all right: he was generous with his wine, and had even offered to get him a couple of girls in the new consignment he'd ordered to replace the ones lost in the earthquake, but they weren't going to be real friends.

The fact was that the whole plan was unravelling. In truth, there was not much he could tell Mohan about how to hunt with hounds, because it was not going to happen here. There'd be no master of the hunt riding over the Kathmandu Valley – not in a hundred years. And where were the rolling hills and upland moors where he and the rulers of Nepal would one day shoot grouse? They were absolutely nowhere. The only thing that kept Francis hanging on in the ruined city was the prospect of the virgin forest and grassland of the Terai, and the elephants, tigers and rhinos he knew were roaming the plains, asking to be bagged.

Drink often made Francis angry, and his temper flared. He needed to sort out the problem of Ellie, and this was the time to do it.

'Mohan, old man, as we're such good friends, I need your help in a delicate matter.'

'Anything for you, Francis.'

'It's my wife, you see.'

'You need another one?'

'Not exactly. The problem is, she has a history.'

'Of what?'

'Mental illness. It started when she was a child. Hard to believe, but her family were killed in the San Francisco earthquake.'

'Good grief. Such bad luck.'

'She's scarred, you see. She takes a sedative used for mental patients. She's addicted to the stuff, and the attacks she has are absolutely terrifying. It's as if she's in their house in California with her dead brother beside her. I feel disloyal telling you this, and I do my best with her, but she's out of control. This earthquake has brought it all back to her; she's mixing up losing her brother with losing our son. She's deranged. I worry she'll do something to herself, maybe even to Lizzie.'

'It sounds like hell, Francis,' Mohan said, looking at him through bleary eyes.

'A fellow doesn't like talking about these things, but I'm

getting desperate. What if there's a scene? What if she loses her marbles completely?'

'I think you should get a new wife.'

'Probably a good idea, but first I need to deal with this one. I thought a spell in Ranchi might be just the ticket.'

'Ranchi? The asylum?'

'They call it a mental hospital these days.'

'It's a good plan.'

'That's what I thought, but I need your help.'

'Tell me, and it will be done.'

'I'm going to send them a wire, but what I need is a letter from a doctor recommending she be admitted. And I need guards to take her to the Indian border. Davies can go with her, but I can't have anything happening to her on the way. Who knows what she's capable of in her condition?'

Mohan gave loud instructions to his servants, and then fell back fast asleep on the chaise longue. Francis stood, staggered and stopped to look at him. He seemed to be covered in a dusting of snow.

'See you tomorrow, old man,' he said, and weaved his way to the door. 'I appreciate your help.'

The crack in the ceiling had widened, and tiny bits of plaster were falling gently on to the Maharaja's nephew.

Twenty minutes later, a bearer found Francis urinating on the base of a giant Chinese vase set in an alcove of the reception hall. He was utterly lost. The bearer began to lead him to his room.

'Do you have a wife?' Francis asked the man, leaning heavily on his arm.

The man smiled at him. He didn't speak a word of English.

'They're bad news, take it from me.' Francis hiccuped. 'I feel a bit sick,' he said. 'That bloody wine must have been off. Trust a wog to serve corked Burgundy.'

The man steered him up the stairs. Francis missed his footing and stumbled half a dozen times.

'Don't marry. That's my advice. I had to. Short of cash, you know, and see where it's got me.' Francis paused, swayed and tried to focus on the man. 'You're young. Don't make the same mistake as me. Don't get yourself saddled with an old mare for a wife. By God, if I could go back and change things, I would. She killed my son, you know.' He shook the man's arm.

'Sahib,' the bearer said, embarrassed.

'Did you hear me?' Francis said loudly. 'She killed my son. She brought him here when everyone said it was dangerous. I tell you, my friend, she deserves what's coming to her.'

The bearer manoeuvred him towards the bed, laid him down and took off his shirt and trousers.

Shushila sat up, and in the dim light the bearer stared at her bare breasts. She poked Francis. He lay unresponsive, like a corpse, and he didn't smell good either. He was so drunk he'd lost consciousness.

Shushila threw herself back on to the bed, her black hair spreading over the pillows. 'Get out,' she said to the bearer. As he closed the door, she turned on her side and kicked Francis hard on the thigh, once, twice, and the third time with such force her big toenail broke and a sliver of it embedded itself beneath his skin.

Francis was still drunk next morning when the curfew ended. The bearer showed Hugh to his room, which was in darkness, the shutters closed and the air fuggy with the smell of stale alcohol. Shushila slipped from the bed, and Hugh was startled. She snatched a sheet to cover herself and tiptoed out as if tiny, quiet footsteps would make her less visible. Hugh watched her go, his anger rising. So Francis is having an affair, he thought, and he's hiding his mistress in plain sight.

'Northwood,' he said. Turning to the bearer, he told him to open the shutters.

'What the . . .?' Francis groaned.

'I have a lead. I'm not sure the information is reliable, but it's worth checking.'

Francis squinted through one groggy eye at Hugh. His mouth and lips were stained purple by wine. 'For God's sake,' he mumbled, closing the eye and covering it with his arm.

'There's a fair-haired boy in Bhadgaon,' Hugh said. 'It's about eight miles from here.'

'That's good,' Francis sighed, drifting back to sleep.

'I came to you first because I didn't want to raise your wife's hopes. It might be nothing.'

Francis was unresponsive.

'Northwood,' Hugh said, his voice rising in anger and frustration.

'Sorry. What?'

'Are you coming?'

'Where?'

'To look for your son.'

Francis rolled over and pulled the pillow over his head. It muffled his voice. 'Not sure I'm up to it today.'

Exasperated, Hugh strode from the room, and then paused in the doorway, wondering if there was another tremor. The palace seemed to creak and shift within its bamboo cladding.

Ellie strode along the hall, dressed for another day trawling the city. Hugh was relieved she hadn't been there a few minutes earlier and seen the ayah sliding out of her husband's room. She smiled at him, and he grinned back a little too fulsomely, hoping his discomfort wasn't transparent

'What is it?' she asked, sensing something unusual in his manner.

I'm such a hopeless dissembler, he thought.

She came closer. 'Has something happened?'

'No,' he lied.

'You've found him.' It was a statement rather than a question.

'No. Well . . .' He sighed, and then paused, knowing he would regret whatever he said.

The road to Bhadgaon, the second largest of the valley's three ancient royal cities, had only just been reopened to cars. The going was slow and their journey was constantly interrupted by pedestrians, porters, and carts transporting building materials. Everyone weaved back and forth to avoid fissures that had spewed soil and sand. Hugh had rented a sedan at an exorbitant rate from the Ford car showroom in Lazimpat, and Ellie wondered whether the suspension would last. She sat in the passenger seat, Tom's one-eyed lamb on her lap.

She thought nothing could be worse than Kathmandu after the quake, but as they travelled east, the devastation became more extreme. Entire villages had been levelled, leaving nothing but low heaps of bricks. She had started the journey talking excitedly; by the time they reached Bhadgaon, she was silent.

Hugh stopped on the outskirts of the city. He got out and

gazed at the forested hills that formed the eastern rim of the valley. Landslips scarred the hillsides. They had cut deep lines into the forest and swept away sections of terraced fields. Somewhere under the eastern hills was the epicentre of the earthquake, the place where the Indian subcontinent had thrust north, sliding itself under Asia and jolting the Himalayas upwards. Four thousand people had died in the valley, but just as many had perished in the hills to the east, in poor villages and mountain bazaars.

Ellie and Francis walked slowly through Bhadgaon.

'How do you know where to go when you've never been here before?' Ellie asked.

'I've read every book written on it, and I've looked at every sketch and map ever drawn,' he replied, trying to sound more confident than he felt. 'This is Durbar Square,' he said, standing in a rubble-filled space. 'It's one of the marvels of Nepal. And that,' he continued, pointing to his left, 'is the Palace of Fifty Windows.'

Its roof was gone and so were many of the carved windows.

'That must have been the Bhairab Temple,' Hugh said. It had been transformed into a giant pile of bricks and wood when its three tiers collapsed, one on top of the other.

'Hugh,' Ellie said impatiently. She wished he would stop grieving over old buildings. Somewhere in the city, maybe just around the corner, Tom was waiting.

Hugh snapped out of his trance and they moved on.

Away from Durbar Square, Bhadgaon was different from Kathmandu. The buildings were taller, three and four storeys high, and the winding lanes were narrow. Old brick houses, some with overhanging balconies, leaned into the street so that at the top there was only a few feet between them, and down at ground level the sun rarely shone. One lane was impassable; the houses had folded into the street.

Hugh stopped to talk to a group of men. He spoke slowly, the men wrinkling their faces as they tried to understand him. Bhadgaon was very much a Newari town, and the language of the Newars was different from Nepali. They switched to Nepali and the conversation began to flow. Ellie's gaze flitted from one to another, trying to gauge from their expressions what was being said. They were pointing up a narrow lane.

'What are they saying?' she asked.

Hugh shook his head. 'I think we're too late.'

Ellie recoiled. 'No!' she exclaimed.

'A fair-haired boy has been here,' he said. 'But they said it was only for a few days.' He gestured to the second floor of a building. Cupping his hands around his mouth, he shouted. No one appeared. He called again, and a woman leaned out of a first-floor room. Strings of onions and chillies hung from her window, and the edges of a drying sari fluttered in a faint downdraught. Hugh struggled with his words for a second time, mixing Nepal and Newari and making the woman laugh. He smiled at her, and she laughed again, amused by what he was saying.

'Stop flirting, and tell me,' Ellie said, suddenly cross with Hugh and with the lack of information.

'She says the family living above her took in a small boy with white skin and fair hair after the earthquake. She hadn't seen him before and they kept him inside.'

'Are they there now?'

'They've gone. She says she never liked them. The wife was

from Nuwakot, and she didn't fit in here. Their rooms were damaged during the earthquake. Apparently there's a hole in the ceiling and a crack in the wall, and that's why they left.'

He called up to the woman again and she stuck her head out of the window a second time. When she finished speaking, he turned back to Ellie.

'They left yesterday at dawn.'

'Where did they go?'

'Nuwakot.'

'Where's that?'

'Somewhere we can't go.'

While Ellie and Hugh were in Bhadgaon, Nanny Barker took Lizzie for a walk around the palace gardens. She thought it would be good for the child to run off some of her energy, and it was safer than being cooped up inside the fragile building. The gardens made a sorry picture. The fountains had dried up because the earthquake had shattered the water pipes. Most of the statuary was broken, and a giant trench ran across the great sweep of the lawns down to the wall enclosing the compound, where it split the brickwork and left a three-foot gap on to the road. One of the follies had tumbled into the ornamental pond, and the roof of the largest summer house had detached itself from the rest of the structure and slid neatly on top of a bed of orange canna lilies.

Nanny Barker looked round for Lizzie. The child had run off again. I'm too old for this, Nanny thought: it's a young woman's job. For once she wished Shushila was there to lend a hand, because the girl could certainly move fast when she put her mind to it. The ayah, however, had devoted herself to nursing injured survivors of the quake, and spent night and day bandaging wounds in the corridors of Bir Hospital. I've misjudged her, Nanny thought, feeling guilty. Perhaps it's only in a crisis that you see people's true colours.

Nanny did a circuit of the lawns and began to panic. God in heaven, she thought, what if I lose the second twin? What if a native kidnaps the child? She prayed Lizzie wouldn't go scrambling over the collapsed wing of the palace. It smelled bad there, and she was sure the search parties hadn't retrieved the bodies of all the servant girls. Worse still, Lizzie might escape through the gap in the wall, and then what would they do?

She ran to a group of porters who were removing debris. They were trudging down the drive, their wicker baskets filled with broken bricks. She spoke to them, telling them about Lizzie and explaining the urgency. They smiled, and plodded on.

Nanny headed for the bushes and stood in a pretty glade, trying to think clearly. She listened intently, hearing only her own rasping breath and a distant temple bell. A sound to her left made her whip round. It was coming from a little summer house that had survived the quake. She charged towards it, flung open the door, and reeled back. A couple lay on the floor, a man's white buttocks pumping between a girl's dark brown thighs. The man didn't stop. He was so engrossed in his thrusting he hadn't even heard the door crashing open. The woman turned her face to Nanny Barker. It was Shushila, and she stared at Nanny, expressionless.

Nanny retreated in a horrified fluster. Leaning against a monkey tree, she tried to catch her breath. Her heart was beating too fast, and she felt dizzy. Slowly the thumping in her chest subsided, and the pulsing at the back of her eyes stilled. From behind a flaming red bougainvillea she heard a child's chatter. She tiptoed round and saw Lizzie sitting on the lawn next to an old gardener in tattered clothes. He squatted beside her, smiling, and then gave her a strange foreign fruit. In a paroxysm of misdirected anger, Nanny thundered towards them, knocked the fruit out of Lizzie's hand, grabbed her arm, gave the man a savage glare, and marched the girl back towards the palace. The old man picked up the fruit, looked at its yellow skin and bit into its crisp cream flesh as he watched the broad back of Nanny Barker disappearing with the child. Chewing without the aid of teeth, he spat out the stalk, took the wide curved blade of his kukri from his belt, and began to cut the grass.

In the summer house, Francis stood up, his trousers falling to his ankles. He looked down at Shushila and wrinkled his face as if to apologise. He couldn't finish the job. His head still hurt too much, his mouth was parched, and his leg was throbbing. He must have injured himself last night, although he had no recollection how it had happened. Perhaps he'd fallen on something sharp. He buttoned up his flies, and walked back to the palace with a slight limp. The gardener glanced up at him, and then watched Shushila follow a few minutes later.

The old man collected the mown grass. He piled it in his basket and squatted to catch another moment's rest. He'd worked since dawn, and soon the dusk would mean he could eat and sleep. He gave thanks, because every joint in his body ached. He looked up at the darkening sky, his attention caught by something new. There was a change in the light; the afternoon sun never looked like this. He stood and turned around. A funnel of grey-white smoke was spiralling from the neighbouring palace. It rose into the air and then, high above, began to drift westward. He watched for a minute as the smoke turned darker and began to billow from the open windows on the second floor. Then he tucked the kukri back into his belt and ran with the speed of a young man towards the palace, calling the alarm, forgetting his worn joints and the cut grass left scattered over the drive.

Hugh drove back from Bhadgaon more slowly than Ellie liked. He was acutely aware of the children who kept darting into the road, and the old people who hobbled into the path of the car. Cows meandered wherever they wished, and porters struggling with heavy loads paid little attention to the sedan creeping along one of the valley's few passable roads.

'I'm going to Nuwakot,' Ellie said.

'It's not allowed,' Hugh said.

'I don't care. I'm going.'

Hugh glanced at her, at the firm set of her jaw and the intensity of her gaze. He liked it when she looked like that.

'How far is it?' she asked.

'To where?'

'Nuwakot.'

'About sixty miles to the north-west.'

'Can you drive me?' she asked.

Hugh laughed.

'What's so funny?' she said.

'Ellie, this valley is the only place in the Nepal Himalayas where there are cars. Outside the valley there are only trails, and the one to Nuwakot is going to be only fractionally better than the road we took through Sisaghari.'

'I'll walk.'

'I'm sure you could, if they would allow you, which I can assure you they won't. Foreigners aren't permitted beyond the edge of the valley.'

'I'll sneak over the hills.'

'There'll be check posts and guards along every trail. And there'll be government people in the villages who'll report anyone suspicious.'

Hugh slowed the car to a crawl as he saw a group of ragged children chasing a herd of goats.

'Will you come with me?' Ellie asked.

'You haven't been listening to what I'm saying. You don't understand how tightly controlled this country is. The Ranas want to keep foreigners out. They're scared of new ideas because they think they'll encourage people to change the political system. The Indian nationalists want the British out of India, and the Ranas think their own people could learn from them. You've seen what Nepal is like: a few of them live in a luxury we can barely imagine, and the rest are wretchedly poor. The Ranas will do anything to keep it that way. That includes stopping foreigners visiting, and keeping them in the valley if they do. They're not going to let you go wandering around the hills.

'And anyway,' he went on, knowing she was unconvinced, 'we don't know he's actually in Nuwakot. It doesn't fit with the story that he was rescued by a Tibetan man. Those people in Bhadgaon were Newars, not Tibetans.'

'The Tibetan man could have given Tom to them.'

He slowed the car again, and looked at her. She was pale and clutched Tom's toy lamb, wringing its legs. If she ever gets to give it back to the boy, he thought, it will be mangled beyond recognition.

'How many blond-haired children do you see here?' she said.

'None, but I've seen Indian children who are so badly nourished that their hair turns red or blond.'

'Do they have white skin too?'

'No.'

'I'll ask Francis to speak to the Maharaja's nephew. He can arrange for us to travel.'

'I'm not sure it will do much good.'

'But he's the Maharaja's favourite nephew.'

'That's not what I've heard.'

'What do you mean?'

'I mean the Rana family is enormous. There are many sons and nephews, both legitimate and illegitimate, and they all have a claim to power and riches. Can you imagine the jealousy and the intrigue? It's happened before. Basically, they kill each other off to make sure they get a bigger share of the cake. From the gossip going round Kathmandu, it seems there'll be another purge soon, and your husband's friend is unlikely to do well out of it. He'll be lucky if he escapes with his life.'

'I'd never have guessed,' Ellie said softly.

'We can speak to Colonel Smith, the surgeon at the Legation,' Hugh suggested. 'He's bound to be sympathetic. The eldest son of a peer of the British realm can't simply be lost.'

'He thinks Tom's dead. And I'm sure Francis told him I'm crazy. I saw them talking, and the way Colonel Smith looked at me was weird. So I'm not waiting round for all the diplomatic niceties. I'm going.'

'You can't.'

'Have you heard of a woman called Alexandra David-Néel?'

'Of course.'

'I met her, and I've read her books. She walked all the way to Lhasa.'

'It's easier to travel in Tibet than here, I promise you.'

'Look, we're living in a damn catastrophe, right? Do you really think I'm going to be followed by police and spies? Haven't they got more important things to do?'

'My God, Ellie, have you been listening to anything I've said?'

Hugh stopped the car and examined Ellie's expression. She's formidable, he thought, and strangely lovely, and he wanted to reach out and touch her cheek. He wanted to kiss her, but knew she would be horrified. He was there to help her, not make love to her, and it would be wrong to take advantage of this moment when, under all the bravado, she was desperate and vulnerable.

Her eyes moved from his and she stared past him out of the window. Hugh turned to look in the same direction. Just to the north of Kathmandu's old city and the pagoda roofs of its remaining temples, a column of smoke rose high into the sky. The sun, sinking behind the western rim of the valley, touched it with orange.

'Where's that fire?' Ellie asked in a small voice.

'I'm not sure,' Hugh lied.

He put the car into gear and they began moving again. Ellie didn't take her eyes from the smoke as it began to billow and drift across the valley, enveloping the Buddhist stupa of Swayambunath on top of its wooded hill.

By the time they reached the city, dusk was falling, and the orange glow of a massive blaze spread from the north.

'Lizzie!' Ellie cried, and Hugh heard hysteria in her voice.

They drove closer, moving against the flow of people fleeing the fire. And then they stopped, unable to go any further. The road was blocked by two trucks that had collided. Ellie scrambled out of the car and began to run, Hugh close behind her. He grabbed her arm and pulled her back. Even from a distance, the heat of the fire prickled the skin of his face. Flames two hundred feet high shot into the night sky, and in the centre of the inferno, the skeleton of the great palace burned.

'That's not where you're staying,' he said, wrapping his arms around her. He felt her shaking. Her legs twitched and her breath was fast and ragged. 'Look,' he said. 'You're staying next door.' He moved her whole body round so she faced the neighbouring palace.

She looked up, and his eyes followed hers. Glowing cinders fell out of the smoke. Some sank slowly; others plummeted into the gardens and on to the roof of the Maharaja's nephew's sagging palace.

Ellie was too terrified to say anything. She was paralysed by fear, although it wasn't only the fear of losing Tom. It was the old fear, the unbearable pain of remembering that had shadowed her for most of her life: fear of losing everything; fear of the dark; of walls falling in; of a city consumed by fire.

On the other side of the earthquake-damaged palace, Lizzie was with Nanny Barker in the back of a golden limousine. The atmosphere in the car was rank and heavy. Shushila smelled of singed hair, Nanny smelled of perspiration, and there was a faint smell of wee from Lizzie, who had been so frightened by the fire she couldn't help the accident. When Major Thapa got in to check on the ladies, and to seize the opportunity to be close to Shushila, he got out again quickly, preferring the acrid smell of the fire.

A large cinder fell on to the long bonnet of the car. It glowed red at its edges and burned yellow at its heart.

'Someone should move this car further away,' Nanny said. 'It's dangerous here; we're far too close.'

Lizzie was mesmerised by the flames shooting two hundred feet into the air. Nanny was more interested in watching the efforts to stop their palace combusting. Men scrambled about on the roof, frantically beating out fires with wet cloths and passing buckets of water from hand to hand. And then her attention was caught by two figures who flew past the car towards the house.

'Lady Northwood, Mr Douglas,' she shouted, and banged on the window. She got out and shouted again.

Ellie turned. Recognising Nanny Barker, she ran towards the car. She saw Lizzie's pale face pressed against the window, her tears streaking the glass. 'Mama, Mama!' the girl cried.

Ellie dived into the back seat. 'Thank God. Thank God,' she whispered as she hugged Lizzie.

Nanny got back in, and she and Shushila noticed a new smell in the car: Ellie reeked of fear.

Hugh climbed into the driver's seat, coughing badly. The smoke was dense and he was struggling to breathe, a familiar tightness beginning to wind itself around his chest.

Shushila didn't look at him: he was a chota sahib – a little white man – so not worth bothering with. She wished though that he'd stop spluttering and spreading his nasty foreign bodily fluids in the close confines of the car. She put up with enough of that kind of thing from the burra sahib, though since he was an important white man, the insult to her body and religious sensibilities was forgivable.

Hugh reversed the car down the drive and through the open gates on to the road. They couldn't head for Kathmandu because he knew that way was blocked. The road also ran past the burning palace, now reduced to a shell. Its roof had collapsed together with the third floor and parts of the second. In the west wing the only things left standing were a few walls and a couple of Corinthian columns, around which the flames danced with so much energy it seemed they would never stop. At their base, the remnants of the palace glowed yellow and orange.

Hugh turned the car in the opposite direction and drove it only a short way before the road became an impassable track. He stopped, and they opened the windows to expel the smell and the fear.

'You can't go back there,' he said.

'Do you think our palace will burn too?' Nanny said.

Ellie didn't seem to be listening; hypnotised by shock, she rocked Lizzie to and fro, her eyes fixed on the back of the driver's seat.

'I'm not so worried about the fire,' Hugh said. 'The building was so badly damaged in the earthquake, it should be condemned. No one should be living in it.' He stopped talking, paralysed by a cough, and Shushila, sitting in the passenger seat, leaned against the door and put the end of her sari over her mouth.

When his breathing steadied, he continued. 'You can go to the government guest house for foreigners down in Thapathali, near the river, although that's been damaged too. That's why I rented a house in Lazimpat, very close to here. You can stay with me and my daughter if you like. The house is clean, and the servants are good. You will have to share a room, but of course it won't be for long. We'll all have to leave soon.'

The thought of leaving the valley without Tom snapped Ellie out of her trance. 'Lizzie is not going anywhere near that palace again,' she said. 'It's a tinderbox. And fires can start at any time after earthquakes. They can destroy whole cities. Imagine if one started in Kathmandu, with all its wood carvings. I want to be as far away from there as possible, so we won't go to the government guest house. We'll go with you to Lazimpat. Nanny and Shushila will help me pack our things tomorrow.'

'I can't,' Shushila said. 'I have to stay here for my work.'

'Your work?'

'In Bir Hospital.'

'But you work for me.'

'Actually,' Shushila said in the voice of an English memsahib, 'I work for your husband. And he wants me to help the wounded in the hospital. He said, "We must do our bit," so that's what I'm doing. You wouldn't want to stop me helping the sick when you already have one ayah to tend your daughter.'

'I'm a nanny, not an ayah,' Nanny Barker said, the slur bringing more colour to her already hot cheeks.

'But you do what an ayah does,' Shushila said. 'The only difference is you are white and you have that smelly uniform.'

Nanny gasped.

'You can go to Bir Hospital from Lazimpat,' Hugh said, knowing what Shushila's response would be.

'The palace is nearer,' she replied.

It was untrue: the distance was the same. Hugh looked at her, and she glanced at him for the first time. Illuminated by the radiant light from the enormous fire, his eyes were shrewd. They both knew she was lying. Francis would stay at the palace if it wasn't razed by fire, and Shushila wanted to be with him. What was more, Hugh would bet she'd never even set foot inside Bir Hospital. If the other women hadn't been in the car, he would have said so, but how could he reveal to them that Shushila's work had never been to look after the children, and that Ellie's husband hid his beautiful mistress right under his wife's nose?

Rain drew the fire's teeth and saved the Maharaja's nephew's palace. It started shortly after midnight and fell steadily until dawn. Hugh drove Lizzie and the sleeping women the short distance back to the palace as a chink of bright light peeped over the mountains and the sun rushed into the valley.

Dozens of weary, smoke-blackened men roamed around. Every soldier, servant, porter and peasant in northern Kathmandu had been pressed into fighting the fire. Next door, they had failed. The three-hundred-room building that belonged to one of the Maharaja's brothers was laid waste. The fire that still burned in its centre was almost spent, though the carcass of the great palace would continue to smoulder for days.

Ellie wondered what part Francis had played in saving his friend's home. When she looked at him lying in bed, feverish and bad-tempered, she realised he'd slept through the inferno.

155

'What fire?' he asked, opening dull red eyes.

'You could have been burned to death in your bed,' Ellie exclaimed. 'And no one would have known.'

'Don't overreact, Ellie,' Francis mumbled. 'You turn everything into a drama.'

'I came to tell you I'm going to Nuwakot to find Tom.'

'What?'

'He wasn't in Bhadgaon, but the woman said they'd taken him to Nuwakot.'

'What the hell are you babbling on about?'

'Hugh told you we were going to Bhadgaon because a blond boy was there.'

'The hell he did.' Francis tried to sit up but dropped back on to the pillows. 'Look, Ellie, I'm in no shape to discuss any of this with you. I'm feeling a bit queer. I'm quite delirious, if you must know. So just run along, there's a good girl. And fetch the doctor while you're at it.'

Ellie looked more closely at him. His face was covered in greasy sweat. She touched his forehead: he was burning up. This isn't another hangover, she thought. He really is sick.

The personal physician to the Maharaja's nephew took a long time examining Francis. Ellie waited outside the room with Hugh, Major Thapa and the Maharaja's nephew. The door jammed when the doctor came out to deliver his diagnosis because the frame and the walls around it were buckling under the pressure of the collapsing ceiling. He had to throw his weight against it to open it.

'It is a most unusual case,' he said, brushing dust from his sleeve. He furrowed his brow. 'He has septicaemia.'

'What's that?' the Maharaja's nephew asked.

'Blood poisoning. He has some nasty wounds on his thigh. There's some bruising and what look like deep scratches typical of an animal's claws.'

'Yes,' said the Maharaja's nephew. 'Even a minor wound from a big cat's claws can become badly infected.'

'Precisely, your excellency,' the doctor said. 'But the question is, how did he come by these wounds? Although he is delirious most of the time, when he is lucid he says that he has not been hunting. Are we to suppose a leopard or a tiger has strolled around this fine palace?'

'The earthquake has made several gaps in the walls surrounding the garden,' Major Thapa reminded them.

'I think my husband would remember being mauled by a tiger, Major Thapa.'

'Not if he was as drunk as he was yesterday,' Hugh added. 'He was three sheets to the wind.'

'Can I see the wounds?' Ellie asked.

They assembled round the bed and a bearer opened the shutters. The bright light showed the mottled red and purple skin of Francis's leg in full and hideous colour. Five inflamed scratches ran down his thigh, and one was beginning to ooze pus.

'If you will stand back,' the doctor said to the onlookers, 'I think I can extract some debris from this wound. I'm afraid this will hurt, your lordship, but it is absolutely necessary to remove the source of the infection. You must brace yourself.'

He fiddled with a bottle of iodine and some gauze, and then opened the wound with his forceps.

Francis screwed up his face and yelled, 'Fuck!'

The doctor stood straight and examined the thing caught between the tips of his forceps.

The Maharaja's nephew darted forward. 'It is a leopard's claw.'

The doctor placed the offending item on a little dish. Hugh struggled to stifle a smile, because he was looking at a sliver of human toenail.

'My assistant will sterilise and dress the wounds,' the doctor went on, 'and I will return tomorrow. For now, he must rest and be given plenty of fluids. I will prepare one of my special poultices to apply to the wounds, and within the hour I will send a boy with a tincture that he must be given immediately.'

'Will he be able to go to Nuwakot?' Ellie asked.

'My dear lady,' Major Thapa said, 'foreigners do not go to Nuwakot. It is forbidden. You must be thinking of somewhere else.'

Hugh gave her a warning look. 'Don't you mean Nargakot, on the edge of the valley?'

'Indeed, that is what you must mean, Lady Northwood,' Major Thapa said with a laugh. 'The views from there are the very best. We can see Everest on a good day.'

'Nargakot is out of the question,' the doctor said. 'Lord Northwood cannot travel. He is still in some danger, though I'm confident this fever will pass.'

Francis slept while a servant girl mopped his brow with a cool towel.

'We'll hear the story about Mr Spots when he's recovered,' the Maharaja's nephew said as they left the sickroom. 'Poor fellow,' he sighed. 'Such are the dangers of shikar.'

Hugh and Ellie found Shushila at the grand entrance to the palace. She was relaxing by the side of the dried-up rose-water fountain after another testing spell at Bir Hospital. Ellie marvelled at how faultless she managed to look, her sari immaculate despite the gruelling work. And Hugh looked at her feet, at the long nails, and the one very short one on the swollen big toe of her left foot. They are the feet of a Bengal tigress, he thought, and we all need to watch out for her claws.

Ellie lay awake all night in Hugh's house in Lazimpat, desperate for the dawn. Nanny Barker's snores were so loud and deep they made the air quiver and the small objects on the cabinet vibrate. Ellie hoped Hugh would know it was Nanny making the farmyard sounds. Hugh couldn't have slept much either; he'd coughed all night and the wooden walls made it feel as if he were lying next to her rather than on the other side of the partition.

She kept her eyes on Lizzie, and occasionally glanced at Nanny. With the practice of years, she avoided looking at the walls and rafters. Her small oil lamp shed only a tiny, clearly defined circle of amber light that didn't extend to the shadowy corners of the room, where the demon might be crouching on his haunches.

As the faintest hint of dawn crept over Kathmandu, Ellie tiptoed out of the stuffy bedroom and into the main room. Below, some of the servants were starting their work. Quietly she opened the creaky shutters, inch by inch, and looked over the narrow, potholed road, through the tall trees and across the fields. The sun hadn't risen above the western hills and the light was still hazy. There was no fog to spoil the view, and the morning air was crisp and cold, and very clear. She shivered and picked up a wool blanket from the floor.

It was thick and matted and smelled of animal, but she wrapped it around her shoulders regardless.

Maya and Hugh's maps were all over the table, and she began to scan them, thankful Hugh hadn't tidied them away before he went to sleep. She walked round trying to read them and establish her bearings. Which way was north? Where were they now? Where was the road from Bhimphedi? And most importantly, where was Nuwakot?

This big map is no good, she decided; it's only of the valley. She took a smaller one that looked as if it had been removed from a book, and dragged it across the table, scattering the little clay markers. The big map moved, and the pins marking ancient sites ripped holes in the paper. Ellie examined the small map. It lacked detail and the scale was very tiny, but there was Nuwakot, to the north-west of Kathmandu. It was just over the edge of the valley, she thought. I could get there today.

'How dare you,' Maya said, striding in and trying to snatch the map from Ellie. 'What on earth do you think you're doing? It's taken me days to prepare this map.' She looked aghast at the rips in the paper, at the markers strewn over the table, some rolling on the floor. She stepped forward and one crunched under her foot.

'I'm sorry,' Ellie said. 'I should have realised this was important.'

'You stupid woman. Everything is ruined.'

'The whole goddam valley is ruined,' Ellie said, thinking the girl was overreacting.

'You don't understand,' Maya said, and her eyes flooded with tears. 'We can't let so much history be lost without there being some kind of record.'

'Well,' Ellie said, bridling, 'it seems like you've got your priorities all wrong. What's the point of digging up old statues when there are people to dig out of the rubble? You've got a few days to make a list of damaged temples, while I'm going to search for a real person. I'm going to Nuwakot to fetch my son.'

'You'll get lost.'

'I have this map.'

'You're mad.'

Ellie looked at her sharply. 'Plenty of people tell me that,' she said.

'That map isn't to scale.'

'Maya's right,' Hugh said, coming into the room. He sounded croaky after all his coughing. 'It's a short distance as the crow flies, but the paths are never straight. It'll take a long time.' He stood next to Ellie and pointed to the map. 'It's the road to Kodari, one of the two old trade routes from Kathmandu into Tibet. It means it'll be busy, and you don't look like a Tibetan, an Indian or a native Nepali trader. You don't look like a pilgrim either.'

'I'll darken my face,' Ellie said, remembering Alexandra David-Néel's efforts to disguise herself as a Tibetan. 'I can pretend to be a Nepali woman.'

Hugh laughed. 'You are a foot taller than a Nepali woman.'

Nanny Barker hovered by the door, still groggy with sleep.

'You don't walk like one either,' Maya added, sounding huffy and cross. 'Hill women have a particular way of walking, if you haven't noticed. They carry their head and back very erect, and they roll their hips.' She stood a little straighter herself as if to make the point.

'Then I'll dress like a man,' Ellie said.

She'll make a believable man, Nanny Barker thought, and

then checked herself, knowing she was being cruel. Ellie was trying to do her best to find her son, even if the search was pointless.

'You don't speak a single word of Nepali,' Maya said.

'Your father is fluent.'

'But he's not going.' Maya looked at Hugh, and her face dropped. 'You aren't going, Father. Please tell me you're not.'

Both Ellie and Maya were staring at him. He glanced from one expectant face to the other. 'We'll be Afghans,' he said, decisively.

'No. It's impossible,' Maya stated. 'Your Pashtu and Dari are poor. There isn't time. And you're not well.'

'I've always wanted to go to Nuwakot, and I'll be able to see what damage has been done to the old palace and the Bhairab Temple.'

'You were coughing all night,' Maya exclaimed. She turned to Ellie. 'You heard him.'

Ellie didn't respond. She didn't care about Hugh's cough; she cared only about getting Tom back.

'Shall I take Lizzie to the palace?' Nanny Barker said.

'No,' Ellie and Hugh said in unison.

'Stay here with Maya,' Hugh added. 'We'll be back in a few days.'

'You hope,' Maya said, and Ellie noted the bitterness in her voice.

'Mama,' Lizzie said, and tugged at the tassels on Ellie's blanket. Ellie knelt down and pushed the loose curls from her daughter's face. 'Where are you going, Mama?' the girl asked.

Ellie looked Lizzie straight in the eyes. 'I'm going into the mountains to fetch your brother.'

4

The Journey to Nuwakot, January 1934

From Kathmandu, the road to Kodari passed first through Thamale and then through an avenue of willows to Balaju. Late in the morning of a dazzlingly sunny winter day, two Afghan moneylenders moved quickly along the smooth path that ran along the banks of the Mahadev Khola.

'Slow down,' Hugh said. 'You look like you're in a hurry.'

'I am,' Ellie said, barely slackening her pace.

'Remember we're on our way from Bengal to Tibet, and we've just stopped in the Kathmandu Valley to make a few loans to victims of the earthquake. I guarantee, no one would move fast on that kind of journey, so if you don't want to attract attention, you need to change your pace. If you don't, we won't make it out of the valley.'

Ellie's strides remained long.

Hugh stopped. 'If that argument doesn't persuade you, think about the climb you're going to make. We're on a nice level path here, but you see up ahead? Where the ground rises? That's Jitpur, and from there we'll be going uphill. You were lugged into this valley in a doli, but you'll have to walk out of it, because no Afghan man would be carried unless he was dead or dying. You have to save your energy.'

Ellie walked more slowly. She glanced at Hugh several times, wondering how anyone could believe they were Afghans, although in truth she had little idea what an Afghan looked like. She had only his word that they could pass for the real thing. He'd made her promise not to speak within anyone's hearing, however, because although she was as tall as a man, she didn't sound like one.

'Shouldn't we have black hair and brown skin?' she asked him.

'Some Afghans have pale skin and red or blond hair. A few have the most incredible blue or green eyes.'

'You mean they have hair like you?'

'Yes, although I don't have any Afghan forefathers, as far as I know. But the Afghans who look something like me are said to be descendants of the soldiers who came to Asia with Alexander the Great. Clearly they liked the place so much they settled down in the hills of Afghanistan, and their children inherited their looks.'

Ellie wasn't convinced, and tucked a piece of blonde hair back under her pagri, the traditional headgear of the Afghan men Hugh had met in the bazaar. The cloth was wound into a roll so it made a kind of flat hat or turban, and the long ends dangled over her shoulder. She was sure it was full of lice, and the thought of it made her scalp feel itchy. If they'd had time, she would have washed it, but as they were already late leaving the city, she'd jammed it on to her head the moment Hugh returned from the bazaar. He'd bought two sets of clothes straight off the backs of a couple of mystified Afghans, and when she'd pulled on the trousers, long tunic and waistcoat, Ellie was certain they were still warm from the body of their previous owner. They certainly still smelled of the Afghan trader, and as the sun beat down, the aroma became sharper. At least the outfit was comfortable, Ellie thought. Despite infrequent laundering, the fabric was softened by age and wear.

Above Jitpur, the road became steep and its surface was covered in loose stones. They passed through intensively culti-vated land where the hillsides were intricately terraced, and although some of the fields were a mere two feet wide, they were perfectly constructed and immaculately maintained. Here and there, the walls of the terraces had been breached by the force of the earthquake and the ground had been swept away by landslides. Farmers were busy repairing the terraces, while others worked on their winter crops, paying little attention to the two travellers on the Kodari road.

They increased their speed when they passed through the small villages of thatched two-storey houses, most covered in earthy red and ochre paint. Ellie manoeuvred around goats, chickens and young children who strayed or tumbled into her path. She didn't look too long at the children, who were bare-foot and ragged, with long strings of silvery snot hanging from each nostril. She didn't make eye contact either with the women, who sat outside their homes weaving baskets, grinding flour or checking their offspring for lice.

In a place where there were fewer houses, and no one appeared to be working, Ellie and Hugh sat in the shade of a pipal tree. Hugh offered Ellie water from a metal flask. She had drained her own because she was unable to pace her drinking properly.

A girl of eight or nine appeared from nowhere and stood too close to them. She examined Ellie's face. Ellie turned her head, but the child moved round so she could stare at her.

'Beat it,' Ellie said. The girl jumped and ran off.

'I told you not to speak,' Hugh said sharply.

'Sorry. I forgot.'

The girl reappeared with a friend, and they inched closer. Hugh began talking to them in Nepali. The children laughed, and after a while, they lost interest and scampered away.

'If they come back with reinforcements, it's good to know that this is the least dangerous place to be caught,' Hugh said. 'If we're stopped, we can say we are guests on our way to the British envoy's summer residence in Kakani.'

'He has a place up there?'

'A bungalow. He has a golf course too, right on top of the ridge.' Hugh stood up. 'Come on. It's not far now, but it will be dusk in a couple of hours and we need to find food and a place to stay.'

Ellie winced when they began walking again. She had refused the Afghan man's boots, insisting that her own, bought in Calcutta, were perfectly fine. They had done her good service in Kathmandu, but her feet must have swollen on the walk, and the boots that were once so comfy were beginning to rub.

They climbed through forests of rhododendrons, forty feet tall. In the spring they covered the south-western slopes of Kakani in pinks and reds, and their trunks were furred with every shade of orchid. In January, though, they only hinted at the splendours the next few months would bring.

Ellie slackened her pace as they neared the top of the path. Her thighs ached, and her calves felt tight. Hugh kept stopping, waiting for her to catch up. His cough had eased, and he seemed perfectly well despite the altitude and the arduous climb. He stood ten yards ahead, egging her on. The late sun shone on him and Ellie was struck by how handsome he looked. The clothes of the Afghan trader no longer looked tatty and comic, but charming and faintly heroic.

'You made it,' he said as she clambered up the last few feet. He offered her his hand, the palm turned upwards.

Ellie didn't reach out to take it; she was suddenly acutely self-conscious, imagining that he'd read her mind, and was only saved from more embarrassment by the view. Taking her eyes from his outstretched hand, she looked northwards to the crest of the Himalayas. The panorama was breathtaking. It was as if the earth had been squeezed and forced to crumple, forming wave after wave of tightly packed ridges and deep valleys. The forested hills rose in ever higher steps, tier upon tier, towards the snow-capped roof of the world. East to west, the mountains stretched as far as she could see.

'Everest,' Hugh said, pointing right towards clouds massing over a far-off peak.

Ellie turned round to look back at Kathmandu. From a distance, the valley looked serene; a bright green oasis among the hills. A breeze blew over the mountain and Ellie wrapped the ripe-smelling blanket she had brought from the house in Lazimpat around her shoulders. In the summer, the cool wind was a blessing for those seeking respite from the stifling heat of the valley. In January, though, the breeze carried a recent memory of glaciers and mountain snows, and its chill bit into her.

'Where's Nuwakot?' she asked.

Hugh studied his map, read a few pages torn from one of his books, and then scanned the landscape.

'You can't see it from here, but it's just over the other side of that ridge.' He pointed to the first great fold in the hills. 'You see this valley below us?'

Ellie looked down to where a river ran in a narrow valley. The scale of the land was immense, because even that first valley was miles away.

'And now look west, over there to where the valley meets another one. That's the Trisuli River. We're going to walk along its banks, and if I'm correct, we'll find Nuwakot above the river.'

Maya had been right. The silly little map was not to scale. It would take them hours to get into the first valley, never mind along the Trisuli and up to Nuwakot.

'Do you want to turn back?' he asked, seeing her startled expression.

'Never,' she said, with so much determination she sounded angry.

A jolly family party, probably returning from the blessing of a newborn, greeted the odd strangers with polite smiles. The men said, 'Namaste,' and the children whispered and sniggered while looking at Ellie, who for once looked nothing like a man. When the long, noisy cavalcade had disappeared down the trail, Ellie and Hugh began walking again.

On the edge of a collection of ramshackle buildings, he left her sitting by a tree, well out of sight of the road.

'I won't be long,' he promised.

She watched the sun setting on the mountains, turning the

snows orange and pink. The sky above the peaks moved through tones of blue and violet to a deep, dark purple. None of the colours approached the rich coral-red of the Tibetan lama's poetry. The sun sank. It no longer shone on the snow, and its refracted light retreated until she was left in a dusk that was fast turning to night. She shivered with fear as much as cold.

'Sorry,' Hugh said softly. His voice made her jump. 'The owner of the first lodging house was too inquisitive, the second place was already full, and the third was a doss house. There's a decent lodge a bit further on, and the owner is friendly without being nosy.'

They picked their way slowly towards it, though Ellie was surprised by how much she could see in the moonlight.

'I'm afraid it's not the envoy's bungalow,' Hugh whispered.

'Anywhere will do,' she sighed, and meant it.

Before they entered, he pressed his finger against his lips and reminded her to be silent. She took a final look across the valley and mountains. The moon illuminated the silvery-white snow, and the sky was a deep indigo. Tom is on the other side of that dark ridge, she thought, and hoped he had a warm blanket.

The smell of wood smoke almost made her gag. She stopped on the threshold, and it was only the surprised expressions of the lodge keeper and his son that made her continue walking. She followed Hugh into a cramped back room furnished only with a couple of bedding rolls and bamboo mats on a hard wooden platform. Hugh dropped their packs on to a floor of beaten earth and motioned Ellie to sit on the mats, aware of the eyes of the lodge keeper on their backs.

They ate *dal bhat tarkari* brought in on metal plates by a sickly-looking boy with a patch of mange on the top of his head. Fortunately, the lodge keeper and his son were distracted by a nasty argument over the young man's prospective bride and paid the travellers scant attention, which was good because no knives and forks had been provided. Ellie had none of Hugh's practised dexterity and struggled to eat with her fingers. She watched him pinch the rice, dal and vegetables into neat little helpings and put them cleanly into his mouth. Ellie tried and failed, dropping bits everywhere. In the end, she picked up the metal plate and shovelled the food into her mouth, using her hand like a scoop. Hugh raised an eyebrow.

'Tasty,' she said. She wiped her mouth with the back of her hand and her fingers on the length of cloth dangling from her pagri.

'The epitome of grace, Lady Northwood,' he said.

She gave him a fiendish grin, and then lay down on the mat and quickly shut her eyes.

The proprietor had stopped arguing with his son and returned to check on his odd guests. He eyed them sharply, always wary of strangers, and was satisfied. He saw the man sitting in silence, running prayer beads through his fingers, while the lanky boy lay on the floor, looking like a stick dressed in rags. The lodge keeper didn't like Muslims. They were like the white people in India; they disturbed the sanctity of his country and its sacred places. But he was also a practical man, and lodging house owners couldn't be fussy.

Ellie had never slept on a hard floor, and it was impossible to fall asleep, even though a dragging tiredness spread through her body and into her very bones. She couldn't get comfortable, and would have shifted around if Hugh hadn't been lying right next to her, in a deep and restful sleep. A soft light from the other room kept her demon at a distance, but as the house quietened and shut down for the night, she became aware again of the smell of wood smoke. Her heart jumped, and began to beat faster. She inched closer to Hugh, finding comfort in being near him. She concentrated on his face. Although he had his back to the light and his features were in shadow, she could make out the angle of his cheekbone and his jaw. Tracing the outline of his face made her heart beat slower and more steadily.

Suddenly he opened his eyes, and they looked at each other, only a foot of darkness between them. He reached out and pulled the blanket higher over her, and underneath it, his hand searched for hers. This time, she took it. He closed his eyes again, and they both slept.

When they left the lodge in the early dawn, every muscle in Ellie's body ached. She hobbled after Hugh, who had stopped a porter carrying winter fruit to sell in the valley. He asked how far it was to Nuwakot.

'A day,' the man said. 'You'll get there before nightfall if you hurry.'

Hugh looked at the porter's thin, knobbly legs. Despite the enormous weight of the fruit on his back, he seemed to spring and dance down the path to Kathmandu. It will take us a lot longer than him to cover the ground, Hugh thought. Ellie was slow, unsure of her footing, and his own chest felt tight and wheezy.

Going down from Kakani was easier than the climb up from

the valley. The incline was gentler, the stony road not as loose. They pushed on, stopping only to fill their flasks from a spring. By mid-morning, Hugh could see that Ellie was flagging, so they found a patch of grass next to a thicket and tore open a stack of roti wrapped in a cloth. Cooked before first light on the lodge's wood stove, the flatbreads were softened by a coating of ghee. They would have been delicious at any time, but when they were so ravenous after four hours of marching, the bread was sublime, and the spring water tasted sweet.

Ellie lay back. This place, just off the path, was peaceful and the sun was warm on her face. A gentle breeze rustled the trees. She closed her eyes and listened to birdsong and the drone of insects. Hugh sat beside her, finishing the last roti.

'Why did you come with me?' she asked, opening one eye and squinting at him. 'Everyone else thinks I'm crazy.'

'Maybe I'm crazy too.'

'I'm being serious, Hugh.'

He looked down at her and thought for a while. 'I think all of us – everyone who came that day over the hills from Sisaghari – are here because we're looking for something.'

'I came to look for the coral-red mountains,' she said. 'And I've ended up searching for my son.'

'Coral-red mountains?'

'I heard about them from a Tibetan lama. I thought they might be here.'

He gazed over the green of the valley, and up into the darker hues of the forested hillsides on the other side of the river. 'They aren't here,' he said. 'They're over the crest of the Himalayas, on the Tibetan plain, in the high deserts.'

'You've seen them?' She sat up quickly.

'Once.'

'Were they beautiful?'

'Yes, but don't go thinking you'll find something mystical there. That idea is peddled by loony spiritualists who keep popping up all over Europe and America. They only get away with claiming things like that because no one is likely to go there and prove them wrong.'

Ellie was disappointed to hear him talk that way. She'd thought he loved the mountains and their secrets as much as she did.

'And why did you come to Nepal, Hugh?' she asked.

'To catalogue the monuments of the valley,' he said.

'But why?'

'Because . . .' He considered for a moment, trying to artic-ulate something he hadn't actually acknowledged himself. 'Because I need to understand this place and its history.'

'Why?'

'So I can possess some tiny part of it,' he said hesitantly.

'Then you do love the mountains,' she said.

'Of course I love them; I grew up among them.'

They got to their feet, and Ellie winced. Her heel felt raw.

'Come on,' she said, seeing him hesitate.

'You can bathe your feet in the river,' he said, sprinting after her. She was moving fast, with a new burst of energy.

She had to get to Tom. She would run if she had to. Her heel could be rubbed to the bone, but she was going to find him.

The sun had already passed the midway point in a cloudless sky when Ellie took off her boots and walked over the stony riverbed and into the shallow water of the Tadi Khola.

The temperature of the crystal-clear river made her jump back in shock. It was icy, only a degree or two above freezing. She inched in, and forgot about her blisters as the meltwater from the high glaciers rushed over her feet and throbbing ankles. She wanted to shriek in pain, and only Hugh's finger pressed against his mouth silenced her. She hobbled back on to the bank, the sun-warmed stones returning feeling into the numbed soles of her feet.

'Wait,' he said as she reached for her socks and boots. 'Don't put them back on yet. We have to cross the river here.'

They waded across, the water sometimes at calf height, at other times reaching their knees. Hugh gasped, not yet inured to the cold, and covered the last few yards in a couple of strides.

Ellie dried her feet with the loose end of her pagri, reasoning that the hat would dry quickly. Hugh pulled a bottle of iodine and a bandage from his pack, and, ignoring her protests, dabbed her blisters with iodine then began to wind the bandage expertly round her foot, adding some lint to act as cushioning over her heel. He made her eat some tinned corned beef, which tasted divine, and some chewy dried rice he conjured from a little cloth bag.

'Will we make it?' she asked, resuming the march.

'Yes.'

'Today?'

He glanced at the sun beginning to move behind the mountains. One side of the valley was already in shadow.

'If not tonight, then tomorrow.'

She accelerated, forgetting about being an Afghan trader. She paid no attention to the farmers in the fields, to the children who ran from a tiny hamlet to greet them, to the pedlar selling metal goods, his pans, plates and bowls stacked high in a wicker basket that was held together by a net. She didn't register the Trisuli River rushing beside them, or the orchards lining its banks. This valley lay at a lower altitude than Kathmandu. Its winters were warmer and its summers almost tropical, so a wide variety of fruits could be grown here for the delight of rich people in the cities.

The shadow of the mountains spread over the bottom of the valley, and up its far side. Soon the sun was gone, and dusk began to fall.

'We'll have to stop,' Hugh said.

'We're almost there.'

'Nuwakot is a two-hour climb from here, but we mustn't jeopardise the plan by appearing out of the night like a couple of crazed foreigners. We'll stay in the village up ahead and then start at dawn. Agreed?'

'Okay,' she said, reluctantly.

When he left her to look for lodgings, she wondered whether she could make the climb alone. Tom was so close, she felt she could almost reach out and touch him. Hugh was taking a long time, and there was just enough light to see, so she began to walk up the path. She knew he would be angry, but he would understand. He always understood.

She walked for twenty minutes and the dusk turned to night.

'Where the hell are you going?' Hugh said, making her jump in fright. He put his hand on her shoulder and spun her round. 'You can't walk through a forest at night.'

'I need to find Tom now,' she said, shocked at the anger in his voice. She flung his arm aside and stomped off up the path. A minute later, clouds covered the moon and the path disappeared.

She was in darkness, and for the first time she heard the sounds of the forest. Hugh wasn't with her; there was no familiar voice, just the chatter and shrieks of animals in the undergrowth and between the trees. She walked faster, then stumbled, her boot catching on her loose Afghan trousers. It was dark, too dark, and she wished she hadn't stormed off. She wished Hugh was with her. The path forked and she couldn't see which way to go.

'Come back,' Hugh said softly. He'd been behind her all the way. He took her arm, and they walked slowly down into the valley.

Tomorrow I'll find him, Ellie told herself, and she rooted around in her rucksack and drew out Tom's lamb. Its one eye glittered in the firelight from the lodge's stove. She lay down on another bamboo mat, and the room grew dark, but by then she wasn't awake. She slept with the toy in her hand and Hugh's breath, gentle and soft, in her ear.

'You speak good Gorkhali for a Kabuli,' the lodge keeper said when Hugh woke at first light. 'Does the lad speak it as well as you do?' He beamed at Hugh and watched him pack his canvas bag and roll a few items tightly in a blanket.

'He doesn't talk much in any language,' Hugh said.

Ellie was still asleep on the matting, a shawl pulled over her head.

'It's strange to have people like you here,' the man said. 'Kabulis don't come this way. We had spice traders last year, and a few selling dried fruits, but there have been no money-lenders on the Kodari road for a long time.'

'We're looking for business in Tibet,' Hugh said, trying to

stay calm and dampen a rising sense of panic. The man was asking too many questions, and he was coming far too close. He's guessed, Hugh thought, and cursed silently.

'You won't find much trade there either,' the lodge keeper said. His smile had altered slightly, and looked more like a sneer.

A cockerel crowed and Ellie shot up, disorientated for a second. Hugh was glad it was still dark in the narrow, damp room, because the shawl was framing her face in a very unmanly way. She looked truly beautiful, and he wondered why he hadn't noticed it before.

'Get up slowly,' he said to her in a bright voice. 'Don't look alarmed. Act like everything is fine. This lodge keeper is getting suspicious. He won't understand anything I'm saying but he'll pick up on any strange body language, so act relaxed. And for God's sake, try to make yourself look ugly, because at the moment you look like the prettiest Afghan man I've ever seen.'

Hugh put Ellie's few things into her rucksack. He stuffed Tom's lamb on top and hoped the man hadn't spotted it. He had to get her out of there as quickly as possible. Even if their speedy departure rang alarm bells in the lodge keeper's mind, it wouldn't be as bad as him getting a good look at Ellie's beardless chin.

Ellie did up her boots. Hugh saw her tying the laces and wondered if the man had noticed her long, fine fingers and soft, pale skin. She stood, hitched up her trousers, and pulled the shawl well down over her head so she could hardly see where she was going. Hugh hoisted all their bags on to his shoulders.

'You won't stay to eat?' the lodge keeper asked. 'My daughter-in-law is making parathas.'

'No time,' Hugh said, guiding Ellie to the door. 'We have a lot of ground to cover.'

They began to walk, slowly at first because they didn't want to look as if they were fleeing danger. Then they accelerated, needing to put as much distance between themselves and the lodge as possible. Hugh glanced back and his heart sank: the man was watching them from the doorway.

'That was a close shave,' Ellie said.

'It's not over yet. We'd better make the climb quickly, because I think we're going to have company.'

The morning was misty, the air dense with moisture. It clung to everything. Ellie's face felt wet, and her shawl was covered in fine droplets of water.

'We won't take the main route,' Hugh said when they came to a junction. To the right, the trail to Nuwakot branched off the Kodari road.

'Won't that be slower?'

'Yes, but we'll have more chance of getting there. We need to be able to take cover if we're followed.'

They began to climb through forest, along trails used by farmers. The main road wound its way up the mountains, but these minor paths were steeper and more direct. Sometimes they petered out into tangles of vegetation; other times they led over rocky ravines and slippery red earth.

Ellie scrambled upwards, drawn by the thought of Tom at the top of the mountain, and pushed on by her fear of the men who might be gathering behind them.

A voice shouted from somewhere downhill. It sounded urgent.

Hugh stopped.

'What did he say?' Ellie asked.

'I couldn't tell.'

'Is he close?'

'I don't think so.'

They continued in silence, and then two voices hollered through the trees.

'They're closer,' Ellie said.

The forest thinned out into a patch of scrub. A little rocky spur thrust out over the trees, and Ellie and Hugh peered down. A hundred feet below them, the main road appeared out of the mist and snaked round a corner. Six men marched along it, and then disappeared, like the road, behind a dense wall of trees.

'Cops?' Ellie asked.

'Army.'

She turned and began to run over the grass, around the scrub, heading for the main road. Please, please, she thought, don't let me fail just before I get there. I have to make it. I have to get to Nuwakot.

She joined the road, hoping it would be quicker. Her heart hammered against her ribs and she gasped for breath. She slowed as a tall building appeared out of the mist. It was six or seven storeys high, its carved black windows the same as some of those in the cities of the Kathmandu Valley. She was almost there.

She gained a new wind and ran faster, leaving Hugh far behind. Her shawl dropped on to the road and she grabbed her loose trousers to stop them falling. On and on she flew, her hair loose, her clothes saturated to the waist because she had brushed against the grasses and bushes lining the road.

At the top of the mountain she skidded to a halt. Nuwakot lay before her. It was a surprisingly small place, with splendid red-brick buildings, remnants of a glorious past when it had been the winter residence of rich Newars and, later, the Gorkha kings. Now, though, it possessed only a few dozen three-storey buildings, and a single main street flanked by tatty houses and shops. Ellie walked along the street, composing herself a little, and putting her head round every open door. She needed Hugh with her to ask where she could find the boy with golden hair. Impatiently she hurried back to the end of the town and looked down the path. Hugh was dragging himself up slowly, looking grey, and for a moment Ellie thought he was having a heart attack. He forced a smile, and wheezed, 'Asthma.'

Satisfied that he would live, Ellie rushed back into the main street. Several people had come out of their houses to look at the dirty, mad white woman in men's clothes. Ellie saw Hugh speak to a couple of men. He was taking his time, still struggling to breathe, his hand on his chest. Then from the corner of her eye she spotted children moving in the dark interior of a run-down building. Forgetting the outrage she'd caused when she'd blundered into the house in Kathmandu, Ellie plunged into the room. Her eyes took a few moments to adjust. The children stared open-mouthed at her, and then one began to cry. Two others joined the chorus.

A woman poked Ellie with a stick and shouted, and Ellie took a step back, shocked that she could have frightened the children so much. Tom wasn't there, and she tried to retreat. The woman pushed her back against the wall with her stick. I must seem like a lunatic or an evil spirit, Ellie thought, and she smiled at the woman, though later she wondered if it had looked more like a lopsided leer. She glanced though the door and out into the street. Soft sunlight was dispersing the mist. She saw several men, a woman, and Hugh, who no longer had his hand on his chest. Behind him, half hidden by his legs, a small child with fair hair bent down to pick something up from the ground.

'Tom!' she shouted, and lunged forward, knocking aside the woman's stick. She charged into the street, pushed Hugh out of the way, and fell at the boy's feet, wrapping her arms around him and sobbing, flooded with relief. He was alive, warm and familiar in her embrace. She kissed him and pushed the blond hair from his face, and was instantly emptied of joy. She was looking into the eyes of a child she had never seen before. His skin was so white it was almost translucent, his eyelashes and eyebrows so fair they were nearly invisible, and his hair wasn't golden, it was white. Only the sun shining on it gave it a hint of colour. The boy was an albino Nepali child. A woman prised him out of Ellie's arms and gave her an outraged look.

Ellie stood up. She was too shocked to cry. She looked uncomprehendingly at Hugh and saw his mouth moving, although she couldn't hear the words. She saw his pained expression. She saw the men marching towards them, and she was rooted to the spot. The little boy was being led away. She gazed at him, at the miserable street, at the tilting temple and the top of the magnificent old palace, damaged in the earthquake. But it was as if she was looking through someone else's eyes.

She felt a jab in her back.

'Ellie. Ellie,' Hugh said, his face inches from hers. 'Ellie,' he said again. This time the blurriness in her head cleared a little, and she registered his voice.

'What's happening?' she asked.

They were surrounded by men in uniform, and by the townspeople, who were observing the scene with a mixture of puzzlement and anxiety.

Hugh squeezed her hand. 'We're under arrest.'

5

Kathmandu to Ranchi, February 1934

ELLIE AND HUGH weren't marched back to Kathmandu in chains. The pace of the journey, though, was a punishment in itself. From his door, the lodge keeper watched in satisfaction as the spies were hustled away. When they passed through villages, everyone paused in surprise. Even the goats stopped eating and looked at the disgraced foreigners. Ellie would have felt embarrassed if she hadn't been so utterly drained. She'd been so sure Tom was in Nuwakot, so sure he was still alive, and now, scrambling back up to Kakani with six soldiers of the Nepali Army ordering her to move faster, she didn't know what she thought. She hardly had time to breathe. Hugh had told them she was an English lady, like a princess, and that she should be treated with respect and carried in a doli. They looked at her filthy clothes and tangled hair, and laughed.

It took precisely two hours for them to be released from the Central Jail on the orders of the Maharaja's nephew. They were escorted, on foot, to the palace by an armed guard, headed by a General Rana, who was a favourite grandson of the Maharaja and no more than fifteen years old. His moustache was a line of fine down on his upper lip, and medals were plastered across his narrow chest.

'You will have to make arrangements to leave Nepal,' he said to Hugh at the gates of the palace.

Hugh nodded. He turned and began to walk back to the main road.

'Where are you going?' the general asked.

'To Lazimpat.'

The general looked confused.

'That's where I'm staying,' Hugh said.

The general ordered two of his men to escort Hugh, while he himself accompanied Ellie into the palace.

The building was clad in such a dense web of bamboo scaffolding that it was hard to find a way in. The general tried the main doors; they were jammed.

'Where are the servants?' he asked, worry making tiny beads of sweat form on his moustache.

Ellie put her shoulder against the door and heaved it open. The stench of something rotten made them pause before they entered. The rose-water fountain in the grand entrance hall was working again, the statues were all upright, every piece of crystal and broken mirror had been swept from the floor, and yet the interior of the palace looked more warped and grotesque than the outside. Ellie approached the fountain, then stepped back hurriedly. The water was stagnant, like the smell of flowers left too long in a slime-filled vase.

'I need some air,' she said, retreating though the web of scaffolding into bright sunshine.

The general spoke to an old gardener who was repairing

large scorch marks on the lawn. The man pointed to a summer house among the trees and ornamental bushes.

'I must give you to your husband,' the general said.

'Because I can't be trusted if I'm not under his care?'

'This is my order, lady.'

Francis was in the summer house, convalescing on a wicker chair, his leg resting on a stool. His eyes were closed and he was smiling. Shushila was sitting by his side, gently running her fingers through his hair. Ellie watched them, unobserved, through the window, and felt shock, but surprisingly little pain. It was, in fact, quite easy to watch this tender scene because she had spent four years being stripped of the idea of love. I'm such a sap, she thought. Why didn't I see this? She paused. Perhaps I did see it, she told herself. Perhaps I chose not to acknowledge it because the consequences would be too difficult to deal with.

The young general coughed, uncertain what to do. 'That is your husband, lady?' he said.

She smiled ruefully at the boy. He saluted and walked back down the drive to rejoin his men, the end of his long cere- monial sword dragging on the ground.

Francis opened his eyes and stared at Ellie in her Afghan clothes. For a few seconds he didn't recognise her.

'Is that you, Ellie? ' he exclaimed. 'What the hell are you doing in that ludicrous garb?'

Shushila continued stroking his hair.

Francis was too annoyed with Ellie to be uncomfortable about being caught in this compromising situation. He sat up straighter, and winced as he moved his leg.

'I've heard all about your escapade. For God's sake, we are guests in this country, and you've flouted all the rules.'

Ellie didn't get a chance to say a word. Francis was in full flow, hardly pausing for breath.

'The Maharaja's nephew had to pull plenty of strings. It's a good job I've friends in high places here, otherwise you could be spending years in prison.'

Ellie glanced at Shushila and did a double-take. She was wearing trousers, and they seemed very familiar.

'Are those my pants?' she asked.

Shushila shrugged. 'Yours are longer.' What she meant was that she'd had Ellie's trousers turned up by a tailor so they would fit her perfectly.

Francis continued his tirade. 'It's the most ridiculous thing I've ever heard,' he said. 'You've been halfway across the country hunting a pitiful albino boy who was orphaned in the earthquake and taken in by his aunt.'

'It could have been Tom.'

'It couldn't have been Tom, because Tom's dead. You've got to accept it. It's not what you want to hear, but he has gone.'

He shoved Shushila's hand away from his temple. 'I know what grief can do,' he said, tensing every muscle in his face. 'My mother spent ten years grieving for my brothers. She thought more about them when they were dead than she did about me, even though I was the only one still alive.'

He looked as if he was about to cry, and Ellie didn't know whether it was from rage or sadness.

'You went off on your jaunt and left Lizzie with Nanny Barker in some wretched native house that isn't much better than a shack. The picture Major Thapa paints of the place is horrifying,' he said, clearly angry rather than sad. 'You left her with Douglas's by-blow, or whoever she is. You are not fit to be a mother.'

Ellie listened to his voice, loaded with entitlement and authority. He was treating her like a spoilt child rather than a mother intent on finding her son, and she was sick of hearing him pontificate as if he had some God-given power and knowledge. Damn it, she thought, who is he to judge anyone else? He's been having an affair with Shushila right under my nose. How disrespectful is that? Everyone must have known. He's turned me into a laughing stock. And he's spent the last week convalescing because, as usual, he got so drunk he didn't know what he was doing, and this time he was attacked by an animal. The absurdity and unfairness of it made her fume.

'Don't expect me to apologise, Francis,' she said, putting her shoulders back and lifting her chin. 'I'd do the same thing again if I had the chance.' There was a new tone to her voice, and she stood in a different way, as if she was no longer embarrassed by being so tall.

Shushila looked in surprise at the memsahib. She'd never seen her like this. Ellie had the makings of a formidable opponent even in those filthy rags. Shushila considered for a moment, and then slid out of the summer house unobserved. Dealing with this new woman demanded a different strategy, and she needed time to plan.

'I'm going to Calcutta,' Ellie declared. 'I'm going to hire every private detective I can, and I'm going to bring a search party here.'

Francis laughed. 'You think the government is going to allow a posse of foreigners to traipse through the country? You've behaved like an ass and got us into a bloody awful mess. It was your wanderings that got Tom killed in the first place, and you've just been incarcerated in a native prison. What the hell will you do next?'

She paused, and the silence seemed to last for minutes.

'I'm going to divorce you,' she said.

His eyes popped. 'What?' he said, so quietly it was almost a whisper. Despite all his anger, and his lack of interest in the tall, outrageously dressed woman before him, he was genuinely surprised. 'Why?' he asked.

'Because you don't love me. Because you married me for my money. Because you have a mistress you keep in the same house as me.'

'Shushila?' he exclaimed. 'But Ellie, she means nothing to me.' He lifted his hands in a 'so what' gesture. 'Look,' he said, 'she's "below stairs". She doesn't count. Most of the time I've been stinking drunk and she throws herself at me. And you've been distant, and no fun. You're just so serious and, well, often you're terribly boring. I mean, what's a fellow to do?'

Ellie's face didn't soften, and he began to worry.

'I'll make it up to you.'

'Like hell you will.'

'I'll send her away.'

'I don't care, Francis. Do what you want.'

Oh God, he thought, why can't she be like other wives? Why can't she look the other way?

'When I get to Calcutta, I'll start the legal process,' she said. 'I guess the real work, though, will have to wait until I get to London.'

'Don't be hasty, darling. You must give this some thought.'

'I won't change my mind.'

'Don't follow the example of that ridiculous friend of yours, having a crack at every young buck she meets, and getting married and divorced with no mind to what people think.'

'Momo isn't ridiculous; she's just unlucky with men. And I don't intend to have a string of marriages and divorces. I am having one of each; that's enough.'

He had never seen her look so resolute. It wasn't a good sign, he thought. What if she really did it? How much was he likely to get as a settlement? Not enough to keep up the great house and become a world-renowned sportsman.

'We need to stay together for Lizzie's sake,' he said.

She shook her head.

Hell, he thought, I can't appeal to her motherly instincts. I'll have to play hard.

'You can't divorce me,' he said. 'You haven't any proof. Who is going to corroborate your story? And if you had any idea about divorce law, you would know that the person petitioning for divorce has to be innocent. That means they mustn't be carrying on themselves, which you clearly are.'

'I am not,' she said.

'You've taken up with that Douglas fellow, though what you see in him, I can't imagine. He's a pretty low sort really. Mind you, I don't suppose you could do much better than the junior ranks of the Indian Army.'

'You weren't in any army,' she said.

He blanched; she knew his weak spots. 'That's not fair. You know Mother forbade it.'

Francis saw she was momentarily off balance, surprised by her own malice, and he seized the opportunity to steer the argument away from talk of divorce. 'Why don't you go and find me a whisky?' he said, forcing a smile. 'Some wog witch doctor has been plying me with infernal local medicines, when all I need is a stiff drink.'

'I haven't taken up with Hugh Douglas,' she said, ignoring his request. He could ask Shushila to get him a drink if he was so desperate for one. 'He is a friend; the only person who's stood by me through all this. But he isn't my lover.' An image of him lying next to her in the lodge at Kakani, and the memory of her hand in his, came to mind, and she thought for a moment that she liked Hugh Douglas far more than if he had been just her lover.

'Everyone knows you've been spending nights with him. You have no evidence of my adultery, but there will be plenty of people prepared to swear to your infidelity.'

She was unmoved. 'I'm taking Lizzie with me,' she announced.

'No court is going to give you custody of a child,' he said. 'You abandoned her in a veritable slum, and you are certifiably mad. It's well documented, isn't it? You've seen every shrink in California, and it didn't help. And you spend half your time stuffed to the eyeballs with Veronal.'

'I've told you I don't take it any more.'

'But you will. When the attacks get bad, you'll reach for your bottle of pills.'

It was a pity, he thought, that he hadn't got her to Ranchi before this divorce drama began. It was sod's law. Everything had been so neatly planned. The Maharaja's nephew had had his doctor write to the medical superintendent of the hospital and recommend Ellie's admission; Francis had telegrammed to confirm she would soon be on her way; and Davies was surprisingly enthusiastic about taking her to India.

'You're not going to keep telling me I'm mad,' she said. 'You've spent our entire marriage undermining me. But I tell you, I'm not crazy. I've never felt saner.'

She turned on the mud-encrusted heel of her boot, and walked away.

'You can't just up and leave,' he called after her.

'Watch me,' she said.

'But we've been happy, haven't we?' he shouted.

When she didn't reply or even pause, he struggled up and hobbled back to the palace.

'Change of plan, Davies,' he said as his gunman woke from a nap on a gold satin sofa in the grand reception room. 'You're taking her right now.'

Davies and four Nepali guards had to run to catch up with Ellie. They reached her when she was within sight of Hugh's house.

'Not so fast,' Davies said, blocking her path.

'Get out of the way,' she said. She was weary and wanted to change her clothes and take a bath.

'You're coming with us,' Davies said, and placed a firm hand on her shoulder.

'I'm not going back to the palace.'

'That's right, you're not.'

Ellie tried to move round him, but Davies sidestepped and she bumped against him.

Davies smiled so she could see yellow teeth between his wide, thin lips.

'Get your hands off me,' she said, her anger rising.

'Take it easy. Don't lose your rag. This is for your own good.'

Davies turned her in the opposite direction. Two women who were doing puja at a little shrine stopped to watch the spectacle, and a group of children gawped.

'We can do this the easy way or the hard way,' he said as he walked behind her down the road to Kathmandu. He poked her in the back to make her hurry.

'Are you taking me to jail?'

He laughed. 'You're going to India.'

'No!' she shouted, and stopped so abruptly Davies slammed into her. 'I'm not leaving Kathmandu without Tom.'

'Your husband will look for the boy, and you're going somewhere you can be dealt with. They're expecting us.'

'Who is?'

'The people we're meeting in Raxaul.'

Ellie remembered the dusty Indian town on the other side of the border with Nepal.

'Who's meeting us in Raxaul?'

'The people from Ranchi.'

'Ranchi?'

Davies guffawed, tickled perhaps by the thought of her in that place.

'The *pagalkhana*. The madhouse, Lady Northwood.'

'No way,' she said, and tried to bolt.

He grabbed at her, missed, and then caught her arm.

'You're not taking me anywhere.' She shook her arm, trying to loosen his grip, and when he just laughed, she opened her mouth and sank her teeth into the flesh of his forearm.

He shouted, and lashed out with his free hand, hitting the side of her head.

'You're a fucking bitch,' he seethed. He seized both of her

hands and yanked them behind her back. 'Now walk,' he ordered.

'No. No,' she said, wriggling and stumbling.

The crowds stopped to look at the sad sight of the mad white woman dressed in filthy men's clothes being marched in disgrace towards the car that would take her to Thankot and the start of her journey to the *pagalkhana*.

The road to India was busy. Porters carried giant loads of building materials, and merchants brought food they knew they could sell at high prices in the cities. This time there was no doli and no bearers to carry Ellie. She walked in her old boots and Afghan clothes, Davies close behind her, and with two guards in front and another two taking up the rear. She was alert, looking for a chance to escape; to cut back through the Chitlong Valley, over the Chandragiri Pass and back to Lizzie in Kathmandu. Escape, though, was impossible. Davies watched her every second. He even followed her into the forest and waited close enough to hear the splash of her urine on the dried leaves, and higher in the mountains, on the thick blanket of pine needles. He saw, or heard, every move she made.

In Sisaghari, the government guest house was a ruin. Less than two weeks before, Ellie had eaten dinner on its veranda and slept fitfully in a smoky bedroom. Now, its first storey had concertinaed on to the ground floor, two of the servants had been killed and the chowkidar was missing. Several other buildings had been damaged, and there was a shortage of accommodation in the bazaar. Davies said they were lucky to find a lodge, and although there was only one room left, he seemed pleased.

'Probably for the best,' he said. 'We can share the room. I need to keep an eye on you, don't I?'

He left her with two armed guards while he went to the bazaar. When he came back, he was drunk and reeking of local liquor, his face crimson. He booted the guards out and pointed out of the window to the veranda, where he told them to remain on watch.

'Fucking idiots,' he muttered when at last they understood.

'Looks like you'll have to share a bed with me, Lady Northwood,' he said, and though she didn't look at him, she could hear the relish in his voice. 'I've never slept with an aristocrat before.'

'I'll stay on the floor,' Ellie said, and lay down on the bare wood.

'Too good to share a bed with me?' he laughed. He hauled her to her feet and pushed her on to the bed.

She curled up on the far side, semi-paralysed by fear. She pressed herself against the wall, her hands feeling the roughness of the timber. Davies settled on the bed with a sigh, and the frame creaked as he rolled over. She could feel the warmth of his body against hers, feel every point at which his body touched hers, and she shrank further away, willing herself to be smaller so she'd take up less room and create a space between them.

Davies was enjoying himself, savouring her fear. It entertained him because she had nothing to be frightened of except what was going on in her head. He pressed his groin against her, taunting her, and chuckled when he heard her gasp.

'What kind of man are you?' she whispered, her voice trembling, her body paralysed with terror 'What kind of man forces himself on a woman?'

'Don't make me laugh, you stupid cow,' he said, rolling over on to his back. 'I'd never touch you.'

Ellie heard him opening a pack of cigarettes and lighting one. He sucked on it and she saw the smoke rings he blew across her. Slowly, she turned over.

'I wouldn't waste myself on you,' he said. 'I mean, what are you? Forty? Forty-five?' His eyes raked over her. 'Though to be honest, you look more like fifty-five these days.' He pulled a hip flask out of the pocket of his jacket and took a slug. 'Want some?' he said, offering it to her. 'It tastes like shit, but it's got a kick. You'd like it. It's better than those funny pills you keep taking.'

Ellie shook her head. Looking down at herself, she saw the top of her tunic gaping, revealing her small breasts in a grubby white bra. She clutched at the material.

Davies smiled, and belched loudly, releasing a blast of hot, alcohol-saturated breath. 'Bet you'd like me to grab a handful of those, wouldn't you?' he said.

Ellie pursed her lips, and turned away to look at the wall.

'You think I'm scum. You reckon I'm not a proper white feller because I'm not a toff like your bleeding husband. But I know your old man pays you no attention because he's always at it with the Indian tart, and I've seen you looking at me. Deep down, I know you want a real man, but you just can't bring yourself to ask me for it. Well, Lady Northwood, I'm pleased to say you're not in luck today.'

He leaned over her and spoke in her ear, his mouth wet with saliva. 'You know I like them young, don't you, so it's no good offering me those saggy tits. And I don't like my girls hairy either, you know what I'm saying? Women like you look more like men the older you get, and it bloody disgusts me. I wouldn't fuck you if you begged me.'

Ellie lay still, her breathing slow but shallow. A memory of a little girl with a heart-shaped face came into her mind, and the shock made her flip over.

'You bastard,' she said, her face inches from his. 'That poor little girl.'

Davies pulled back from her and widened his eyes in surprise. 'I thought you was on to me,' he said, then paused. 'Mind you, you're slow on the uptake. You never noticed your husband's been shagging the ayah for months.'

'How can you do it? The girl I saw was a child. I saw her coming out of the house where you said you were resting.'

'It's a brothel, not a house.'

'She was so young.'

'Don't get fucking righteous with me. It's different here. I'm doing them a favour; they're poor and I've got money. They need some help and I give it to them. And the children aren't like the ones at home. They're more natural here. It's a way of life to them, and they start early. There's no harm done.'

'You can't get away with it.'

'Who's going to stop me? Not the madam who takes my money, that's for sure.'

'I'm going to stop you.'

'I thought you'd try. That's why I'm helping your husband get you to Ranchi.'

'I'll tell everyone.'

'No one will believe a bloody crackpot,' he laughed. 'And I know another way to keep you quiet.' He pulled her towards him and held her so tightly she could barely breathe. 'You wouldn't be able to tell anyone if I smashed your head in. You could have a nasty accident on the way down to Bhimphedi. Remember how steep the climb was when we came up to Sisaghari? Well, tomorrow we're going down that same path.'

Ellie struggled as he squeezed the air out of her.

'And there's another reason you'll keep quiet. As soon as we're in Raxaul and I've handed you over to the people from the madhouse, I'm going back to Kathmandu. I'm going back to your husband, and your lovely little daughter. And if I hear any accusations . . . if any reports come from Ranchi . . .'

She stilled immediately and his grip on her loosened. She gasped, filling her lungs. 'Don't you touch her,' she rasped. 'I mean it, don't do anything to her.' Her voice was breaking. 'Don't do any of those disgusting things.'

He frowned. 'Do you think I'm a bloody animal?'

'You're worse than an animal.'

He laughed and shrugged his shoulders. 'She is a pretty little thing,' he said.

They crossed the Terai in a cart and then in a truck, because the railway to Amlekhganj had been damaged in the earthquake. The tracks had been wrenched apart when sand and water spewed from geysers that opened like blowholes in the earth. The road they took instead was long and rutted, but Ellie was glad to sit as they jolted slowly through the thick scrub and jungle dividing Nepal from India. She had walked up and down the foothills of the Himalayas for two days, and her legs felt as if they were no longer hers, and that if she stood, they'd be unable to bear her weight.

Two representatives from the psychiatric hospital were waiting for them in the ruins of Raxaul, very near to the railway station. Mr Atkins, a tall young man who wore glasses right at the end of his nose, stood with Sister Drayton, who was middle-aged and had dry, red-rimmed eyes and hair that was parted in the middle and pulled back very severely into a tight little knot at the nape of her neck.

'I'm afraid Lord Northwood can't be here to see her ladyship into your care,' Davies said. 'He's injured.'

'In the earthquake?' Sister Drayton asked.

'Yes,' Davies lied.

Ellie remained surrounded by the Nepali guards as Davies talked with Mr Atkins. Sister Drayton gave her a chilly smile. 'Is she a dirty patient?' she asked Davies.

Ellie was still in her Afghan clothes and had no luggage.

Davies sighed. 'She hasn't had a bath for a week and she won't give up those rags.'

'I mean, does she mess herself?'

Davies thought for a moment. 'Only when she's having a bad day. I've a letter here from the personal doctor to the Maharaja's nephew that will explain everything: her medical history, that sort of thing. You must have received Lord Northwood's telegram, because you wouldn't be here if you hadn't.'

'It's been a terrible journey,' Mr Atkins said, wiping the sweat from his brow with a greasy yellow handkerchief. 'There's not a foot of railway line in Bihar that hasn't been affected by the earthquake. We had to take a car for the last seventy miles, and it's been hell.'

'I'd better let you get off then, seeing as you have another long journey to make.'

'Come along, dear,' Sister Drayton said, while Mr Atkins and Davies guided Ellie to the car.

'Goodbye, Lady Northwood,' Davies called through the open window as the car began to pull slowly away from the station. 'I'm on my way back to Kathmandu right now, and I'll take special care of your girl. Trust me.'

Ellie sank into the back seat, sandwiched between Mr Atkins and Sister Drayton. Davies was lost in a cloud of dust kicked up by the wheels of the car.

'Thank God. Thank God,' she sighed. 'You can't believe how good it is to get away from him. He's a monster.'

'You'll be quite safe at Ranchi. It's a hill station and the climate is excellent,' Mr Atkins said.

'But I don't want to go to Ranchi, and I'm not crazy. My husband says I'm mad because the ayah is his mistress and he wants my money, and he doesn't believe my son is still alive, but an old woman told me she'd seen him being pulled from under a collapsed building and now he's with a Tibetan man in a red coat. I have to get back to Kathmandu quickly. I have to find him, and there are other things going on, things I can't explain because Davies will do something terrible if I do, and I must go back to stop it, and if I don't, Tom will be lost forever and he'll be so frightened, and so will the little girl with the face that's like a heart. She's very tiny, and her eyes are blank, like they're dead.'

'Lady Northwood,' Sister Drayton said slowly and deliberately, as if she were talking to a dim-witted child. 'Do you need the bathroom?'

'Now you won't want to be keeping these old rags will you, Lady Northwood?' Nurse MacLennan said without waiting for Ellie to reply. She spoke in a Scottish bur and Ellie found it hard to understand her. She almost wished she was back in the car with Sister Drayton and Mr Atkins. Nurse MacLennan poked the pile of clothes with a stick and Ellie looked at the engrained dirt on the bra straps and felt a twinge of shame.

'They'd best be burned because I'll no be surprised if they're full of lice. Sister Drayton says you're very fond of this particular costume, but I know we can find you something much nicer after you've had your bath.'

Nurse MacLennan ushered her under a shower. 'Sister Drayton also says you're not always good about going to the WC, but I'm sure we'll have no trouble like that today.'

Watched by two attendants, Ellie washed dust from her sticky skin, and her hair turned from a dull brown to gold.

'When can I see the doctor?' she asked when the water was turned off with a creak of a rusty tap.

'After your treatment,' Nurse MacLennan said.

The two Indian attendants accompanied them down a corridor and into a room where steam rose from a large tub.

'But I've only just had a shower,' Ellie said when the attendants took off her robe.

'Hydrotherapy calms excited nerves,' Nurse MacLennan said. 'Most of our patients have water therapy when they first arrive and they find it very soothing indeed.'

Ellie looked at the canvas hammock strung inside the bath, and turned to leave. The attendant snapped the door shut and turned the key.

'In you get,' Nurse MacLennan said.

The water was warm, and the attendant added more so it

lapped over Ellie's shoulders. The women lowered a heavy canvas sheet over the tub, adjusting it so her head poked out of a hole in the fabric.

'It's time to relax,' Nurse MacLennan said.

The shutters were closed over the windows, and Ellie could just make out the two Indian attendants observing her from chairs placed against the wall. Nurse MacLennan had gone, and the only sounds she could hear were distant laughter that faded to weeping, and the drip, drip of water on the stone floor from pipes feeding the bath.

She didn't know what time it was when she'd been put in the tub. It must have been around midday, because the sun was shining in a sharp and very fine beam of white light through a crack in the shutters. The shaft of sunlight sparkled, turned yellow and then orange, and then was gone. Soon the only source of light was a pale pink strip under the door.

The attendants were replaced by other equally quiet women who refused to speak to her, or even to each other. Ellie's treatment consisted of water, silence and the dark.

'I've been in here hours,' she said when Nurse MacLennan did her rounds.

Nurse MacLennan checked her watch. 'We'll keep you in a little longer. You'll sleep wonderfully well tonight.'

Ellie had had enough. She kicked her legs and thrashed her arms, and the water sloshed around in the bath, slapping against the underside of the canvas sheet. 'I have to get out.'

Nurse MacLennan slipped out of the room.

The hammock held Ellie tight. I'm trapped, she realised. Trapped by Francis's intrigue in an asylum in the middle of India. If I wasn't crazy before I came here, she thought with growing dread, I will be very soon. It was dark, the water dripped, and the bath felt like a tomb. It squeezed her, the canvas tightening around her. She couldn't breathe, and her scream, when it came, was a whimper.

Someone was standing at the end of the bed. Ellie opened her eyes wider and saw a woman with curly red hair.

'Momo?' Ellie said.

'You've been asleep for a whole day and night,' the woman said. Ellie's spirits sank: it wasn't Momo. Her accent was British, and when Ellie looked closer, she saw she was heavy set and wore frumpy clothes.

'This is the best room,' the woman said. 'You have a lovely view over the garden and it catches the afternoon sun perfectly.'

Ellie sat up, and remembered the bath and the journey. She thought of Tom and Lizzie in Kathmandu, and the desperation to be with them was so strong it hurt her head. Her guts twisted in despair.

'Is this the asylum?' she said, confused because the room looked nice, like something you would find in a guest house. There were no straps and restraints, and the doors didn't have bars but opened out on to a veranda.

'It's the Ranchi European Mental Hospital.'

'I shouldn't be here.'

'Neither should I. My husband is a district commissioner and my name is Mrs Knox; Mary Knox.'

Ellie jumped off the bed and almost fell because her legs were wobbly. She tottered out on to the veranda, which ran around a courtyard and a little garden full of flowers.

'Some patients here are genuinely insane,' Mary said, following her outside. She lowered her voice to a whisper. 'Alice, the woman in the next room, is a serious case,' she said, pointing to a closed door. 'The poor thing thinks she's being followed everywhere by Mrs Darling and her baby who were killed in the Cawnpore Massacre. They were butchered with meat cleavers and thrown down a well, and now Alice is great friends with Mrs Darling, and looks after the baby and tries to sew up its wounds in the needlework class.'

Ellie wasn't interested in talking about Alice.

'How do we get out?' she asked.

'Out?'

'How do we leave the hospital?'

'Oh, we don't. There are walls and gates.'

'You mean it's like a prison and we've got to bust out?'

'No,' Mary laughed. 'It's a bit like being at school and can be quite good fun really. And we can take a stroll in the grounds. It's actually rather pleasant. I'll show you the ropes, but first you'll have to get dressed. If you walk round in a nightdress, people might think you've gone doolally. Come to my room when you've freshened up. I'm next to Alice.'

When Ellie knocked on Mary's door twenty minutes later, there was no answer. She knocked again and pushed gently at the door. It swung open slowly. Mary was lying naked on her bed.

'Sorry,' Ellie said, grabbing the door and pulling it shut.

'How dare you enter my chamber!' Mary shouted. 'I am Nefertiti, Queen of Egypt, and I am waiting for the sun god to bless me with his seed.'

The Indian doctor looked too young to know anything. His hair was soft and fine, almost like a baby's, and when he smiled at her on the third occasion she sat in his office, he looked more nervous of Ellie than she was of him.

'What exactly do you think is wrong with me, other than that I've been incarcerated because my husband wants to get rid of me?'

'It's far too early to make a diagnosis, but I am sure your husband has done what he thinks is best for you. I'll continue your assessment over the next few days, and then our medical superintendent, Colonel Berkeley-Hill, will see you when he gets back from Delhi.'

'I've told you everything already, so you must be able to see I'm not mad.'

That wasn't entirely true. Ellie hadn't told him about Davies, but she had explained about the earthquakes and her childhood, and Francis and Nepal, and the Tibetan man who had Tom, and while she spoke, the nib of the psychiatrist's pen scratched at the paper. She jumped up and looked over his desk and spotted 'delusional disorder' scrawled across the top page. He slammed the file shut, and began to talk about grief and bereavement and the slow process of recovery.

'Would you like to tell me about your son?' he said. 'Was his name Bobby? I don't think I wrote it down.'

It's ridiculous, Ellie thought. The man said he wanted to understand her story but he wasn't listening. She glared at him and he recoiled at her rage.

'I think that will be enough for today,' he said. 'We'll continue with the water treatment every morning, and in the afternoons I'd like you to join one of our occupational therapy groups. How are you at needlework?'

'When is this Berkeley-Hill coming back from Delhi?' Ellie asked.

'In a few days.'

Damn it, she thought, as she stormed out of the room, followed by her two attendants. She had to waste more time strapped in the bath, entombed in the silence and the dark; more time with Alice and the dead baby, and Mary, the Egyptian queen, spending whole afternoons doing needlework. And the worst thing was that, in Kathmandu, Tom was missing, and Lizzie was in danger. The horror of it reeled through her head; the world was mad and turned upside down. She wondered who knew where she was. Did Hugh know? And Nanny Barker? And if they did, would anyone come to rescue her from this nightmare?

In Kathmandu, a guard had been placed at the gate of Hugh's house. The young man spent most of his time snoozing in the sun, and at night he was replaced by an elderly chowkidar who disappeared for hours on end. The Nepali police and army were engaged in rebuilding the city and there were few competent men to spare for guard duty. In the confusing aftermath of the quake, Hugh wasn't summarily expelled from Nepal, but he was given a few days' grace to gather his things before setting out on the journey back over the Chandragiri Pass.

When Ellie didn't return from the palace after a few hours, Hugh began to worry. Perhaps the young general had her under house arrest. In the evening, shortly before the curfew began, a messenger brought him a note, scribbled by Francis, saying that Ellie was feeling ill and needed to rest, and that she would come to collect Lizzie as soon as she was better. It was odd, Hugh thought, that she hadn't written herself. Perhaps she really was seriously sick.

The next day, Ellie didn't return to Lazimpat, and there was no note from the palace. Something wasn't right, Hugh was certain. And so the following morning, three days after they'd been released from the Central Jail, and roughly at the time Ellie was being sandwiched between the psychiatric nurses in the back of a car in Raxaul, Hugh walked past the crystal rose-water fountain in the crooked palace and was escorted to Lord Northwood's room, where a masseur was pummelling Francis's back while he lay on the bed.

Francis sat up and the masseur retreated into the shadows. 'I'm surprised you're here,' he said. 'You've got a bloody nerve.'

'How is she?'

'Delicate,' Francis said, knowing it was probably the truth. He did a quick calculation and reckoned Davies and Ellie must have crossed the border into India by now, but that Ellie almost certainly wasn't safely in the confines of the hospital. Once she was admitted, he knew the doctors would see she needed institutionalising. I'll have to stall Douglas, he thought. I don't want the interfering do-gooder prying into my family's affairs.

'Can I see her?' Hugh asked.

'Of course not. She's in the women's quarters. She's exhausted and mentally fragile. She needs to rest. As soon as she's strong enough, I'm sending her back home to England with Nanny Barker and Lizzie.'

'I wanted to say goodbye to her. We're leaving in a couple of days.'

'She doesn't want to see you. You've already done enough damage. You can't go round interfering in other people's lives and trying to destroy their marriages. It's bloody irresponsible.'

'There's nothing improper in our relationship. She's been completely faithful to you, I give you my word.'

'I'm not sure what your word is worth, Douglas,' Francis laughed. 'You've encouraged her in her fantasies. You've kept her hopes up and taken her on a ridiculous journey that's made her ill.'

'She was going to go to Nuwakot with or without me.'

'She wouldn't have set foot outside Kathmandu without your help.'

On this, Francis was right, and Hugh had no reply. 'I'll send Nanny Barker and Lizzie here,' he said. 'It'll do Ellie good to see the girl, though to be honest, I'm alarmed at the state of the building. It should be condemned. You can't have them staying here.'

Francis thought for a moment. It wasn't such a good idea to have Nanny and Lizzie back quite so soon; Lizzie would surely want to see her mother. 'Give it a day or two,' he said. 'She needs complete rest and I'm rather busy with the preparations.'

'Preparations?'

'For the shoot. The camp is being set up and we're going next week.'

Hugh looked at Francis in disbelief. In the aftermath of a catastrophe in which his son had been lost and his wife shattered by grief and illness, Francis was going hunting.

Hugh left the palace feeling like a fool. He had misjudged so many things. He shouldn't have taken Ellie to Nuwakot; he shouldn't have raised her hopes or placed her in danger. She didn't know this place, or anything about this part of the world except some mystical nonsense she'd heard about coral mountains.

He was the one with the knowledge of the country and its people, and he should have been more objective. But he had let emotion rule his head, and although he was right when he told Francis that Ellie had been a faithful wife, he knew that was not what he himself had hoped for. He had gone to Nuwakot to find Tom, but what he really wanted was Ellie.

Davies marched very quickly back into the Kathmandu Valley, unencumbered by Ellie and by the nagging worry that she was going to drop him in the shit. He felt happy, pumped up, and it had nothing to do with hunting. He was on a mission, and he had it all planned out. He was going to stay in the valley a little longer, and then he was going to India. He'd seen the mess the earthquake had made of Raxaul; the town looked as if it had come under heavy shelling, and he'd heard it was bad all over Bihar. It's perfect, he thought; that's just the place I'm needed.

He hauled himself up to the palace, reluctant to play the part of a servant any longer. He paused before he went inside. Something wasn't right. The building looked crooked, as if it had been built on a slant. It was slowly warping, twisting in on itself. If Northwood stays in there much longer, he thought, it'll be his bloody tomb.

'Good man,' Francis called gleefully when Davies eventually managed to force the bedroom door open. 'Job done?' he asked.

'Consignment delivered,' Davies said.

Shushila was sitting on the bed, wearing a pair of Ellie's trousers. She was also wearing her memsahib's blouse, which was too small to comfortably contain her breasts. The sight of the ayah in a white woman's clothes made Davies as uneasy as when he'd looked at the crooked palace. Some things were just plain wrong.

'Well, Davies, it seems as if we're off to the Terai,' Francis said.

'I'm not sure about that,' Davies said.

'Plans are very advanced. Mohan says the camp is ready.'

'Well, I've got my own plans now, see.'

'What's that?'

'I'm heading to Bihar. It's in India.'

'I know where it is, Davies. Why are you going there? Someone told me it's a bloody hellhole. It's wretchedly poor, flat, full of flies, and there's no decent game. Mind you, that sounds like most of India.'

'They were hit badly in the earthquake.'

'What's that got to do with you?'

'The Red Cross are there, so I'm going to muck in and give them a hand.'

'What for? You're still employed by me.'

'Not any more.'

'I don't like your tone, Davies.'

Davies shrugged. 'I'm leaving; probably tomorrow.'

'You can't.'

Davies left the door wide open. He heard Francis shouting from his room, and smiled. Walking away from the palace, he felt a lightness of heart and spirit. This is the life, he thought, enjoying the sunshine on his back. It's been good here, but all good things come to an end. The opportunities in Kathmandu were drying up, and he could see the way the wind was blowing. Some of the local big shots wanted to run the relief operations entirely by themselves, and he needed to go somewhere he'd be given the responsibility his race and experience demanded. He wanted food and materials to distribute, and an audience to listen to his advice.

He strolled down a now familiar lane, and the children melted silently into the shacks and the alleys running between them. He'd miss a lot about Kathmandu, but there were sure to be compensations in Bihar. A pretty young woman with dark, glittering eyes squatted by a doorway. He looked at her and wondered where her little sister was. The girl held his gaze, and spat in the dirt as he passed.

The madam didn't smile as Davies grinned at her. She shouted down the path that ran round the back of shacks, and the girl with the heart-shaped face dragged her feet as she appeared out of the shadows.

The next day, the maps had been rolled up, Maya's pins and clay markers were back in their boxes, and the books were piled carefully in small crates. Nanny looked at the sun streaming through the carved lattice window and the hundreds of dust motes floating in the light. Watching the packing was such a relief. She and Lizzie were going back home with Lady Northwood. Mr Douglas said Francis was arranging it, and she was counting her blessings because it meant that all the horrors in the Land that Time Forgot were going to end. She'd return to an ordinary life, where the most exciting things were found between the pages of a book and where she wasn't surrounded, night and day, by incomprehensible people in a place that some higher power had wrenched from the earth and shaken in a giant malevolent fist.

'When are we going to see Mama?' Lizzie asked.

'Today, I think. Mr Douglas is going to take us to the palace.'

'I miss Mama,' Lizzie said, pulling out a tuft of her doll's hair. Jean had a bald patch on the back of her head, and her eyes no longer closed but remained permanently open in a disconcerting stare.

Maya bundled her clothes untidily into a box. She took it downstairs to the storeroom where they were collecting their luggage ready for the journey 'Do you know,' she said when she came back into the room where her father was relacing his boots, 'I'm sure we're taking back more than we brought here.'

'We just haven't packed it efficiently,' Hugh said.

A bearer knocked at the door and came in with a note. Hugh opened the envelope made of thick, hand-made local paper and read the copperplate handwriting. He folded it, placed it in the empty hearth and set it alight.

'Father?' Maya said.

Hugh was already leaping down the wooden stairs, and if he heard her, he didn't reply.

The entrance to the women's section of Bir Hospital was crowded with patients and relatives. Hugh paused by the door as a family charged in carrying a young woman on their shoulders.

'Where can I find Dr Prasad?' he asked the first nurse he met. The woman was wearing a uniform marked by some alarming stains. She indicated the end of a long corridor, and Hugh picked his way between the patients who were lying on the floor, row upon row, surrounded by their relatives.

Dr Prasad was bending down, listening to an old woman's faint breathing. When he looked up, he stuffed his stethoscope into his pocket. Hugh was taken aback. The doctor had aged. His face was drawn and he'd become an old man.

'This way,' Dr Prasad said, and motioned Hugh to follow him. They went into a small wooden cubicle that was sectioned off from a large ward.

'There'd better be a good reason for asking me to come here,' Hugh said.

'My younger son was arrested a few hours ago. The older one got away, and I assume – or at least I hope – he's making his way to India. I'm not sure that he'll make it, though. They'll come for me too very soon. In fact I don't know why they're taking so long.'

'What the hell's happened? Why are they on to you?'

'I don't know. Maybe someone talked.'

'Well, being seen with me will only make matters worse.'

'You don't need to tell me that.' Dr Prasad spoke in a rasping whisper, as if there were spies lurking on the other side of the flimsy wooden door. 'Do you still have everything I sent you?'

'Of course, but what's so urgent you asked me to come? Why put yourself in more danger?'

'A patient is worrying me.'

'How can I help?'

'She was brought here last night by her sister. They're from a poor family. I think they're orphans, and I believe the older girl may be a prostitute, although that's not something she's likely to admit.'

Dr Prasad paused, and Hugh wondered what all this had to do with him, and why he had to come to the hospital so quickly.

'You'll understand better if you see the child,' Dr Prasad said, and opened the office door.

As they walked through the ward and down the corridor, relatives of the patients called out to Dr Prasad, and he responded saying he would be back soon.

'Most of them have crush injuries,' he told Hugh, his voice weary. 'There's almost nothing I can do for them.'

He stopped to speak to a young doctor, who blinked as he listened, his eyes red with lack of sleep. 'Adil,' Dr Prasad said, 'please can you check the woman from Lalitpur in the first ward? I think the leg will have to come off. See what you think.'

At the far end of the second ward, Dr Prasad stopped by a small figure lying under a blanket on a thin bamboo mattress. He winced as he knelt down beside her, before breathing out through gritted teeth. Then he fastened his gaze on the girl, and took her wrist to feel her pulse.

Hugh couldn't tell whether the child was deeply asleep or unconscious, but her temperature was clearly raised. Her face was flushed and covered in perspiration.

'What's so special about this girl?' he asked. There were so many injured people in the hospital, he couldn't see why this one child was exceptional. How could her suffering be different or worse than that of the others around her?

'She wasn't injured in the earthquake, but she has internal injuries,' Dr Prasad explained. 'And now she has a fever because they have become infected.'

Hugh knelt on the other side of her and watched the rapid rise and fall of her chest under the blanket. 'Is she going to die?' he asked.

'I don't think so, but it's been touch and go for a while.'

'What exactly is wrong with her?'

'She's been raped.'

Hugh looked at him in disbelief. 'But she is a child.'

'Clearly that was of no consequence to the man who did this.'

Hugh was rocked. It's impossible, he thought. Impossible anyone could do this to a child. 'Who was it?' he said.

'Her sister wouldn't say much. She gave the barest details. I believe they live in a lane on the outskirts of town, close to the road to Swayambhu.'

'Does she have any idea who did it?'

'She didn't say. I don't know whether she's scared of repercussions if she speaks out or if she genuinely doesn't know. And I'm surprised she's not here now: she's devoted to this little girl. She's hardly left her side. You'll know the older girl if you meet her because she looks like this one, although she has the blackest eyes.'

Dr Prasad rubbed his hands over his face. 'The thing is, Hugh, when I first examined her, she was semi-conscious, and she talked; not to me, you understand, it was a kind of delirium, but it was also quite clear that she was terrified of a white man, a foreigner, a man she called Davvy.'

Hugh looked up sharply. 'My God,' he whispered. He gazed back down at the girl, at her black hair braided with blue cotton, at her little pointed chin and her heart-shaped face. 'The bastard,' he said.

At the far end of the ward, Adil, the young doctor, shouted a warning.

'They're here,' Dr Prasad said, standing up. 'I leave this in your hands.'

Hugh inched back and then slipped into a side room while

Dr Prasad walked towards his jailers, an old man with the weight of the world on his shoulders.

I'll go one last time, Davies thought, just to say goodbye. The lane with its bamboo and khas grass shacks looked almost pretty in the late-morning sun. A few of the younger children scampered away, and some of the older girls gave him shy smiles. These blacks are funny little things, he thought, smiling back. They were uncomplicated, and he loved their sweetness and simple ways. He knew what they liked: give them a bit of bakshish and they'd be happy.

They must have known he was leaving, because the older sister, who usually had such a hard look about her, garlanded him with a string of marigolds. When she smiled, her face became soft and more like her sister's. He looked around for the child – Laxmi, was it? – but he couldn't see her. He stepped through the doorway and squinted until his eyes adjusted to the lower light levels. He moved to the back room. The boy who dressed as a girl was lying on the mat, and he looked up and waved and said something in Nepali that Davies didn't understand, but he knew the freakish boy was pleased to see him because he beamed at him, and then jumped up and smoothed out a blanket for him to sit on.

'I can't stay long,' Davies said, though clearly no one understood because the boy-girl gave him a big joint of ganja. Davies was going to refuse – he planned to leave early next morning and needed a clear head – but then a new child appeared, one he'd not seen before. She was framed in the doorway, and she looked so guileless and fragile he couldn't resist. He took the ganja and motioned her to sit by him.

Two other girls, around the same age as his pretty little friend, came to the door, and giggled. Like all the other children in the lane, they were barefoot and skinny. These two wore glass bangles on their delicate brown wrists, and their plaited hair was threaded through with strips of blue cotton. Davies was struck by how perfect and bright they looked. One of them brought him a cup of beer. She held it in both hands before him like it was an offering. It tasted rank but he drank it anyway, because he couldn't refuse those big limpid eyes. He began to wonder whether he should stay in Kathmandu another day.

'Where've you two been hiding?' he said to them with a chuckle. The ganja was good, perhaps even a bit stronger than usual.

Laxmi's big sister beckoned to him from the door, and when he stood, unsteadily at first, the two new girls danced around him like tiny butterflies. They tugged gently at him, and jabbered in that lively way native children did.

'All right. All right,' he said, laughing and joining in the fun.

'Uncle,' the older sister said, 'we are sad you are going; you have been good to us. You have given us money, and we are grateful.'

Davies wished he'd learned some of the lingo, but he knew what she was saying from the look in her eyes. Yes, he thought, they've done well out of me. They've probably earned more in two weeks than they normally would in a year.

'Come,' the sister said. She pulled him towards the street, and the two new girls fluttered around him.

He turned, wanting to ask his new friend to come with him, and as he flicked his head in the direction of the street, he staggered a little. Shit, he thought, that ganja is good. He mustn't have any more, though, because if this afternoon was going to shape up the way he thought it might, he needed to be sober. The girls were planning something special for him; a kind of leaving present, a sweet farewell. They wouldn't do business with a feller with his kind of money every day, so they were making hay while the sun shone. For all their sweetness and timidity he knew that, underneath, these Orientals were a canny, scheming bunch, desperate to make money. They'd sell anything for a price.

'Not so fast,' he said, and guffawed at the excited, happy faces. The children from the hut had been joined by half a dozen others. They frolicked and skipped around him, and then began to move along the road. The older sister took his hand and he followed them around the side of the shacks, along a track that he thought smelled of shit, towards a big mud-brick house at the edge of a field.

The new girls twirled in front of him. He was mesmerised, his mind a bit hazy, and he followed them through the door of the house. It shut behind him.

'What's this?' he said, taken aback. The house had appeared solid from outside, but in fact it was a shell and only the exterior walls were intact. The earthquake damage had made it uninhabitable. The roof had collapsed on to the first floor and there was a gaping hole through which he could see blue sky.

Davies was looking up into the void when the statue of the goddess smashed into the back of his skull. He rocked, but didn't fall; he was too big and heavy to be floored by a girl less than half his size. He was stunned, though, partly by the blow and partly by the beer and ganja the children had laced with more potent drugs. He staggered forward and then turned to look at his little friend's older sister. Terrified and exultant, she hit him again with the goddess, breaking off the idol's head as it struck his temple and crushed the bone around his eye socket. He swayed, and the girls with the bangles pushed at his legs. He fell face up on a pile of bricks, and the children stopped laughing and gathered around to stare at the unconscious man. Blood spurted from his eye socket, and they watched as it spread, bright red against the dull brown of the bricks. One of the children began to whimper and back away, and the older girl caught her arm and spoke to her calmly.

They began to move quickly, as if they had a well-rehearsed plan. The older girls rifled through his pockets and found a wallet and a leather pouch full of coins. Together they rolled him over, tied his hands behind his back and bound his legs. The big girl stuffed a rag into his mouth and gagged him with a strip torn from an old sari.

'Will he wake?' the youngest girl asked tearfully, upset by what the giant would do if he broke loose.

'He can't free himself even if he does,' her sister said.

Davies stirred. He moved his head, and the blood spurted a little more.

'Quickly,' the older girl said. She threw the bag of coins to the boy who was dressed as a girl. 'Buy as much wood as you can, and we'll meet you where we arranged. Don't haggle over the price. There's enough there to buy a forest.'

Davies opened his good eye. The injured one flickered, a mass of pulverised flesh and jelly. He saw a face peering closely at him. He couldn't move; he was paralysed, restrained by ropes. He tried to twist sideways, to wriggle his hands out of their bindings, but they were tied fast. He felt hands on him, grabbing his clothes, and then he was being dragged over bricks, through the door and out on to the track.

Bloody little bitches, he wanted to shout, but his mouth was full and he could only grunt. They heaved him on to something that was lying in the dirt, and then he saw nothing but white and red because someone had thrown a sheet over him.

The bigger children took hold of the bamboo staves of the bier and lifted it. They were chattering now, more at ease, and began walking briskly and unsteadily, hardly able to bear the weight of the big foreigner. Davies was jolted and shaken. He groaned, the sound coming from his chest, and a roar rose from deep within his gut. The children beat drums and chanted loudly to drown his protests.

Few people paid them attention as they carried the bier to the Bagmati River. Four thousand people had died in the valley alone, and one more body on its way to the ghats aroused little attention.

Outside Bir Hospital, a man asked why children and not adults were taking this corpse to the ghats.

The older girl rubbed her eye as if wiping away a tear. 'This poor man was our neighbour,' she explained. 'His whole family were killed in the earthquake, and now he has died of his injuries. There is no one left to carry out his funeral rites. Alas, this duty has been left to us.'

The bystanders nodded. It was indeed a tragedy that so many funerals were being conducted without the proper rites.

The children paused by the statue of Jung Bahadur Rana because the road was blocked. An elephant lumbered past with a bejewelled howdah on its back, and a beautiful woman, wearing odd clothes, stared down at them.

'Faster,' the girl said to the children when they began moving again. Davies was twitching a little more vigorously now.

The boy-girl was waiting by the banks of the river. They had chosen a spot far from the temples, well away from the ghats, where many corpses were still waiting to be burned. Quickly they began assembling a pyre. A middle-aged man who was working the fertile soil of the vegetable fields by the river glanced up and watched the children, but in that time of chaos and catastrophe the little group busily building a pyre in an unconventional place wasn't especially remarkable. The man returned to cultivating his onions and didn't see them heave the jerking Davies into the heart of the pyre.

At last Davies understood what was happening. His drugged state and the concussion was wearing off, and he was less confused. His good eye saw clearly, and he was terrified. He watched the children stuff dried grasses around him and place timbers over him. He turned his head sideways, and through the gaps between the wood he glimpsed a burning torch. The older sister brought it close, poking it through the stacked wood so that the dried grass caught fire. At first the kindling smouldered, a slender spiral of white smoke drifting around the pyre. He prayed the fire would die, but then, just a few inches from his eye, he saw it sputter and burst into life. Through the gap in the wood and the smoke that was now billowing in clouds, he saw the children watching, stony-faced. The flames crackled, and Davies silently screamed.

When the goddess smashed into Davies's skull, Shushila was sitting in a jewel-encrusted howdah, under a gold-fringed canopy. The mahout perched on the elephant's neck stabbed it behind the ear with a stick. Shushila could see puncture wounds from previous strikes in the animal's wrinkled grey skin, and she didn't like it. The elephant turned the way the mahout wanted, and plodded down Kanti Path. The howdah swayed, and the Maharaja's nephew used the movement to slide closer to Shushila.

Apart from the time Hugh Douglas had driven them a short distance down the track to escape the fire, Shushila hadn't been outside the palace since they had first arrived in Kathmandu. She hadn't noticed much about the city then because she'd been too tired to bother looking. Now, from her vantage point twelve feet above the ground, the centre of the city looked like a vision of hell. At its heart, several of the pagoda-roofed temples were still standing, but many of the buildings around them had been levelled. Hundreds of tents had been erected on the Tundikhel. She stared over the top of Ellie's sunglasses at a strange little cart, piled high with old clothes, being pushed by a boy between the tents, its front wheels wobbling. The twins' Silver Cross pram had found a good home.

Shushila sat back, enjoying the shade and the faint breeze on her face. She liked being transported like a maharani. She glanced surreptitiously at the Maharaja's nephew. She didn't want to give him the impression she would grant her favours easily. Men like him needed to feel they were great hunters stalking valuable quarry. He was wearing his splendid headdress, with the bird-of-paradise plume, though in this light Shushila was surprised to see it was purple at the tip. The jewels embedded in the cap must have been worth a fortune. They would look better on me, she thought.

It was good to be away from Francis: he was a demanding patient and she was a terrible nurse. The idea that anyone could have believed she spent her time bandaging the wounded in Bir Hospital made her chuckle.

'You are enjoying yourself?' the Maharaja's nephew said, hearing her laugh.

'Yes,' she said. She could think of nicer things to do than looking at piles of broken bricks and poor people in tents, but it was better than playing nursemaid. Shushila didn't even like being with Francis when he was well. She wished he'd go off hunting and that she'd only have to see him for an hour or two now and again. When she spent too long with him, the strain of feigning affection and desire began to tell.

At least the blood poisoning had curbed his passion. In hindsight, she shouldn't have kicked him so hard. He could have died and left her without any gifts or money, or even anywhere to live. It would have been a rotten investment of all her time and effort. She needed to be rewarded; these were her best years and she couldn't waste her youth on poor men, or rich ones who didn't pay.

By the statue of Jung Bahadur Rana, the mahout jabbed at the elephant and it stopped. A cart loaded with timber had lost a wheel and was blocking the road. A funeral procession weaved between the coolies and round the elephant, and stopped next to the animal. Shushila looked down. The body on the bier was large. It must have been a big fat man, she thought. A girl accompanying the mourners stared up at Shushila and then hurried the procession through a little gap in the traffic. Shushila looked again in surprise; under the white sheet the body seemed to writhe for a moment. She shivered, thinking of ghosts, and then decided that the breeze must have ruffled the sheet.

A net of bamboo scaffolding was being erected around the

stump of the Bhim Sen Tower. The Maharaja's nephew leaned over to get a better look, and pressed his thigh against Shushila's trouser-clad leg. This time she didn't move away. The poor man needed consoling; he'd lost his favourite concubine. Shushila hadn't seen her but had heard she was just a hill girl, and so she judged it wouldn't take him long to forget her if he had the right distractions.

The mahout turned the elephant and they began the journey back to the palace.

'You speak excellent English,' the Maharaja's nephew said. 'If I may say so, you speak it rather better than Lady Northwood. She has such a dreadful American accent.'

Shushila took off her glasses, looked at him directly, and then dropped her gaze so her jet-black eyelashes fanned, long and very glossy, over her cheeks.

'Thank you, your excellency,' she said.

'Please call me Mohan.' He leaned closer. 'That is a wonderful fragrance,' he said.

She smiled prettily. It was the memsahib's perfume. Ellie had left it, like she'd left so many of her things, when she'd gone to stay in a poor man's house with the chota sahib, Douglas.

The elephant lumbered wearily towards Mohan's palace, and Shushila winced as the mahout jabbed it repeatedly in one of its flapping ears.

'The builders will begin renovating the house tomorrow,' Mohan announced. 'Although I'm thinking of starting from scratch and having a new place built. What do you think? You have an eye for beauty.'

'It is a charming palace,' Shushila said. 'But it is a little . . . crooked.'

'What do you think makes a good palace?'

Shushila didn't have to think. 'Wide verandas, ceiling fans, flush toilets, and a giant swimming pool with a diving board.'

'I'll see what we can do.'

In the drive, the mahout made the elephant kneel. The man ran down its trunk and held out his hand so Shushila could step with elegance and poise out of the howdah. Mohan followed, and as he clambered out, Shushila grabbed the stick that had been thrust so often into the animal's ear and used it to dig the mahout sharply in the middle of his back. He yelped in pain and surprise.

Mohan hardly noticed the cry, because by then, Francis was limping towards them at high speed, shouting at Shushila, 'I say, where have you been? What the hell is going on? I'm laid up for a while and everyone decides to bugger off and leave me.'

Mohan surveyed the lawns and the ornamental gardens. 'I think,' he said, pointing to the waterless fountains surrounded by beds of deep red canna lilies, 'that is the ideal place for your swimming pool.'

Shushila looked from Francis to Mohan. This, she thought, was what the sahibs described as 'tricky'. Which one was the better bet?

'Shushila,' Francis demanded. 'Come with me.'

She hesitated and then walked towards him.

'You've been neglecting me.'

'I've been busy.'

'Doing what?'

'Working in the hospital.'

Francis's face twisted as if he was trying to understand the impossible. He looked at her stony face and realised she wasn't her usual warm and lovely self.

'Look, I know I've been a bit of a pain recently, but I'm going to make things right now.'

'How?'

'Well, we can get you new clothes and some jewels.'

She sniffed, thinking of the treasures on Mohan's spectacular headdress.

'Do you think the memsahib will be happy about that?'

'You don't need to worry about the memsahib.'

'Why not? She will see the new clothes and jewels and wonder why an ayah is wearing them.'

'She won't see them because she won't be here.'

'She's gone home to her family?'

'She hasn't any family. She's gone to Ranchi.'

'Where's that?'

'In India. Far away from here. I've sent her to the asylum.'

The skin between Shushila's dainty eyebrows puckered. 'What is an asylum?'

'A hospital for people who are mad.'

Shushila flinched as if she had been struck. 'You mean the *pagalkhana*,' she said in a flat voice.

She knew about the *pagalkhana* in Calcutta, a place where the patients were chained, where gangs of them were forced to clean the streets, where their lives were said to be worse than their deaths. The thought of it made her shudder. She didn't like the memsahib; she wanted her to go back to England or America, wherever she came from, but she couldn't stand the thought of her in the *pagalkhana*. She wasn't mad; she was just plain and getting old, and she had lost her husband long ago, if she had ever had him at all. It wasn't right. What the sahib had done was wicked, and Shushila realised that she hated him even more than she disliked the memsahib.

She watched Mohan's men forcing open the door to the palace and the flourish of the bird-of-paradise plume on his cap as he climbed the steps to the portico. She walked down the drive, almost skipping in her hurry.

'Where are you going?' Francis called after her.

She didn't respond, and at the gates she smiled at a young guard. 'You know the chota sahib, Mr Douglas?' she asked him.

He gawped at her and shook his head.

'The *mleccha*. The man with red hair?'

This time he understood.

'Quickly,' she said. 'Take me to him now.'

Hugh was not at the house in Lazimpat when Shushila arrived, and Maya didn't know where he had gone. While Shushila waited impatiently, tapping her foot on the floor and ordering the bearer to bring endless cups of tea, Hugh was walking down an unmetalled lane, edged by shacks. He paused and spoke to an old man who squatted by his open doorway smoking a *bidi*. The old man jerked his head right, towards a closed door made of rough bamboo.

'Hello?' Hugh called outside the door.

It swung open and a middle-aged woman with sharp eyes gave him a hard look.

'What do you want?' she asked.

He hesitated for a moment, sure the woman was a madam, but uncertain what to say.

'We're not open today,' she said. 'Come back tomorrow.' She

began to shut the door, the bottom of it scraping though the dust of the road.

'I'm looking for someone.'

'So are all the customers, but I said we're not open.'

'I'm looking for a girl.'

Her eyes narrowed. 'What kind of girl? We don't have young ones here. Not any longer. You can clear off if that's what you want to spend your money on. I'm sick of foreigners.'

'I don't want to spend any money.'

'In that case, stop wasting my time.' She shut the door in his face and he could hear her chuntering inside the shack.

He was convinced now that this was the place. Then, from the corner of his eye, he saw a crowd of children trudging up the road through the dust. They were headed by a girl, almost a woman, with brilliant black eyes and a heart-shaped face.

The girl looked at him warily, and while the others fled, she stood still.

'Your sister's in the hospital, isn't she?' Hugh said.

She nodded.

'Who did it? Tell me, and I promise no harm will come to you or her.'

She stared at him, unmoved.

'I can help you,' Hugh said. 'I can stop this happening again. The man needs to be punished. Just tell me his name.'

'Davvy. A white man. He's been here many times, and not just with my sister. I know what he does. I know she is not the only one. He goes round this city and he does these things and it is a secret because no one knows, or they pretend not to know. No one does anything about it because they are scared. He is such a good, big man, everyone says so, and so no one will believe us when we say he is a demon and he's possessed by evil spirits.'

'I believe you. He mustn't be allowed to get away with this. He will carry on and others will be hurt. You understand? We have to stop him.'

'He won't hurt another child.'

'You can't know that.'

'I do.'

'Men like him don't change. They don't stop.'

'Sahib, I see you believe me. I see you want to help, but you have to trust me when I tell you he won't harm anyone else.'

Hugh knew he couldn't persuade her. She was firm and resolute.

'Now leave,' she said. 'I'm going to the hospital to see if my sister is still alive.'

The girl went into the shack and spoke to the madam. When she came out, she began to run back down the road into Kathmandu.

A boy who was dressed as a girl whistled from an alley between the huts. He beckoned Hugh and they walked in silence along a path behind the shacks that smelled of shit. When they went into the carcass of the ruined house, Hugh saw blood on the bricks and marks on the floor. At first he thought he was looking at the place where the little girl had been raped, but then he saw the blood was still fresh and that there was a lot of it. And whoever had been dragged out into the road was big and heavy.

The boy-girl began to walk into Kathmandu, along Kanti Path and then down to the river. It was a long way, and Hugh wondered whether he should be following this silent boy-girl in his ill-fitting sari. They walked through the fields, and the man who had earlier been cultivating onions was now tending to his spinach. He looked up and saw a white man following the same *hijra* child who had been so sad when the body had been cremated in the afternoon.

Hugh stood beside the pile of ash. It was still warm. What, he thought, was this boy-girl trying to tell him?

'Why have you brought me here?' he asked.

The boy-girl pointed into the heart of the funeral pyre. 'The demon,' he said.

Hugh flinched in shock. 'Davvy?' he asked.

The boy-girl nodded.

'Who did it?' Hugh said.

'We did.'

'Who's we?'

'Me and the others.'

'The girl I talked to?'

'Yes, her and the small ones. We all did it.'

'Did the madam know?'

The boy-girl shook his head.

Hugh took a stick from the riverbank and poked among the ashes. The only solid thing he could see was part of a thigh bone that had been too thick and heavy to be completely incinerated. He raked the ashes again and saw something else. He moved a little closer, feeling the heat rising from the embers. Carefully he picked it out with the tip of his stick, and saw a pair of scorched dog tags swinging on a metal chain. He tried to hold them, but they were too hot to handle, and so he put them in the grass and sprinkled river water over them. They were too badly warped by the heat of the pyre to see the identification numbers, but he knew they belonged to Davies. He had been killed in that house and dragged here so the evidence of his murder could be destroyed.

Hugh knew he should inform the police and that the children couldn't take justice into their own hands. But then he thought of the child in Bir Hospital, and her defiant, angry sister, and the sad boy-girl in his drooping sari. What would happen to them if they were convicted of murder? He took a last look at the dog tags and flung them as far as he could into the depths of the Bagmati River.

6

Kalimpong, February–October 1934

EIGHT DAYS HAD passed since Ellie was taken from Kathmandu. For five days she had lain each morning in the canvas-covered bath. She had seen the young doctor every afternoon and had been excluded from needlework therapy because she was disrupting the other patients. She was confined to bed for the rest of the time because the nursing staff said it would soothe her. It hadn't soothed her in the slightest. In fact, she was livid, so furious she could have bitten and spat and been the dirtiest patient they had ever had in their goddam madhouse.

When Colonel Berkeley-Hill came back to his asylum, she was going to tell him he couldn't force treatment on people who didn't need it. She wouldn't be calm, and she wouldn't be quiet. She would rage, because she knew the demon was here in Ranchi, and it would be prowling in Kathmandu. It was going to take everything from her. It would take her children and her sanity, and there was nothing she could do to stop it unless they let her go. She had to be free to fight it, to kill it before it killed her and everyone she loved.

On the fifth day, she was allowed to have lunch with the

other patients. In the dining room, the pure whites congregated on one side of the room and the Eurasians on the other. Ellie saw the flurry of excitement as a man toured the tables, talking to the patients.

'That's Colonel Berkeley-Hill,' Mary said, now in her guise as the District Commissioner's wife. 'He really is a first-rate psychiatrist. I have complete faith in him.'

Ellie watched the rather insignificant-looking man and couldn't imagine what it was like to have complete faith in anyone. An image of Hugh came to mind, and she pushed it away. He wasn't going to get her out of this mess; she had to fall back on her own resources.

Mary shut her eyes and Ellie worried she was turning into an ancient Egyptian, but then she opened them again and said brightly, 'He married an Indian woman but we mustn't hold that against him. He has some very progressive ideas.'

Ellie wasn't so sure about how progressive his ideas were, and as she'd spent a lot of time with psychiatrists, she felt she knew something about the subject. That afternoon she was taken to Berkeley-Hill's office, which was like an Englishman's study. Ellie thought it was rather too much like Francis's room in the gaunt house on the edge of the Fens, full of dark furniture and sofas that were supposed to relax the patient but were too hard or too soft, or faced the wrong way.

'I'm glad to meet you at last, Lady Northwood,' Berkeley-Hill said.

Ellie smiled stiffly and nodded without speaking, because she didn't know why she should be friendly with a man who had agreed to incarcerate her on the say-so of her husband. He smiled gently, and all of a sudden her resolve to speak her mind vanished. Instead of spewing forth all the anxiety and fear she'd harboured for the last week, she let him speak.

'I've been reviewing your case and have looked at the notes my colleagues have made,' he said, sifting through her file. He pulled out a sheet of thick hand-made paper. 'I have here a letter from none other than the personal physician to one of the nephews of Nepal's maharaja.' He put the letter at the back of the file. 'I have also had some necessarily brief correspondence by wire with your previous doctors, one of whom is a dear friend of mine from Stanford.'

'I'm not mad, I can promise you that,' Ellie interrupted.

Berkeley-Hill looked at her, weighing her up. 'Well, you're not a dirty patient, as we first thought. You are not violent, although you are subject to outbursts. You do not have syphilis, and although there may be some signs of delusion—'

'No!' Ellie cried.

'Let me finish,' Berkeley-Hill said. 'We're not in the business here of punishing people. We don't believe in restraints and chains. We listen. We try to understand. We hope we are one of the foremost mental hospitals in the world, not just in India.'

'You don't need to sell the place to me. It's not like I have any choice about being here.'

Berkeley-Hill cleared his throat and rifled through the documents in his hands. 'I have telegrams from your husband – two of them, in fact – and another more recent one.'

'Yeah, they'll all say the same thing: I'm crazy.'

Berkeley-Hill closed the file and drummed his fingers on it. 'Will you take a walk with me?' he asked.

Ellie didn't think it would help her cause if she refused, and so she accompanied the doctor round the grounds. As they walked, she told him about the earthquake, and Tom and Lizzie, and Francis's affair.

He paused under the dappled shade of the pine trees. 'And Mr Douglas? Where does he fit into this story?'

She hadn't talked about Hugh; she hadn't mentioned him once. 'He's not my lover. Francis is wrong. He's my friend.'

'And would you like to see him again?'

'Yes, when I get back to Kathmandu.'

'I don't think it would be wise for you to return to Nepal, and I know you won't be permitted back into the kingdom. Besides, Mr Douglas isn't in Kathmandu.'

'How do you know?'

'Because, he's here.' Berkeley-Hill stepped on to a wide veranda and opened a door. Ellie didn't see the other people waiting in the room; she saw only Lizzie, who squealed and ran to her. Ellie swept her up.

'Mama, Mama!' Lizzie cried. 'You were lost like Tom.'

Hugh got to his feet, and when she put Lizzie down, he held out his hand and she shook it. The formality of it was strange, but his grin was not.

Nanny Barker dozed on a reclining chair, and Maya nodded to Ellie as if she still harboured a twinge of resentment because Ellie had taken her father to Nuwakot, and spoiled her maps.

Berkeley-Hill shook Nanny awake. 'Will you look after the child? I need to talk to Lady Northwood and Mr Douglas in my office.'

Nanny stirred, but was still groggy with fatigue. She had left Kathmandu because when Mr Douglas took them back to Francis, they found he had already gone shooting in the Terai. He'd left her a short message giving instructions to stay in the wrecked palace until he got back. The idea was terrible: she would be the only white woman in a place full of natives, and she was sure the ceiling was going to drop on her head. Francis was her security; he was going to give her a pension and a cottage on the estate, but with everything that had happened in the Land that Time Forgot, she no longer felt so confident he would remember her. So instead of obeying Francis, she'd left with Mr Douglas. She'd brought Lizzie on the awful long journey where there were no dolis, no trains and no decent roads. She was, she knew, far too old for all this travel and upheaval.

'Lizzie can stay with me,' Maya said, and the old woman drifted back to sleep, her mouth hanging open and her jaw slack.

Berkeley-Hill led Ellie and Hugh into his office. Ellie was still in a daze, and she glanced briefly but often at Hugh as if she couldn't quite believe he was there; as if perhaps she had conjured him out of thin air the way Mary Knox did with the sun god.

'You're probably wondering how this has come about,' Berkeley-Hill said to Ellie. 'When I was going through your file earlier, I said there had been a telegram quite recently. It wasn't from your husband, but from Mr Douglas saying he was on his way. And this morning I've spoken with both him and your nanny, though it seems the conversation has exhausted the poor woman. Anyway, I'm satisfied you should not be here.'

'I kept telling that young doctor I wasn't mad,' Ellie said.

'I know you didn't warm to him, Lady Northwood, but he actually agreed with you. He recommended that you be discharged into the care of someone who will help you recuperate.'

'I don't need to recuperate, and I've got to look for Tom.'

'It's quite clear to us that the earthquake and losing your son has revived painful memories of your brother and your parents, but it does not mean you should be a patient here. You must take time to rest, though, and you mustn't overexcite yourself.'

Berkeley-Hill left Ellie and Hugh alone while he went to arrange her discharge from the hospital.

'Did Francis tell you I was here?' Ellie asked Hugh.

'He said you were in the palace and didn't want to see me.'

Ellie's laugh was bitter. 'Then who told you?'

'Shushila.'

Ellie's intake of breath was sharp. 'I'd never have believed it. I thought she hated me.'

'She probably does, but she has some sense of justice, and she knows about the old *pagalkhana* for Indian patients in Calcutta.'

'Hugh, there's something important I need to tell you,' she said, suddenly injecting an urgency into her voice. With Lizzie in the next room and no longer in danger, Ellie was free to tell the world about the monster stalking Kathmandu. 'Davies isn't what he appears to be,' she said. 'He's not a hero.'

'I know what you are going to say,' he said.

'He abuses children in the most terrible way.'

'Yes, I know. Dr Prasad treated one of the girls.'

'We have to stop him.'

'He's been dealt with.'

'He's in prison?'

Hugh shook his head. 'Trust me,' he said, 'there's no more danger from him.'

Ellie frowned, wondering what Hugh could mean.

'Is he dead?' she whispered.

He didn't reply.

'Hugh, did you kill him?'

His silence chilled her, and she sat wondering if she herself would have killed Davies if she'd had the chance, and if it was the only way to stop him. Then Hugh turned to look at her, and she knew by the softness of his eyes that he wasn't a murderer. He couldn't be.

In the quiet of the room the sounds of the hospital were amplified. Someone was singing tunelessly, and in the distance there was a shout and a burst of unmodulated laughter that echoed through the corridors.

Hugh was hiding something about Davies, but she took him at his word: the children of Nepal and India were safe. Now it was time to think about Tom and how she would find him.

'Thank you for coming here,' she said. 'It looks like you are my saviour. It seems you are always around when I'm in trouble. And I can't tell you how glad I'll be to be out of this place. I'm going straight to Calcutta and I'm going to hire every detective I can find.'

'Detectives there won't know the first thing about the Himalayas. I have a much better idea: come with us to Kalimpong. My home's there. It's on an offshoot of the Old Silk Road, one of the most important trade routes from India to Tibet. British intelligence is utterly inept in India, but it's pretty good on the north-eastern frontier. We know a lot about what happens and who moves through the passes. The bazaar in Kalimpong is full of information, and if anyone knows about a fair-haired boy travelling with Tibetan traders, we'll hear about it.'

He spoke with a surety born of years spent in the Himalayas. 'It's a deal,' she said.

The next day they took a train to Siliguri and then travelled the forty-two miles to Kalimpong by car. The Teesta Valley Road was one of the most beautiful in the hills. It followed the river for around twenty miles before crossing the three-hundred-foot-wide gorge on a suspension bridge. Then it rose up through the hills, through immense sal forests, the tall, straight trunks of the trees soaring above the tangled under-growth of the forest floor. Hugh drove slowly, anxious not to let the truck that was carrying their luggage out of his sight. It trailed them at a distance, and he kept glancing in his mirrors to check it was still there. Later they passed through tea estates and beside terraced fields, the road cutting back upon itself time after time, looping first up and then down the steep mountainsides until they had to stop for Lizzie to be sick in a thick patch of ferns.

The earthquake that had wreaked such devastation in central Nepal had caused only minor damage in this eastern flank of the Himalayan foothills. A few buildings were damaged in Darjeeling and Kalimpong, but none had collapsed. Ellie spotted a couple of landslides on the way, but Hugh said later that they had probably been caused by soil erosion and weren't the direct result of the earthquake. Even so, he was concerned enough about hidden dangers to check over his house and gardens the moment they arrived.

Ellie stood with Lizzie and Nanny in the drive, surrounded by their few tatty bags of possessions, like down-at-heel nomads. She'd expected Hugh's home to be in a local style, because he seemed so in love with India and Nepal and the mountains. But although Roseacre's walls were made of local stone, and its interior was panelled with local timber, it looked like an English gentleman's country residence. Ivy grew around the front door, wisteria climbed over the east wall and the gables, and if it wasn't for the wide verandas on the south and west sides of the house, and the dull red corrugated-iron roof, it wouldn't have looked out of place in a sleepy part of Kent. It wasn't a particularly old building – it must have been built fifty years before – but it had the solidity and patina of age. It was, Ellie thought, shockingly pretty.

She looked at Hugh, who at that moment couldn't have seemed less like an English country gentleman. He was tanned and wore a short-sleeved khaki shirt, which had ripped over the shoulder. His hair was a bit too long, curling into his neck and flopping over his forehead, and he had a week-old beard that suited him very much. The whole look would have created a stir on the Mall in Darjeeling.

Hugh took Ellie, Nanny Barker and Lizzie on a walk through the gardens that spread in front of the house and down the hillside in a succession of four wide terraces, covered in fine lawns. The deep beds were filled with bushes and ferns, and the flowers of India's cold season and an English summer. Before the gardens ended and the trees began, a chain of lily ponds sparkled in the golden sunlight. And then, beyond the jungle fringe, the land fell away into a deep gorge where a river crashed and foamed over smooth rocks. When Lizzie stopped chattering, Ellie could hear the faint rush of swiftly moving water.

Tea covered the surrounding hillsides, and the deep valleys were forested in many shades of green. To the north and west, the mountains rose into the peaks of the high Himalayas, and above them all towered Kanchenjunga. It appeared so close, Ellie felt she could reach out and touch it, and feel the cool bite of the snow on her fingers. She had seen Kanchenjunga from Darjeeling before the monsoon clouds had dropped a cloak over the mountains. But this time it felt different, because now she was imagining the spaces beyond the peaks, the plateau on the other side, the place where she used to think she'd find the coral-red mountains but where she now believed she'd find Tom.

'Let's go to Kalimpong and ask around,' she said as Hugh walked back to join them after double-checking that the terraced lawns had escaped earthquake damage and weren't about to slide into the gorge.

'What?' Hugh said. 'You haven't even been inside the house yet. We've been on the road for almost two weeks. The doctor said you had to rest.'

'But I don't want to.'

'It'll be dusk in an hour and it'll take half an hour to drive into Kalimpong. Besides, tomorrow is Saturday; it's the weekly bazaar. That's the best time to go. The town will be full of traders.'

Reluctantly Ellie followed Hugh into the house. Lizzie was sliding on the polished wooden floors, and Nanny Barker was flustered. She looked tired and overheated despite the lateness of the day and the cool temperature in the shady interior of the house. A man wrapped in a thick woollen jacket was laying a log fire in an open hearth in the sitting room, and Ellie thought they might need the extra warmth when night fell.

Maya had the servants make up a bed in a little room under

the eaves for Nanny Barker, and Ellie and Lizzie were given a room at the front of the house with a view over the gardens and up towards Kanchenjunga. The view inside the room was less spectacular: the furniture was old, the fabrics faded by the sun, and everything seemed a little worn, as if nothing had been renewed since the house was built.

'Sorry,' Hugh said, leaning against the door jamb. 'We're a bit behind the times here. We can't rely on the electricity and there's no hot water in the bathrooms. I've asked the water boy to bring you plenty.'

'I washed in the river on the way to Nuwakot,' Ellie said. 'I think I can manage here.'

She bathed Lizzie in a big red tin bath that the water boy filled with hot water, and later she sank into the tub herself, the heat easing the tension in her muscles. By nine o'clock she couldn't stay awake any longer and left the side of the roaring fire in the sitting room. When she climbed into bed, she found a hot-water bottle taking the chill off the sheets. The linen, although soft with age and laundering, smelled fresh and new, of English lavender and roses on a balmy summer evening. She fell into a deep and dreamless sleep, glad that her daughter was beside her in the big old bed, and that her son was, perhaps, not so far away.

A mule train clip-clopped along the road leading to the bazaar. The animals wore brightly coloured woven head decorations and bells around their necks. Ellie stood aside to let them pass, and thought the loads slung on either side of their backs seemed too heavy for such small creatures. The hardy little beasts walked doggedly on spindly legs through Kalimpong, their bells sounding tinny as a muleteer and a couple of traders on horse-back drove them forward.

The heart of the bazaar was packed with shoppers and merchants. Some of the better stalls had corrugated-iron roofs to protect them from rain and sun. Ellie stopped to watch a stallholder hanging gold earrings on a red cloth, and another spreading fancy cigarette cases and watches over a table. Hugh went from one stall to another, speaking to everyone he could. He bent down to talk to the poor women who sat on the ground selling a pound or two of rice, or a few vegetables they had placed in a neat pile in front of them. Ellie saw them smile as they spoke to him.

A rosy-complexioned Tibetan woman whose cheeks were a mass of broken veins from a life spent in the sun and wind was selling a selection of felt and fur hats. Hugh had a loud conver-sation with her as she stood with her hands on her hips. She swept her arms from side to side, and pointed left and right.

'Does she know something?' Ellie asked, springing forward.

'She says she saw a boy with blue eyes come through the market a few weeks ago. But it can't be Tom. He was Tibetan. He had dark skin and hair. She remembers him because of his eyes: she felt sorry for him.'

'Why?'

'Many Tibetans associate blue eyes with blindness,' he said.

Ellie trailed after Hugh for an hour, always hoping the next conversation would bring a bit of news. Nobody, though, had seen or heard of a golden-haired boy travelling to or from Tibet.

'I'm going to speak to the muleteers, and the wool and salt traders,' Hugh said to Ellie. 'Why don't you take your film to be developed, then we'll have a photograph of Tom to show people.' He meant the picture Ellie had taken of Tom and Lizzie in the doli on the top of the Chandragiri Pass.

They agreed to meet an hour later, but when Ellie arrived at the meeting place, Hugh wasn't there. She stood in the shade of a stall, eyed warily by a man selling dried plants, bones, and assorted withered things. She couldn't tell whether they were dehydrated flesh or mushrooms. Either way, she didn't like the smell, and she moved away.

In her new spot, she could see the street barbers shaving clients as they sat on the pavement. A group of children gathered around her; thankfully, she thought, they weren't quite as mesmerised by her oddness as the children in Nepal had been. They were accustomed to seeing foreigners in Kalimpong. A couple of Tibetan men wrapped in especially heavy tunics, secured by thick belts, shooed them away with a shout. The men beamed at her, laughed at a shared joke and continued on their way.

Ellie was standing in the sunlight now, and feeling hot and uncomfortable. Hugh had been gone a long time. A line of porters walked by, carrying loads that seemed heavier than those borne by the mules. They were bent by their burdens, their faces set with the effort. Ellie stepped back, and teetered on the edge of a pothole. She moved again, this time between the stalls selling fabric. A band of chattering women jostled her. She was a foot taller than them, and she felt suddenly and frighteningly out of place, surrounded by tiny people who spoke in loud, brash voices, whose bangles shook and long earrings jangled. They seemed to be laughing in her face.

She bolted in the direction Hugh had taken, stopping at the northern edge of the bazaar, where the buildings were in the

Tibetan style. She still couldn't see him. There were so many men talking in little groups. Others milled around, greeting friends and old trading partners. Although Hugh was usually easy to spot because of his height, many of the Tibetan traders were tall too. She scanned the area, and her gaze fastened on a man in a long red coat. She began to dodge through the crowd towards him, and then stopped, confused, her eye caught by something else. Three, four, then five men walked out of a building to her left, grinning and hollering to one another. They looked as if they had just finished celebrating a good business deal with a hearty meal and plenty to drink. All wore red coats.

'Where've you been?' Hugh said, and turned her round. 'I've looked all over the bazaar for you.'

'I came to find you. See over there,' she said, spinning round. 'All the men in red coats.'

'I've spoken to them already.'

'And?'

'They don't know anything, but they are going to ask everyone they meet. So are half the people in this bazaar. I'll talk to the priests, the Tibetan lamas, the police and the army as well. The message will spread.'

'How quickly?'

'Tibet is a big place, but the trading networks are dense. I'm optimistic we'll hear something soon.'

Hugh's optimism was unfounded. A month later, as the cold season turned to spring, and almost as quickly into an early summer, not a single scrap of information about the missing golden-haired boy had reached the traders, gossips and spies of the Kalimpong bazaar.

Ellie rarely went into the study: it was Maya and Hugh's domain. Hugh had shown her around the room when she first arrived. The windows opened on to the veranda, one with a view over the drive, the other looking out over the side lawns to where the kitchen gardens curled around the mountainside. Two walls were lined with shelves, which were slightly bowed with the weight of the books on them.

'It's like a library,' Ellie said.

'Try telling that to Maya. She's always complaining she wants more books and needs to study in a real library in Calcutta or London.'

'Does she need to?'

'Not if I can help it.'

'Why?'

'She's still a child.'

Ellie looked quizzically at Hugh. 'She looks very young but is she really a child?'

'She is to me.'

Ellie stopped and examined a collection of framed sepia photographs.

Hugh pointed to a man in uniform. 'That's my father when he was in the 5th Gurkhas.'

Ellie thought she could see some resemblance to Hugh, but not much.

'And here's my mother and father on their wedding day.'

The photograph was badly faded and Ellie moved closer.

'You take after your mother,' she said.

She paused by another photograph. 'Who's this?' An Indian or Nepali woman was standing with two small boys in a garden.

'It's me with my ayah, Kamala.'

Ellie glanced outside and then looked back at the photograph, recognising the stone birdbath in the picture. 'It was taken here, right?'

'Just outside,' he said, closing the study door behind them. Maya was busy at her desk and disliked chatter when she worked.

'Don't let Lizzie play in here when I'm out,' Maya called after them. 'I don't want her scribbling on my work.'

Ellie didn't return to the room until three weeks later. She watched Maya from the door, her head bent over a sheet of paper, and thought how odd it was for such a young girl to be so devoted to her work. She might as well be in a convent. It was a strange, sequestered kind of life, but then Ellie remembered that people must have thought the same about her when she was a girl, because she too had been reluctant to go out, and lived more in her daydreaming mind than in her body.

'Will you show me where we are, on your maps?' Ellie asked.

Maya looked up, surprised.

'I was wondering how far we are from Tibet,' Ellie said.

Maya put down her pen, searched through a folio case and pulled out a map. She spread it on the table. 'We are here,' she said, pressing her finger over Kalimpong. 'All this is Nepal.' She waved her hand over to the left. 'There's Kathmandu. You see how the mountains run along the north of India?' She drew her finger over the map. 'And all this to the north is Tibet.'

Ellie knew this; it was like a basic geography lesson. What she really needed was detail. Exactly how far was Tibet? Where were the passes? How did you get there? She didn't say this to Maya, though, because it was the first time the girl had spoken to her without there being a cold, clipped edge to her voice that wouldn't have sounded out of place among the memsahibs in the Planters' Club.

'How do I get to Tibet from here?' she asked.

'This way,' Maya said. 'There are lots of small passes but these are the two best, the Nathu La and the Jelep La. They were closed for a few weeks because of late snow, but they're open now.'

They looked as if they were close, but Ellie remembered how Nuwakot had seemed a mere stroll from Kathmandu on the map.

'Is it hard to cross the passes?'

'You should ask my father. He has been over them many times.'

'Why?'

'He worked for the government, and the British are very interested in Tibet. They want to keep it friendly and under their own control because they think that way they'll protect their rule in India. They don't want the Russians interfering in Tibet, spreading their influence south and disrupting the Raj.'

'So your father's a spy?'

Maya laughed. 'A diplomat.'

'But he hasn't worked for the government for a long time, has he?'

'No.'

'Why did he leave his job?'

'It's complicated.'

'Tell me, please.'

'He fell out of love with them, and they with him. And his health wasn't good, so he stopped travelling for a while, and

247

was invalided out of the Political Service. I think it suited everyone.'

'But he went to Kathmandu.'

'Try stopping my father doing what he wants. He's always doing things that aren't good for him.' The old harshness came back into Maya's voice, and the expression in her eyes was like an accusation.

Ellie wanted the girl to soften again; she wanted them to be friends, because the alternative was stressful. They were all living here, miles from anywhere, in the shadow of Kanchenjunga, waiting for news. Maya had spent the last month avoiding her, or sitting frostily at the dinner table. She thinks I want to replace her mother, Ellie thought. She thinks I want to be mistress of this shabby old house.

'How far is it to the passes?' she asked.

Maya shrugged. 'Three or four days. But don't think you can go alone.'

'I won't.'

'And you can't go with my father, either.'

'I'll hire a guide and a muleteer.'

'Good.' The girl brightened. 'And before you go, I'll draw you some maps.'

'Thank you,' Ellie said, delighted by Maya's sudden warmth and desire to help. Perhaps we can be friends, she thought as she left the girl to her labours. Maya looked at Ellie's retreating back, and scowled.

Nanny Barker was feeling better. The hill diarrhoea that had assaulted her with such force and randomness hadn't struck since they'd arrived in Kalimpong, and she thought the gremlins were finally vanquished. The weather was good here; there was a snap to the air, especially at night, which reminded her of home. The sanitation was basic, but the house was kept spotlessly clean by servants. Nanny was pleased, though, that there weren't too many of them. She didn't like being surrounded by natives all the time, the way they were in the palace or, worse, when they were in Calcutta. It was disconcerting to be swamped by a sea of dark faces.

It was different here: the servants were friendly, and they understood most of what she said, especially the cook, Tenzing, who would have been a good-looking man if he wasn't black. He was a Lepcha, from the tiny kingdom of Sikkim to the north of Kalimpong, and his English was wonderful because he'd worked for Hugh Douglas for years, and for his father before him. He wanted to know all about England, and they spent a couple of hours most afternoons, while Lizzie was having a nap, drinking tea and talking about all kinds of things, because the cook was a sociable man and liked telling stories as much as listening to them. At night he gave Nanny Barker strong millet beer and told her about the Yeti, the giant wild glacier ape that walked in the mountains and swung through the jungle. Nanny was riveted, remembering the creatures in *The Land That Time Forgot*. She sipped the beer, sure that it was settling her stomach.

It was good to get back into a routine; children thrived on routine, and all the travelling round India and Nepal like gypsies had been disruptive to poor Lizzie, who was fractious and demanding because she didn't know what time of day it was, and where she was going to sleep next. Nanny thought it was cruel to drag a little one from pillar to post. Francis and Ellie had just been thinking of themselves. They were globetrotters, hunting for magnificent game, or searching for a mystical place, when they really should have been putting the children first. Even now, after everything that had happened, Ellie wasn't thinking of Lizzie very much; she was far too obsessed with finding Tom.

Ellie let Lizzie sleep in her bed every night, and Nanny didn't approve, saying it would spoil the child. But that was about the extent of Ellie's interference, and in some ways, Nanny thought it might be a good thing, as she herself was left to organise Lizzie's day, just as she would have done in the nursery at home.

One morning, as Nanny Barker and Lizzie played with Jean on the veranda, dressing the doll and putting her to sleep in a wicker basket, Maya was wandering around the garden, deep in thought. When she came back to the house, she paused on the veranda, watching Jean being tucked into bed. Lizzie patted the doll's head roughly.

Ellie rushed by, making for the car. She was going to meet Hugh in Kalimpong and undertake another fruitless investigation in the bazaar.

'Nanny, please check Lizzie's milk has been boiled right,' she said.

It was an unnecessary instruction, because the cook was meticulous about boiling the milk they got from a neighbouring farm.

Ellie drove off, trailing a little cloud of acrid blue smoke.

Maya looked at Nanny. 'What's your name?' she asked.

Nanny looked puzzled. 'Nanny Barker,' she said.

'I mean your real name.'

Nanny was flummoxed.

'The one you were given when you were born,' Maya said.

It took Nanny Barker several moments to process the question. No one had called her by her Christian name since her mother had died.

'My name?' she said.

Maya waited.

'My name is Sarah.'

'I'll call you Sarah from now on,' Maya said, and walked back into the house.

Sarah Barker rocked the doll's wicker basket. She didn't know how she felt. Was the girl being cheeky? After all, being called 'Nanny' was better than being called by your real name, like any minor servant. Or was Maya being kind, acknowledging that she was a person and not just a job? Sarah rolled the name around her mouth like a sweet she'd not eaten for years, and was surprised to find that she'd forgotten how it tasted.

'But Father, of course I will be all right. I've been driving since I was sixteen,' Maya said, when Hugh and Ellie returned home.

'Not all the way to Darjeeling,' Hugh said.

'I drove half the way to Darjeeling last year.'

'With me in the car.'

'I know the way.'

'That's not the point. The roads are dangerous.'

'Not at this time of year. There's been no rain. Please, Father.'

Hugh shook his head.

'You let her drive,' Maya said, pointing to Ellie.

'She's been driving for years.'

'Not in India.'

'Ellie drove to Kalimpong, not all the way to Darjeeling.

251

Look, I'll drive you myself, but I can't do it tomorrow. I have to go to the bazaar to meet someone; it could be important.'

'I want to go tomorrow.'

'No.'

'Father, you are always stopping me doing what I want. Why is it that you can do all the things you're not supposed to, and I'm not allowed to do something as simple as drive thirty miles on a road I know. I'm not a child any more. Please, Father, let me go.'

Hugh hesitated, then nodded. Maya flung her arms around his neck and hugged him. As she skipped off, she looked like a child in her exuberance. It was startling to Ellie, because Maya usually looked so sombre and serious.

'What can be so exciting about Darjeeling?' she asked Hugh. 'Is there a party or something?'

'I am sure there are lots of parties, but not ones where Maya will be welcome.'

'Then why Darjeeling? And why tomorrow?'

'The Oxford Bookstore.'

'A shop?'

'We go four times a year and Maya looks through all the new books. Only we haven't been for our usual visit for a long time. First there was the trip to Nepal, and now I'm busy here.'

'Will that old jalopy make it to Darjeeling?'

'It looks bad, and it's a bit smoky, but it's in good working order. It's done the trip more times than I can remember.' Hugh said it as if he was trying to convince himself.

'Well, you don't like Darjeeling anyway, do you?' Ellie said.

He nodded, clearly still preoccupied with the thought of allowing Maya to go alone.

'No, I don't like it. And I think the feeling is mutual.'

'Why aren't you more popular in town?'

'Because I have a different view of the world from the people there,' he said, with a shrug. 'I used to think like them, but then I abandoned the faith. I'm a kind of apostate.'

'What turned you into a disbeliever?'

'It's too hard to explain.'

'Try.'

'I was in the Indian Civil Service in Bengal. It was a poor district and I thought I was there to help the peasants. I thought I was protecting them from landlords and moneylenders. And I did. But then I realised that my obsession with saving the poor from these evil people was obscuring the greatest exploitation of all.'

'What's that?'

'Us. Us being here at all, pretending we're bringing justice and peace to a less civilised people when it's actually about stripping the country of its riches.'

Ellie glanced round at the beautiful house and its even more magnificent gardens, and wondered if Hugh included himself in this damning verdict. She didn't ask, because he had already gone. She watched him lift the bonnet of the car and lean over the engine. It was a chance for her to look at him properly, at the colour of his hair, the shape of him, and the way he moved. She only did this when she was sure he wasn't aware of her, when he was engrossed in conversation with Maya or one of the servants, or when he was busy fixing something, intent on a task. It was too unsettling to look him in the eyes, because then she might have to acknowledge that some of the fears she knew Maya was harbouring – the fear that she loved Hugh –

might actually be right, and that the girl could sense something Ellie wouldn't admit to herself.

Ellie didn't see Maya leave early the next morning, half an hour after first light. She was asleep next to Lizzie until the mad cockerel, which often strutted around the garden, crowed with bloodcurdling vigour below their bedroom window. Lizzie shot up in terror and her mother pulled her back down again into the soft pillows.

'It's only that silly old rooster,' she said, stroking the girl's hair.

The cockerel, which enjoyed crowing all the time and not just at dawn, was furious in the morning, scratching the flower beds near the weeping cypress trees. When Hugh returned on his horse from Kalimpong, disappointed again because his contacts had no news, the bird paraded angrily around the horse's hind legs, narrowly missing being kicked by the irritated mare. In the late afternoon, it chased Nanny Barker across the middle lawn, pecking at her ankles, and then turned on Lizzie in a storm of feathers. The girl screamed, Nanny tried to kick the bird, and then Hugh grabbed it. It squawked and thrashed, scratching him with its spurs, until he released it into the yard behind the stables, where the hen coop stood.

Ellie sat on the veranda, comforting Lizzie, who was snuggled up on her lap. Hugh flopped into a cane lounger next to her and used a handkerchief to wipe the blood from his arm. He was worried, and he didn't need to look at his watch to know it was getting late. The last of the sun shone on the sweet peas climbing over woven frames in the flower beds nearest the house. The faint breeze fanned the fragrance over the veranda. Below them the soft yellowing sun glinted on the lily ponds.

Hugh dabbed at his wounds with iodine, aware that Ellie was watching him. He'd often noticed her doing that, and it was odd, because she rarely looked him in the face. He wished she would; that way he thought he might be able to judge what she was thinking.

'I shouldn't have let her go,' he said abruptly, anxiety making him speak more loudly than he'd intended.

Lizzie thought he was angry, and her face crumpled. Ellie rocked her, and she curled up again, resting against her mother. Nanny Barker snored loudly on a chair at the far end of the veranda, and Jean lay abandoned on the lawn.

'She should be home by now,' he added, lowering his voice.

'She's probably been distracted,' Ellie said.

'Maya doesn't get distracted.'

They sat in silence. The late sun tinted the snow orange and pink, and then was gone.

Nanny Barker woke and took Lizzie off for supper and a bath.

Hugh paced the veranda. 'This is when I regret not having a telephone.'

'You're worrying without real reason,' Ellie said, and thought how often people had said the same thing to her. 'I'm sure there's a sensible explanation.'

'I'm going to ride to the next tea garden. I'll borrow their car and drive to Darjeeling. Maybe she's broken down. Or she might have gone off the road.'

'Don't say that. You can't think the worst.'

Hugh went to the stables and Ellie stayed on the veranda.

She was looking over the garden filled with the soft, bluish light of the new moon when her attention was caught by headlights moving along the road.

Hugh rode out of the stable yard holding a hurricane lamp in one hand. A rifle was strapped to his back.

'Wait,' Ellie said, holding the horse's bridle.

Hugh dismounted as the Baby Austin pulled into the drive.

Maya jumped out. 'I had a good time, but I'm glad to be back,' she said, grabbing parcels and bags out of the passenger seat.

'Where's Sarah?' she asked. 'I've got a book for her.'

'Sarah?' Hugh and Ellie said in unison.

'Believe it or not,' Maya laughed, 'Nanny Barker has a name.'

She flew into the house with her purchases, and Hugh leaned on the overheated car and sighed with relief.

'I think I need a drink,' he said.

'You don't drink.'

'I will tonight.'

Hugh found a bottle of Scotch in a cabinet in the sitting room and opened it on the veranda. Above them, Kanchenjunga glowed in shades of blue and purple, and the sky turned a deep indigo.

'You want some?' he asked, filling a second glass without waiting for an answer. He looked at the whisky in the lamplight. 'It's from the land of my ancestors.'

She tasted it, and it wasn't as awful as she'd remembered. After a few minutes she began to feel a warm glow spreading through her limbs.

Hugh leaned back in the chair, still feeling shaken. He knew he shouldn't have let Maya drive such a long way, no matter how persistent she'd been. She was too young and inexperienced.

Ellie saw the frown lines on his forehead. 'You can unwind now. She's home safe,' she said.

'But she might not have been. I don't know what I was thinking. It's not like me. I've a duty to protect her.'

He was staring glassy-eyed at the moonlit mountaintops.

'You love her, so of course you worry about her, but there's no need to overdramatise this.'

Ellie paused, asking herself if she had actually said that – she who made a drama of every dark place, wisp of smoke and clap of thunder.

'You must have loved her mother very much,' she said in an effort to sound supportive.

Hugh focused directly on her, surprise in his face. 'Oh no,' he said. 'I loved her father.'

Ellie almost choked on her whisky. 'But you *are* her father.'

'I am now, in every way that matters, but she's not my biological daughter. I didn't even know her mother.'

Ellie felt suddenly, frighteningly confused. She had to rethink everything. All her assumptions had been wrong. Hugh Douglas wasn't the man she'd thought he was.

'And you loved Maya's father?' she asked, failing to keep the tremble from her voice.

He laughed, seeing the way her mind was working. 'Not like that,' he said. 'He was my brother.'

She put her hand over her glass as he tried to refill it. Her mind was fuzzy and she wanted to understand what he was saying. The moths flung themselves against the lamp, the bullfrogs croaked down in the lily ponds, and she listened as he told her the story of his brother, and a war, and a love he wished he hadn't betrayed.

'Do you remember that photograph you looked at when you first arrived? The one in the study of me and my ayah, Kamala?' Hugh asked.

Ellie nodded.

'There were two boys in the photo, not just me. The other boy was Suresh, Kamala's own son. When my mother died, Kamala became my wet nurse as well as my ayah. Suresh and I were the same age – we were born only weeks apart – and so we grew up together. We were like brothers. Everything he did, I did. That's why I speak Nepali like a villager. Ironically, it's my mother tongue. And I know the hills and mountains around here because that's where Suresh and I used to play. We were so happy, both of us. Really happy. Then it all changed, because I turned into a sahib.'

Hugh blew out his cheeks and Ellie thought he might get up and leave; he clearly wasn't happy talking like this.

'Actually, I turned into a burra sahib. It didn't happen overnight, because you have to learn how to be a sahib. No one is born with that sense of entitlement and superiority. My school in England taught me well. After school, I went to Cambridge, passed the exams to enter the Indian Civil Service and got a posting as an assistant district commissioner in a wretched district in Bengal, which is the place they send the least promising officers, because they think it's a shit hole, and they're probably right.

'I came back ten years after I'd left. It was half my lifetime, and it was a shock because it was as if I'd never been away. It was like coming home, only there was a problem, a sort of unease. I couldn't be myself any more. I was some stupid parody of a sahib. I remembered India but I couldn't remember who I was.'

Hugh took another sip of his whisky and then put the glass down. He could see Ellie looking at him intently, and he didn't want to return the gaze in case it broke the spell binding her to him.

'I came back here on my first leave. I was desperate to see the house, and to see everyone, but I was scared too, because it was the place I'd always dreamed about. I'd thought about it every day in England, especially at the start, when I could have died of homesickness. I hadn't seen my father since he sent me away to school, and for a moment I'm sure he didn't recognise me. The last time he'd seen me I was twelve years old. He'd changed a lot too: he was an old man, and probably dying, though I didn't know it then. Kamala looked older as well, but she was still full of energy, working around the house at odd jobs. It was only Suresh that I failed to recognise – and that's because I didn't want to see him. I didn't want to know him.

'On the first afternoon, I was sitting here, in almost exactly this spot, and he was down there, where the middle tier of the lawn ends. He was weeding the flower beds, because in the ten years it had taken me to become a burra sahib, Suresh had become a *mali*, a gardener. He ran up here, just the same way he did when he was a boy. He was excited, and he smiled at me, and one part of me saw he was exactly the same, but I couldn't acknowledge him. I pretended I didn't recognise him, and then I gave him a stiff little smile and a nod, the way a sahib acknowledges a loyal servant.

'And that was the way it went on for the full two weeks of my leave. I snubbed him constantly. When he came to speak to me, I brushed him off. He loved me; he still thought of us as brothers. And I couldn't bear to look at him. I couldn't stand it. I hated his bazaar clothes, his bloody cheap sandals, the way he smiled at me. I'd changed and he hadn't. In the end, he gave up. He was proud, and I humiliated him time after time, until he got the message and went about his work without looking up at the house.'

Hugh's voice cracked, and Ellie reached over and put her hand on his.

'God, if only I could go back and change things. He'd shared his mother with me, we had played together every day for years, and I couldn't even speak to him.' Hugh used his bloodied handkerchief to wipe his eyes.

'I went back to my district and barely thought of him at all, until I got a letter saying Father was ill. I came home to find him dying. Suresh had left the house two months before, and to be honest, I was glad, because it saved me embarrassment. It was the first year of the Great War, and he'd joined the 8th Gurkha Rifles. He'd married just before he left. Cook said she was a pretty girl, though I can't vouch for that as I never saw her myself. Her name was Ishwari, and her family had come from Nepal to set up a tea shop. I suppose Suresh thought being a rifleman was a step up in the world for a newly married man.'

Hugh laughed. 'God, if only he had known what it would really be like. The 8th Gurkhas lost hundreds of men at Festubert, and in the middle of winter they were in the trenches still wearing their Indian weather clothing. Father was gung-ho about the war and he wanted me to keep up the family tradition, so I joined the 5th Gurkhas, just like he had. It was a sort of deathbed promise. Only I wasn't in the 5th for long, because they moved me to the 8th. They'd lost so many men and officers, they needed reinforcements to take part in another big battle. I checked the rolls and saw Suresh's name in the list of riflemen, so I knew he was still alive. I joined the 8th just before the Battle of Loos. Have you heard of it?'

Ellie shook her head, and then, realising that Hugh was looking at the mountains, she said, 'No. I try not to think about the war.' She wanted to add that she had too many bad things to think about already but it didn't seem the right response.

'When I arrived, an artillery bombardment was already softening up the enemy. It looked promising, but a couple of days later the weather changed and rain filled the trenches. It was a foot deep in places. On the day of the battle we launched a chlorine gas attack at dawn. It was the first time our boys had used gas, and what a bloody mess it was. At the last moment, the wind turned and blew the gas back on to our own lines.

'I was on the left flank and the gas missed us, but I saw what it did to the other men. A lot of them had gas masks, but they weren't up to the job. You couldn't breathe through them and the eyepieces fogged up. The men were vomiting and coughing up green foam. An hour later many of them were dead; their skins had turned green and black, and their tongues stuck out of their mouths, covered in a thick, dry fur. I kept thinking I'd find Suresh like that, but thank God he'd escaped it.'

Hugh's voice had gone flat, as if he couldn't imbue his words with emotion because if he did, he wouldn't be able to speak them.

'We went over the top. Again, it didn't go to plan. The wire hadn't been cut in front of our lines, visibility was terrible and we were under heavy fire. The Germans positioned machine guns in front of us. They were bombarding us with shells and it was utter confusion. I can't remember what happened next; not clearly. My only firm memory is of a young subaltern being hit by a shell a few feet from me. His head and arms flew over my head. Then something hit me. It was like a thud, and it wasn't painful. Then there was nothing.

'I can't have been unconscious for long, because the sun still wasn't high when I opened my eyes. I was lying on my back in a shell hole that was slowly filling with gas. I tried to move, but the pain in my chest paralysed me. I knew that even if the wound didn't kill me, the gas definitely would. I tried searching for my mask, but I'd lost it. A searing pain cut into my lungs, and then I passed out. When I came round again, I wasn't in the shell hole; I was being dragged across no-man's-land, a foot at a time. The bullets whistled around me. I turned to find out who was pulling me and saw a hand around my wrist, and then a face I knew. Suresh looked at me. He didn't speak. I heard him groan with the effort as he heaved me another foot, and another. Then I was gone, into the blackness again.

'I woke in a field hospital, hanging over the side of the bed frame so my lungs would drain of fluid. My chest had been punctured by shrapnel, and my lungs were scorched by chlorine gas. I should have died in that shell hole. But the irony is that I lived, and the man who saved me didn't. Suresh had seen me and my men in the middle of a mortar attack. He saw I'd been hit and he crawled through no-man's-land to find me. He was shot twice, once on the way there, and again on the way back. It took him two hours to drag me back to our own lines, but by then he'd lost so much blood, there was nothing they could do. The orderlies told me he died half an hour after the stretcher bearers got us to the hospital. Apparently it was one of the heroic stories that came out of that pointless battle.

'He was awarded the Victoria Cross,' Hugh said, his voice cracking. 'He lost his life fighting in a war that wasn't his. It was my country's war, and that battle was for inches of land. He died for an inch of European soil.'

'No, Hugh,' Ellie said, feeling as choked as Hugh sounded. 'He died saving you.'

'It's a bloody farce, isn't it? They said it was the regiment's Valhalla, and a magnificent display of bravery. But do you know what that actually means? We started that morning with ten British officers, eight Gurkha officers and five hundred and two men. By evening there was only one British officer and forty-nine men left standing.'

'My God, that's terrible,' Ellie said, and thought how pathetic and weak her words were. How was it possible to respond to such trauma with the intensity of emotion the events required? So in the absence of a better way, she did what she was accustomed to doing in the face of tragedy: she withdrew and became small. That way the great waves of sadness would not drown her, and she would bob along on the surface, fragile but still buoyant. She stroked Hugh's hand, and wished she knew how to hold him and comfort him.

Instead she said, 'But you are well now, aren't you?'

'I was in hospital and a convalescent home for over a year. My lungs are shot. I mean literally shot. They're full of shrapnel wounds and the doctor said there are still a few pieces left in there. You mustn't get me near a magnet.'

It was meant to be a joke, and when Ellie realised, she laughed, though it came out sounding silly and shrill.

'You never did have asthma when you were a child, did you?' she asked.

He shook his head. 'It seemed the best way to explain my cough without having to rake up this terrible story.'

'Did you go back into the army?'

'I was invalided out. I went back to an ICS job, back to a district very like my first, only this time in Bihar, on the northern plains. It was bad for my chest; too much heat and dust. Luckily I was transferred to the Political Service and moved back here in 1920. I worked in Gangtok, and it was good while it lasted. The hills are better for me, and I could use my Nepali and Tibetan, which is not actually as good as I like to think it is.'

He was sounding more like the old Hugh, and Ellie began to relax.

'For a while I couldn't face coming back here. I was afraid it would make me remember things I'd rather forget. I dreaded seeing Kamala, knowing that her only son had died because of me. And I was worried about the empty house, and its memories. I am such a bloody coward, Ellie. You don't know what a weak man I really am.'

'You're not a coward, Hugh,' Ellie said. He'd had the strength to tell her his secrets, the things that troubled him, whereas she had talked to no one, not even the kind and patient doctors who had sat with her and encouraged her to confess her fears of the dark. We are both damaged, she thought. I was injured by a natural disaster, and Hugh by a man-made one. Hugh carries the scars in his body, while I am damaged in my head.

'But one good thing did happen,' Hugh said. 'When I came back, Kamala was here as I'd expected. I'd paid her wages and those of the other staff ever since my father died, so I knew she wouldn't have left. But she also had her granddaughter, Maya, with her. You see, Suresh had left his bride pregnant; I've no idea if he even knew he had a child. Ishwari, Maya's mother, died in the Spanish flu epidemic a few months after the end of the war, and so the little girl was being looked after by her grandmother.

'When Kamala died, I took Maya on as my own. I adopted her. She is Suresh's daughter, and she is mine too. She looks like him, and I am repaying a debt I will never be able to settle. Over the years, I've blamed everyone for this situation. I blamed the generals for the war that killed Suresh. And I blamed the bloody Empire, and the school where they turned me into a man I didn't want to be. But most of all, I blame myself, because it takes individuals to make a culture, and I chose to be a sahib and cast off the best friend I ever had, because he was too poor and too black.'

Ellie moved her chair towards him, its legs scratching on the tiled veranda. She put her arm around his shoulder and pulled him towards her, his head resting against her cheek. She stroked his hair, feeling it thicker and softer between her fingers than she'd imagined. He smelled of sandalwood, and she tipped her head so her lips touched his hair in a kiss that wasn't a kiss. From inside the house, she heard Maya and Nanny Barker laughing. Ellie pulled away from Hugh, and in a sudden surge of madness that she didn't see coming, she cupped his face and kissed him full on the mouth, only once and only for a second. Then she stood, smoothed her blouse, and walked quickly into the house. Her lips were wet and she tasted the saltiness of tears.

Spring in the Himalayan foothills was short, and summer began in April. Darjeeling was packed with heat-raddled escapees from the dusty plains. The white people who could afford to leave Calcutta came to the hills, to a place that looked like home, only it was better than the Lake District or the Cotswolds or any of the other scenic places in Britain, because in India, they could still afford plenty of servants.

May was the hottest month in Kalimpong, but here the strength of the sun was tempered by the altitude, by the deep shade of the forests and by cool air sweeping down from the high peaks. The days were balmy and the nights were fresh. If it hadn't been for the thought of Tom, which gnawed away at Ellie, she would have been content, because she knew, without actually having the heart to feel it, that this was a perfect place. But every time she began to relax – on the veranda, walking in the gardens, or riding with Hugh along the dirt roads through the neighbouring tea estates – Tom's disappearance, and the knowledge that he was somewhere across the crest of the Himalayas, pulled her back into herself, so there was no rest from the worry and the waiting, even in the warmth of an afternoon sitting on the lawn, with Lizzie playing by her feet, and Hugh dozing on a blue and yellow blanket, in safari shorts and a short-sleeved white linen shirt, while the butterflies danced above him and insects flew past, some slow and droning, others whizzing by, invisible and without trace, except for the lingering buzz they left in her ears.

Towards the end of May, on a blisteringly hot morning, Ellie was surprised to see an old man sitting with Hugh on the veranda. She didn't recognise him, but she knew his hat was a Nepali topi, and there was something about the way the two men talked, their heads close together, each intent on what the other was saying, that made her pause and take a step back into the house. When she looked round the door again, the men were walking across the drive and heading for the storerooms around the back of the stables. She waited a minute and then followed, intrigued. They had opened the door to the smallest store. It was usually padlocked, and none of the servants had a key.

The sun shone directly into the room, and Ellie saw Hugh and the man stooping down around a collection of boxes. She went closer, feeling as if she was doing something wrong, but then reasoned it wasn't really like spying, because Hugh and this new man couldn't have anything to hide. She stepped into the room, blocking the sun so the light level dropped. Hugh jumped up from beside an open box, and the old man stared up at her, unable to stand quickly enough. It took her several seconds to realise it was Dr Prasad; he looked twenty years older. A pistol fell from his hand, and she squealed in fright.

'Be quiet, the servants will come running,' Hugh said, and looked round the door to check no one was about. Then he began to open the other crates with a crowbar, trying hard not to splinter the wood. There were four of them, and in the bottom of each, an assortment of guns and ammunition was neatly arranged under bolts of cloth.

'Oh my God,' Ellie said, backing away. 'You keep these things in your store? There's enough here to start a small war.' She examined the boxes and thought she recognised them; hadn't they come with them in the luggage Hugh and Maya had brought back from Kathmandu?

'What are they for?' she asked uneasily. These weren't the kind of guns Francis owned. They weren't for tiger shooting or hunting barking deer.

'They're mine, or at least they belong to a group of my friends,' Dr Prasad said.

'You have some weird friends, Dr Prasad.'

'Hugh brought them back from Kathmandu for me. In fact, he looked after them for me after the earthquake destroyed my house. I had nowhere to store them and they were in danger of being discovered.'

'That's a real nice thing for someone to do for a person they don't even know.' Ellie turned to Hugh. 'When we went to Nepal and we were walking through the Chitlong Valley, you told me you didn't know Dr Prasad.'

'I wasn't being entirely truthful. Actually, I've known him for years. When I was visiting Calcutta, we'd see each other at meetings organised by the League Against Imperialism, or by Congress. But I didn't know he'd be on his way to Nepal at the same time as I was. There was no big conspiracy; it was just chance that we were both on that train. The trouble was, it would do serious harm for Dr Prasad to be associated with a foreigner when he was in Kathmandu. It would raise all kinds of suspicions, so of course I said I didn't know him.'

Ellie recalled a hazy memory of a room in which giant shadows played on the walls and Hugh whispered to a man who looked, in her delirium, strikingly like Dr Prasad.

'You came to Tri-Chandra College the night of the earthquake, right?'

'I did,' Dr Prasad said. 'I came to beg for help.'

'And these guns were supposed to start a war?' she asked.

'They were supposed to begin a revolution in Nepal. We were going to topple the Ranas, but the earthquake struck before we could act. You might say it was fate, Lady Northwood.'

'Are you part of this revolution, Hugh?'

'No,' he said. 'But when Dr Prasad came to Tri-Chandra College and asked me for help, I couldn't refuse.'

'What would have happened if you'd been caught?'

Hugh sighed heavily. 'I don't really know what would have happened to me. I'd probably be imprisoned and there'd be some diplomatic fracas. But if Dr Prasad was found with these armaments, it would mean certain death.'

'You risked all that to get rid of the Ranas?' Ellie asked the doctor.

'It would be a sacrifice worth making,' Dr Prasad said.

Hugh scanned the crates. 'Everything is here, isn't it?' he asked. 'Nothing's missing?'

'It's all there,' Dr Prasad said.

Hugh began fixing the lids back on, tapping in nails to secure them.

'I'll have a couple of men collect them this afternoon,' Dr Prasad said, walking back out into the sunlight. 'I'm sure you'll be glad to have them off your property. I would have arranged it sooner, but they didn't release me until last month, and it's taking me some time to regain my strength. Prison takes an especially heavy toll on the elderly.'

'Was your son released too?' Hugh asked.

'He was executed by firing squad last week, and then they hung his body from a tree on Kanti Path as a warning to others.'

'No. My God!' Ellie gasped, and covered her open mouth with her hand.

'My other son is well, though. He managed to escape and I'm joining him in Calcutta as soon as I can. Then we are going to make new plans.'

'You are going to carry on after what happened to your son?' Ellie asked. 'Haven't you suffered enough?'

'We won't stop until my country is free. I'm physically broken now, and the only reason they didn't put me before a firing squad is because they'd be wasting a bullet. I won't live long, but after I've gone, there will be others to replace me. We have the support of King Tribhuvan, and one day the Ranas will no longer govern Nepal.'

Ellie took his arm and led him to the veranda, where she helped him lower himself into one of the cane chairs. The bearer brought him a plate of *dal bhat tarkari*, the food of Nepal. The rice was fragrant and brilliant white; the dal earthy and laced with ginger and garlic; and the vegetables were colourful and sweet, and shot through with fiery chillies.

'Do you remember the girl you were treating, the one you took me to see?' Hugh said when the doctor had finished eating. 'I wonder if she recovered.'

'She did. When I was released, I went back to the hospital and found Adil, the junior doctor, who treated her after I was arrested. He said she survived, though she has no chance of ever being a mother.' Dr Prasad fixed Hugh with an intent look. 'Did you investigate?'

'I did, and it was Davies, the gunman. He won't be doing anything like that again.'

'You took matters into your own hands?'

Ellie stared at Hugh, worried about what she was going to hear.

'I didn't have to,' Hugh said. 'A girl with the blackest eyes did that, and the evidence is at the bottom of the Bagmati River.'

Ellie sighed, and for the first time in months, Dr Prasad smiled.

The monsoon was late and the Himalayan summer continued with cloudless skies. Temperatures rose in Kalimpong, and anxious farmers looked south for signs that the wind would bring rain from the Bay of Bengal. The tea gardens needed downpours to start the third and fourth flushes and provide the biggest, if not best, harvests of the year. The mists and hailstorms that usually preceded the rains didn't arrive, however, and although black storm clouds gathered over Sikkim to the north, the monsoon did not break.

Ellie was waiting, but not for the rains. The monsoon was of no consequence to her when all she cared about was hearing news that never came. In the bazaar, the traders and their customers smiled sadly when shown the familiar picture of Tom on the Chandragiri Pass. 'No,' they all repeated, 'we have heard nothing.'

The Assistant District Superintendent of Police was tired of seeing Ellie and Hugh in his office, always asking the same questions. Derrick Williamson, the Political Officer in Gangtok, the capital of Sikkim, was courteous and very helpful, and said he would do what he could to find Tom. He promised he would send word through the network of British spies. But Ellie also listened to Williamson's warnings that Tibet was a vast country and British influence didn't run as far and as deep as he would have liked. The chances of finding a missing boy were slim, to say the least.

Hugh had used all his contacts to find the boy, and he'd spoken to almost every trader who'd passed through Kalimpong bazaar. But there was something else he was waiting for just as much as news of Tom. He wanted Ellie to soften. He wanted her to kiss him again the way she'd done on the veranda the night he thought Maya was missing. Since then she'd grown distant, and was more self-contained than usual. He'd told her he was a coward, a man who put social convention before friendship. Perhaps she'd believed him and taken him at his word. Maybe, he thought, she's beginning to dislike me.

Hugh was wrong about this: Ellie didn't dislike him. In fact, the opposite was true.

She watched the syce bring Hugh's horse to the front of the house.

'I'm going to the army checkpoint,' Hugh said, and pulled his Terai hat firmly on to his head. Before she'd kissed him on the veranda, Ellie had gone with him to the checkpoint almost every day. Now she gave different reasons to stay at home: Lizzie wanted to play games; or the child was feeling poorly; or Nanny Barker's puffy legs had swollen up again. They were feeble excuses, and Hugh knew it. At times he thought she was unreachable, that she would never soften, never be his, and he despaired, not knowing what he could say or do to chip away at the barrier she erected around herself.

The harder he tried, the more aloof she became, and it was unbearable. He wanted her more every day, his longing so acute she erased the memory of the women he'd known before: the Anglo-Indian women he'd courted in Calcutta; the girl from the fishing fleet who'd come to India to bag a husband and who'd been his fiancée until she visited the flyblown district in Bengal that was to be her home. Standing in the drive, looking at Ellie's serious, intense face, he found he could hardly recall what that girl had looked like.

Hugh moved closer to her, and Ellie was sure the air between them vibrated with tension. She wanted to reach out and touch him right there and then, but she kept her hands by her sides. Most of all, she wanted to do what her friend Momo would have done without a second thought, and the idea of it crowded her waking hours and interrupted her sleep. In truth, she didn't want to stay in her own room at night. She wanted to get out of bed and walk down the corridor to Hugh's room. She wanted to lie with him on sheets that would smell like him, of sandal-wood and the sun. She wondered how his skin would feel against hers. Would it be cool or warm? She imagined his hands stroking her, cupping her breasts, and his mouth on hers in a kiss that was not like the hard, quick one on the veranda, but long and slow, his tongue on her lips, and between them. She slammed the door shut on those thoughts, and gave Hugh a composed, unreadable look.

The monsoon drove a strong, swift breeze before it. It whistled through the forest, bending the trees, and when the first rain came, it was icy, as if it had brushed against the snow-capped peaks that were suddenly hidden behind clouds. By the middle of June the rains were warm, heavy and sustained. The downpours drummed on Ellie's umbrella, and thundered on the tin roof of the house. They washed away the hot season's red dust, turning the hills around Kalimpong glossy and emerald green. In the valleys, the jungle sweated with humidity, and higher, on the forested slopes, streams dashed over their rocky beds, accelerating as they drew closer to the deep gorge of the Teesta River. The hill terraces filled rapidly with water. The narrow fields were like mirrors to the sky, glassy and black while the storms gathered, blue and white and sparkling when the sun edged briefly from behind the clouds.

Heat and moisture made everything grow. The tea pluckers couldn't work fast enough, the bushes producing more fresh tips than they could harvest. Orchids grew in profusion in the forks of the trees, and the creepers, tree ferns and vines all flourished as rain fell, day after day, on warm earth. When it wasn't raining, mist rose from the valleys, and lingered in nebulous clouds that dissolved in long, vaporous fingers over the hillsides.

In Kalimpong bazaar, Ellie did her rounds of the stalls with Tom's photograph. She glanced at her watch to make sure she wasn't going to be late meeting Hugh, who was doing his own rounds of the tea shops and the less salubrious toddy shops. The watch face was misted up on the inside, and she could only just make out the time. She stood under her umbrella as the rain pelted it, the force of the deluge making the handle tremble.

Hugh strode towards her, rain dripping off the brim of his hat.

'There's nothing,' he said, shaking his head.

'The bazaar is emptier than usual,' she said.

'There are fewer wool traders during the monsoon. The damp isn't good for wool. It'll be quiet until the autumn.'

'When's that?' Ellie said, alarmed.

'September or October.'

Her whole body contracted and she seemed to shrink three inches. That's another two months at least, she thought. Two more months of waiting. It was far too long. Tom had been gone for five months, and five months was a long time in a small child's life. Perhaps he would forget her. Perhaps, when she found him, he wouldn't even know she was his mother.

Hugh registered her panic and took her arm. He guided her back to the car, and it was only when she was sitting inside that she realised thunder was booming around the valleys and echoing off the hills. Sheet lightning crackled among the clouds.

'It will pass soon,' he said, and held her hand. She didn't pull it away.

They sat in silence as the thunder receded. The rain bombarded the car. A couple of Tibetan lamas ran by with blankets held over their heads, and two half-naked boys cavorted in the waterfall spilling from the corner of a roof. When the rain slowed to a drizzle, Hugh cleared the misted windows and drove home slowly on roads of greasy red clay.

Tom's lamb sat on the chest of drawers in Ellie and Lizzie's room, its one glass eye staring out of the window to where Kanchenjunga was masked by cloud. Downstairs, in the study, Maya also kept one eye on the window. She was looking for the dak wallah, though he only came to their house about once a week, and when he did, she was always disappointed that he had nothing but newsletters and book catalogues for her.

'Why do you run to the door whenever the post comes?' Hugh asked.

Maya shrugged, wrinkling her nose, and went back to her work.

Hugh watched her typing the manuscript of their book, the keys of the old typewriter jamming for a moment every time she pressed 'A'. He wondered if she was waiting for a letter from a boy, though he didn't know how it would be possible for her to meet anyone without him knowing. She spent all her time in the study and only went out to take walks near the house. The only time she'd spent by herself was when she went to Darjeeling and came home so late. She hadn't had time then to start a romance, he decided, but even so, he felt uneasy. It was as if she was growing out of his control, and out of his care.

It was another hot, sultry afternoon, and the sweeper came silently into the study and began spraying the corners with Flit to combat the mosquitoes. Hugh started to back out of the room, but not before he'd breathed in a lungful of pesticide and a band had tightened around his chest. He gasped, then coughed, and Maya jumped up in fright. He lifted his hand, motioning her to sit as he left. In his room, he sorted through the medicines on his chest of drawers and coughed up a spot of bright red blood into his handkerchief.

Maya's letter came at the end of July. Hugh saw her reading it in the little mosquito-proof, mesh-covered outdoor room on the southern side of the veranda. He saw her biting her lower lip. Her feet were moving, tapping the floor as if she was excited. He sat next to her, and when she wouldn't look him in the eye, he knew it meant trouble.

'Is it from a boy?' he asked.

'A man.'

He bridled. A man, he thought. Jesus Christ, she's only a girl.

She saw the horror on his face. 'No, Father, it's nothing like that.'

'Are you going to tell me?'

'I will, if you promise not to be cross.'

Nanny Barker walked across the lawn carrying an armful of cut flowers from the garden. Hugh noticed she wasn't wearing her brogues; instead she wore sandals from the bazaar. She stopped and looked over at Maya and Hugh. They resumed their conversation, but switched to Nepali, and Nanny Barker continued on her way, her feet squelching on the sodden grass.

'I can't promise not to be angry, Maya, because I don't know what you are going to say.'

She took a deep breath. 'You remember when I went to Darjeeling? Well, I didn't just go to do shopping. I went to a lecture at the town hall by Mr Cartwright, one of the curators from the Indian Museum in Calcutta. It was advertised in the paper.'

'I see,' Hugh said. 'And what's the significance of that?'

'I wanted to talk to him. I wanted to tell him about what we do. About what *I* do.'

'And was Mr Cartwright impressed?' He spoke in a measured voice, because this confession sounded a lot better than Maya meeting an unknown man and beginning a disastrous romance.

'Yes, yes,' she said, excitement making her jiggle in her chair. 'They have no one at the museum who can read as many languages and scripts as me. I asked if I could assist them in their archaeology department. I discussed it with him there, and later I wrote to him. This is his reply, Father, and it says I can go. They won't pay me, but I can work with them, and who knows, maybe they'll give me a job when they know how good I am. And even if they don't, think of the things I can learn. Just think of it.'

'No, Maya, absolutely not.'

'Why?'

'You can't live in Calcutta.'

'Why not?'

'It's dangerous for a girl.'

'Father, I am not a girl. I am almost twenty years old. And I can find lodgings in a decent place. You know I can.'

'This is your home.'

'Yes, it is, but I don't want to stay all my life in one place. I'll always come back home, but I'm not like you, Father. You want to be here; you need to be here. And I don't. I want to see the city. I want this chance. I don't only want to read the books in our house and the ones I order from the bookshop and from catalogues. I want to sit in a big proper library.'

'The university and colleges don't admit women.'

'Then I'll study on my own. I can do it. I know I'm smarter than all those boys in the university. I was the smartest girl in school. Please, Father, let me go.'

'It's impossible. Your home is here, and I have a duty to look after you.'

'Please.'

'No.'

'You can't make all my decisions for me. You're not my father. You're not my real father,' Maya shouted, and stomped out of the mesh room, slamming the flimsy door behind her.

She sat in the study and sobbed at the injustice. Nanny Barker put a vase of flowers on the table, and stroked Maya's bent head. Maya glanced up at her, and howled.

'Whatever it is, you won't feel so bad tomorrow,' Nanny said.

Maya dried her eyes on Nanny's apron.

'I will, Sarah,' she said in a wobbly voice. 'He's turning me into a prisoner.'

Nanny Barker couldn't imagine why Maya wanted to leave her home in the hills. In the early mornings, in the quiet of her room, Nanny gazed through the haze of the mosquito net at the open window and the low slanting ceiling. Unlike everyone else in the house, who seemed to be waiting for something important, Nanny Barker had found peace. The mad cockerel crowed outside, but it was an undemanding sound because it didn't call her to action. Under the eaves, she didn't have to listen for babies and children the way she used to in the night nursery. She could lie and think, luxuriating in the freedom of not being on duty. At night Lizzie stayed with her mother, and for the first time in forty-five years, Sarah Barker's sleep was undisturbed.

Nanny was surprised to find she liked eating with Tenzing in the cookhouse. He sat cross-legged on the floor to eat his meals. When Nanny had tried this, she couldn't get up and had to be hauled to her feet. After that, Tenzing fetched a chair, and she balanced her plate on her lap. He was thoughtful in other ways too: he made sweet milky puddings and cakes like they had in the nursery at home. He said they were for the Missy Baba, but Nanny knew he really made them for her, not Lizzie. If she had been a young woman, Nanny might have thought Tenzing was courting her, but as she was old and white, and he was old and Indian, she knew he was just being kind.

Ellie liked Lizzie to have cookies and milk in the afternoons, and every day Tenzing diligently boiled the milk and baked fresh cookies – though Nanny insisted on referring to them as biscuits, because that was what they were called in England. While Lizzie had her snack, Nanny read her a story in the shade of the mesh-covered outdoor room, and then put her to sleep in a little string bed. The girl needed to have a good afternoon nap, otherwise she became ratty and unmanageable long before bedtime.

'This is a story about a boy who never grew up,' Nanny Barker said, getting comfy and arranging the cushions on the cane sofa.

Lizzie climbed on to the sofa and settled down, leaning against her. 'What's his name?' she asked.

'Peter Pan.'

It must have been the bearer's day off, because Tenzing appeared carrying the milk and biscuits. He put them on the table in front of Lizzie, and as Nanny began the story, the little girl began to gobble the biscuits and drink so fast it left a big white milk moustache on her upper lip. Ten minutes later, when Lizzie was dozing, her head heavy on Nanny Barker's arm, Nanny looked up to see Tenzing still at the mesh door.

Later, she went to the kitchen to fetch a glass of cold water. Tenzing stopped sifting through the dried lentils and said, 'Do dogs look after children in England?' There was a twinkle in his eye.

'You like stories from England?' she asked.

'I do.'

That night, in the cookhouse, Tenzing presented Nanny with a steamed treacle pudding and custard. Despite the heat of the evening and the fact that she had already had dinner, it made her heart and stomach glad.

'I have a new book here,' she said. 'It is brand new. Maya bought it for me as a present.' She took *Lost Horizon* by James Hilton out of the cavernous pocket of her apron. 'Shall I read it?' she asked. 'It's about a perfect valley called Shangri-La in the middle of the Himalayas where life is so good no one grows old.'

Tenzing drew up her chair, poured two small glasses of millet beer, and settled himself on the floor.

Nanny ran the spoon around the last of the custard clinging to the side of the bowl, and glanced at him as she put it in her mouth. He really is a fine cook, she thought. And he's got a lovely face for someone his age. She opened the book and took a sip of beer. It tasted good. He grinned at her, and she smiled. They were too old for romance, she thought, but not too old for stories.

The monsoon began to withdraw as August turned into September. The rice seedlings grew tall in the flooded terraces, the rains slackened, and sunlight shone through gaps in the mist and moved in patches over the tea. Thunder echoed less often in the valleys, and on some days the clouds lifted from the mountains. Fields drained, the rice ripened, turning from green to gold, and the farmers prepared for the harvest. The heat and humidity slowly diminished, and autumn settled, bright and warm, on the Himalayan foothills. Early mornings carried a snap in the air, and nights were chilly again.

Traders began to return to the bazaar, and pilgrims gathered at the gompas and temples. In the house, Ellie waited anxiously. Hugh continued to be patient and observant, while Maya fumed, resentful and short-tempered, and Nanny Barker drifted from nights of contented sleep into days of good food, millet beer and storytelling, while wearing a brand-new pair of felt boots bought by Tenzing from the bazaar.

Ellie did not hear much from the world beyond Kalimpong. She heard nothing from Francis, despite sending him several letters to the palace in Kathmandu and to the house in England. She'd let him know they were staying at the Douglas family home in Kalimpong, but Francis hadn't written to ask about her or Lizzie, or how the search for Tom was unfolding. She received no letters apart from correspondence from her bank, which queried several large cheques Francis had drawn on one of her accounts. In October, a letter told her why.

Francis's barely legible handwriting, which deteriorated into a scrawl, indicated that he had written the letter while plastered, and probably just before passing out. It began by stating that he'd intended to rush to Kalimpong to apologise on bended knee for being such a rotten ass, and to ask Ellie to forgive him his mistakes so they could start afresh. He'd been in Calcutta making plans for the journey when, quite by chance, he'd met a girl at the Tollygunge Club who was out from home for a few weeks. She was one of those horse-mad debutantes, and although Ellie had been the love of his life, he wrote, this girl, who was called Elizabeth, might help heal his broken heart after Ellie had chucked him for that marriage-wrecker, Douglas.

Francis insisted he didn't hold anything against Ellie; he'd been a miserable drunk and a cad, and she deserved a better husband. But now the damage was done, he'd reconciled himself to settling for second best. In which case, he continued, perhaps they should get a divorce so he could forget the traumas of the past and start anew. He was sailing on the tide for Kenya, where he and Elizabeth would live in Happy Valley with all the other aristocratic exiles, and where the big-game hunting was still good and the servants cheap.

He was sorry to tell her that, in the end, the Maharaja's nephew had turned out to be all talk: there was no hunting with elephants in the Terai, and they had turned back before reaching camp. In fact, the Maharaja had disinherited his supposed favourite nephew along with a lot of other members of the overly large Rana family. To top it all, the nephew had been the most terrible host and had abandoned poor Francis in the sagging palace, vanishing one night with a haul of Nepal's most priceless treasures, together with that hopeless and disloyal ayah, Shushila.

Could Ellie, Francis suggested, come to an agreement with him? Some sort of settlement? Ellie could have custody of Lizzie, and perhaps, as a gesture of goodwill, she could make a small contribution to his future, a way to repair his damaged life. Half a million dollars would do the trick.

After she'd deciphered the address where he would be staying, she wrote two letters and gave them to the chowkidar to take immediately to the post office in Kalimpong. One told Francis he could have his half a million dollars; the other instructed her lawyers. She watched the chowkidar run down the road, skirting around a couple of lamas, who walked slowly, spinning hand-held prayer wheels. She stepped back into the shade of the house and was on the verge of crying with sorrow and relief when she saw the lamas turning into the drive. They sat by a low wall next to the gates and placed bowls in front of them. They had come to beg for alms.

Hugh stepped on to the veranda through the study doors. He walked over to the men and bent down to talk to them. Then his head moved up sharply and his back straightened. Ellie felt the tiny hairs on her arms prickle. Anticipation fluttered in her stomach. As she walked on to the drive, her heart beat faster.

The men wore felt boots and long, heavy robes, stiff with grease and dirt. They beamed at her and spoke a greeting. Their faces were serene and friendly under their bright yellow hats.

'These lamas have been pilgrims for years,' Hugh said. 'They travel between Tibet, Nepal and India. They visit every Buddhist shrine and monastery.'

Ellie stopped breathing and stared, knowing exactly what Hugh was going to say. She willed him to speak the words.

'They've seen Tom. He's in Tibet. In a town called Gyantse.'

7

The High Himalayas and the Tibetan Plateau, November–December 1934

GYANTSE WAS A three-week march from Kalimpong. They would have to travel through Sikkim, over the High Himalayas, and across the Tibetan Plateau. Hugh went to Gangtok again to see Derrick Williamson, the Political Officer, and use what influence and goodwill he had left. It speeded the process of getting frontier permits to enter Tibet, but although it took three weeks rather than the usual two months, Ellie was frantic at the delay. Winter was approaching and she was anxious the passes would soon be blocked. Several times a day she looked north to the lowering snowline on the mountains, and despaired.

The long wait meant there was a chance Tom might no longer be in Gyantse, which was the last place the British had any practical influence in Tibet. Foreigners weren't allowed beyond the town, with or without a permit.

They left in a rush one Tuesday morning at the end of November. Their permits were approved, and Hugh had secured permission for them to use the dak bungalows on the road to Gyantse. Shortly after dawn, he bought provisions in Kalimpong. Marmalade, macaroni, biscuits, tins of Campbell's soup, cheese, tins of milk, cocoa, flour, tinned meat, candles and kerosene were piled in a tower of crates in the bazaar.

'Can't we buy things on the way?' Ellie asked.

'Not in Tibet. We have to carry what we need,' Hugh replied.

He added presents to give to Tibetan dignitaries: red ceremonial scarves, boxes of English toilet soap and bottles of scent. Elsewhere in the bazaar he bought bedding, and then greatcoats, warm tweed clothing, gloves, snow goggles and Gilgit boots, which were fur-lined and reached the knee. Ellie was taken aback at the sheer quantity of things they needed.

Working fast, Hugh talked to a group of muleteers and looked over their pack mules, examining their backs and checking them for girth galls. He waved aside five, tapped a dozen on their heads to indicate that he would take them, and the deal was done. He chose two Bhotia ponies, which the Tibetans had trained like mules, and then negotiated the services of a bearer and a sweeper. Turning to Ellie, he told her they were ready to go.

'Now?' she said.

'We've a long journey today, and the days are getting shorter.'

Ellie was unnerved. She'd waited so long, and so impatiently, but now they were going, she wasn't prepared. She hadn't given proper instructions to Nanny Barker, and she hadn't explained to Lizzie what was going to happen. So while the muleteers loaded the pack mules and the syces prepared their ponies, Hugh and Ellie returned to Roseacre to say their goodbyes.

'We'll be back in around six weeks,' Hugh said as the members of the household assembled outside.

Ellie bent down to hug Lizzie, who was dangling a bald, naked Jean by the arm.

Maya was scowling, and Hugh nudged her arm, motioning her to move away from the others. He didn't want to leave this way, not with so much bad feeling between them.

'You're in charge, Maya,' he said. He gave her the keys to the car.

Maya's smile was wry. 'You leave me in charge of a house, a child, and a car, but you won't let me go to Calcutta.'

He sighed.

'You shouldn't go on this trip,' she said. 'It's against everything the doctors have advised. Why can you do exactly what you want, while you don't allow me to do anything?'

She searched his face and he looked into her eyes. They were exactly like her father's, and for a few seconds Hugh was thrown off balance.

'Why are you doing this?' she asked, frustration and anger making the smooth skin of her forehead bunch into lines.

'Because I know the boy is out there. He's not a figment of her imagination.' Hugh's eyes darted to Ellie and he took a deep breath. 'And because I love her,' he said. 'I've loved her since we were in Kathmandu and I saw her digging through the rubble to find her son. I have to help her.'

Maya's mouth and eyes opened in surprise. 'But she's such a peculiar woman. She's so . . .' She paused, and thought. 'She's so distant. Yes, that's it. It's as if she's not quite here.'

He smiled. Maya had it exactly right.

'Father,' she said, gently. She could see he meant what he

said, and her heart softened. She didn't like the way Ellie had established herself in the house and the way Hugh deferred to her like she was the new memsahib, but if she made him happy, Maya would tolerate her. He deserved that much at least.

He looked at her intently. She hadn't said 'Father' like that for a long time, not since she'd insisted he was not her real father. There was warmth in it, and he felt a lump in his throat.

'Be careful,' she said. She leaned against his chest. 'I don't know what I'd do without you.'

He lifted her head, cupping her small chin in his hand. 'You would probably go to Calcutta,' he said, and grinned.

She gave him a small, cracked smile.

He paused, staring at her, and saw the young woman she'd become. He'd been living in the past, thinking she was a child, when he really needed to let her go. His job was done. 'In the spring,' he said, 'we'll go to Calcutta and find you a good place to live.'

She gasped. 'I can go?'

'Yes, and, in the meantime, you must finish the book on your own. There's not much more to do. You'll have to add the final touches: confirm the references and double-check all the transliteration.'

Maya was so thrilled about the future, she forgot her fears about the present.

'Will you drive us to the bazaar?' Hugh asked.

She nodded enthusiastically.

As they were about to join the others, she took his fingers and pulled them. 'I didn't mean it, you know,' she said.

He looked sideways at her.

'When I said you weren't my father. I didn't mean it.'

'I know,' he said, and for the first time since she'd spoken the words, he believed her.

They left Kalimpong on the lower road to Tibet. They climbed the first seven miles on a stony, shadeless path, passing two mule teams heading in the opposite direction. Ellie's mount was a strawberry roan pony, which she decided to call Ruby. Ruby walked good-naturedly until she spied some tasty vegetation and veered off the path. It took a tap from the syce to head her in the right direction, and Hugh spoke sharply to the men in Tibetan, worried that Ruby wasn't going to be reliable on the dangerous paths.

Ellie's backside began to ache, and as they entered the forest, she dismounted and walked. Her wool socks drooped and then fell down inside her boots. When her heels began to rub, she climbed back on to Ruby for the final five miles before they reached the first dak bungalow in Pedong. It felt like torture. They'd done a double march, twenty-one and a half miles in a day, and although a lot of it had been borne by Ruby's legs, Ellie felt sore and fatigued. She wanted to lie down, but first they had to show their passes to the frontier guards, because they were now in Sikkim.

The dak bungalow was one of many built by the British for official and private travellers going as far as Gyantse. They were also staging points for the dak wallahs taking post from India to Tibet. The bungalows themselves were basic; they had beds without bedding, and fires without fuel. Ellie didn't care, and fell fast asleep on a thin mattress under a mound of thick blankets. She was too exhausted by the march and by emotional strain to be aware that the kerosene lamp Hugh placed in her room ran out of oil long before dawn.

The next day they lost a mule on the road to Sedonchen. Where the narrow path veered around a boulder, the animal skittered and lost its footing, tumbling over the precipice and falling to the rocky bottom of a valley, its neck and legs breaking on impact. The descent was too difficult for any of the men to retrieve the two packs, each weighing eighty pounds, that had been strapped to the mule's back and now lay smashed on the valley floor.

They pressed on through forest, climbing higher on a staircase of cobbles to a lonely bungalow. It looked back over the road they'd already covered, and to the south they saw Darjeeling straggling untidily over its ridge.

Ellie wasn't too tired to notice that the bungalow was a lot more uncomfortable than the one at Pedong. The chowkidar who was supposed to look after the building wasn't there, and when Hugh tried to light a fire in the hearth, the smoke billowed out of the chimney into the bungalow. Ellie scrambled outside, holding her breath. She heard Hugh cough as he put out the fire, and she felt guilty because she knew he shouldn't be in such a smoky atmosphere. It was bad for his chest, whereas for her it was just bad for her mind. She went back in to help him dampen the fire, and then they both fled into the clean mountain air.

They cooked over an open fire in front of the bungalow, watched by the bearer and sweeper, who couldn't understand why the rich foreigners hadn't hired a cook. Hugh had bought goat meat in a village before they began the steep ascent to the bungalow. He threaded the chunks on to a wire and hung it on a flimsy metal frame over the flames. The meat sizzled and the juices dropped into the fire with a hiss and a crackle. Ellie drew closer, staring at the flames. It was cold, and she pulled a blanket round her shoulders. The wind blew through the forest, swirling dead leaves around them and making the flames bend and flicker. Hugh gave her a piece of the meat. It was hot, and she passed it from hand to hand; when it had cooled slightly, she bit though its crisp, salty crust, and thought it was the best thing she'd ever tasted.

Hugh took some of the meat to the muleteers and the servants in their quarters set apart from the bungalow. He came back deep in thought.

'Are they okay?' she asked.

'Listen,' he said.

She heard singing in the distance.

'They're drunk,' he added.

By morning, the servants, muleteers and syces were clear-eyed and sober.

'Stay on Ruby today,' Hugh told Ellie. 'We're already at over nine thousand feet. By the end of the day we'll have climbed another four thousand. You mustn't walk. If you get mountain sickness, we'll have to turn back to a lower altitude as quickly as possible. If we had time, we'd climb more slowly and stay at a lower elevation to acclimatise, but we have to press on.'

'Is it because Tom might be taken somewhere else?'

'No. A storm could be gathering.' He pointed north and west to clouds banking over the mountains. 'If there's heavy snow, the passes will close and we won't even find the next bungalow because it'll be deep in drifts.'

The Kupup bungalow at the end of the glacial Bidang Lake was dusted with powdery snow when they arrived. The ground and the lake were frozen solid, but at least here, high among treeless mountains, the chimney was clean and a chowkidar built them a roaring fire, which cost them several rupees more than the going rate in the other rest houses because the wood had to be carried up from the forest.

Ellie had a slight headache and felt dizzy when she moved fast, and when she tried to walk around the lake in the late-afternoon sun she became breathless and returned listlessly, realising she'd been foolish. Hugh sat on a smooth boulder near the bungalow, conditioning himself to the altitude, because tomorrow they would climb higher, up to the Jelep La, the pass that would take them into Tibet.

From the Kupup bungalow, a steep path zigzagged to the pass. Ellie and Hugh rode part of the way, and where it became too difficult, they dismounted and walked carefully up the icy path. The peaks surrounding them were wreathed in grey cloud that made the barren mountainsides appear austere and bleak. Hugh stopped, breathed deeply and then followed the mules, their bells ringing through the thin, misty air.

A stone cairn stood at the very highest point, and ragged prayer flags flapped on poles that had been bent by the gales. Above and behind them, snow clouds massed, but to the north, the sun shone over Tibet. Range after range of weathered hills faded into the distance, and occasionally sharper snow-capped mountains jutted into the sky.

Ellie took out her camera.

'Stand next to the cairn,' she said to Hugh.

He leaned towards the stones, lifted a hand and smiled. Her fingers were cold and she fumbled with the Leica, hoping the shot would work. Behind him, bare brown and grey mountains stretched as far as she could see. None were coral red.

Descending the steep path into Tibet was more difficult than climbing up to the Jelep La. Ellie's thighs ached, and her knees felt as if they would buckle at any moment and she would slide down into the picturesque Chumbi Valley on her backside. When the incline eased, she got back on Ruby, who ambled through the pine and rhododendron forests, crossing and recrossing a river, until they came to Yatung where the British Trade Agent had a surprisingly pretty bungalow with a glassed-in veranda and terraced gardens. The agent wasn't in residence, so Ellie and Hugh settled in the dak bungalow further up the valley.

The sun hadn't yet set behind the mountains as they made camp. The syces attended to the ponies, the muleteers unloaded the supplies, the sweeper checked the bathrooms, the bearer made up the beds, and the chowkidar who supervised the bungalow lit fires in the bedrooms and the small room that functioned as an office and sitting room.

Ellie looked through a shelf of tatty books left by previous guests. Most must have been purchased to provide travellers with inspiration. There were two books by Sir Francis Younghusband, who had brought his military force over the Jelep La on his way to subdue the Tibetans in Gyantse thirty years before. There were novels by Rudyard Kipling, several memoirs by great men who had served the Empire, and a book by Sir Charles Bell, *Tibet: Past and Present*. The book's spine was broken and Ellie opened it carefully. On the title page was a signature in faded ink: 'Hugh Douglas, 1924'.

'I wondered where I'd left it,' Hugh said, looking over her shoulder.

'You were here in 1924?'

He thought. 'Twenty-five. That was my last visit, the year I left the service. This place doesn't seem to have changed much, though. It looks like they've still got the same mattresses.'

Hugh watched her flick through the dog-eared pages. She stopped now and again to read some of the comments he had written in the margins. 'It's worth reading,' he said. 'Charles Bell is a fine scholar. Better than I'll ever be.'

'And better than Maya will ever be?'

'I'm not sure about that.'

'Why does she spend all her time studying ancient history?'

'Not just any ancient history; it's the history of Nepal. That's where her grandparents came from, so I suppose it's her way of knowing something about herself when both her parents are dead and she has a white man for a father.'

He looked sad, and Ellie furrowed her eyebrows, as if to ask him what the matter was. He understood her expression because he had spent so long studying her face.

'She told me I wasn't her real father,' he said. 'You must have heard it. She said it after she received that letter from the Indian Museum.'

Ellie shook her head. 'I heard a lot of shouting, but you were speaking in Tibetan or Nepali or something.'

The last of the sun had gone, and dusk swallowed the Chumbi Valley. The bungalow grew dark. Hugh crouched by the fire and threw on another log. He watched it begin to burn and crackle, the resin bubbling out and filling the room with the smell of pine.

'I think,' he said, 'I haven't been such a good father after all. I've treated Maya like a fragile child because I thought I owed it to her father to protect her from danger. But all the time I was raising her, I was thinking about Suresh. I was thinking about the debt I owed him and not what Maya really needed. We've stayed in the hills, like exiles, because I thought I had to do that to make amends. If I'm honest, I've spent the last years living more with Suresh's ghost than his daughter.'

Ellie squatted down beside him. Her weary legs protested and the pain made her whimper.

'You are a wonderful father,' she said. 'I've watched you with Maya, and I know she loves you, whatever she said in a moment of anger.'

She was close to him, closer than she usually ever came, and he thought this might be the moment he'd waited for, the moment she broke through the invisible barrier that kept her from him. But she didn't come nearer; she inched away.

She watched him prepare food, boiling macaroni in a pot and heating unappetising meat out of a tin. The force that had pulled her towards him weakened, and she was disappointed, and relieved. The chowkidar came in and tended to the fires in the bedrooms. The bearer checked on them and left because there was nothing to do. The sweeper brought hot water for the bathrooms, and then went to his own lodgings. Outside, they heard the muleteers heading off to the tea shop in Yatung that sold girls and chang, the local beer.

Hugh took a kerosene lamp into Ellie's bedroom. Then they said a formal goodnight and went to opposite ends of the bungalow. Ellie lay in bed, listening to the fire spit and crackle. It died slowly and collapsed into a heap of red embers. There was no smell of smoke, no rising panic in her mind.

Both Hugh and I have lived with ghosts, she thought. He's been so concerned with the past that he holds too tightly to its remains. And I'm so obsessed by bad memories and scared to lose what I love that I push away any chance for happiness.

She sat bolt upright and cast aside the layers of blankets and the greatcoat that topped the pile. She walked out of her room and across the bungalow to Hugh.

He was awake, and he pulled her under the sheets beside him. His skin was warm, his body hard, and even in winter he smelled, as she'd always known he would, of sandalwood and the sun. There were no ghosts in the room, no demons in the dark corners; there was only the joy of the present, and of love after long waiting.

The next day, they made a late start. The muleteers were recovering from their hangovers and Ellie and Hugh lay under the blankets whispering and laughing. It was only the sound of the chowkidar raking out the hearth and lighting a new fire in the sitting room that made them get out of bed. Ellie felt guilty because, for the first time, Tom wasn't at the very forefront of her mind.

They began the journey, Hugh pointing out frozen waterfalls. Where the valley opened out and a river meandered through a plain, he drew her attention to a monastery perched on high cliffs. Ellie was attentive and happy, and the distance that usually separated her from those around her had vanished. She was living in this moment, with a man she loved.

The road grew steeper, and the softness of the Chumbi Valley was replaced by a wild, rocky landscape. The next dak bungalow was as miserable and cold as the scenery. But once the door was closed and the fire was lit, they were in a world that was warm, and theirs. At night they slept by a slow fire, and Hugh told her of all the times he had waited for her, all the times he'd watched her, remembering everything she did and said. He was content: she had come to him again, her guard down, her face readable, and he was sure she wouldn't leave.

Ellie ran her fingers over his chest and he shivered, partly with the brush of the cold air on his skin, and partly with the newness of it, because no one had touched his wounds apart from surgeons and nurses. He worried she might think him grotesque. In the faint light the scars shone silver and white. She didn't recoil and she drew him close.

'Do they ever hurt?' she asked.

'Not the scars on my skin. Sometimes my chest is tight, but it always passes quickly.'

The next morning he coughed loudly in the bathroom, and the tightness didn't pass quickly.

They left the bungalow when the sun had begun to thaw the white frosting on the sparse grass. The road was steep and strewn with boulders. In the higher altitude, the air was thinner. The temperature dropped, and even in her fur-lined gloves, Ellie felt the sharp prick of cold at the end of her fingers. The trees petered out and only stunted bushes grew alongside the rocky road. Hugh didn't walk at all now, but rode his pony. He smiled at her often, though he was quiet, and had stopped his running commentary on the scenery.

The town of Phari stood on a dry, barren plain at the head

of the Chumbi Valley. It was nicknamed 'Phari the Foul' by its foreign visitors, and was described, with good reason, as the filthiest town in the world. Decades of refuse and human waste had accumulated in the streets. The road passing though the centre of the town had risen to the height of the buildings' first-floor windows, and tunnels had to be cut through the waste so the inhabitants could enter their homes through the original doors.

The muleteers halted at the edge of town. A strong wind, laced with tiny slivers of ice, bit into Ellie's face, and she was glad to follow Hugh into the warmth of an inn. While the feeling slowly came back into her toes and fingers with a painful tingle, she sat and watched as a Tibetan woman wearing a multicoloured apron prepared butter tea. She cut a chunk off a hard block of black Chinese tea, and put it in a kettle of boiling water over a fire. When it had bubbled for several minutes, she and a boy poured the dark brown liquid into a long wooden cylinder. The woman added a large knob of butter and a spoonful of salt, and the boy churned the tea while the woman talked animatedly to Ellie.

'She says she's going to make the tea extra special for you,' Hugh said.

Ellie smiled, thinking she wouldn't care how special it tasted as long as it was warm.

The churned tea was tipped into a kettle and reheated. When she judged it hot enough, the woman poured Ellie a large bowl and put a dollop of white mutton fat on top. As Ellie watched, it melted and floated to the surface in a thin, shiny layer. She sipped and recoiled. Her mouth was full of oil. It was revolting, and she struggled not to retch.

'Blow off the film of fat,' Hugh said, and demonstrated the technique when the woman wasn't looking. 'Try not to think of it as tea. Imagine it's chicken broth.'

Ellie decided it was either the foulest chicken broth or the foulest tea she'd ever tasted. Under the greasy layer, the liquid was salty and slightly rancid.

The friendly woman, who was clearly proud of her butter tea, offered them a plate of dumplings.

'It's *tsampa*,' Hugh said. 'It's the staple food of Tibet.'

Ellie looked at the balls, unconvinced.

'Try it,' Hugh said, and took a bite. 'It's roasted barley mixed with butter tea and rolled into balls.'

The woman brought a plate of something withered.

'And this,' Hugh announced, 'is dried yak meat.'

Ellie fled outside. She turned her back to the wind so it didn't blow into her face.

Hugh followed. 'Was it the smoke?' he asked.

She shook her head. 'It was the tea. I couldn't stand the smell.'

'This is Tibet,' he said. 'You'd better get used to the smell, though the mutton fat is reserved for special guests.'

Ellie's stomach lurched.

In the dak bungalow, which was some distance from the town, Hugh laid cakes of dried yak dung on the fire. On the Tibetan plains, the lack of trees meant wood was scarce and expensive, and far too good to burn. From Phari onwards, the fires were fed only with dung.

The windows had been boarded up to protect the bungalow against the winter storms, and Hugh opened the door a fraction to check on the weather. A whirlwind of tiny snowflakes was blasted into the room. He snapped the door shut quickly and grimaced. On the following day they would cross the Tang La, and good weather was crucial.

'Tomorrow will be the hardest day,' he said as he drew her into bed early in the evening.

'I thought crossing the Jelep La was the worst,' she said.

'The Tang La is the real pass on to the Tibetan plateau, and we have to cover twenty-one miles to get to the next bungalow.'

Hugh's voice was steady, and yet he was uneasy. He curled around her, her body warm in the icy sheets. She shivered.

'I wonder if we will remember this next summer when we're at home, sitting in the garden in the sun,' he said.

'You mean how cold it is?'

'All of it. How cold. And how wonderful.'

He turned her round and made love to her with an urgency he'd not shown before.

The morning was bright and bitter on the plain. In the distance, the snow on Mount Chomolhari shone brilliant white against the surrounding brown hills. While the syces prepared the ponies, Hugh looked south, to where clouds gathered over the passes to Sikkim. Then he looked north, to the Tang La. Once over that pass there would be no turning back. They could stop now, and if they hurried, they could return to Kalimpong before snow blocked the Nathu La and Jelep La. A syce helped Ellie on to Ruby's saddle. She looked at Hugh, eager to start the journey. He handed her a scarf to tie around her face, leaving only her eyes uncovered. She pulled her hat lower so the flaps covered her ears. The wind gusted and propelled Hugh forward.

A group of pilgrims walked past, apparently unconcerned by the freezing temperature. They carried prayer wheels and chanted, 'Om mani padme hum,' not quite in unison. One man, who wasn't part of the group, prostrated himself after every step. He knelt, pressed his head to the ground and then stood up so he could take another step closer to the holy city of Lhasa. The large weeping ulcer eating away at his forehead was aggravated every time he touched his head to the road.

Hugh nudged his pony. The foreigners who were hunting for a lost boy, and who were pilgrims of a different kind, began to move north.

An unrelenting gale blew over the Tang La, despite the sunshine. The climb was steady, and there was no clear high point. The pass rose over a flat, windswept upland. Ellie thought it was the most desolate, awful place on earth. She hunkered down, curling into herself to keep out the bitter wind, but it forced its way into the gaps between her greatcoat, hat and scarf, and through the densely woven fabric of her clothes.

By a cairn that marked the crossing on to the Tibetan Plateau, the prayer flags had been shredded into thin strips of tattered material. Ellie stopped. Hugh was a few yards behind. Like her, he was bent over his pony, his head tucked into his chest. She shouted to him over the roar of the wind, but as his pony walked past, he didn't acknowledge her. Perhaps he didn't hear me, she thought. She watched him sway, his head at a strange angle. She kicked Ruby on and drew alongside him.

'Hugh!' she shouted.

He lifted his head slowly, as if he was hearing her from a

long way off. All she could see were his eyes. He lifted his gloved hand a few inches in a gesture that said, 'I'm fine.' His pony plodded on; it knew which way to go.

The small town of Tuna, and the next dak bungalow, looked close from the Tang La. In Tibet, though, sight could be deceptive. The altitude and thin air gave a clarity and luminosity to the light. Colours were both mellow and heightened, and in the vastness of the open spaces, distant towns and mountains seemed closer than they really were.

The mule train trudged over a track that ran across a gravel plain: an ancient dried-up lake bed. They were following the telegraph wire connecting Sikkim to Tibet, installed twenty years before by the British. The telegraph poles threading their way to Lhasa made a lonely picture. They stood, sometimes at odd angles, in a bare high-altitude desert that had no trees, and only a few stunted bushes to soften the landscape.

The dak bungalows on the plateau were different. They were enclosed by walled compounds, to keep out the wind and the Tibetans. Tuna was the coldest bungalow, and the yak dung fire took a long time to get going. Hugh sat, with an unhealthy pallor, on a chair near the hearth.

When the bearer had gone and the chowkidar had his back turned, Ellie stroked Hugh's face and kissed him. He was ill, and she didn't know what to do. Perhaps they should turn back, return to Kalimpong and plan a new journey to Gyantse.

'You're not well,' she said.

'It's mountain sickness. It'll pass.'

'We should go back.'

'We've come this far; we've got to go on. Besides, retracing our steps over the Tang La won't do me much good. We're two thousand feet lower here, so I should feel better soon.'

'Is Gyantse lower?'

'It's the same. Most of the plateau around here is about thirteen thousand feet.' Hugh stood and walked to the bedroom, taking slow, careful steps. 'I think I'll have a rest.' The bearer had made up only one room, because servants were smart and knew as much about the sahibs' private lives as the sahibs did themselves.

Hugh slept without eating, and when Ellie lay next to him, he didn't make love to her. He curled around her, cupping her against him, and she listened to his breathing. Dread flooded her for a moment, though it was not the familiar dread of the dark: his breath was shallow and laboured, and far too fast.

Hugh had recovered by the morning. He talked to her during the journey, pointing out the black tents of nomad shepherds and yak herders. He ate a lunch of crackers and cheese, and a big bar of chocolate, and there was a sparkle in his eyes. At night his breathing was strained, but only because they made love twice in the dark, under the blankets that had begun to smell of mule.

The great vistas started to get wearisome on the next day's march. Ellie was tired of the endless flat lands, the weathered brown hills, the distant snowy peaks. Even the cobalt sky was monotonous in its endlessness. Where the hell is Gyantse? she thought. How far can it be? How much more damn wilderness is there? Hugh had shown her on the map, so logic told her they were close, only a few days' march. It just didn't feel like that. It felt never-ending.

Occasionally they met other travellers. Traders with mule teams went south, and at one point, a high-born Tibetan lady on a magnificent horse, accompanied by a retinue of servants, passed in a stately procession. Several times the mail service sped by, racing south towards India or north to Lhasa. Ellie wanted to follow their example. She wanted a horse, not an old pony like Ruby. She wanted to gallop across the flat land and not stop. She would race through the moonlight because she could not wait; because Tom could not wait.

Instead, they moved at the pace of the mules, plodding across the frozen desert in blinding sunshine, and at night they slept in the cold, fortified dak bungalows. Hugh was feeling better, and he began to cook again in the evenings. In Kala, which was little more than a collection of hovels, they bought dried fish, a local speciality, which was bony and utterly tasteless, but made a welcome addition to the crackers and Campbell's soup.

After four days and nights in the unrelenting vastness, Ellie drew Ruby to a halt. A tree, bent and wizened, grew out of a hollow. Further along the road, five more trees, which almost amounted to a forest, clustered around a dried-up pool. Soon there were fields, willows and a stream. The fields became bigger and greener, and the villages more prosperous.

The approach to Gyantse could not have changed for hundreds of years. A massive *dzong*, built to guard the valley leading to Lhasa, sat on top of a giant spur of rock. The sheer walls of the fort leaned inwards, making the structure appear even more immense. Below the fort, flat-roofed houses spread over the valley floor, and at the opposite end of the city, the golden-topped monastery was surrounded by the 'Dragon's Back': the high defensive walls running along the crest of the hills and intersected by tall watchtowers. This was the place besieged, and subdued, by the British three decades earlier. Ellie wondered if the citizens of Gyantse had long memories, and what they would think of the foreigners arriving in the latest mule train.

The dak bungalow was about three-quarters of a mile from the city and had excellent views of the *dzong*. It was set among willows in a pretty garden and was by far the best bungalow since they'd left India. Ellie wanted to abandon the supplies and head immediately into town, but Hugh insisted they visit the British Trade Agency before they entered the city. All visitors had to register their presence there. As far as the British and the Tibetans were concerned, they had reached the end of the road. Only those with special permission from the Tibetans and the government of India could move beyond Gyantse.

The Trade Agency was like a little fort itself. It was surrounded by thick defensive walls, and the windows in the two-storey building had been boarded up against the winter weather. Hugh and Ellie sat in the sun with the Agent, Captain Hailey, and the medical officer, Captain Guthrie, in the shelter of a windbreak.

As Hugh explained why they were there, Captain Hailey filled his pipe, drew on it several times, and nodded. He leaned back in his chair, puffed away and closed his eyes. Clearly, the long months spent in this outpost of the Empire, holed up with a couple of other British men and a contingent of Indian Army troops, had done quite a bit to relax the usual formality of the British colonial official.

'We've heard quite a lot on this topic,' the agent said. 'We've had a number of letters and a telegram from the Political Officer in Sikkim explaining about your son, Lady Northwood.'

'Did he say that Tom has been seen in Gyantse?'

'Well, yes, and of course we immediately made enquiries in the town.' He sighed. 'I don't want to be the bearer of bad news, but we suspect you've been misinformed.' He lifted his feet and put them on the table. 'As far as I can tell, your son has never been in Gyantse.'

'I believe our sources are good,' Hugh said.

'By all means ask around, but be careful. Most Tibetans are a peaceful lot, but a few aren't. There's been some trouble with bandits, so I'll have a small number of troops accompany you.'

'Please, there's no need,' Hugh said. 'It might do more harm than good.'

Captain Hailey pulled long and hard on his pipe. 'I can't recommend it.'

'I speak Tibetan.'

'You do?'

'And I've been here before.'

'Really?'

'I was in the Political Office some years ago.'

'Must have been before my time,' Captain Hailey said. 'Anyway, don't leave the town, whatever you do. It would cause a diplomatic upset, and is too dangerous in any case.'

They left with a promise to heed his advice, and within two days had broken it.

The smell made Ellie's throat constrict as tightly as if she was being throttled. Something in Pelkor Chode, the great monastery of Gyantse, smelled sour and sickly, like sweetened cream left to turn rancid in the sun. She gagged and ran out for air. Hugh was made of stronger stuff; he stayed inside the dark shrine painted in reds and oranges, strung with banners, and lit only by butter lamps. Ellie peeped around the door and saw him talking to a couple of elderly lamas in a low voice.

She leaned against the wall and watched shaven-headed monks stroll around the monastery in maroon robes. Younger ones, some only boys, sat in groups, arguing in a peculiar way. One would stand up, shout, slap his hands, and then sit down as another jumped up to start the same shouting and hand-slapping. She knew she should have been intrigued – this was the kind of thing Alexandra David-Néel had walked across Tibet to see – but Ellie found no spiritual connection with the monastery and its spectacular buildings. The shrine felt oppressive and she didn't like the big red Buddha covered in scarves. She hated the darkness, the flickering lamps, the chanting of the monks kneeling on long strips of carpet. It was so far outside her experience, it felt outlandish. And the smell was nauseating, a mix of incense and dirt, and scorched, tainted butter. Please don't let Tom be in a place like this, she thought. He'll be terrified.

'They've not seen him,' Hugh said as he appeared from the dark and strode into bright sun. 'Let's ask in the bazaar.'

Gyantse's bazaar was held inside the walls of the monastery. Stallholders spread their wares in the streets that ran between the buildings, and the better stalls were covered in awnings.

Ellie followed Hugh, holding her photo of Tom. It was a new copy because the first one had fallen to pieces through constant use. She showed it to the traders while Hugh talked. Two men spun wool on to spindles as they sat beside a sheet on which they'd arranged heaps of dried plants. They carried on spinning while they looked at the picture and listened to

Hugh. They glanced up at Ellie and both of them smiled, sadly, their eyes crinkling into dozens of deep lines.

Further down the crowded street, Hugh began talking with a Nepali trader who'd come to buy carpets. He'd heard nothing about a golden-haired child either.

By late morning, the wind was beginning to blow hard, and the stallholders huddled in the shelter of the monastery walls. Hugh had questioned fifty or more people and Ellie had shown Tom's picture to many more. She had the sinking feeling she used to get while touring the bazaar in Kalimpong. Maybe the Trade Agent had been right.

Outside the walls of the Pelkor Chode, a tall, striking man with long black braided hair and silver earrings strode past them. Hugh called to him and the man stopped. He looked handsome and fierce, and Ellie recoiled a little until she saw that his smile was friendly and at odds with the large knives he wore in his belt.

'Show him the picture,' Hugh told her.

The man glanced at the photo and then pointed down the road. Hugh frowned. The man found a stick and crouched down to draw something in the dirt. If it was a map, it was unlike one Ellie had ever seen. Hugh looked perplexed, and the man beckoned them to follow him. He walked fast, accustomed to the altitude. Ellie struggled to keep up, and Hugh's breathing was audible over the sound of the wind.

They passed some fine two-storey houses that were whitewashed and had fabric pelmets over their black-painted windows. Then they turned into a less affluent street, dodging the goats and cattle tethered in front of the dwellings. A Tibetan mastiff barked ferociously from a doorway until its mistress silenced it with a kick. A minute later, they were on the edge of town, where the buildings were shabby, run-down hovels. A few seemed to be subterranean and cut into the rock.

The man pointed to a low doorway.

Was Tom in there? Ellie's heart beat fast with excitement and the exhaustion of the short march.

The man slapped Hugh roughly, as if they were old friends, and then left.

'The woman who lives here knows everything that goes on in town,' Hugh told Ellie. 'At least that's what I think he said.'

Ellie stared at the low door and prepared herself for another disappointment.

The door was ajar. Hugh shouted and knocked, and someone called back. He pushed the door open and went inside, bending because it was no more than four and a half feet high. Ellie followed. The only light in the house shone from the door and through a small opening in the ceiling. Their eyes, used to the blinding winter sun, didn't adjust immediately, and they were disorientated and sightless. A voice spoke in the darkness. Slowly Ellie began to regain her vision. She saw a polished kettle and a glow from smouldering yak dung. The woman laughed, and Ellie opened her eyes wider, as if that might help her to see. No one seemed to be in the room.

Hugh began to talk, and the invisible woman replied. Ellie looked in the direction of the sound and eventually saw her; or more accurately, she saw a set of bright teeth and the white of the woman's eyes. It took longer to make out the rest of her, because she was blackened from top to toe. Smoke from the yak dung fire had coated the old woman, her possessions and her home. Only her teeth, eyes and the copper kettle she polished every week remained untarnished by the accretion of years. Ellie edged forward, unsure of her step, and her shin brushed a low table.

The woman was chattering to Hugh. They were laughing, and Ellie wished she could understand what was being said. It was frustrating to wait and then have everything translated.

'Tell me what she's saying,' she said, interrupting the conversation.

'Most of it is irrelevant,' Hugh said. 'She's telling me about the weather, and the floods they had a couple of years ago.'

Ellie could have screamed in exasperation. 'Ask her about Tom.'

'Sit down,' he said. 'She's going to give you tea.'

'Oh Christ, no,' Ellie moaned.

The old woman handed her a bowl of butter tea. Ellie squinted up at her, and blinked a few times because the smoke was making her eyes sting. She pinched her nose, hoping the woman wouldn't notice, and sipped the tea. It tasted as foul as she remembered.

Hugh cleared his throat and spoke again. The old woman launched into an explanation, waving her hands and talking loudly. Ellie took the opportunity to put the bowl down, the vile butter tea barely touched.

Hugh turned to her, speaking softly while the old lady continued. 'She says a boy with yellow hair was staying with a family in the city a few weeks ago. He wasn't their son, she is sure of that. The father is called Dorje. He's a merchant and lives near the entrance to the Pelkor Chode. She says they kept the child inside because his eyes were so blue they thought the sun would blind him.'

'Is she sure? Did she see him?'

Hugh talked with the woman for a long time before he answered.

'She didn't see him, but she knows about him.'

'How can she know? Does she know someone who saw him?'

'She knows everything in this town.'

'How?'

'The man with the silver earrings said she was a witch. I think a better name for her is a shaman.'

Ellie was startled. The woman certainly fitted the image of a witch in one respect: she was old. But under the sooty layer, her face was kind and her eyes were warm and not those of a cunning crone.

The woman grabbed Ellie's hands and held them tight. She closed her eyes and chanted, and then began speaking urgently, her face a few inches from Ellie's.

'What's she saying?' Ellie asked.

'She says there will be joy and sadness.' Hugh seemed to be confused for a moment, and then carried on. 'She says we will find him, but we have to be quick.'

'Why? Is he in danger?' Ellie's voice rose to a higher pitch. Her nerves were ragged. I mustn't panic, she thought. I have to stay calm; I can't break now.

The woman hustled them to the door, still gripping Ellie's hand and speaking loudly. Hugh handed her some silver coins, and the woman slipped them inside the folds of her blackened clothes.

She watched them from the doorway as they hurried to find the merchant's house. Hugh wheezed and coughed, and Ellie's heart thumped from fear and lack of oxygen. When they turned to wave goodbye, the old woman had already returned to the darkness.

The house of Dorje the merchant was a fine two-storey building in a street of other fine buildings. Its walls were thick, and its heavy door was of carved black wood. The material of the pelmets above the windows and door was new, and two of the windows were glazed with opaque glass. The others, like the rest of the houses in the street, had only white cloth to keep out the cold and wind.

A servant answered the door and was astonished to see two foreigners. He took a step back and stared at Ellie, his gaze settling on the hair that had escaped from under her hat. Hugh asked to see Dorje, and the servant turned into the dark interior of the house, closing the door behind him. He returned a few minutes later and motioned them inside.

They passed through a room filled with boxes, rolls of carpet, and tightly wrapped bundles. The next room was the living space of someone who was clearly wealthy. It was painted in mellow colours, the yellows and reds muted by the thin layer of smoke that must have adhered to the interior of every Tibetan home. Two tall lacquered cabinets stood against the far wall. Carved and painted wooden tables were dotted around, and cushions and carpets covered the floor. A lamp cast a small pool of light in the far corner, and the sun shone weakly through the glass panes of a single window.

A woman swept into the room, bringing a new level of tension with her. She seemed to be wearing her family's wealth. Her black hair was worked into an elaborate headdress and threaded with coral and turquoise. Her silver and pearl earrings were long, and her thick robes were covered in silver necklaces and turquoise brooches. She was a woman of substance. She was also very nervous.

When Hugh spoke, his tone was apologetic and soft, and the woman relaxed a little. He handed her the photograph of Tom and she took it to the window.

'Tashi,' she said with a muffled sob. She looked at Ellie, then drew her to the window and turned her to face the light. Ellie pulled off her hat and the woman touched her hair. It was brighter than it had been for many years, bleached by months in the Himalayan sun.

The woman sat on a low couch and told them both to join her. Then she began to talk, slowly, giving Hugh enough time to translate. For once, Ellie listened without butting in.

'My name is Pema; I'm the wife of Dorje the merchant. Dorje isn't in Gyantse. He's on his way to Shigatse. That's where he was born and where many of his family still live. He's taking our youngest son to join the monastery there. He's ten years old, and is ready to become a novice monk. His uncle, my husband's brother, is an influential lama in the Shigatse monastery. He'll take care of my son.' Pema paused and looked from Hugh to Ellie. 'My husband is also taking another boy to the monastery. His name is Tashi. He is much younger than my son, and he has golden hair.

'Last winter, Dorje was in India,' she continued. 'He's often away for many months. He travels with his men between Tibet and India. Usually he goes to Kalimpong through the Chumbi Valley, and then on to the Indian plains. They take wool to Kalimpong, and normally they buy household goods in India, which they bring back to sell in Gyantse and Shigatse. Last year they did something different. They went to Kathmandu to see what was for sale. If there was something good, they could transport it here along the Kodari road. Only it was a wasted trip, because the Newaris had a stranglehold on the best trade, and the Kodari Pass was closed by heavy snow. It was a pointless journey, and then, to make it worse, as they were preparing to leave, an earthquake killed one of his men in the main bazaar and a house collapsed on some of our mules, killing five of them. Dorje said the city was in ruins.'

Ellie nodded, desperate for the woman to get to the heart of the story. She wasn't interested in hearing about trade.

'After the quake, one of Dorje's men was picking his way through the streets when he saw something move in the debris. It was a child's hand. Well, he had to stop and dig the child out. The boy was covered in dust and dirt. It was amazing he'd survived at all, and sad too, because the rest of his family weren't so lucky. Everyone in that house was dead. An old woman told him the whole family was crushed. So what could Dorje's man do? Could he leave the child there? No. He brought him to my husband, who took pity on him because he was like the white-haired, white-skinned children you hear about in India who cannot tolerate the sun. The boy couldn't speak. He was mute. And he didn't seem to understand Nepali, or Newari or Tibetan. My husband wasn't sure he would live, but he did, and in the spring Dorje brought him back here for me to look after. I called him Tashi, because it means lucky.'

Ellie was rocking to and fro, her arms wrapped around her legs.

'I kept him inside because whenever he went out his skin turned red and I was worried about him. And he was so quiet, you wouldn't know he was here. But then, around harvest time, he began to speak. He spoke Tibetan words. Not many, but I was happy because I knew he was getting better. We took him to the Oracle to ask for advice, and the Oracle said he should be dedicated to the religious life. I thought he was too young, but maybe that was his destiny. He was made for some special purpose. Perhaps he was a reincarnation of an important man, and that was why he was spared when all his family had died.'

'What is the Oracle?' Ellie said.

'He's a kind of medium,' Hugh said. 'You ask the gods a question and they respond through him. The advice is valuable because they think it's divine.'

Ellie thought for a moment. 'But how can they send Tom to a monastery when he is only three?'

'It's quite normal for children to be sent for an education in the monasteries when they are five or six. A few go even sooner, especially if they are thought to be reincarnations.'

'They can't think Tom is a reincarnated monk, can they?'

'If they do, they'll certainly look after him well.'

Pema watched Ellie and Hugh as they talked, and then she began speaking again.

'I can see now that he's not a Nepali boy. He's your son,' she said, patting Ellie's knee. 'He looks like you. His hair is the same, and his eyes, and you both do this.' She wrinkled her nose, knitted her eyebrows and pursed her lips, and Hugh laughed because he recognised the expression. Ellie pulled that face whenever she was concentrating. 'And why would you come all this way if he wasn't your son? I would do the same too,' she said. 'If any of my boys were lost, I would cross the sea and walk to the end of the earth to find them.'

Ellie looked around the room, imagining Tom there, trying to feel his presence. Pema watched her, and when she spoke, Hugh translated immediately.

'She says he used to stand on that box,' he said, pointing to a wooden chest under the window. 'He looked into the street as if he was waiting.'

He was waiting for me, Ellie thought, her heart almost breaking.

'Come with me,' Pema said, and led Ellie upstairs. Ellie didn't need an interpreter now, because she understood Pema's words. One mother was talking to another.

Pema took her into a bedroom. 'He slept here,' she said. 'I made a bed for him next to mine.' Ellie bent and touched the blankets on the little cot, as if they would still contain the heat from his body. Tom's head had lain on this pillow, and she wondered if he'd slept well. If he'd had nightmares, she knew Pema would have comforted him.

Downstairs, Hugh questioned Pema closely for a few minutes.

'She says they are on their way to Shigatse and that they left two days ago. But she says they are making a detour first. Her husband wants to do some trading. They're staying at one of the small monasteries about a day's walk from here.'

'Will they still be there?' Ellie asked.

'She thinks so,' Hugh said.

'Let's go now in case they leave.'

'It's too late today.'

Pema clasped Ellie to her. She was a big woman, almost as tall as Ellie, and she hugged her tightly. In that moment, Ellie knew that this woman had loved Tom like a mother.

Pema spoke directly to her, emotion flooding her face. Ellie hardly needed Hugh to explain her words.

'She is saying she would not have let him go if it hadn't been for the Oracle's advice. She would have kept him with her, but she knew he would be safe with her own son, and her brother-in-law.'

Pema sat and slowly began to write a note in a careful, controlled script. She rolled the paper into a tight cylinder, then, opening a little silver charm box that hung round her neck on the end of a turquoise necklace, she put it inside and fastened the box. She lifted the necklace over her elaborate headdress and handed it to Ellie.

'She says you must give this to her husband. You must show him the photograph of Tom, you must take off your hat to show him your hair, and once he has read the note, everything will be fine.'

At the door, they said farewell.

'Tell her, thank you for looking after Tom,' Ellie said. 'I am so grateful.'

'Come and see me when you bring him back to Gyantse,' Pema said.

The sun was low, and soon the temperature would plummet.

'We'll leave first thing tomorrow,' Hugh said.

'Not now?'

He appeared slightly exasperated. 'You know how cold it gets and how quickly we lose the light. It's a long day's march, and there are no dak bungalows on the way. This is the end of the line as far as the British are concerned. We can't go any further.'

'But we will, right?'

'Of course. But we have to be clever. We have to let everyone think we are returning home.'

Hugh was standing in a pool of weak afternoon sun, and Ellie focused properly on him for the first time for several hours. He spoke with energy and excitement, but that wasn't reflected in his skin, which looked ashen under his golden tan.

'Are you all right?' she asked.

'Nothing that a good night's sleep won't fix.' He sounded his usual confident self. 'Come on,' he said. 'First we need to buy you some new gloves in the market.'

'I've got gloves.'

'You need better ones. It's getting colder, and you need Tibetan cat-fur gloves.'

Ellie gave a squeak of revulsion.

'And then we need to hire a guide and a couple of guards,' he added.

'What kind of guards?'

'Armed ones.'

The muleteers who had brought them to Gyantse were undecided when Hugh asked them to take them to the monastery in the hills to the west of Gyantse. It wasn't a route they knew; they stuck to the old trade road, wary of bandits who might roam the less travelled paths. It was only when Hugh offered them triple rates that they agreed to take half the mule train. The bearer and the sweeper were adamant that they wouldn't accompany the party; they were men from India, and had no intention of travelling further into Tibet than they had to.

Hugh and Ellie were both breathless when they got back to the dak bungalow. The post from India had just arrived, strapped to the backs of two ponies. Ellie watched it being unloaded, and when she went to their room, Hugh was already resting on the bed. She lay next to him, and her breathing gradually slowed.

A sudden gust of wind buffeted the building. Ellie was sure it made the thick walls vibrate. In this bungalow, they had the luxury of a wood-burning stove. It stood at the side of the room and radiated heat within a four-foot circle. Beyond it, the air felt frozen.

'Are you hungry?' Ellie asked Hugh.

He didn't reply; he was asleep.

She opened a tin of macaroni and waited while it took forever to heat in the thin air. Then she sat on the bed and ate it. When Hugh stirred and opened his eyes, she offered him some. He took one look at the rubbery mess and got up slowly and moved to the bathroom.

'I don't fancy eating just now,' he said.

She heard him coughing. It wasn't his usual wheezy cough. When he returned, he looked pale and drawn.

'I think I'm coming down with a bloody cold,' he said, as he rooted through his rucksack and found a bottle of medicine. He took a carefully measured dose and flopped back down on the bed.

'I'll be fine in the morning,' he said.

He coughed all night. Ellie lay next to him and rubbed his back, although she knew it made no difference. He vomited twice, and she could tell by the way he winced when she talked that his head was pounding.

By dawn he was no better.

'I'll send a message to the Trade Agency and ask Dr Guthrie to come,' Ellie said.

'It's not necessary. It'll pass. It's just a bad cold that's gone to my chest. I'll be back on my feet in a few days.'

He could see her working this out. If they stayed here too long, Dorje would leave the monastery and take Tom further into Tibet.

'You'll have to go alone,' he said.

'I can't leave you,' she said.

'Nonsense. The guide, the guards and the muleteers will be here very soon. It's one day's journey, and if you leave within the hour, you can be there by tonight.' He paused to catch his breath. 'If all goes well, you can return tomorrow. You'll be back by nightfall.'

It felt wrong to leave him, and just as wrong not to. Ellie was pulled in two directions. Should she go and find her son, or stay and care for the man she loved?

Hugh heaved on his greatcoat and hat and went out into the dawn light. The wind had stilled. He talked with the guide and supervised the loading of the mule train. They were taking six mules, and Ellie would ride Ruby.

Back inside the bungalow, he gave her brief instructions, telling her to give gifts to the abbot of the monastery, to wear glare goggles if it snowed, to be brave, but not so brave that she put herself in danger.

'Now go,' he said. 'The longer you leave it, the more likely word will spread that you've gone beyond Gyantse, and then you'll either have a contingent from the British Agency on your tail, or you'll be a target for the local bandits.'

He led her to the waiting guide and syce. He kissed her on her forehead and then watched her struggle to climb into Ruby's saddle. She was wearing so many layers of thick clothes, she could barely move. The massive cat-fur gloves restricted the movement of her fingers and stopped her holding the reins properly.

He smiled at her, and she knew he wasn't pretending. He was glad she was going.

'I'm getting back into bed,' he said.

'Promise you'll send for Dr Guthrie if you don't feel better soon.'

'I promise. And I'll have something nice prepared for your supper tomorrow night. Corned beef and crackers maybe.'

He tapped Ruby on the rump and the pony walked out of the bungalow's compound and on to the road north out of Gyantse.

Ellie's new gloves and the long, fur-lined Gilgit boots kept her hands and feet warm until mid-morning, when the wind began to blow. They had left the plain around Gyantse and were among the mountains, climbing up steep trails and then down into rocky valleys. Ruby faltered and shied as she walked over flimsy wooden bridges and others of worn stone that crossed gushing streams and narrow, bottomless gorges.

The wind blew harder as the day wore on. Streams of high cloud flowed from the south and washed the colour from the cobalt sky. Heavy clouds gathered over the mountains.

They rounded a spur of rock and began to climb again, and when they had breasted the ridge, the guide shouted and pointed up. A collection of whitewashed buildings clung to a distant mountainside. Ellie's stomach did a somersault, and she immediately reined both herself and Ruby back. She mustn't do what she'd done in Nuwakot; she mustn't race towards her goal like a lunatic. She was going to be measured, and she reminded herself not to get too excited. She needed to prepare herself for the fact that Tom might already have gone, or that Pema had made a mistake. Even if Tom was there, he might not recognise her. He hadn't seen her for almost a year. That was a third of his life. Perhaps he might not remember anything before that terrible day in Kathmandu. Perhaps he'd been so damaged by the trauma, so terrified at being separated from his family that he'd never be the same again. Like Ellie, he'd bear invisible injuries.

The monks thought she was a man because she was tall and wore men's clothes. When she spoke, they looked startled, and the guide stepped in, talking quickly. Ellie hoped he was explaining why they were there.

A servant led her into a building that faced on to a small courtyard. The windows were small and let in little of the early-evening light. In a room panelled with dark-painted wood and lit by butter lamps, the servant pointed at a low chair and asked her to sit. He left her alone, and she breathed deeply to quell her nerves. She didn't even notice the smell of the butter lamps mingling with incense. In front of her, a gilded statue of the Buddha was wreathed in scarves; below it, a tiered altar was cluttered with vases, ivory carvings, paper flowers, offerings of food and a dozen brass bowls filled with fresh water.

An elderly monk, whom she assumed was the abbot, appeared from behind a red curtain, followed by a tall, well-built man with the long braided hair of a layman. Behind them she thought she saw a child, and a hint of brightness that could have been blond hair. She jumped up. The curtain closed and the two men looked at her. She spoke to them but they clearly didn't understand.

Remembering Hugh's instructions, she pulled the ceremonial silk scarf, the perfumed soap and the biscuits from her rucksack, and offered them to the abbot. It was the wrong thing to do, or she was doing it the wrong way, because he seemed surprised. He called for a servant, who appeared from nowhere and whisked the presents away.

She searched in the pockets of her greatcoat and found the photograph of Tom. The men struggled to see it in the dark and took it to where a cluster of butter lamps made a pool of soft light. While they examined the picture, she took off her hat. The men talked softly and then turned their attention to her.

'I'm Ellie,' she said, pointing to herself. 'Ellie,' she repeated, patting her chest. 'I'm looking for my son.' She mimed a little story to the bemused men, first rocking an imaginary baby, then holding her hand at around the level of Tom's head. She did an impression of the earthquake, shaking, and then demonstrating how the buildings fell down.

Oh my God, I look insane, she thought.

She patted herself again and repeated her name.

The abbot tapped his own chest and said something that might have been a name, though it sounded impossibly long. The man with the braided hair held his hand over his heart and said, far more simply, 'Dorje.'

Ellie could have whooped with joy. It was the merchant, Pema's husband. She undid her coat, searched under the layers of clothes and pulled the turquoise necklace over her head.

Dorje was taken aback when she handed it to him. He recognised it, and was astonished.

'Look in there,' she said, tapping the little silver charm box.

He fumbled with the clasp, his big fingers struggling with the intricate fastening. He pulled out his wife's letter and, unfurling it, went over to the light. When he had finished reading, he rolled it up and put it back in the box. Ellie held her breath. She watched him walk across the room and disappear behind the curtain. It gave her an odd feeling, as if she were in some bizarre magic show. The abbot was silent, and they waited, both staring at the curtain. Slowly it was drawn back, revealing another room, this one sunk in even greater darkness. Dorje stood in the doorway.

Ellie's intake of breath was sharp and sudden. A child with fair hair had its face buried in the folds of Dorje's long, heavy coat. Ellie moved closer and crouched down. Dorje spoke softly, and the child turned its head so that one frightened eye peeped for a second at Ellie and then looked away, back into the safety of the wool coat.

'Tashi,' Dorje said.

His name isn't Tashi, Ellie thought. It's Tom. Her heart soared. The journey was at an end, although this was not how she'd imagined it would be. She'd dreamed of this moment for almost a year. She'd thought she'd see joy and love in Tom's face when he recognised her; that he'd run to her and throw himself into her arms. But as she crouched, just feet from him, she was a stranger to him. He'd forgotten her; he was scared of her. She began to cry, as much from sadness as relief.

Dorje put his hand on Tom's head. His large brown fingers, covered in silver rings, stroked the boy's hair.

'Tashi,' he repeated more loudly.

Tom peeped at Ellie again.

'Tom,' she said. He didn't respond; just stared at her sorrowfully.

She scrambled over to her rucksack and searched inside.

'Look, Tom,' she said, hurrying back to him. 'Look who's come to find you.'

She straightened out the lamb's limbs, which had become squashed and distorted in the rucksack. The toy's single eye sparkled in the light from the butter lamps. Tom turned to face her, and focused on the lamb. He hesitated, and then walked slowly towards her. He reached out and touched the toy's pink felt nose. He came closer, and closer still, and then he was hugging the lamb to his chest. He lifted a hand and tentatively touched his mother's hair. She was crying, and smiling, and his eyes were big and wide, and wondering.

'Mama,' he whispered, as she took him in her arms.

They left soon after dawn. Ellie had forced down a breakfast of *tsampa* and butter tea because she knew she needed the energy and warmth it would give her for the journey. Tom had wolfed his. Dorje arranged for one of his men to accompany them, and provided a shaggy black yak to carry Tom. He was wrapped in furs, and Dorje lifted him into a pannier on the yak and checked he was secure. A roll of carpet was put in the pannier on the opposite side of the animal to balance the load.

Dorje talked with the guide for several minutes. The men looked at the sky, their faces grave. Ellie thanked the merchant, sure that he would know what she was saying even if he couldn't understand English. He had cared for Tom for months, treating him, she was sure, like his own son. Dorje was brusque and efficient, not wanting, Ellie presumed, to show his emotions. He pointed at the sky. He must think there's going to be a storm, she thought. Then he slapped Ruby on her rump to send her ambling out of the gate of the monastery, and as the yak swung on to the road, he called something to Tom, who gazed at him over the top of the pannier.

We're on our way home, Ellie thought, with a feeling of warm satisfaction. Her quest was completed. She'd begun this long journey looking for an enchanted land and coral-red mountains and had found neither. Instead she'd found her son, and Hugh.

Now that she had Tom, she had to hurry. She had to get back to Hugh, and to Lizzie, who had been without her for almost a month. Nanny Barker and Maya would be taking good care of her, but it was a long time for a child to be without her mother.

The gale that usually started at mid-morning began to blow earlier that day. Layers of cloud that were stacked high over the mountains suddenly coalesced to form a billowing black mass that sank on to the peaks. A minute later, tiny, sharp flakes of snow, as dry as fine sand, began to cut into the skin round Ellie's eyes. The wind drove it over the scree, over the stony mountainsides, whipping it into crevices and into drifts. It stuck in Ruby's mane and swirled around Tom in the pannier, settling like a thick white crust over the boy. Where the path broadened, the guide pulled alongside Ellie and shouted. His meaning was clear: the weather had set in and they had to turn back. Ellie drew Ruby to a halt. She was supposed to return that day; Hugh was expecting her, and he wasn't well.

'No!' she shouted, pulling the scarf from over her mouth and nose. She pointed ahead. They had gone perhaps a third of the way back to Gyantse. Surely, she thought, it would be better to press on? It would be just as hard to retrace their steps. The muleteers had different ideas. Swaddled from head to foot, they gathered together, their backs to the wind, and spoke with their heads down. Their body language told her they were annoyed.

'Come on,' she said, and pressed her legs against Ruby to start her walking again. The guide reached forward and took the reins.

The muleteers and the mules were already heading back up the path to the monastery. Dorje's man turned the yak around.

'The trail is still clear,' Ellie shouted. 'Look, the wind is blowing the snow away.' She glanced along the path, which was now completely white, visibility down to less than fifty yards. The guide pulled his hat down and his scarf up over his face, and led Ruby back to the monastery without saying a word or looking at the snow-blasted figure crouched over the saddle.

For five days the storm slammed against the monastery walls. Even in the shelter of the courtyard, the gusts were strong and sudden enough to knock Ellie off her feet. Horizontal lines of snow blew across the tiny windows, only a few protected by glass, the rest boarded up by heavy shutters. When the wind died and the snow stopped falling, she looked out on a crisp, crystalline world that sparkled in the sunlight. The air was clean and unalloyed, and the visibility so sharp she could see for miles.

Again the mule train left the monastery just after dawn. This time Ellie wore glare goggles to guard against snow blindness, and she stopped every few minutes to adjust Tom's glasses, because they were adult size and a poor fit on a small boy's face. The mountainsides were frosted. On the leeward side of boulders, and in gullies sheltered from the wind, the snow was three feet deep, but in other places the wind had scoured the ground and left bare swathes of rock and scree.

When they stopped to eat, Tom played in a snowdrift, and Ellie ran her cat-fur gloves over the surface of the snow. It was powdery and pure, and so perfectly dry it reminded her of being a child and playing with Bobby in the warm sands of south California's beaches.

The further they travelled, the shallower the drifts became, until by the time they reached the plain around Gyantse, no snow lay on the ground. The wind had stripped it from the flat land, although traces of snow lay in clefts in the frozen earth.

The dak bungalow looked pretty, like a picture, the willows and poplar trees surrounding it still covered in ice in the late afternoon. The chowkidar and the men who worked in the stables came out to meet them. With the help of Dorje's man, she lifted Tom out of the yak's pannier, and balanced him on her hip, then rushed on to the veranda of the bungalow. She couldn't wait to see Hugh and let him know she'd found Tom – that they'd both found him. It was a scene of triumph she'd anticipated for six long days and nights.

She swung open the heavy door and shot into the main room. Hugh wasn't there. She lifted Tom and shifted him to her other hip. He'd grown much heavier in the months they'd been apart.

'We're back,' she called, striding into the bedroom. The bed was stripped, and there was no sign of Hugh.

She called again, putting her head around the storeroom door. The chowkidar was following her, talking loudly. She ignored him, and instead shouted Hugh's name as she walked into the empty second bedroom. He must have gone into Gyantse, she thought. 'British fort,' the chowkidar said, enunciating the words slowly and carefully while thrusting his arm in the direction of the Trade Agency.

Poor Ruby had another journey to make.

Three British men walked out from the Agency as Ellie rode up. Tom was perched on Ruby's saddle with her.

'I found him!' she cried in exultation.

One of the men lifted Tom down, and then Ellie dismounted.

'You didn't believe me, did you? You thought I was some crazy woman, but I knew he was alive.' She spoke excitedly, pumped with adrenalin. 'The lamas in Kalimpong said he was here, and I believed them because there was something about them. They were so sure, and I just felt it in my gut. I knew he was here.'

The men hadn't spoken. They listened to her, and smiled.

'Where's Hugh?' she said. 'If it hadn't been for him, I would never have got Tom back. He was the only one who believed me, and he came all this way to help me, and it was so sad that he wasn't there when I found him. I would've loved to have seen his face.'

'Lady Northwood,' Captain Hailey began.

'Ellie,' she said, cutting him off. 'I'm getting divorced.'

'Ellie,' Captain Hailey said softly. 'Your friend, Mr Douglas . . .'

'Yes, where is he?'

'Would you like to come inside and take a seat?'

'Is he with you? I thought he might have gone to Gyantse. He likes the bazaar.'

'Not exactly, Lady . . . I mean, Ellie.'

For the first time, she looked at the men properly. They were sombre, their stiff British faces betraying a level of emotion that wasn't usual, and which she didn't like. It felt wrong, and something heavy sank within her, like a stone being dropped through clear water into a bottomless sea.

'He's ill?' she asked.

Captain Hailey shook his head. 'He came to us four days ago, just after the storm started. It was amazing he made it. The boys from the dak bungalow carried him to our hospital through the blizzard.'

'And how is he now?' she asked, not wanting to hear the answer.

'Come this way,' Captain Hailey said.

He led her across the compound and into the main Agency building. Ellie looked around, hoping to see Hugh.

'Please, take a seat,' Captain Hailey said.

Ellie sat Tom on her lap. 'Tell me,' she said. 'Please don't keep me in suspense.'

The agent looked up as Captain Guthrie took a chair opposite Ellie.

'We did what we could,' Captain Guthrie said. 'The combination of the altitude and his lung condition meant he really didn't stand much of a chance. Once the thing had got a hold of him, it just wouldn't let go.'

'What are you saying?' Ellie asked.

'I'm so sorry.' Captain Guthrie looked at her steadily. 'Mr Douglas died yesterday.'

Ellie sat completely still. She made no sound, though a voice inside her was screaming. No, she thought. This can't be happening. I can't find Tom only to lose someone else. He was ill when I left; he wasn't dying. He said he would be fine. He said he would make a good meal when I returned. We were going to have corned beef and crackers. I wouldn't have gone if I'd known; I would have stayed.

She pulled Tom to her and kissed the top of his head. But would I? she wondered for a fleeting moment. Would I have stayed and risked losing Tom?

'What happened?' she said, so softly it was barely audible.

'You know he had a lung condition?'

Ellie nodded.

'It was a damned unlucky combination of the fact that he'd lost almost his entire right lung to shrapnel, together with the damage done by exposure to gas. It's incredible he survived as long as he did. And then on top of that, there were complications brought on by the altitude. Basically, his lungs filled with fluid.'

'You mean he drowned?'

'He had massive organ failure, though it happened over several days.'

'Did he suffer a lot?'

'He was prepared. He was well aware of his condition. And he was a brave man.'

'Where is he now?' Ellie said, her voice catching as she spoke. Please, please, she thought, don't crack now. Don't let the floodgates open; don't cry here in front of these reserved, detached strangers. I can't let Tom see me go to pieces, not when I've only just got him back. He needs a mother who is sane and steady, someone who makes his world solid and strong.

'We buried him in the British cemetery this morning,' Captain Hailey said. 'Every autumn we have a grave dug before the ground freezes just in case we should need one. Your friend – he was, I believe, a good friend – is buried there.'

'He was more than a friend,' Ellie blurted out.

'Yes, that is what he told me,' Dr Guthrie said.

'I can take you to the grave, if you wish,' Captain Hailey offered.

Ellie felt too numb to get up; there was no strength in her legs.

'Here,' Captain Hailey stood, 'let me take the child. You've had a terrible shock.'

A bearer brought them tea and a plate of stale biscuits.

'Mr Douglas left you a letter,' Dr Guthrie said. 'He wrote it in the hospital and asked me to give it to you.' He handed Ellie an envelope, and the men withdrew to the far side of the office as she looked at her name, written in slightly shaky handwriting. She opened it and began to read.

My darling Ellie,
You've been gone for three days now, and the storm that started yesterday morning is worse than ever. I'm confident you are safe. The guide I hired is experienced and knows these mountains well, so you are in good hands. As I lie in this odd little hospital that has only one ward and three beds, I imagine you are in the monastery and that Tom is with you. I feel this with absolute certainty, and it brings me peace.

Storms like this can last for days, and I'm not sure you'll be back in time for me to say the things I need to say to you, so I'm writing them down. If the weather improves and I get no worse, you won't have to read this letter. I will be able to tear it up, and say a proper goodbye. I doubt this will happen, though, because I feel pretty bad, and it's an effort for me even to write. You'll have to excuse the handwriting. It's hard writing in bed, and at such a peculiar angle. If I'm right, you'll find yourself in a few days from now sitting in the Trade Agent's office reading these words because I'm no longer here to tell you them myself.

There's no easy way to put this, but I'm dying. It's not such a shock for me because in reality, I've been dying for years. I've been living on borrowed time since Suresh pulled me out of that shell hole in France. I cheated death then, but it seems it's now caught up with me. At the time, I didn't understand why I was spared, although now I know it was to raise Suresh's daughter – my daughter – and to fall in love with you, Ellie, and to help you find your son. I can't think of better reasons for living.

I've written to Maya too, and told her not to hold you responsible for what's happened. She knows I could have died at any time – that's why she was always so adamant I shouldn't do too much or take too many risks. I shouldn't even have made the journey to Kathmandu, although, if I hadn't, I wouldn't have got to know and love you. Fate works in remarkable ways.

Maya is well aware, from her own experience and her desire to leave home and go to Calcutta, that to take no chances is not a good way to live. I've realised, very late, that I have to apply this way of thinking to her too. I have kept her too close to me, and she is a young woman who needs to fly.

I have made good provision for her in my will – she has the house and a modest income – but I'm still worried about her. She's headstrong and has the idealism of youth, and I don't want her hopes to be destroyed. Please take care of her. See her through this time of change. Make sure she is safe.

Never blame yourself for what has happened to me, Ellie. I knew that coming to Tibet was dangerous, and I didn't hesitate. There was a time, just before we crossed the Tang La, when I wondered whether we should turn back, but I decided against it. I knew that if we pressed on to Gyantse I might die, but equally, I could have died at any time in the gentle warmth of Kalimpong. And I wonder too, if we hadn't made this journey, would you have come to me the way you did? Wasn't it something about the danger, and being away from everything you knew, that made you willing to take a chance on loving me?

I'm glad you did, Ellie. I waited for you for so many months, and there were times I thought you'd always keep your distance. In truth, I've loved you since I saw you digging through the ruins in Kathmandu – and I always hoped you would love me as much as I love you. I'm happy that, in the end, I believe you did. We won't have another summer together in the hills, but we had several wonderful cold days on our journey through the Himalayas and into this, quite literally, breathtaking land. It's been worth it, Ellie, and I'm so grateful I was given the time to be with you. You've been the love of my life, my only real love, and if these things are measured in depth of feeling rather than length of time, I've been the luckiest man on earth.

If you are in Kalimpong next summer, think of me. Sit in the garden and listen to the sounds of the hills. And if you have time, go back to the dak bungalow at Yatung, where you first told me you loved me. The Chumbi Valley is perfect in late spring and early summer. The rhododendrons are magnificent and the flowers are too beautiful to describe. My book is still there: I left it again, along with a piece of my heart. The rest is with you, Ellie, wherever you will be.

Goodbye, my love. Live your life well, and without fear.

Hugh

Ellie lifted her gaze. Tom was standing next to her, staring solemnly into her eyes. He pushed his lamb on to her lap, leaned against her legs, and, reaching up with his little fingers, touched the tears on her face.

Author's Note

T HE HIMALAYAS AND the Tibetan Plateau are sacred for Hindus and Buddhists; they are the abode of gods and places of pilgrimage. For centuries they have also held a fascination for Westerners for whom the mountains and high altitude deserts were thought to be unchartered, unchanging and pristine. In the late nineteenth and early twentieth centuries, some Westerners who despaired at the spread of industrial capitalism, and then the brutality of the First World War, imagined the Himalayas as the repository of ancient wisdoms and a peace lost to the modern world. Such views were fantasies, but they were powerful ideas that still resonate today. In many ways, I suppose, I am a descendant of those who dreamed of the Himalayas as a refuge and an untainted space, because although I don't believe the mountains to be other-worldly, I know them to be spectacularly, and unforgettably, beautiful.

I had the good fortune to live in Kathmandu for two years in the early 1990s when my husband of the time was working for the British aid programme to Nepal. During the months when the skies were clear, I woke each morning to see the vast wall of the Himalayas from the roof of our house. And I can promise that there is nothing quite so pleasing to the senses as walking along quiet trails in spring when the yellow flowers of the mustard crop gild the emerald green Kathmandu Valley under a cloudless, cobalt sky.

I am indebted to another group of Westerners who have gone before me and who also loved the Himalayas and their peoples. During the British Raj, this region, which was on the periphery of the empire, was administered by some exceptionally committed men who were also scholars of the culture, history, and flora and fauna of the Himalayas. Today they may be seen as representatives of a discredited colonial regime, and all were unquestioning supporters of British rule. However, most were also passionate in their desire to understand and record the world they saw around them. Brian Hodgson, British Resident in Nepal in the nineteenth century, and Sir Charles Bell, Political Officer for Sikkim, Bhutan and Tibet in the early part of the twentieth century are among the best known of these scholar-administrators, but there are also less exalted figures who have left an important legacy in books, photographs and films. I have used their work extensively, especially in the sections on Kalimpong, Sikkim and Tibet.

I am beholden, in particular, to the wife of one of these men. Margaret Williamson lived with her husband, Derrick, in Sikkim from 1933 to 1935. He was the Political Officer in Gangtok and their house, which is now the official residence of the governors of the Indian state of Sikkim, influenced the depiction of 'Roseacre', Hugh's home in Kalimpong. Margaret's memoir of her life in the Himalayas,★ and her travels with

Derrick, inspired significant parts of *The Himalayan Summer,* especially their journey into Tibet in the autumn of 1935, when Derrick insisted on travelling to Lhasa despite suffering from a chronic illness. When he was taken seriously ill, they were unable to retrace their steps over the passes and he couldn't be evacuated by air because planes in those days were unable to take off at such high altitude. Derrick died and was buried in the British cemetery in Gyantse, leaving Margaret a widow at twenty-nine years old. She never remarried and devoted the rest of her life to the memory of her husband and his work.

Margaret's memoir is a fascinating glimpse into a world that is now lost, partly because of the simple passage of time but, more traumatically, because of the Chinese occupation of Tibet. Her book is also a poignant testimony to enduring love. As Margaret said of her time with Derrick in the Himalayas, 'The two and a half years that I spent with him were the happiest and richest of my whole life. In a sense that brief period was my life.' I have a notion that Ellie would feel something similar.

*Margaret D. Williamson, *Memoirs of a Political Officer's Wife in Tibet, Sikkim and Bhutan*, London: Wisdom Publications, 1987.

The 2015 Nepal Earthquake

A DEVASTATING EARTHQUAKE struck Nepal on 25 April 2015, and was followed, three weeks later, by a major aftershock. Over 9,000 people were killed in the worst natural disaster to hit the country since the great Nepal-Bihar earthquake of 1934 when roughly the same number of people died. Both events were calamities for Nepal, which is one of the poorest countries in the world, and one badly prepared to face the challenges of rescue and rebuilding.

Nepal lies in a vulnerable seismological region where the Indian tectonic plate collides with the Eurasian plate. Earthquakes occur every few decades, and catastrophic ones every century or so. The mighty Himalayas appear strong and unchanging but they are, in fact, fragile. They are the world's highest peaks and some of the youngest, and they are still in the process of being created.

I had already completed a first draft of *The Himalayan Summer* when the earthquakes of 2015 occurred, and I was appalled to see my descriptions of events in 1934 being repeated. I wondered whether I should abandon the novel but instead decided to rewrite the book, shifting its focus and removing whole sections of it in order for it not to appear grossly insensitive. I hope I have achieved this.

Today, the Nepali economy is heavily reliant on income from tourism. Inevitably, the 2015 quakes had a massive effect upon tourist numbers and revenue from foreign visitors has dropped. I would urge anyone who has the means to visit Nepal to do so; it is a spectacularly beautiful country, rich in history, and its people are unfailingly warm and welcoming.

Many Nepalis are still suffering from the after effects of the earthquake: some are injured; families have been deprived of breadwinners; and people have lost homes, livelihoods and loved ones. Although the Disasters Emergency Committee has closed its Nepal appeal, several charities in the UK are still – as of November 2016 – fundraising to help victims of the tragedy. They include Age International, CARE International, Christian Aid, Oxfam, Plan UK, World Vision and Tearfund. All can be found online. Please give what you can. Nepal is an exceptional country, filled with exceptional peoples, and it needs our support.

Acknowledgements

I COULD NOT have written this book without the help of a great many people, especially those in my family. Joanne and David Miller deserve special mention, as does my daughter, Lorna Nickson-Brown, who has read, criticised and improved every draft of the story. Most of all I want to thank my mum, Julie Brown: *The Himalayan Summer* wouldn't have been finished without her.

My agent, Caradoc King, has, as always, been a source of support and good advice, and my editor, Imogen Taylor, provided me with superb direction and the benefit of her wisdom while I wrote the novel. I also need to say a big thank you to Jane Selley whose meticulous copy editing kept me on my toes, and to Amy Perkins whose organisational skills made the whole process of getting a book from draft into print appear so effortless.

Eden Gardens

Louise Brown

Calcutta, the 1940s. In a ramshackle house, streets away from the grand colonial mansions of the British, live Maisy, her Mam and their ayah, Pushpa.

Whiskey-fuelled and poverty-stricken, Mam entertains officers in the night — a disgrace to British India. All hopes are on beautiful Maisy to restore their good fortune.

But Maisy's more at home in the city's forbidden alleyways, eating bazaar food and speaking Bengali with Pushpa, than dancing in glittering ballrooms with potential husbands.

Then one day Maisy's tutor falls ill. His son stands in. Poetic, handsome and ambitious for an independent India, Sunil Banerjee promises Maisy the world. So begins a love affair that will cast her future, for better and for worse. Just as the Second World War strikes and the empire begins to crumble . . .

This is the other side of British India. A dizzying, scandalous, dangerous world, where race, class and gender divide and rule.

REVIEW

ISBN 9781472226105

Cartes Postale from Greece
Victoria Hislop

...k after week, the postcards arrive, addressed to someone Ellie ... not know, each signed with an initial: *A*.

...ese alluring *cartes postales* of Greece brighten her life and cast ... spell on her. She decides she must see this country for herself.

On the morning Ellie leaves for Athens, a notebook arrives. Its pages tell the story of a man's odyssey through Greece. Moving, surprising and sometimes dark, *A*'s tale unfolds with the discovery not only of a culture, but also of a desire to live life to the full once more.

'Impressively imagined' *The Sunday Times*

'Hislop's passionate love of the country breathes from every page' *Daily Mail*

'This wonderful, illuminating novel is a perfect escape' *Woman & Home*

REVIEW

ISBN 9781472223210

Victoria
Daisy Goodwin

In 1837, less than a month after her eighteenth bir
Alexandrina Victoria – sheltered, small in stature, and *fen*
became Queen, not only of Great Britain, but of s
countries in the Empire beyond. Alexandrina had always
tightly controlled by her mother and her household, and
surely too unprepossessing to hold the throne. Yet from t
moment her uncle died, the young Queen startled everyone
abandoning her hated first name; insisting, for the first time in
her life, on sleeping in a room apart from her mother; resolute
about meeting with her ministers alone.

Lord Melbourne, a minister and confidante, became Victoria's
private secretary. Her cousin, Prince Albert of Saxe-Coburg and
Gotha, was destined to become her husband. But Victoria had
met Albert as a child and found him stiff and critical: surely the
last man she would want to be married to . . .

'The research is impeccable, the attention to detail perfect,
and it brings the formidable figure of Victoria
to sparkling life' *Sunday Mirror*

'Goodwin demonstrates her admirable ability to fuse
wide-ranging knowledge of the period with
lively storytelling skills' *The Sunday Times*

REVIEW

ISBN 9780755396115